Porch Swings & Picket Fences

LOVE IN A SMALL TOWN

Porch Swings & Picket Fences

BERGREN • HICKS • ORCUTT • PIZZUTI

WaterBrook
PRESS

PORCH SWINGS & PICKET FENCES
PUBLISHED BY WATERBROOK PRESS
5446 North Academy Boulevard, Suite 200
Colorado Springs, Colorado 80918
A division of Random House, Inc.

Scripture quotations are from the *King James Version* of the Bible
and *New American Standard Bible* (NASB). © The Lockman Foundation
1960, 1962, 1963, 1968, 1971, 1972, 1973, 1975, 1977. Used by permission.

The characters and events in this book are fictional, and any resemblance
to actual persons or events is coincidental.

Library of Congress Cataloging-in-Publication Data
Porch swings & picket fences : love in a small town / [Lisa Tawn]
   Bergren . . . [et al.] — 1st ed.
      p.   cm.
      Contents: Tarnished silver / Lisa Tawn Bergren — Twice in a blue
moon / Barbara Jean Hicks — Texas two-step / Jane Orcutt — The boy
next door / Suzy Pizzuti.
    ISBN 1-57856-226-0 (pbk.)
     1. Love stories, American.   2. Christian fiction, American.
3. City and town life—United States—Fiction.   I. Bergren, Lisa
Tawn.   Tarnished silver.   II. Title: Porch swings and picket fences.
PS595.L6P67   1999
813'.08508—dc21   99-22466
                                          CIP

Printed in the United States of America
1999—First Edition

10 9 8 7 6 5 4 3 2 1

Contents

Tarnished Silver

by Lisa Tawn Bergren

For John and Hope,

who love with a small-town-forged sort of love

and molded a boy into a fine man for me to marry.

Thank you for making me your "daughter-in-love."

Chapter One

Jemma Stuart lowered her sunglasses on her nose to see if she had read the banner correctly. CORNHUSK CRAFT SHOW, SUNDAY 3–6 P.M., BAPTIST CHURCH. She shook her head as she drove under the banner. That was a sign she would never see in Manhattan, and she was glad of it. Cornhusks? How many ways could one do crafts with them anyway? Things sure were different in Stillwater, Iowa, than in her native New York. But certainly this was just like a thousand other American towns.

The old, rounded stoplight ahead turned red, and Jemma took the opportunity to look around and observe the locals. The people on Main Street seemed to ignore the stifling Midwest heat of early summer. A girl with a jump rope skipped away from Jemma, and two boys held triple-scoop cones that threatened to melt before they were eaten. Women window-shopped and men emerged from a hardware store that looked like it hadn't changed since the 1950s. *Mayberry,* she thought. *I'm in Mayberry. Where's Aunt Bee?*

One thing was for sure. She needed to find this church she had been contracted to fix up, get the job done, and get out. She needed the culture, the action of New York. Her soul seemed to crave it. How long had it been since she had been home? Ten months. For ten months she had been on the road, moving from one town to another on stained-glass jobs. If this one hadn't sounded so unique—a turn of the century cathedral being renovated to house a new nondenominational congregation—she would be on the open road right now in her shiny, candy-apple-red Miata. *That's right,* she mused, losing track of time, *the top pulled down, the wind in my hair*—

"Hey, lady!" yelled a driver behind her. "The light's green!"

"Oh!" Jemma gasped, stepping on the gas. She turned left on Coolidge—as in Calvin—and then again on East Third Street, then into the double-cement-track driveway of her rented cottage. *At least the town is easy to figure out in terms of directions,* she thought, referring to her notepad to make sure she was at the right place. The streets were all numbered in gridlike fashion or alphabetized as the last names of presidents. *Three-twenty East Third Street,* she confirmed. This was it. She smiled for the first time as she gazed at the Craftsman cottage.

Obviously built around 1920, the two-bedroom house had a porch that ran the entire width of the front and was painted eggshell white with forest-green trim. At either side were huge banks of lilac bushes, just now hitting full bloom and filling the air with intoxicating perfume. It was very late for lilacs; perhaps Iowa had had a cold spring. The lawn had been impeccably mown and the hedges trimmed. Jemma smiled again as she climbed the wooden steps. To one side were wicker chairs with big, welcoming cushions. To the other side was a porch swing. Above the door was a beveled-glass entry window, a classic, and it looked to be in good condition.

She fished a key out of her jeans pocket. *Maybe Mayberry won't be so bad,* she thought, looking over her shoulder to see kids playing football in the street, as well as spying on her. Probably weren't too many newcomers around here. Undoubtedly, she would be the talk of the town for a while. She shut the heavy, solid wood door behind her and felt her smile fade. In contrast to the charm of the porch, the interior was sparsely furnished. She noted a dining table with two mismatched chairs in the far corner—outside what she assumed was the kitchen—a rocking chair near the front window and a coffee table. "What'd you expect, Stuart?" she whispered to herself. Since her housing was part of her fee, the church was bound to make it as inexpensive as possible. "I just hope I have a bed."

The smell...Jemma fought to place it. *Just like at Grandma's,* she decided. Mold, old paint, resin from aging wood. The aromas were unmistakable. She dropped her heavy bag from her shoulder and went to explore the rest of the cottage. The kitchen had been remodeled...in 1940. The bathroom still had a deep, brass-footed tub, a definite plus, but no shower. The bedroom was tiny, with a bed that folded up like a taco around her when she lay down on it. *At least there's a bed,* she chided herself. No way around it, she would just have to make the best of it. *Find something to enjoy, like the lilacs outside and the chance to walk to work without fear of being mugged.* Yep. That was it. It was all in one's mind-set.

After stowing the rest of her belongings in an antique dresser and parking her mountain bike in the backyard, Jemma decided to walk what she estimated to be seven blocks to the church. Hopefully she'd run across a store for some groceries. She changed from her blouse into a T-shirt, and from her trendy loafers with heels into running shoes. Looking into the oval mirror above the dresser, she pulled her long brown hair into a ponytail. Good enough, she decided, for a quick assessment of the job ahead. Checking her watch, she doubted the pastor would be in at this hour anyway. After all, didn't they just work Sundays?

She rifled through the cabinets until she found the one with six place settings of dishes, and then she gulped down a glass of water. It was ice-cold, as if from a well. Jemma moved aside the kitchen's lace curtains to peer into the small backyard. No well. How long had it been since she had come across city water that tasted like it came from a Brita-filtered pitcher? She set aside the glass, walked out the door, and, feeling like a risktaker, left it unlocked. It went against everything she had grown up with, but what was the good of a small town without tiny pleasures like leaving your door unlocked?

Jemma hopped down the steps, waved at the boys in the street, and walked quickly north toward New Life Christian Church. All along the street, neighbors were in their yards or on their porches, many just getting home from work and settling in to enjoy an early summer evening. The heat was beginning to break as the sun sank in the sky, filtering through the giant maples that crossed the street in an arch, forming a leafy green bridge. Everything was veiled in a hazy, golden light, as if she were looking through sunglasses. The air was still.

She waved at people who looked up at her with tentative, curious smiles and waved back. The houses were well cared for and the people obviously friendly. All in all, it wouldn't be a bad place to spend a couple of months. It might not be exciting, but at least her neighbors would be nice.

In ten minutes she arrived at the church and let out a long, low whistle. The old cathedral was huge, built of gray stone blocks. The outside of the stained-glass windows had been covered in horrific rusted screening in the sixties—an obvious effort to protect them from vandalism, but it dulled the light that made them magnificent from the inside. It would have to go. Plexiglas could accomplish the same thing without shading the glass. There were five windows on either side, each towering twenty feet high and five feet wide. At the front was a huge round window.

Next came the part she loved—seeing the windows from the inside. Her heart skipped a beat as she opened a huge, red front door, entered the narthex, and paused to let her eyes adjust to the dim light. From somewhere near the front, she heard pounding, but she ignored it. Instead, her focus was on the windows, the glorious windows. She walked down the center aisle, pausing before each set, looking left and right in awe. *The old masters were so good at what they did,* she mused. It was tough to get craftsmanship like that anymore. She winced as she noted holes patched haphazardly here and there with mismatched glass, signs of a congregation in decline. How long had the church been in decay?

"They're something, aren't they?" came a voice in front of her, startling Jemma so much she jumped. Her eyes swept from the depiction of Jesus in Gethsemane to the man before her. "Y-yes," she stammered, a bit taken aback by the handsome guy. Tall and gorgeous, he had broad shoulders easily seen under a tight T-shirt that met jeans at a narrow waist. He had wavy brown hair under a baseball cap on backward, and big blue eyes. She loved baseball caps worn backward. It seemed so playful, so boyish.

Jemma willed herself to look away, back toward the windows. "I've been called here to work on them. I haven't seen anything of this quality in some time." She glanced back at his hand, which held a hammer, then quickly into his eyes, then away. "You the carpenter?"

He laughed, a deep, rich sound. "Carpenter, janitor, carpet layer. I'm doing it all."

She smiled. "Wow. They'd better be paying you more than I'm getting."

He smiled back at her. "It's enough. It's worth a lot just to be able to work in here. It's holy, don't you think? Just being in here?"

Jemma nodded. "Yes. You're right. As in, *holy cow,* there's a ton of work to be done. This place is a disaster." She glanced up at old chandeliers, looking precarious on dusty, cobweb-laden chains. Up and behind the main floor was a balcony with an ornate, giant organ supporting pipes that reached the ceiling. *I wonder if it works?* In front was an altar area, where this guy was obviously hard at work. "You restoring that?"

"Tearing it apart," he said, flashing her again with his electric smile. "The church wants to target the younger crowd, and as a whole, they like something lighter."

Jemma frowned. "You're taking it all out? What bozo decided

to do that? Some pastor with no artistic vision? It will leave the windows high and dry not to have something up front that complements them."

"It'll work," he said confidently. He tapped his ball cap. "I see it up here."

"Oh," she said with her eyebrows raised. She could feel a blush rising up her neck. "Sorry. Sometimes I speak before I think. I'll just concentrate on my windows."

"No need to apologize. I like to hear what people think. And you're wrong. I'd guess you say exactly what you're thinking, a different habit than speaking before you think. It's okay to have an opinion."

"Not if I'm offending people left and right. And, uh, I wouldn't want that smart-aleck comment to get back to the pastor. Again, I'm sorry. My name's Jemma. Jemma Stuart." She reached out her hand.

"Samuel," he said, enveloping her hand with his big fingers and warm palm. "But my friends call me Sam."

"Nice to meet you, Sam."

"And you, Jemma. Where'd you get such a pretty name?"

"It's British—a family name."

"Ah," he said, pulling back a bit to look her over while still holding her hand. "Should've guessed. The aristocratic nose, the narrow face, the ivory skin, large eyes. Bit of Scottish and Irish too, if I guess right. Does royalty run through your veins, milady?"

Jemma pulled her hand away, wondering if he was making fun of her or flirting. "I have some blue blood in me," she said in a superior tone that implied he clearly did not.

"There're quite a few people in this town who can trace their lineage to royalty," he said, turning back to his project at the front of the sanctuary. "My sister," he grunted, pulling out a nail a century old, "is something of a genealogy buff. Loves it. She has all the equipment—a high-powered computer, a microfiche machine. She'd have a blast with a Stuart."

"Yeah, well, I won't be here long enough to do some major search for long-lost ancestors." Her eyes returned to the windows at her right. There would be quite a bit of work to do. They would all have to be taken down, out of their frames, and worked on. Someplace level…

"Won't be here long, eh? Seems like those windows will take some time."

"Yes. There is quite a bit to do." She reached up to run her fingers along the leading of a damaged piece of glass and felt the warmth of outside air entering. "To keep any heat in here, let alone for esthetics. But it's nothing I can't handle." Her hands went to her hips. "Small-town life isn't my cup o' tea. I intend to do my job and get out of here."

Sam took a nail out of his mouth and wiped his brow. "Do your job and get out? You make it sound like a prison sentence. Surely Stillwater hasn't turned you off already."

"No," she said, attempting to backtrack. Who knew how long this guy had lived here? She didn't want to offend anyone. "I'm just missing Manhattan, that's all."

"Well, you should give it a chance."

"I have. I mean, I will."

"Right." Sam reached to his tool belt and pulled out a screwdriver. "You've already written it off. I can see it in your eyes." He met her gaze levelly. "I'll bet you a hundred dollars."

"A hundred dollars? On what?"

"That I can convince you before you leave that Stillwater is as excellent a place to live as Manhattan."

"In your dreams!" she snorted. It was out before she could stop it. She was committed. "There's no way a town like this could compare to *Manhattan*."

"That's where—beggin' milady's pardon—you're dead wrong."

"Okay," Jemma said, lifting her chin and letting out a small laugh. "You're on. Easiest hundred I'll ever make." Now she was flirting! What was happening to her? She hadn't flirted with a man since Mark had dumped her last year. Since when had she felt like flirting? And with a carpenter on a job? She turned away and started walking up the aisle. "I had better get to a store or I won't eat tonight. Where's the nearest grocery?"

"Corner of Second Avenue East and East Second." He laughed at her puzzlement. "Two blocks toward your house and one to the right."

"How do you know where I live?"

"Jemma Stuart, welcome to Stillwater, Iowa. Nothing's a secret in this town. It's part of the charm."

Chapter Two

"Early riser?"

Jemma's spine tingled as the warm tones of his voice met her ears. "Apparently earlier than you, Sam. Hope you don't mind that I borrowed your ladder." She was ten feet up, working with her awl to examine the disintegrating soldering of a window. It crumbled away as she worked at it, and she paused to wipe her brow. It was already warm.

"Cup of coffee?"

She turned to look at Sam, still standing below her with a steaming mug. "No thanks. I don't do more than my breakfast caffeine. I'm already scary enough with that in my system."

"High energy, eh?"

"You could say that."

"I like that in a coworker. How'd you sleep last night?"

"Back's a bit sore. The church cheaped out on me and left an old taco bed at the house."

"Taco bed?" Sam asked with a smile.

"Yep. You lie down on it, and suddenly you're the meat and it's the shell. I had horrible dreams of being eaten by some ravenous teenager." She smiled over her shoulder. "Kidding."

"Well, maybe we can do something about that—"

"Sam!" came a female voice from the narthex. "I brought doughnuts!"

Here we go, Jemma thought. *The girlfriend.* But then another woman came in behind the first. Sam probably attracted women left and right. *Put it out of your mind, Stuart. You're here for a couple of months, and he's not worth the competition.*

"Alison, what are you doing up?" Sam asked. He went to greet them. "And June! You're never up this early!"

They hemmed and hawed, protesting that no, that wasn't true, weren't they up for first service every Sunday? "Besides," Alison said, moving forward to the front pew and throwing Jemma a glance, "we figured you'd need help today."

Sam's hands were on his hips. "Why today?"

"Why not today?" June asked, leaving Sam in the doorway and joining Alison near the front. "I have to go to work at noon. The store manager needs me there to cover lunch break."

Jemma climbed down the ladder and turned to the young women. It was clear they were there to check her out, not help Sam. "I'm Jemma. Don't worry"—she lowered her voice—"I'll be out of town by August."

"Why would we be worried?" Alison asked, her forehead furrowed in confusion. There was something familiar about her eyes…

"I'm not in the market," she said softly. Sam was getting closer.

"For what?" June asked, speaking just as loudly as Alison had.

"For a man!" Jemma said. "For him," she said under her breath, just as he reached the trio.

Both women burst out laughing. "You think," June giggled, "we're interested in him? Ha!"

"Not in a thousand years," Alison said, punching him on the shoulder. "Even if he wasn't my brother."

"Oh," Jemma said, feeling a blush start creeping up her neck. There she went again, saying exactly what was on her mind. She moved the ladder, anxious to climb up to the next window and appear busy.

"I'm Alison, and this is my sister June. We call Samuel, here, our big bro." She looked Jemma in the eye. "To be honest, we had to come see the new artist he was gabbing about last night over dinner. For heaven's sake, you'd think he didn't already have a hundred women in love with him the way he went on about you."

"Alison—"

"Oh shush, Sam. You know you're the eligible bachelor about town."

"Yeah," June put in, "I wish you had more friends. Get a life, would you? There's more to Stillwater than this church."

"Not for him," Alison said. "He can't think of anything but this church. He's on a mission from God," she said to Jemma.

"Like the Blues Brothers?" Jemma asked. It was impossible not to take part in the fun.

"Exactly!" Alison said, her laughing eyes telling Jemma she had found a kindred spirit.

"Lucky for him the church was being renovated."

The laughter stopped. "Lucky, shmucky. This guy made sure it happened."

Jemma frowned. "Made it happen?"

"Well sure," June said, weaving her arm through her brother's. "Who else but the pastor would care so much?"

Sam could tell Jemma was angry as she put two and two together. He silently chastised himself for not coming clean with her yesterday. He really hadn't had the opportunity, and she had gone about putting her foot in her mouth before he could set the record straight.

"You're Samuel *Tucker? Pastor* Tucker?"

"Uh-oh," June said, dropping Sam's arm and slapping his bicep. "You didn't tell her you're her boss?"

"Way to go, champ," Alison said, tipping off his ball cap. "We'd better head out. Nice meeting you, Jemma. We'll talk more when you're not ready to kill my brother. Don't want witnesses around if you're set to off him." The sisters hurriedly walked away. "See ya later, Sam!"

"My...boss?" She turned away from Sam, running her lovely long fingers through her bangs.

"Jemma—"

"All those things I said...you let me ramble on..."

"I'm sorry, Jemma. Every time I thought to try...I'm sorry. I should've interrupted you. I should've told you. It really started out innocently. You mistook me for the carpenter—"

"Yes, you should've interrupted me. Excuse me," she said, following his sisters down the center aisle. "I need to go home for some tools I forgot."

He watched her go, angry at himself that he had blown it. When the door closed behind her, he sank into the front pew and reached into the Dunkin' Donuts carton for a chocolate éclair. "Well, Lord, I blew that one," he mumbled around the crumbs in his mouth. He tossed the rest of the doughnut back in the box. Were these doughnuts day-old bargains? Knowing Alison, that's where she had purchased them. She was notoriously cheap and had the biggest mouth... "I know, God. I know! It's not Alison's fault. It's just that sometimes having sisters is the pits. I would've come clean with Jemma today. You know that. Please, Father, please let her give me a chance. We'll be working together a lot, and I'd like it if we could at least be friends."

Sam wondered about his plea. Was it more than a friendly interest that made him beg God to influence Jemma? If he was honest with himself, he had to acknowledge she was attractive and interesting. Was it because she was an outsider? His sisters always claimed that he set his sights on unattainable women so he wouldn't have to settle down. Jemma Stuart would be here for no longer than two months, tops, by her own account. But it didn't feel like an evasion to Sam. Jemma was the first woman he had been attracted to, truly drawn to, since college. His interest had moved him so much that he had blathered on last night over dinner at his folks' and set himself up for disaster. He should've seen it coming when his sisters had shared a cloistered glance at the table.

"Oh, brother," he whispered, remembering that moment. "I blew it, Lord. Let her give me another chance."

She returned an hour later and walked straight up to him.

"You want me to continue the job, or would it be best if I just left now?"

"Wh-what? Leave? Because you made a few smart remarks?"

"Because you played me for a fool."

"No. No, I didn't! Come on, Jemma. Would you have given me half a chance to be your friend if you knew I was your boss? A pastor? Most women I meet don't give me the time of day after they hear that, especially if they see this place." He gestured about him.

He saw her falter, clearly uneasy. What had he said? Oh, *now* he had done it. He'd gone and let her know he was interested. Maybe she wasn't. Was he bordering on sexual harassment? He'd read the pamphlets sent out by the state. A man couldn't have a sincere interest in a woman he worked with these days without worrying about false accusations.

"Give me a break, Tucker. Your sister said it herself; you have a hundred women in love with you. You don't need me. And yes, by the way, I would've given you a chance to be my friend, as well as my boss."

"Maybe, maybe not."

She looked him in the eye and his heart skipped. *Man, she is beautiful.* Hazel eyes that looked into a man's soul. And those lips… He forced himself to recall Scripture to bring his mind back to holier thoughts.

"I'm only here for a couple of months, and then I go back to Manhattan," she said, continuing to stare into his eyes. "I don't think it would be wise for us to date."

"Who said I wanted a date?" he retorted. What was she, a mind reader? "We'll just be…friends. And maybe, just maybe, you'll let me earn that extra hundred. The place needs it, don't you think?" he said, gesturing about him.

"It needs more than a hundred. Um, about what I said, you know, about the pastor being cheap—"

"Don't worry about it. You didn't say anything I wouldn't have said myself."

"Really?"

"Really. Now will you forgive me?"

"I guess so. I mean, what am I supposed to say to a pastor asking for forgiveness?"

"You're supposed to forgive Sam Tucker, the man."

"Okay. I forgive you. Now can we get back to work?"

"By all means. Doughnut?"

"No thank you."

Jemma worked all day, acutely aware of Sam working not fifty feet away. It was just her luck to be developing a crush on a pastor. A pastor, of all people. While she had given her heart to Christ many years ago, she had never fancied herself as the wife of a *pastor*. She couldn't make a casserole to save her life. *Whoa,* she thought. Wife? Where did that come from? And how could it even be an option? He was just so adorable that it would drive any woman to wild thoughts. Being friends with a small-town pastor would definitely be enough for her. Definitely.

She jammed her awl in a crack too hard and winced as a piece of glass splintered. It was her friends' fault, she decided. They were the ones who were always talking about the men in their lives. In the last year, five of her closest girlfriends had gotten married. If she had to sit at another round table making wedding-day chitchat with family members and friends, pretending she was so glad the newlyweds had found true love when she hadn't, she would throw up.

It was their fault marriage was on her mind, making even Pastor Sam Tucker a potential suitor.

"Can I walk you home?" he asked from the bottom of the ladder, startling her. Good grief, he was handsome. She longed to tip off his ball cap like his little sister had, do anything to make him a little less appealing. *Lord, I'm confused by what I'm feeling,* she prayed silently. *Help me to cut this off now. My heart can't take it. Not since Mark, anyway.*

Her relationship with Mark Haverfield seemed to have left her heart in as bad a condition as the windows in the church. She wouldn't let that happen again. "Oh, no thanks. I can make it home all right. I'll see you tomorrow."

"Come on, Jemma. Let me see you home. How am I supposed to collect on my bet if I can't start convincing you that Stillwater is at least as wonderful as Manhattan?"

"We should probably cancel our bet, Sam. I don't think this is wise—"

"Maybe not. But, hey, no risk, no gain. Come on. Let me walk you home and we'll discuss the bet."

"No. You can walk me home. But that's it."

"Fine. Shall we?" He gestured down the aisle.

"Are you going to replace the carpeting?" Jemma asked as they walked, eager to return to neutral territory.

"I'm taking it out. There are beautiful hardwood floors beneath that I'd like to refinish. Better for acoustics too."

"Where are your members? Don't you have help? I mean, I'm assuming you have a congregation—"

Sam laughed and locked the door. "Yes, I have members. We meet at the elementary school right now. The church came up for sale, and I put everything I had into it. It meant a lot, being my grandparents' church and a town landmark."

"Good location too. You mean, you put your own savings into it?"

Sam shrugged as they walked. "As I said, it meant a lot. And my congregation only numbers a little over a hundred. New kid in town. I mean, even if I am a hometown boy, I still have to prove myself as pastor, you know?"

"I understand. It's still a lot, taking on the whole church renovation."

"Oh, others come and help. Every Saturday. During the week, they all have jobs and households to run."

"If my fee is too much—"

"Nonsense. As I said to you that first day, the windows help make the sanctuary holy. You deserve your going rate to make them shine again. And hold the heat in."

Jemma colored slightly at the mention of her comment. "Why'd you come back? Why not start up somewhere else after seminary?"

"Because I love it here. Remember?" he asked, skipping ahead to walk backward in front of her for a moment. "I'm going to show you why. Show you why you should love Stillwater as much as Manhattan."

It was impossible to remain angry with him. "I thought our bet was off."

"We'll see," he said, returning to her side.

"Pastor T!" a boy called from the street. "Go long!"

"Goin'!" he yelled, jogging out into East Third. The ball sailed through the air, just under the canopy of maples. Sam grabbed the football with his fingertips, then ran for an imaginary end zone. "Touchdown! And the crowd goes wild! Ahhhh!"

She watched as the neighborhood boys swarmed the young man, giving him high-fives and secret handshakes. They obviously adored him, and she could see why.

Sam Tucker wasn't one of the pastors of her youth. He was the boy next door.

Chapter Three

Jemma hung up the phone in Sam's office, content that tomorrow she would have the manpower she needed. In the morning, four carpenters would be at the church, ready to take down the windows for repair and replace them with temporary plastic sheeting.

"Can I give you a lift?" Sam asked, leaning against the doorjamb with his arms crossed.

"A lift? No, I think I can make it home."

"Not to my folks' house. It's quite a walk." He grinned, pulled off his baseball cap, and twisted it in his hands before replacing it. "My mom wants me to invite you over for dinner. And my sisters want a second crack at ya."

"Taking me home to meet your mother, huh?" Jemma flirted. *Stop that.* "I suppose as good Christians you all feel obligated to take care of the new girl in town."

"I suppose," he said, his eyes showing he felt no obligation. "So, can you make it? Should I call Mom and tell her to set another place at the table?"

She studied him for a moment before saying, "Sure. If it's not too much trouble." What safer way to be with a man in the presence of his whole family? She gathered her things and rose. "I know you have two sisters. Do you have any brothers?"

"Three."

"Three? Big family."

"You betcha. Best kind."

See, Jemma? He'd never be happy with the two kids you want to have. He'd want a whole pack of 'em. "Are the brothers all at home?"

"One. He's the baby, still in high school. The other two are in college but home for the summer."

"So you're the eldest?"

"Yes." He opened the door for her, then shut and locked it behind her. "It goes me, Alison, June, Keith, Nick, and John. How about you? Do you have brothers or sisters?"

"Nope. Just me. Mom went off and left Dad when I was nine. The marriage wasn't a good one."

"Ah. I'm sorry." His eyes were compassionate. "Do you have a good relationship with your mother now?"

"No. When she left, she never looked back. I don't even know where she is." She tried to make her tone nonchalant.

Sam stopped, and Jemma squirmed under his gaze. "I'm really sorry, Jemma. I hate it when families split up, especially when there are kids involved." Jemma was relieved when they continued walking around the building to the parking lot. "So is your dad a Christian?"

"Yep. He's the best. Gave me my foundation, taught me what I needed to get through life."

"Is that what you do? Get through?"

"I don't know. I suppose." Jemma felt defensive. Was he judging her now for how she lived life? She glanced up at him, shoulders tense, but there was no condemnation in his glance back at her. Only concern. "Life is...challenging. There's always something new to get through."

"I prefer to think of life's challenges as opportunities."

"Ah. Always the positive thinker, eh?"

"I try."

"I'm a bit more of a pragmatist."

"I'll try not to hold that against you." He stopped in front of an old motorcycle and handed her a helmet from the backseat.

"You ride a motorcycle?"

"Sure. Ever since I bought her when I was sixteen."

She looked at him and shook her head. "You're one surprise after another, Pastor Tucker."

"Sam," he said with a grin, pulling on his own helmet. "Please, call me Sam."

They rode out of town, and Jemma had to smile as people openly stared. The young pastor, on a motorcycle, with a *girl.* She could hear the wheels turning as the gossip clocks began ticking. Somehow Jemma knew it would be a town triumph if they could get Pastor Tucker married before the year was out. Small towns like this didn't take it well when they couldn't get the eligible young men married off. But how would they like it if he took an outsider as his bride rather than one of their own? *Stop it,* she told herself again. *Stop it, stop it, stop it.*

She tried not to hold on too tightly as they rounded a corner. "You have to lean with me," he directed over his shoulder. "Don't fight it; roll with it." Jemma liked the motion, the easy swing and sway of the bike. It had been years since she had ridden one. She found herself enjoying riding with Sam.

Gradually, the town buildings grew farther apart and eventually disappeared as Sam and Jemma entered the miles of rolling hills that surrounded Stillwater. The cornfields were young, with stalks that barely reached a man's thigh. So was the grain, still green and with thin heads ready for a summer's fattening. The air held the fresh, clean scent of farmland that stretched for a hundred miles. *No smog here,* she thought. *That's something anyway.* There was a simple beauty in the fields, a refreshing reminder that life didn't have to be one challenge after another, but could be perceived as an opportunity to make the most of. Maybe it was this setting that had given Sam his outlook on life.

After a fifteen-minute drive over one dirt road after another, a huge farmhouse loomed on the horizon. It was a classic two-story, with a porch that wrapped around three sides. People milled about on it already, walking up and down the front steps or sitting in wicker chairs and rockers and swings. On the front lawn, three kids were tossing a baseball. "My nephews," Sam explained. "Alison's kids. They're here more than they are at home, which is a farm just up the road."

They pulled up in front of the house, and Jemma could feel the almost-palpable wall of curiosity. A woman she assumed was Sam's mother came out the screen door, letting it bang shut behind her as she wiped her hands on an apron. "Jemma? I'm Rose Tucker."

"Rose. It's nice to meet you," Jemma said with a nod. She was svelte and well-dressed beneath her apron, not at all what Jemma had assumed the stereotypical farm wife would look like.

An older man stepped up from beside the boys on the lawn. "I'm Tom Tucker."

"Tom," she said, firmly shaking his hand. He had kind eyes, the same shape as Sam's but a different shade of blue, set in a weathered, leathery face. "These are my grandsons, Jamie, Christopher, and Neil."

"Nice to meet—"

"Uncle Sam! Uncle Sam!" they yelled, ignoring Jemma. They surrounded him and begged him to wrestle until he acquiesced.

"Sorry about them," Alison said, joining her and Tom. "I try to teach them manners, but you can see how well I've done."

"I'm sure they're fine boys. And you have time to whip 'em into shape. They're only what, five and under?"

"Three, four, and five." She studied the brown-haired youngsters with devotion in her eyes. "Trouble, those three."

Jemma smiled. "I'm sure they aren't trouble all the time."

"Well, maybe not all the time. Speaking of trouble, I'm sure sorry that we caused some between you and my brother yesterday."

"That's fine. It was bound to come out sooner or later that he

was the pastor pretending to be the chief carpenter." She said it loud enough for Sam to hear.

"I understand he owes you an apology," Rose said as they joined her on the steps.

"Now, Mom—" Sam complained from the lawn. He had grass stuck in his hair from wrestling with his nephews, making him look all the more adorable. "I told you I'd taken care of things with Jemma. Don't you go treating me as if I were no older than *these guys,*" he said, returning his attention to the boys, who shrieked their pleasure as he pretended to tackle them.

"Hi, Jemma," June said, raising her glass. "Would you like some lemonade?"

"Sure, that'd be great," she said.

"These are my other boys, Keith, Nick, and John," Rose introduced them, as each stepped forward to shake Jemma's hand and nod. They looked so similar to Sam that Jemma was sure she could have picked them out of a crowd. One offered her his chair and she sank into it, holding her cold glass.

"Which one of you goes to Michigan?" she asked, looking at a car with a Wolverine sticker on the back.

"Me, ma'am," Keith said. "I'm in graduate school there, studying to be a vet."

"Jemma. Please call me Jemma," she said. "You're making me feel old. I'm one of the Fighting Irish. I'm sorry to break the news, but Notre Dame is comin' back this year and is going to squash you guys like the bugs that you are." She sat back, confident in her gloating and knowing that her challenge would warm Keith up. She was right. He immediately settled into a monologue about how the new head coach would make the most of their senior quarterback, and why Notre Dame's running game was killing them.

"You said you're in grad school. Do you want to be a large-animal vet?" she asked, wanting to get away from the topic of sports. With so many men around, if she didn't get it under control right then, they'd be talking about it all night. It was one thing to use it to break the ice, but another to let it dominate their conversation. Alison shot her a knowing glance, and June raised her lemonade in a silent, covert toast.

"Yeah. Wasn't cut out to be a corn farmer," Keith said. "Mom and Dad plan to leave this place to Nick and John. They're the ones who love it."

"My husband and I have a spread a few miles from here," Alison said. "We raise corn too."

"You'd think it was next door, considering how often they're here," Keith ribbed her.

"Yeah," Nick and John agreed, laughing. They obviously thought Keith was everything they wanted to be.

"And I work in town," June offered, ignoring her brothers. "I run a flower shop on Main."

"I always thought arranging flowers would be fun," Jemma said. "Are you married?"

"No. But I'm working on it."

"Oh, come off it," Nick said. "Judd is never going to figure it out."

"Sure he will," June defended. "He just wants to get settled at the Merc before he asks Daddy for my hand."

"Hope he takes the rest of you too," Keith said with a snort.

"Yeah," said his Greek chorus of younger brothers.

"The Merc?" Jemma asked.

"The Mercantile. It's on Main, two doors down from my shop. Judd and I were high-school sweethearts, and just got back together last year when he came home to run his dad's business."

Jemma nodded.

"Sure he isn't sweet on somebody up in Saint Paul?" Keith asked.

"Maybe *you* should just pop the question," Nick added.

"I'll pop you boys if you don't let up on your sister," Tom chimed in. All three immediately fell silent. It did not ruin the mood, Jemma noted, just kept things from getting hurtful.

"Are you the genealogist?" Jemma asked June.

"I dabble in it. Stuart would be a fun project. What town were your ancestors from?"

"I don't know," Jemma said, vaguely startled by the query. She really didn't know much about her extended family, when she thought about it. Something about the Tuckers made her think they could name every last relative.

"You folks all come in and eat," Rose said from behind the screen door, wiping her hands on her apron. "Food's on the table."

Everyone rumbled in, and Jemma, in the midst of the crowd, smiled to herself. How long had it been since she had eaten with a family that routinely numbered twelve or more at the table? She couldn't remember whether she ever had. The Tuckers seemed to take her in like an adopted puppy, never throwing her a strange glance or making her feel uncomfortable. She had the uncanny feeling that she had been eating with them for years. *How do they do it?* she wondered. Maybe it was the knack of big families in small towns, accepting whatever came their way. There was an easiness, a peace, that Jemma couldn't explain. But she liked it. She liked it a lot.

She looked up from her fried chicken and mashed potatoes to see Sam grinning at her from across the table. "What?" she mouthed, wiping her cheek to make sure there wasn't food smeared anywhere.

But he shook his head and turned his attention back to his food, still smiling. He obviously approved of something. *Oh,* she thought, sitting back in her chair. *Our bet.* He thought he had her. Already. Sure, this was nice, but it wasn't home. No sir, there was no way he'd ever get her to agree this place was as good as Manhattan. She bit into fresh string beans and paused. *At least, not yet.*

"Come on, Jemma," Sam prodded as they reached his motorcycle for the ride home. "Admit it. Mom's cooking is some of the best you've ever eaten. You have to give Stillwater a point just for her."

Jemma fastened the strap under her chin and smiled up at him. She was so beautiful, with her hair glistening in the light of the setting sun. Her eyes were *snappy*. That was it—*snappy*. They sparkled when she talked, and it made Sam want to talk to her all night. "I'm willing to give you a point," she said. "A combination point for the charm of a big family and the meals Rose serves."

"Okay, I'll take that." He straddled the bike.

She smiled and then got on behind him. "But to be fair, you would have to come with me to Anthony's Pepperoni Pizza in Manhattan, or eat clam linguini at a hole-in-the-wall restaurant I know of."

He turned around on the seat to look at her. "Why, Miss Stuart, are you asking me to come visit?"

"Certainly not," she said, looking as though she wanted to stick out her tongue at him instead of smiling.

"I see." He revved the engine and they took off a moment later, waving to the remaining relatives who covertly—they thought— looked out the windows at them. No doubt his mom was excited, with him bringing home a girl and all. Married at nineteen, his parents thought him a lost cause at thirty.

They drove home past waving fields, the light just about gone on the horizon. During the summer, it was often light until ten, with twilight lasting a good two hours. To the west were the last vestiges of gold and orange and brick red; to the east the sky was full of stars against a blue velvet sky. It reminded Sam of a place he used to go when he was a kid. He'd have to take Jemma there. He found himself wanting to take her lots of places, share many things.

All too soon they were at Jemma's house. He stopped the engine and took Jemma's helmet from her with a smile he hoped conveyed all he was feeling without scaring her off. She glanced at him and then hurried away. Sam's heart faltered. After a moment's hesitation, he followed her up the stairs, ignoring the neighbor boys calling to "Pastor T" to come and play Mississippi with them.

"Jemma, I—"

"I had a great time tonight, Sam. Thanks. It was really nice of you to invite me. See you tomorrow."

"Okay. Sure," he said slowly. "Tomorrow. And after that?"

Jemma turned the antique knob of the front door and walked halfway through. "And after that?" she asked, looking puzzled.

He felt stupid. Clearly, she felt nothing of what he was feeling. "Well, you know, I was thinking I'd like to visit New York. You know, for the shows."

"For the shows."

"Yes."

"Well, Sam, if you come for the shows, we'll have to get together for dinner sometime."

Did she mean it? Or was she just protecting herself? "Sure. You can have a chance to prove that Anthony's measures up to Mom's cooking."

"Good night, Sam."

"Good night, Jemma."

Samuel turned away as she shut the door behind him, feeling a little sick to his stomach. What was he doing, anyway, flirting with a girl who had no intention of staying? He was here for the duration. Stillwater was his home, and hopefully would be for at least another ten years. It would take that long to get New Life on its feet and rolling.

He pulled on his helmet and angrily looked up at the sky, stars just visible among the heavy foliage of the maples towering above him. "Why, Lord?" he whispered. "Why in the world would you taunt me with a woman now when we can't possibly be together?"

Chapter Four

Jemma could tell she had hurt Sam's feelings the week before. She wanted to say something, tell a joke to ease the tension, but then she stopped herself. Maybe it was all for the best. If they cut it off now it would be a lot less painful than down the road. *Nip it in the bud,* she told herself. *Head it off at the pass.* But it was easier to think about it than to do it.

He had invited her to his church at the elementary school while they were at his folks' house, but she had declined. She worshiped at the Presbyterian church instead. When she returned to work on Monday, she noted that Sam was gone. *Perhaps he's just taking the day off,* she thought. *And what do I care? It's easier if he's gone.* Surely he had church work beyond the rejuvenation of the sanctuary. But then he had been gone for the next four days as well. She threw herself into her work, trying not to think about him, determined not to think the worst. After all, he had no cause to report to her. Maybe he was off on some other church business. Or away on vacation, for all she knew. But on Friday afternoon, she was ready to track down Rose or Alison to make sure he was all right.

She was just taking off her apron after soldering a piece— expertly matched and cut, she thought—into the nativity window when he strolled down the center aisle. In the quiet of the empty

"Am I late?"

"I don't know. I wasn't paying attention to the clock." *Just my watch.* She grabbed her sweater. "What's the deal anyway? Doesn't the church pay you enough to buy me dinner?"

"We can have dinner anytime. I'm on a mission."

"Mission?"

"To convince you that Stillwater is the greatest place to live on earth." He reached out his hand. "Or at least as good as Manhattan."

She took his hand, warm and slightly rough from his carpentry work. It felt so good to have her hand held by another! "One step at a time, Tucker. One step at a time."

He took her directly to the city park, turning down a dirt lane that eventually narrowed to little more than a path. "Where in the world are we?" Jemma asked when they stopped.

"The lake."

"Obviously. But what's this? An old hangout?"

"Could say that." He shouldered a bag and then took her hand again and led her through the underbrush, pushing aside branches as they went. They emerged in a small clearing, made utterly private by the foliage on either side. The lake was almost still, and a silver moon had already climbed high in the sky even as the last line of red faded to the west. It grew brighter as the sun disappeared completely and the night sky took over. Jemma stood beside Sam for a moment, just staring outward. The moonlight reflected on the lake in shimmering flakes, like powdered sugar falling from a baker's sifter.

Without a word, Sam gathered a handful of pebbles from the beach and then pulled her toward an old dock. They walked to the end of it. "Sure we're not going to end up swimming?" Jemma asked.

"And if we did?"

"Never mind. Let's just say I was hoping for a dry date tonight."

"Okay." He sat down. "How about wet feet?"

"All right," she allowed, sitting beside him and taking off her shoes. She rolled up her jeans and dipped her feet in the water. "It almost feels warm."

"Probably because the air temperature's down to about seventy."

"No fish are going to come nibble on my toes, are they?" Jemma asked, mildly concerned.

"None except that largemouth bass. Old Pete is said to have eaten small children."

Jemma laughed. "As long as he goes after the kids and leaves my toes alone."

Sam joined her, his laugh rich and warm. They sat in companionable silence for a while. "Hear that?" he asked her.

"What?" Jemma said, straining to hear anything beyond the *kerplunk* of their pebbles as they took turns tossing them in.

"Exactly," he said, gloating.

And Jemma had to admit that the silence was mesmerizing.

"Come on," he said, pulling his feet out of the water. "I have a new bet for you." Standing behind her, Sam easily lifted Jemma to her feet.

"A new one? We haven't resolved the first one."

"This one's easier." He pulled two jars out of his bag and nodded toward the woods. For the first time, Jemma saw the lightning bugs, blinking on and off. "First one to collect ten gets to sit at a table while the loser buys us a banana split to share."

"You're on," Jemma said. How long had it been since she had grinned so much her cheeks hurt? She laced up her shoes, then took Sam's proffered hand.

Once on shore, Sam looked at her in the dim light. "Ready?"

"You're buying the split, Tucker," she taunted, running toward the biggest group of lightning bugs she could see. She laughed, feeling young and carefree as she swooped at the flying keys to her success. The difficult part, she soon discovered, was keeping those she had caught in the jar while capturing their brothers. She giggled, feeling funny swiping at lights that were there one second and gone the next. Sam's deeper chuckle echoed behind her.

"Done," he said a minute later.

"What?" she asked, whirling. She only had two! "How did you do that?"

"Small-town secret."

"Let me see." She looked inside at the whirling, buzzing insects. It was impossible to count, but it looked like an awful lot. "You sure there are ten in there?"

"Are you questioning my honesty?"

"No, but—"

"Then you owe me a banana split, Miss Stuart."

"Fine," she said, releasing the bugs from her jar.

"You didn't really have ten lightning bugs, did you?" she asked, dipping into her half of the banana split.

"No. That's the small-town secret," he said, flashing her his super-white teeth. "Lightning bugs hardly ever flash at the same time. My younger brothers always bought when I made that bet with them."

"Well, that's practically malevolent, Pastor Tucker."

"Whoa, big word. Never said I had ten."

"You led me to believe you had ten."

"Well, sure. What can I say? My mother used to call me 'a little dickens.' My brothers always trusted me when they shouldn't have." The teasing went out of his eyes, and he reached slowly across the marble table for her hand. "You can, Jemma. You can trust me."

She pulled her hand away with a small smile, conscious that half the patrons in the old-fashioned ice-cream parlor—the only people still up in Stillwater, apparently—were staring in their direction. Sam smiled knowingly, glancing over his shoulder. "They're harmless."

"Possibly," she said, scooping out the last spoonful of fudge sauce.

"Say, you want a caramel apple?"

"No, thanks," she said with a laugh. She'd eaten more than her half of the dessert. "I didn't have much of a dinner," she explained.

"Ah. Shall I walk you home?" They had left his motorcycle at her house after their visit to the lake. She glanced at her watch. It was after eleven! "If you expect me to be up before ten tomorrow," she retorted.

They walked home, chatting all the way about growing up and college. When they reached her front porch, Sam stared into her eyes for a moment, then slowly, reverently, kissed her on the cheek before turning and walking away. He straddled his bike and put on his helmet. "Ten o'clock tomorrow, huh?"

"Better make it eleven."

"See you then, Jemma." He even said her name like he loved the sound of it. She felt as though her heart would burst, she was so happy! He sat there, staring at her, until she realized he was waiting for her to go inside. Feeling like a twelve-year-old with a crush, Jemma turned and hoped she looked carefree as she entered her house and closed the door behind her. She went directly to the darkened window. When he had revved up the engine and was almost down the street, she went back outside and sat on her front steps. She listened to the sounds of the night, wanting to think of other things than Sam but unable to do so.

Jemma pulled off her shoes and rested her head on one knee. *Dear Father,* she prayed, *out of all the men in my world, you had to choose a guy in Stillwater, Iowa?* She was falling hard; she could feel it. And try as she might, she could find not one ounce of courage to put a stop to it.

She was about to protest when he kissed her. Slowly, softly, soundly. Jemma felt a bit dazed as he stepped away. She frowned. "I can't, Samuel. I can't."

"You can't what?"

"I can't stay here."

Sam sighed and looked down the street. She followed his gaze to a banner that crossed the street. FARMERS' FUND ANNUAL COMMUNITY DANCE. "I know where you stand, Jemma. I do. But give me the rest of the time you're here. Give me the chance, at least, to show you another route that might work for us."

"Okay," she said tentatively.

"And go to that dance with me tonight."

"Okay," she said, a smile lifting her cheeks.

After returning home for a shower and a change of clothes, Sam picked up Jemma in an old Ford pickup. He opened the door for her and she laughed. "I thought all you had was the motorcycle. I was worried for you, come winter."

"I only break out the old girl for special occasions," he explained, shutting Jemma's door and gazing at her through the open window. "You look gorgeous."

"Thanks," she said, smoothing her yellow skirt self-consciously. The butter-colored dress had been a last-minute decision in her packing, and Jemma was glad she had brought it. It had a sweetheart neckline, and the tight bodice met a full skirt that reached her lower calves—perfect for dancing.

"You don't look so bad yourself," she said. Sam looked like a young college professor, in a navy long-sleeved polo shirt and khakis. He got in beside her and cranked the old engine. After a second, it turned over and they were off, heading west into the setting sun.

The dance was held in the center of town, on a hastily built platform. Lights were strung around the perimeter, and elderly people sat on the outskirts on folding chairs, drinking punch. It looked like something out of Jemma's grandmother's book of Rockwell paintings. Sam took her hand and led her toward the platform, where the dance was just starting. "I feel like I'm playing hooky," she said quietly.

"Why?" he asked, a bemused smile on his face.

"Out dancing with the pastor! Isn't that illegal or something?"

"For some," he said. "I figure as long as we keep farther apart than I want to be, it's okay."

Jemma smiled, acknowledging the compliment and admiring his ethics. When was the last time she had met an honorable, available man? She couldn't remember. But her mind was soon distracted by her intention to match his dance steps as he led her through one expert move after another. She laughed as he twisted her around and she nearly lost her balance. "Where did you learn to swing?"

"Mom," he said, turning her around again. "Do you mind?" They talked when they were near enough to do so.

"Mind? No. You'll just have to teach me. The most I learned was the popcorn in grade school."

"No square dance?"

"Oh yes, that too. But I'd be hard-pressed to remember any of those moves. Maybe my old dance partner, Buddy Buck, would." The lively song ended and a slow waltz began.

"Buddy Buck, huh? Should I be jealous?"

"Probably. He used to walk me home, and once he told me he loved me."

"In what grade?"

"Fourth." They adjusted their tempo to match the slow number, and Sam pulled her in close. She seemed to fit in his arms just right, and she closed her eyes, wanting to memorize the feeling, the moment.

"Did he carry your books?"

Jemma laughed. "He did. Pretty gallant for a fourth-grader, huh?"

Sam pulled back and looked her in the eye. "I'd have done it for you in fourth grade. You were probably the prettiest one in the school."

Jemma smiled, embarrassed.

"What'd you say when he told you he loved you?" Sam asked. She met his glance and knew he was talking about more than Buddy Buck.

"I told him we were too young, and I just wanted to be friends."

"Ah. Are you still too young for love, Jemma?"

"No. But neither am I too old for friends." She could see that her comment had put him off, but she could not stop herself. Things were moving too quickly. It was dangerous. At this rate, Sam would have her heart on a platter just as Mark had.

Soon afterward, Sam took her home. They stopped for a root-beer float at a local A&W, and never had root beer tasted better to Jemma. But once again she felt something shift between them. As she thought about it, Jemma decided it was good. What if she found she hated Stillwater but could never leave because of Sam? She didn't want to be tied down. Not yet.

Sam hadn't invited her—either reluctant to have her turn him down again or a bit miffed by her subtle rebuff the night before—but Jemma rose the next day and headed to his service at the elementary school. She sat in the back, hoping to simply blend in and watch him at work, but his eyes soon met hers and he gave her a small smile. Jemma had the distinct feeling that he was able to connect with each of his parishioners like that, giving good cause for the packed auditorium. But deep inside, she hoped their connection was special, sacred.

Oh for heaven's sake. What is it, Jemma? Do you want him to think of you as special or just as a friend? Make up your mind, girl! She struggled to concentrate on his sermon instead of *them* and admired him in action after the service—how he listened attentively to those who spoke to him about serious matters; joked with the youth, drawing them in; and genuinely welcomed visitors, encouraging them to come back. He was charismatic and warm, friendly and kind.

He was dangerous, Jemma decided, and she was getting in too deep. At this rate, the windows would be repaired come autumn, but her heart would likely be shattered. She left without speaking to him and avoided her house for the day, climbing on her mountain bike and riding for miles.

"In that box. The chain was sticking through the floorboards. I pulled and the boards gave way. The box was underneath." She studied him for a moment. "It's almost as if she was having another funeral, burying her jewelry box like that."

Sam looked at her and nodded. "You're right. The locket, the letter, and the ring. That was all she had left of my great-great-grandfather. I've heard June ask Dad about her wedding band. I guess she thought that those memories belonged here, where they shared them."

"How'd he die?" she asked, moving toward the door.

"Who?"

"Your great-great-grandfather."

"Oh. Tuberculosis. Had it bad. Died in his thirties."

"Poor lady, your Grandma Emma."

"No kidding. Can you imagine being alone out here? And Stillwater was little more than the general store at the time."

"No, I can't. Listen, I had better head home. Have some miles to cross if I'm to get to Stillwater before dark."

"I can put your bike in the truck," Sam offered, gesturing over his shoulder.

"No. No thanks," Jemma said. She was eager to leave. "See you later, Sam."

"Oh. Bye." She could tell he was sorry to see her go. This "God thing," as he had called it, probably made him think that they were destined for one another. But he was wrong. Like Emma, Jemma belonged in the city. Her dad, her business, her home were there. Not out here. She couldn't make it work. She couldn't ever make it work.

The week went on, hotter than ever before. Jemma couldn't remember sweating so much or working in such humidity. She and Sam danced around one another, careful not to get too close, each clearly wanting something more. But it was better this way, Jemma decided. Better to end it before it really began.

She had just returned from lunch and was walking into the sanctuary when she spied the work crew. There were about twelve men and two women working inside, ignoring the stifling heat in their exuberance. Several were painting, several more were finishing the front area of the sanctuary where Sam had been working for weeks. Others were in the balcony, and it smelled as though they were stripping the paint to refinish the wood underneath.

Up front, one of the last five windows was lying on Jemma's workbench. On top of it was Sam's toolbox. She stifled a yell. His toolbox! On top of her window! She rushed forward and lifted it off, groaning at what she saw beneath it. Two cracked pieces. Two pieces she had labored to cut out of very expensive glass from Saint Paul and work into the window. She had even "aged" the solder to make it look like the rest. It had been seamless work, and now it was ruined. Furious, she grabbed the toolbox and marched to the back where she had glimpsed Sam working.

She dumped it at his feet with a loud clatter. "Thanks a lot!" she said in a barely controlled voice. "Thanks for ruining my window! Are you purposely trying to damage my work so that I have to stick around here longer?"

Sam looked confused, concerned. "What are you talking about?"

"My window! Your toolbox!" She couldn't keep herself from yelling anymore. "You left it on the window and broke it."

"Ah, miss—" came a voice behind her.

"Just a minute!" she barked over her shoulder and tapped Sam on the chest. "If you think you can keep me here through petty...*vandalism*, you have another thought coming!"

"Jemma!"

"Ah, miss—"

"In a minute!" she said, throwing up a hand. "You don't pay me enough to put up with this, Sam Tucker. You paid me to come fix these windows, so do me a favor and let me do my job!"

Sam's face broke into a grin.

"What? What's funny? You think this is funny?"

"No, I don't. Not about the window, I mean. I think your reaction is funny."

"Ah, miss, I'm afraid I'm your culprit."

Oh no. She turned to see a hulking man of about fifty, looking sheepish. "Someone yelled for help, and I had Sam's box in my hand. Didn't think about where I was putting it down. Just did it. I'm real sorry. I'll pay for the damage."

"No," Jemma said, instantly contrite. "No, that's okay. I'm sorry. I'm on edge lately. Really. I can fix it pretty fast."

The man gave her one last rueful look and turned away. Jemma closed her eyes and sighed, then told herself to have the courage to look Sam in the eye. When she did, she saw his gleeful expression. "What? What are you gloating about?"

"It's great."

"What's great?"

"Now, at least I know you care. I thought you didn't feel anything." He walked off and left her there to stew in her own juices.

Sam didn't approach Jemma again until two days later. The heat had continued, the temperatures passing a hundred during the day, and the church youth had a cooling-off event planned. He walked toward her, admiring her as she concentrated on her window, the one damaged days before. He cleared his throat, not wanting to startle her once again. "I was wondering if you'd come with us tonight," Sam invited when she looked up at him.

"What? Where?"

"One of our summer inner-tube parades on the river," he explained. "The youth love it, and we do it several times each summer. The trucks meet at the school at five, drop us off a few miles north, and we ride home. It's a blast. Almost as fun as water-skiing in the irrigation ditches."

"I won't ask," Jemma said.

"Better not to. Really, it is a great time. My sisters are coming, so we wouldn't need a chaperone. And it is one of my last opportunities to collect on my bet. The way you're working through these windows, you'll be gone before the end of August. Come with us, Jemma. I swear, it could be a tourist attraction."

"I didn't bring my inner tube from Manhattan," she said dryly.

"That's fine. We make 'em bigger and better here anyway," he said. "Tractors, you know. We have plenty to go around."

She stood and stretched, all long, lovely limbs. "Okay. What do they wear? Swimsuits or shorts?"

"Either."

"Okay. See you and the gang at five. I'd better knock off now and get some dinner."

"Don't do that. You'll spoil your appetite for pronto pups and s'mores over the bonfire afterward."

Jemma smiled, and Sam felt relieved to see it. She had such a nice smile, and it had been conspicuously absent for days now. "Pronto pups?"

"Hot dogs, for you easterners," he explained.

"It's been years since I've had a hot dog and a s'more."

"Small-town charm," he said with a shrug. "You've probably forgotten how fabulous they taste."

"When you're really hungry."

Sam laughed and nodded. "When you're really hungry. See you at five. Want a lift to the school?"

"No thanks. I'll just see you there."

It was hard maintaining her distance from Sam, but Jemma was determined. At home she had donned a pair of cutoffs, a swimsuit top, and a T-shirt, relishing the idea of a swim. When they got to the slow-moving river, she was delighted to find that it was a

Chapter Seven

O h man, you've got it bad," Alison said, as soon as Sam walked into his mother's kitchen some days later for a weekday family brunch to celebrate Tom's birthday.

"What are you talking about?"

"You can't fool us," June said, coming closer to look him over like rotten fruit. She rested her hand on his shoulder as she examined him. "Yep. Puffy eyes, red face. Samuel, have you been crying over Jemma?"

He shook off her hand, irritated.

"Girls, leave him be," Rose said from in front of the stove.

"I'm not making fun. I mean, I'd understand crying over her," June said, moving to pour orange juice at the table. "She's a great girl. You have to stop her."

"Stop her from what?" Rose asked.

"From leaving," Alison put in. "She's going back to New York in a couple of weeks."

"If she doesn't see what a wonderful boy you are," Rose said, "then she can just go on home."

"Mom—" Sam complained.

"Mom, it doesn't work that way," Alison said. "I think Jemma's head over heels in love with Sam, but she's afraid. Afraid of such big choices as love in the first place, and in the second, moving to Podunk, Iowa."

"I hate it when you call Stillwater 'Podunk.'"

"Sorry, Mom. But it is. You have to be very determined to move here. It's one thing to grow up here, another to move in. Especially from Manhattan."

"You should stop her, Sam," June said again. "Come and buy her huge bouquets at my store and leave one for her every day on her porch swing."

"I'll go broke," Sam said.

"That church needs to pay you more," Rose said.

"No, Mom. They pay—"

"Have you even taken her out for a decent dinner?" Alison asked.

"Sent her a sweet note?" June asked.

"Sent who a sweet note?" Keith asked, dropping into a chair and picking up a roll.

"Nobody!" Sam said. "Listen, if I had known I was going to get grilled over this, I wouldn't have come for brunch. Can't we eat together and talk about something else?"

"What?" Nick said, coming through the door. "What don't you want to talk about?"

"Nothing!" he sighed and shook his head at his mother. "Sorry, Mom. I think this is a bad idea. I need some time to think."

"And pray, sounds like."

"And pray. Do you think Dad would mind if I skipped out this morning?"

Rose went to the table and gathered three fresh rolls in a cloth napkin, along with a wedge of cantaloupe. She handed the bundle to her eldest and led him to the door. "Go, Son. Go and find your heart. Go and find what God wants for you, then follow his lead. You can make it up to your father later."

"Okay, Mom. Thanks." He bent down to kiss her cheek, then

waved over his shoulder at his siblings, who were all talking at once, discussing, it seemed, his love life.

He left Tucker land and rode for miles, thinking of little other than Jemma. When he had passed the barbed wire of smaller spreads and reached the farms that stretched out for miles, he slowed, looking for a spot to eat his breakfast. A mile farther he discovered a stand of willow trees encircling a small spring. He parked his motorcycle, hopped a rotting fence, and went to sit beside the water.

The spring bubbled and flowed, a source of life to who knew how many cattle and farmers that had passed this way. At one time it had been tapped for irrigation, but perhaps it gave too little to be worth the effort anymore; the irrigation equipment had been removed.

Sam continued to wrestle with his predicament while eating breakfast. He had fallen in love with Jemma. He knew it. His sisters were right. From the start, it had been different with her; he hadn't felt this way about a woman in years. What was he to do?

That corny ditty came to mind about if you loved something, you had to let it go, and if it came back, it was yours, and if it didn't, it wasn't yours in the first place. He hated that verse, first because he had heard it way too many times, and second, because it hurt to imagine letting Jemma go, not fighting for the chance to love and be loved.

"Why, Lord, why?" he asked, tears slipping down his face. It had been years since he had cried and a decade since he had cried twice in twenty-four hours. "Why must it go this way? I know you want the best for me. Is this a test? Or part of the plan?"

He could see her face in the waters of the spring. Her snappy hazel eyes and brown hair that glinted with gold highlights in the sun. He could picture her brow furrowed in concentration over her work, and he recalled how she playfully splashed back at the boys who idly flirted with her during their inner-tube trip. Sam wanted a wife, had prayed for a wife. "I'm thirty years old, Lord. Isn't it time? I'm angry with you. Yes, angry! How could you allow this to happen?"

She was everything he wanted: strong, beautiful, a little artsy, faithful. And there was something exotic about her too. "Probably that Manhattan influence," he mumbled to himself.

"I just want someone to come home to, Father. I want a best friend, a lover. Someone to raise a family with. What do you want from me? How can you hold Jemma in front of me like a carrot before a horse? Haven't I waited long enough?"

Sam glumly finished his breakfast and lay down on the grassy bank of the spring. He stared at the water, letting the last of his tears abate. "Okay, Lord. I've complained enough. You hear my cry. Let me listen now. Let me hear your word. Guide me in the way I should go, Father. And I promise, despite any grief I must bear, to follow. Just show me the way, Lord. Show me the way."

Jemma drove past cornfields that now reached as high as her shoulders, her backseat laden with stained-glass windows. The dealer in Fillmore had come through for her as promised and contacted other antique dealers in Camden County. True to his word, they all had come up with windows for her restoration business. None of them was a Tiffany, but several were competitors of the great artist, and the others were of fine quality. She would make a mint from them. It was while she was driving, thinking of how she had missed Sam over the last few days and wondering if she could actually live in Stillwater, that she thought of it.

What was keeping her in Manhattan? Besides the action, the culture, the movement? Over the summer, she had grown accustomed to the almost-spooky quiet of Iowa nights and the sweet breeze that sifted through the cornfields in the evenings. She liked knowing her neighbors and having them know her. She loved the sight of kids playing in her front yard on East Third, and people who practically lived on their front porches. What if she could have both? What if she could have a porch swing and a picket fence in Iowa *and* her industrial, contemporary studio in New York?

What if she could collect windows, first from Iowa, then from other Midwestern states, and refurbish them here in Stillwater? Then she could take them to her studio in Manhattan and sell them. Her profit margin would cover three or four trips east a year, as well as a salesperson for the studio. If she had enough windows, she could even hire some help here in Stillwater. She really liked the town, and if she could get out to the surrounding counties on road trips and take several trips east a year, it would make her feel less claustrophobic, less…stuck.

Jemma hopped into her Miata the next day, feeling more jubilant and hopeful than she had in weeks. As she had finished each church window, she had become more and more discouraged, thinking that each completion took her one step closer to leaving Sam's side. Although they had not pursued their relationship, the idea of it seemed to hang in the air between them like a winning lottery ticket just out of reach. Having slept on the idea of staying in Stillwater, Jemma smiled again. She could do it. She could do it!

She waved to the boys playing football in the street and tuned in her radio to Paul Harvey. It was cooler today, a blessed relief, and her heart pounded at the thought of telling Sam her idea. What if he didn't care anymore? What if he had given up on her? In minutes, she pulled into the church parking lot and hopped up the front steps. As she pulled open the door, she heard someone softly playing a piano in the front of the sanctuary.

Jemma paused, moved by the soulful, soft music. When had the piano arrived and who was playing it? There were a couple of keys that were sticking, but all in all, it sounded terrific. She entered quietly and padded down the center aisle. The musician was Sam, and he was so involved in his music he didn't even hear her come in. She sat down in the second pew, listening as he segued from one song to the next, sometimes picking up portions of an old hymn, other times catching the chorus of a pop song from the radio. Amazingly, it all seemed to meld together perfectly. The music built to a crescendo and then eased away, as if Sam were tiring. It was the loveliest thing Jemma had ever heard. It was as if she had peeked into his soul.

When his hands rested, she spoke, surprising him. "Let me hear how you would express joy," she requested simply. He thought for a moment, and then his hands moved lightly over the upper scales, the music sounding like racing water.

"Sadness," she said.

He thought again, then slowly played a song among the lower scales and minor keys.

"Frustration."

He responded accordingly, pounding on the keys.

"Wonder."

He played a delightful tune that reminded her of being a child and exploring.

"Love."

But he didn't play then. He rose and moved toward her, never pausing, never allowing his eyes to leave hers. He pulled her to her feet, and Jemma's heart hammered in her chest. Sam gently placed his hands on either side of her face and pulled her in for a long, deep, soft kiss.

"Jemma Stuart, I'm in love with you. God help me, I'm in love with you," he said with tears in his eyes. "What am I supposed to do with that?"

"What are *you* supposed to do! What am *I* supposed to do?" She felt the tears well in her own eyes. "Because apparently, Samuel Tucker, I'm in as deep as you are."

Chapter Eight

Jemma reveled in the idea of being Sam's girlfriend, and he seemed to feel the same. They held hands constantly, and once their love had been declared, they became inseparable. Still, she hadn't told him of her idea about staying in Stillwater. Something kept her from talking about it; it was as if she still needed to mull it over. And she didn't want to get Sam all excited over something she wasn't willing to see through.

So they spent the next couple of weeks dating as she continued her work on the windows. They went to his parents' home and to his sister's. They appeared at a church potluck, obviously "together," and set the gossip tongues wagging. Everyone was curious, but kind, and what hit Jemma most was that folks were genuinely happy for the couple, as if celebrating their love.

The last window was completed too soon, and Jemma stalled, taking her time in coordinating schedules with the carpenters to get all the windows back in place. *I really should be heading home now,* she admitted to herself. But she didn't care. And Sam, although he could clearly see that her work was done, never said a word. So she decided to enjoy their remaining time together. And enjoy it she did.

Jemma could not remember laughing or smiling so much. She

couldn't remember the last time she had *played* as much as she did with Sam. They were walking home one evening, a magical night with a hint of a breeze that set the leaves above Third Avenue rustling, when the neighbor boys begged them to play Mississippi with them.

"What exactly is Mississippi?" Jemma asked.

The youngsters—about eight of them—all started talking at once. "One person is it!"

"And they count—"

"Like this: 'One Mississippi, two Mississippi, three'…all the way to ten."

"You say, 'Go! One Mississippi,' and everyone runs. You have to hit all ten bases and get home before you're caught."

Sam turned to her and smiled. "You up for it?"

"Sure," she said, pulling off her sweater and dropping it on her neighbor's pristine lawn. "What are the bases? You boys haven't seen an expert play this game, have you?"

"You've played it?" one asked, eyebrows raised.

"No. But this is kid stuff. I'll have no problem taking all of you," she said.

They smiled at one another in obvious approval over their new neighbor's boast.

"What do you think, Pastor T? Is your girl going to beat you home?"

Your girl. The boy's words rang pleasantly in Jemma's ears. "I wouldn't doubt it," Sam said, throwing an arm around her shoulders in pride. "I wouldn't doubt it."

They played with the boys for over an hour, and Jemma even dived over grassy hills to find hiding spots. How long had it been since she had played anything? Her heart felt like it was going to burst, she was so happy. Around eleven, Sam called it quits, declaring himself overall winner over the loud protests of the boys.

"Catch you later," he said to them. "I'm going to see *my girl* home."

They whistled and whispered among themselves, laughing, and Sam shook his head. "It's time for you all to head in too. Don't keep the neighbors up."

"One more round!"

"No. See you all tomorrow." He waited expectantly for them to shuffle off, which they did. Jemma admired the respect he had earned from the youths. Would it be the same in New York if they were there? Somehow, she thought it would be.

He took her hand in his and they walked to her house. "Want to sit on the porch swing for a bit?" she invited. He nodded, his dark hair glinting in the moonlight.

"Do you want something to drink?"

"No thanks. I just want to sit here with you in the quiet."

They sat down together on the swing and he pulled her close to his side, his big arm around her shoulders. In the quiet of the night, a barn owl called from one of the big maples, the leaves still rustling around him. After screen doors had slammed, signaling the return of the Mississippi kids, the neighborhood was suddenly very still, as if Jemma and Sam were the only ones awake.

They swung back and forth, content in the silence and in one another's company. A waxing half-moon peeked through the branches above the street, and Jemma closed her eyes, wanting to memorize the feeling of the night. Being there with Sam, she could not imagine ever leaving him. She wanted to settle into her cottage and make it a home. She wanted to make a home with Sam. Would it ever work—the small-town pastor and the city girl? She thought of her childhood book about the city mouse and the country mouse.

"Suppose," she said, breaking the silence. "Suppose I were to stay here. To see if this thing we're working on could be long-term."

Sam looked at her steadily. "You would do that? You would consider that?"

"I would. It's not like you can move to New York, with your church and all."

He didn't respond for a moment. "Could you be happy here, Jemma?" he asked quietly. "In Stillwater? I mean, you haven't said I could collect on my bet yet."

She swallowed hard, having difficulty believing she was gutsy enough to say what she wanted. "I think so. I mean, I've been thinking. What if I just expanded my business to the Midwest? You know, collected windows from throughout Iowa and beyond, then took them home to Manhattan to sell. Could you ever go back with me?"

"For how long? It would be hard to leave my congregation."

"I don't know. Maybe I could go back for a month at a time, and you could come for a week of it. I was thinking I'd need to go back every quarter."

He gazed at her evenly and took her hand. "It means a lot to me, Jemma, that you would even consider it. I'd be willing to try any crazy sort of schedule if it meant I could be with you."

Jemma nodded and looked away toward the street, unable to bear the intensity of the moment any longer. "Let's think about it, Sam. Let's both think about it."

Labor Day was the biggest thing to hit Stillwater all summer. There was a tricycle parade in which every child under four—along with a few crazy teens—decorated a trike and hit the road in a huge group. Behind them came the mayor in a convertible, and the town's only fire engine, sirens blaring. There were two police officers throwing candy out their cruiser windows, the high school's marching band—sadly out of sync after a couple months of summer vacation—and then tractor after John Deere tractor. Jemma stifled a laugh. It was hardly the Macy's Christmas parade, but it had its own charm.

In fact, she liked it. There was a remarkable feeling of commu-

nity, and it was all very unpretentious. People didn't take themselves too seriously here, whereas in New York... Still, she missed
Manhattan. As much as she hated the idea of leaving Sam's side,
she felt the pull of the East within her. It was almost as if she had
to go home, to be sure that even considering staying in Stillwater
on a temporary basis was a wise idea.

Sam took her out to his folks' farm for a church corn feed that
afternoon. They all had lemonade while the fresh corn boiled in
huge cauldrons over two open fires. She looked around after her
first ear of corn to check out the rest of the meal, and Sam smiled
at her, seeming to read her mind. "That's it, if you're looking for
other food. This is a corn feed, and we eat it until we feel sick!"

Jemma laughed, then ate two more ears. The winner was
Jedediah Franklin, a hulk of a man who downed fourteen ears.
"Talk about feeling sick," Jemma whispered in Sam's ear. He
laughed and shook his head, then put his arm around her. She was
proud to be his girl, and it felt right to be in his arms. How could
she ever leave? How could she ever break it to him that she had to
leave, even if she planned to return?

That afternoon, Rose sent Jemma and Sam out to the orchard in
back to collect walnuts. As she picked them up from the ground,
she picked up the peculiar smell of citrus.

Sam saw her take a whiff of one and smiled. "They smell like
lime, huh?"

"Yes. That's it! I could have sworn..." Her voice broke off as
Sam walked deliberately toward her. "What?" she asked, backing
up. He had a playful look on his face. He kept on coming until
Jemma's back was against a huge old tree. Putting a hand up behind
her, he leaned forward, kissing her long and hard. He left her
breathless. When he broke away, he took the basket from her hand
and set it on the ground. Then he knelt before her. "Jemma, I—"

"No, Sam, wait." Her heart was in her throat. Horrified, she
realized he was proposing. "There's something I need to say to you."

His eyes studied hers, and he was obviously thinking about going on with it anyway. But when she did not soften, he rose. His head bent toward hers, one eyebrow cocked. "What is it, Jemma." There was no question in his voice, just intensity.

"I have to go home. To Manhattan."

He looked away.

"No. I mean, I don't think it's forever. It's just that before I make a decision to stay, I feel like I need to go home. To make sure that I can even take that next step of 'checking things out,' let alone considering the idea of staying forever."

"I was so sure…I had thought you had decided already. And then I thought, well, if you're going to be here anyway…"

She smiled at him and touched his lips, silencing him. "Hold that thought, Tucker. I think I'll want to hear it out in a couple of months. But first I'm going to Manhattan."

"When?" he asked, so softly she barely heard him.

"The sooner the better, I think. I was even considering going tomorrow. It never seems like a good time to leave, so I think I'll just have to do it. Fast, like ripping off a Band-Aid, you know? The windows have been done for more than ten days now. And I have responsibilities at home I need to tend to."

Sam nodded and looked toward the house. After a moment, he reached out a hand to her. "Then come," he said. "If you're leaving tomorrow, I don't want to share another minute of your time with the others."

Feeling melancholy, she nodded and took his hand.

They rode for an hour on Sam's motorcycle, and when they crested a hill, Jemma noted they were entering an abandoned junkyard for old cars, the latest model probably from the 1950s. Sam zigzagged his bike through the rusted-out frames and paused at the top of a hill. The sun was setting in a brilliant display that reminded Jemma of the approach of autumn colors. Sam got off.

Jemma, still astride the motorcycle, crossed her arms. "This is where you want to spend our last evening together? What are we doing here, looking for a new car for you?"

"Off the bike," he directed lightly, grinning at her with that heart-stopping smile. He had something up his sleeve, obviously. Going to his knapsack, he pulled out two long cables and then popped the hood of an old truck beside them.

"Uh, Sam, I think it's no use," she said with a laugh. "It's dead and it's not coming back. Besides there're no wheels…"

He just held up a hand, silencing her. After fiddling around for a moment, he stepped into the cab—the door was long gone—and turned the knob of an ancient radio. Through the static came the soft tones of Nat King Cole's voice.

Sam looked up at her and grinned again. "Dance with me, Jemma." He clambered out of the truck and stood before her. "Dance with me."

Jemma glanced up at him and laughed. "Here? In the middle of a junkyard?"

"Here, in the middle of a junkyard. Here, where there's only me and you for twenty miles." He took her in his arms, and they began to sway. "Look beyond the rust, Jemma. See the swaying grasses and the setting sun?"

"I do," she said, resting her head against his chest. Being there with him, dancing, was the single most romantic moment of her life. How had she been so blessed to have a man like Sam fall in love with her? How would she do without him, even for a short time? She cast the thoughts out of her mind, wanting only to concentrate on *this* moment in time, like she had that evening on her porch swing.

He sighed as he twirled her around, and every once in a while bent down to softly kiss her. "Do you see? Do you see, Jemma? Even a junkyard can be beautiful if you and I are together."

"Even a junkyard," she said softly.

They danced until the night sky dominated their view, and Sam worried that the battery might be running low on his motorcycle.

When they got back to Stillwater, they sat on her front porch swing until dawn, wanting only to hold one another, unable to say good-bye. As the sun came up, Sam finally rose and pulled her up for a hug. Then he tilted her chin up for a short kiss, turned, and walked away. He did not look back. Jemma wondered if he was crying too.

She cried the whole time she packed her two bags and loaded her car with the windows, her bike, and luggage. And she cried all the way out of Camden County.

Three days later, she was home.

Chapter Nine

Jemma stared out her studio window. The lights were off behind her, so she could better see the fat snowflakes that sifted out of a late-November night sky down to a streetlight below. In sweats, she reached behind her head to loosely braid her long hair, wanting it off her face. She stood there for several long minutes, feeling the warmth of the old radiator at her thigh and the cool fall air seeping around the windowpanes to touch her cheek. It was beautiful, just as beautiful as a junkyard at sunset, if not more so. This was home. How could she leave it?

Her heart ached for Sam Tucker. They had written one another long love letters nearly every day and spoken on the phone almost every night at first. But still, she could not make the decision to leave Manhattan. Now that she had been here for almost three months, it was even more difficult to depart. Iowa seemed distant; Stillwater, foreign. How had she ever felt at home there? Only the memory of Sam's big, warm arms called to her now. But maybe it had all gotten blown out of proportion. Maybe it had been only a summer romance, a fling. Maybe it was time to get past it and move on with her life.

The idea of small-town life was romantic, but who knew if it was for her? And if Sam Tucker truly wanted her to be his wife, he would never have let her go. If she had truly wanted to be Sam Tucker's wife, she would never have left. Didn't she already know all she needed to know? There wasn't any need to return to "check things out." She knew.

She glanced at her watch, struggling to see the time in the dim light. Seven o'clock. It was time to dress. Tonight was the show, the opening of her new gallery and studio. She had invited Sam repeatedly, but he had begged off, telling her he had to be in Stillwater for a congregational meeting or something. If she was important to him, wouldn't he be here? About that time their calls and letters had begun to grow more infrequent.

Jemma sighed and turned away from the mesmerizing flakes. She walked to her closet and pulled out a dress that had cost her a month's pay. She undressed and first slipped on hose, then the long sheath, which reached her ankles. It was made of shimmering polished silk, in a pale green that brought out the best in her eyes. It had spaghetti straps and a matching shawl that she would wear around her shoulders. Jemma slipped on ivory heels and a choker of delicate pearls, then added earrings. She did a quick updo with her hair, first unbraiding it, then pinning it in back with a pearl comb, and finally curling long tendrils at her ears and over one side of her forehead, just beside her right eye.

Smashing, she admitted to her image in the mirror. She paused. If only her smile would come back. It seemed as if she had left it in Stillwater—where she had left her heart. *Enough!* Sam Tucker, as wonderful as he had seemed to be, was obviously not meant to be the One. If he were, she would still be in Stillwater, or he would be here.

You're being stupid, Jemma. Impossible. How could he leave? You know he feels called to be there! They've just gotten into the restored sanctuary and they're approaching Advent. There's so much for him to do… Letting out a sound of disgust, Jemma turned and pulled on her shawl, just as the phone rang. *My cab, probably.* It was.

She dabbed on some pale pink lipstick and wished one last time that Sam were there. It would be so much easier going to these things as a couple. Life would be so much easier as a couple! "Stop it, Jemma," she said aloud. "Stop it, stop it, stop it!" She glared at her mirror image. "You've made your choice, haven't you? Now make the best of it! Think of all you have going for you. Hundreds of people would love to trade places with you, so stop being a whiner!"

She heard the cab horn *beep* and grabbed her purse and keys. After locking the three deadbolts of her front door, she hurried down the steps to the first floor before the cabby could leave her behind.

The show began with Jemma restlessly pacing the wood floors of her remodeled gallery, wondering if anyone would appear. The local newspaper had given her work rave reviews, and the opening was touted as a "must" for the city's elite; word had it that invitations to the event were highly prized. But Jemma doubted her sources. Who did she truly know, anyway, who would know these people? You didn't take people at face value in New York as you did in Iowa. If you trusted a smile, the next instant you could get smacked over the head. Shawna, a close friend and her new gallery manager, constantly reminded Jemma to "always watch your back."

Her words echoed in Jemma's mind as she paced the floor, the hired waiters nervously rearranging cocktail napkins and checking portable ovens to make sure the canapés were not getting burned. She had already invested over two thousand dollars on the caterers, not to mention all the money that had gone into the showroom's renovation. Was it all for naught? Had she been stood up for some other gallery opening?

Jemma wrung her hands and walked past the walls of hanging, restored windows held in place by long chains hung from the high tin ceiling. Her new showroom had once been a bank, and she had had part of the plaster sandblasted away to expose some of the turn-of-the-century brick. The wood floors had been refinished, leaving the flaws exposed. It was a perfect setting for old windows now restored. The lighting was soft, allowing just enough of a glow to make the sparkle come through the deep ochres and sapphire blues. There were over forty windows in place, more than half from Iowa. Each sported a tag about where it had been discovered and the supposed original artist. Some of her favorites were still those she and Sam had found in…*Oh, Sam. I miss you.* What she wouldn't give for a hug from him tonight!

The front door opened and Jemma turned, wishing Sam Tucker were coming through that door. What if he *had* come? What if he came through that door and said, "Come on, Jemma. There's more to life than this. Come home. Come home with me to Stillwater"? What if he walked right up to her, just as he had in the orchard, backing her up against the brick wall and kissing her as she'd never been kissed—

"Hello? Anybody in there?"

Jemma snapped back to the present and saw Shawna peeking around the corner at her. Her tall, blond friend was wearing a little red number that would certainly get her a few invitations for dinner.

"In your own little world there, huh? Well, look alive. There are people arriving in long, black vehicles that aren't hearses."

"What? They're here? Someone's here?"

"Sure! I called and left a message for you today. The newspapers are all—"

"Yes, but here it is, already seven-thirty—"

"The fashionable hour. Honey, you've been in the boondocks too long. Remember how New York lives? This place won't be hopping until ten, and then baby, look out!"

Jemma sighed. Right then, staying up until ten sounded like a lot of work. At ten, she would wish she was on a porch swing in the middle of Iowa…

"Max!" came a shrill voice from the front of the gallery. "Max! Have you ever seen such remarkable work! Yes, please. I'd *kill* for a beverage right now. Oh! Cassandra! Come and see this! Wouldn't it be just to die for in my front parlor?"

Shawna rolled her eyes and nodded at Jemma. It was time. This was it. If her business was to be a success, tonight had to come off without a hitch. Jemma nodded to the waiters. Bring on the caviar. Bring on the canapés. Bring on the crystal flutes. Give New York what it demanded: Something fresh. Something innovative. Something exciting. Something old, made new again. Because at the very least, Jemma had to earn back the two thousand for the caterers, her investment in the original windows, and mortgage money.

By ten o'clock Jemma had a raging headache. Shawna found her outside in the alley, holding a cold cup of cappuccino in her hands. The snow had ceased, but it had left a pristine blanket of white over everything. "Okay, what are you doing out here in subzero temperatures?" Shawna asked. "Waiting to get mugged?"

Jemma smiled. She and Shawna had become buddies in art school and were more like sisters than friends. "I've got a killer headache. If I have to smile at one more person who cares more about what they're wearing than my windows, I'm going to scream."

"Which is why you've hired me, the Queen of Schmooze," Shawna said brightly.

"Exactly. I don't know, Shawna. Something's changed for me. I've been dreaming about this night for years, and here we are, a success, right?"

"Right."

"And it means nothing. I mean, I'm glad that I can meet my mortgage and overpay my gallery manager and cover my debts. I find a certain satisfaction in being considered successful. But what's it all for? Why do it at all? My favorite part is the treasure hunt, finding the windows—diamonds in the rough—and restoring them. This part is…empty."

"You must be kidding! This is the great part! The glory! If my sculpture was received like this—"

"Your sculpture is original. I'm just recapturing someone else's original beauty. Someday someone will discover your work."

"Maybe. Maybe not. The point is that only one percent of all artists ever make enough to live on in this city, and it looks like you're in the club. God is smiling! Don't spit in his face by not reveling in the gift."

"I'm just saying that maybe I made a mistake. Last summer I was thinking about moving. I mean, opening up this gallery, having you run it, then heading back to someplace more quiet to live. Someplace where the pace isn't so fast."

"Someplace like Iowa."

"Yes."

"Someplace like Stillwater with a handsome pastor you fell in love with and left."

"Yes."

Shawna mulled it over for a second then tipped her head back. "Can we talk about this inside? You're looking hypothermic, and I'm on my way there myself."

Jemma nodded, noticing for the first time that she was shivering. Once inside, Shawna wrapped her coat around Jemma's shoulders and looked her in the eye. "For as long as I've known you, we've always encouraged one another to follow God's lead. Is this where he's taking you? I mean, it sounds like it would work to me. Talk about having it all. Love. Work you love. A slave like me to sell the work you love. A killer gallery that the city is wild for. A—"

"Yes," Jemma interrupted. "I think this is God's lead."

"Then do it."

Jemma felt the grin grow across her face, engulfing her cheeks. Once in Manhattan, she had become so wrapped up in achieving her professional goal that Stillwater had seemed to fade into a dream, become almost surreal. She doubted some of it, even wondered if Sam Tucker was all she had made him up to be in her mind. Her heart wanted to trust the long phone calls and love letters that reaffirmed what had begun last summer, but her big-city mind questioned it all. *Watch your back.*

Maybe that was what drew her to Stillwater and Sam Tucker.

There, with him, she felt a certain peace that she had never encountered before, as if her back was being covered already. God's lead, certainly. Maybe God's blessing too. "Father, let me be wise about this," she whispered heavenward.

Jemma felt an uncanny sense of peace when she reentered the gallery. It was as if she had been given new eyes; she was overwhelmed by the compassion she felt for the people who had come to rave over windows and purchase them for homes already overflowing with possessions. They were seekers, desperate for the peace that passed all understanding. What was this peace she was experiencing? It was feeling as free to leave Manhattan as she had been to leave Stillwater. It was all up to her. There was no perfect place to live, after all. Any place had its drawbacks and positive attributes. Maybe a plan like the one she had hatched last summer could work after all.

If Sam Tucker really was in love with her.

She was circulating through the throngs of people again, greeting everyone she met, when an older woman in a wheelchair gained her attention. She was in a classic dress, and a stately man stood by her side, gazing at the same window as she. When Jemma drew near, they turned to her and smiled into her eyes. Jemma was affected by it, since many who attended these shows never let a smile reach their eyes.

"You have done a fine job with these, Miss Stuart," the woman said.

"Fine," the man repeated.

"May I ask why you do this? Take old windows and restore them?" The old woman's eyes were a crystal blue, piercing and alive, though her body below was withering.

"Why? To pay the rent, I guess."

"No. You know why."

Jemma let out a half-laugh at the lady's audacity but was not offended. She paused, thinking, then spoke. "No. You're right. It's beyond the rent. It's my passion."

She turned toward the window before them, one of the Tiffany projects rescued from the back of an Iowa antique store. "These windows are like windows to the past for me. I imagine their creators and the times they lived in. What would they think if they knew I would one day be restoring their pieces? They're like fine silver, covered with tarnish. Wipe that away and you see something remarkable, what it was meant to be."

"Rather like life, eh?" asked the distinguished gentleman.

Jemma thought for a moment, and then nodded once. "Yes. You're right. In fact I've just recently discovered that I haven't been looking for the silver hard enough. Been caught up with the tarnish. But underneath—"

"There's sterling. Wise words from someone so young," the woman said approvingly.

"The wisdom hasn't come readily. Most days, God has to hit me over the head before I see something the way I ought to."

"Well, you're not alone."

"Don't let the tarnish keep you from the wealth," the man said, wheeling the woman Jemma assumed was his wife toward the front door. It was late, almost midnight, and the crowd was beginning to thin out.

"I won't," Jemma whispered.

"Know who that was?" Shawna asked, suddenly at her elbow.

"No."

"Genevieve Tiffany Gabor, heiress to the Tiffany fortune."

Jemma gasped. "You're joking! She hasn't been out in years!"

"She heard you had found some fine Tiffanys. Called and purchased them sight unseen. Raved when she saw their condition and the restoration work you had done on them."

At one A.M., Shawna paid the caterers and they packed up to leave. Jemma collapsed into a chair after seeing out the last of their customers. "How'd we do?" she asked, rubbing her eyes, indifferent to her smeared mascara.

"Over half were sold. Serious interest in another ten, I'd say. They'll be back this week. All in all, I'd say you're as much of a success as the newspapers said you'd be. And I have a job for a bit, if you'll get back out there and restock our showroom."

Jemma smiled and leaned her head against the chair. Closing her eyes was a blessed relief. Outside, a truck pulled to a stop in front of the gallery and the door opened. Jemma, wearily looking up, said, "I'm sorry, but we're—"

Sam.

It was Samuel Tucker. In a tuxedo. A bit disheveled and with oil spattered on his white shirt, but still there, in her gallery, in a tuxedo. His gaze locked with hers.

"Sir, we're closed for the night," Shawna said, obviously wondering what had happened to Jemma's tongue, but then she glanced from Jemma to Sam. Then from Sam, slowly back to Jemma. "You can come back...Wait a minute. Let me guess. Sam Tucker, handsome Iowa pastor?"

"Well, I'll admit to the Iowa pastor part," he said, his blue eyes never leaving Jemma's.

"I'll vouch for the handsome part," Jemma said. "You came. All the way to New York." She rose and went to him, and he took her into his arms for a long, warm hug.

"Man, I've missed you," he said.

"I don't think I realized just how much I missed you until tonight."

"And I'm Shawna, Jemma's best friend whom she's rudely forgotten to introduce," Shawna said.

"Nice to meet you," Sam said with a smile, his eyes still locked on Jemma's. "Got any music, Shawna? Some Nat King Cole?"

"Comin' right up." She clearly enjoyed playing Cupid. Jemma could hear it in her voice. She went to the back office to put on a CD, and Jemma could hear her strike some matches, relighting the huge pillar candles throughout the gallery and dimming the lights, settling a warm, cozy glow about them.

"You came," Jemma repeated.

"A bit late," Sam said ruefully. "In more ways than one. The truck broke down…I'm sorry, Jemma. I wanted to be here tonight for you."

"It's okay. It means so much to me that you tried."

Nat King Cole's voice crooned softly through the speakers. *"When I fall in love, it will be forever…"*

"Good night, Jemma! Nice to meet you, Sam! I'm sure we'll become friends when you can tear your eyes away from my buddy."

"Lookin' forward to it," Sam murmured. The back door slammed shut and they were alone. Sam pulled her into his arms to dance. "I'm sorry, Jemma."

"You tried to get here—"

"No, I'm sorry I ever let you leave Stillwater."

"You had to let me leave. I had to go to figure it out. Had to leave to see what I was missing. And I didn't even figure it out until tonight."

"Figure what out?"

"I was so afraid that I would be missing Manhattan that I never got past the tarnish in Stillwater."

"What?"

Jemma pursed her lips and shook her head. "Bear with me for a moment. Every place is like tarnished silver. *Life* is like tarnished silver. You have to get past the grit and gray to see the stuff that is valuable underneath. It's like finding you in Stillwater—a town I looked down my nose at—and then learning I could be happy there too. Like learning that you can be happy anywhere if you dig down to the good stuff."

"That's when I fall in love with you."

Sam smiled down at her. "Are you saying I can collect on my bet?"

"Maybe. You haven't been with me to Anthony's yet…"

"So you're coming home?" He knelt before her and took her hand. "Will you come home with me, Jemma? To be my bride? If you can scrub away enough of my own tarnish, that is, and see the sterling guy I really am."

"There's not much to scrub, Sam Tucker. I want to build a life with you. I'd love to be your wife."

Sam stood, lifted her into his arms, and kissed her.

But it was difficult to kiss because both of them were smiling.

Twice in a Blue Moon

by Barbara Jean Hicks

Chapter One

It was a foolish notion, of course, after living in Seattle for twenty-five years, to think he could be happy in a little town like Pilchuck. He didn't know where in the world the idea had come from.

You can't go home again, he argued, fighting the buoyant feeling the mere thought of Pilchuck had unexpectedly stirred in his heart. But it was hard to argue with weightlessness. Especially when he'd felt so heavy for so long.

Maybe not to live. But you can visit, he argued back. Besides, there were times in a man's life when he just had to go with his impulse, and Jack's impulse this fine June morning was to get out of Dodge. The old hometown was calling.

So within the hour he was in his car—a ridiculously decked-out gold Jeep Cherokee that had never seen a moment of four-wheeling—heading north on the interstate with his overnight bag and the latest Tom Clancy novel. Just in case he ran out of things to do in Pilchuck.

He hadn't even called his sister to say he was coming; she'd be at the store on a Saturday morning anyhow, and probably busy with customers. Besides, it would be more fun to surprise her.

Fun! he thought. How long had it been since the idea of *fun* had occurred to him?

Too long.

He jumped. He could have sworn the thought had come to him in Helen's voice. As in, "Don't cry for me too long, Jack. Life's too precious. And I should know."

Surprisingly, he didn't even feel sad, thinking about Helen. How could that be?

It's time.

Not words, but an impression. And no question where it came from.

"Thank you, God," he breathed, and then without thinking broke into the chorus of a hymn he hadn't been able to bring himself to sing for three years: *It is well, it is well with my soul!*

This morning, for the first time since Helen's funeral, the words felt like the truth.

His resonant baritone filled the Jeep with song after song for most of the next two hours. Hymns. Choruses. Spirituals. He couldn't remember the last time he'd felt so light. So free.

He exited the freeway just before eleven and approached the bridge that led over the Ruby River into the little town where he'd spent the first eighteen years of his life. *Welcome to Pilchuck,* the sign at the near end of the bridge read. *Town Motto: We like it like this.*

He grinned. Helen had always been so amused by Pilchuck's town motto.

He stopped at the red light just over the bridge. *Gonna lay down my burden,* he hummed.

One traffic signal at the bridge and three more up ahead, he saw as he waited for the light to change. So Pilchuck had grown into a four-light town! They weren't just for show either—the weekend traffic, both auto and pedestrian, was heavier than he remembered it being even several years ago, the last time he'd come for a visit.

Otherwise, Main Street stood shining in the summer sun almost the way it stood in his childhood memory. There was the old square post office building and the ivy-covered brick library. The Apple Basket Market, Fairley's Drug and Fountain, the Kitsch 'n' Caboodle Café—none of them looking much different than they'd looked nearly thirty years ago when he'd left Pilchuck to take on the world.

There were a few new names on the street, of course. Like his sister Bonny's Blue Moon Gallery. It would be fun to see what she was doing with the store.

Fun! There was that word again!

A *Drive-Through Espresso* sandwich board on the curb caught his eye, and he pulled off the street and into line at the window, behind an ancient, beat-up pickup truck with five teenagers crammed into the front seat.

The memory of another Saturday morning suddenly flashed into his mind. A Saturday morning thirty years ago. He'd been sixteen, newly licensed, the first in his group of friends to have his own driving machine—a cherry red '57 Chevy pickup with four on the floor and a souped-up engine.

Cait had been almost as crazy about that truck as he'd been, he thought, smiling to himself. Cait Anderson, his best buddy practically from the cradle on. He'd picked her up the very morning he'd signed the pink slip for the Chevy—Cait and a couple of other friends—and driven them out to Heron Bay to cruise the strip. Later, back in Pilchuck, they'd whooped it up for the seven minutes it took to cruise the town from one end to the other and back.

Jack Van Hooten had been in his element.

Especially when an officer of the law pulled up behind him, siren blaring and blue lights flashing. When had life ever been so exciting?!

It was the sixties, so of course the mild warning the officer issued Jack had evolved into police brutality as the story was repeated, and he and his friends were campus heroes at Pilchuck High School for weeks afterward. Until the senior class president actually got arrested for chaining himself to the front door of the army recruiting center in the county seat at Bellingrath.

Honn-kk!

Jack looked up, startled. The pickup had moved beyond the espresso window, and the driver behind Jack's Jeep was leaning on his horn.

He pulled forward and ordered a cup of black coffee for himself and a mocha for Bonny. A habit he'd learned from Helen—never arriving anywhere empty-handed. Gracious, thoughtful, caring Helen...

He wished they'd made the time to visit Bonny more often. His sister had been only six when he left home, more like a doll to him than a real human being. He liked the person she'd turned into. He wondered if she knew.

Maybe after he'd had a chance to look around the gallery, Bonny would let him treat her to a bite of lunch. The Kitsch 'n' Caboodle had always served a decent sandwich and a tasty soup. If one could get past the painfully tasteless decor.

As for the rest of the afternoon—well, he'd have to see.

Meanwhile, the Cait of Jack Van Hooten's memories—Cait Reilly, she was now—strolled contentedly through the Blue Moon Gallery in Pilchuck, admiring the lovely pieces on display.

In an unconscious ritual Cait performed every time she entered her friend Bonny's craft gallery, she lifted her hands to stroke here, caress there: the smooth, fragile surface of a handblown bowl, the soft nap of a hand-knit angora afghan, the satin finish of a hand-made cherry dining set...

Her eye caught the notice above a display of ceramic tableware: *Lovely to handle, Tempting to hold, If you break it or soil it, Consider it sold!*

She sighed. At least the reminders, posted every few feet along the walls, were elegantly scripted, in keeping with the exquisitely crafted items for sale.

And at least she'd talked Bonny out of *Keep your mitts off!*

"How can you possibly expect your customers not to touch when the pieces practically *beg* to be touched?" she'd asked her friend.

"They're here on consignment, Cait. I'm responsible for them!"

"You want to sell them? *Let the customers touch,*" Cait urged.

So the signs were a compromise.

Not that Bonny should have to compromise—it was her store, after all. Cait did provide the Blue Moon with a line of fanciful evening bags—pieced-fabric clutches embroidered, appliquéd, and embellished with interesting baubles. Eminently touchable, one might add.

And her younger daughters, the twins, did work for Bonny.

But Cait was only one of several dozen artists and craftsmen Bonny represented. And Robin and Rosie were only eighteen, and worked at the Blue Moon only between their more important obligations: during the school year, their community-college schedules. Currently, summer-stock theater. *Phantom of the Grand Ol' Opry,* to be exact.

Still, Bonny might never have opened the Blue Moon Gallery without Cait's support and encouragement. Especially after that flaky husband of hers—ex-husband now—had picked up and left town with barely a good-bye. Just as Cait might never have stuck with her dressmaking business after Joe-Joe had died if Bonny hadn't believed in her so strongly.

Wasn't that what best friends were for? And wasn't Bonny Fairley her very best friend in all the world, now that Joe-Joe was gone?

"Hey, lady!" Cait heard a familiar voice behind her. "D'you have to leave your fingerprints on *everything?!*"

Cait smiled over her shoulder at the tall, slender redhead

pushing through the stockroom doorway, several willow baskets swinging from her arms.

"You have to ask?"

Bonny rolled her eyes. "One of these days you're going to drop something," she said for the hundredth time as she set the baskets on a table behind the cash register. "And more likely a three-hundred-dollar vase than a twenty-dollar paperweight. *Then* what will you do?"

Cait tucked her short blond hair behind one ear. "Be in your debt forever," she said, then added, "as if I weren't already."

"Oh pshaw!"

Bonny was the only person outside the comic strips Cait had ever known who said "pshaw!" She pronounced it in two syllables, the "p" by itself, barely more than a puff of air, and the "shaw" exploding out of her mouth like a circus clown out of a cannon. Bonny made Cait laugh, which Cait had sorely needed after Joe-Joe's tragic accident.

She fingered a brocade and satin crazy quilt draped over a hickory chair, rubbing her thumb across the even feather stitches. She didn't know why she so loved the feel of things, but she did know it was one of the reasons she'd chosen dressmaking as her trade.

She liked the look of things too, of course, and had, as one of her favorite clients put it, "an enviable eye for design." She had to, in her line of work.

But it was the feel of a nubby wool, a plush velvet, a light-as-a-whisper silk chiffon under her fingertips that gave her real pleasure. The same kind of pleasure as the sun on her face, the wind in her hair, the touch of a loving friend. Maybe it was because touch seemed so much more reliable a sense than eyesight. Without her glasses or contact lenses, Cait was blind as a mole.

"This is a lovely piece, Bonny," she said. "You've discovered a new quilt artist?"

Bonny looked up from the tags she was printing. "Olga Pfefferkuchen, believe it or not."

"Really! The woman is full of surprises, isn't she?"

Everyone in Pilchuck knew Olga Pfefferkuchen. And until two years ago, not a one of them would ever have said she was full of surprises. Full of vinegar maybe. Full of resentment and ill will and perversity.

Some of the townfolk were still mystified by old Olga Pfefferkuchen's complete and utter transformation. Not Cait. The good Lord had worked a miracle, plain and simple. No other explanation—even the popular theory that Olga had been kidnapped by aliens and given a personality transplant—made any sense at all.

"I love finding local artists to represent," said Bonny. "Tillicum County seems to have talent in spades."

"It's the clean air. Gets the creative juices flowing." Tillicum County, in the northwestern corner of Washington state, got rain 265 days of the year, give or take a week or two.

"I don't think that's it," said Cait. "I think you're just a first-class Finder of Neat Stuff."

"A first-class Finder of Neat *People*," Bonny corrected her.

"I'm certainly glad you found *me*," Cait said. And she didn't mean just to sell her evening bags either.

In her forty-six years, Cait had been privileged to have three best friends. *Real* best friends. A pretty good record, she thought, when in grade school alone a girl might go through three "best friends" in as many days.

The first eighteen years there'd been Jack, who was born one hour, six minutes, and twenty-four seconds after Cait was, at the same hospital—St. Boniface's in Bellingrath—and lived next door to her in Pilchuck all the way through high school. They were practically twins. "*Siamese* twins," Cait's mother used to say. "Attached at the hip."

Then, like so many young people of their generation, Jack had gone away to college and never come home again. Oh, holidays, of course, but that hardly counted.

She wasn't sure she'd ever quite forgiven him.

Then had come Joe-Joe—a totally different experience than Jack, of course, as Joe-Joe had been her sweetheart and her husband before he'd finally grown into her best friend. He'd been a grand best friend too, and a grand husband. A once-in-a-blue-moon husband. A once-in-a-blue-moon father to their three girls. Until the Almighty had seen fit to take him.

It had come as a surprise, Bonny stepping in to fill the "best friend" gap after Joe-Joe, even though they did live right across the street from each other. Even though they'd both sung alto in the choir at the Pilchuck Church of Saints and Sinners for two years. Even though they'd always been friendly.

For one thing, at thirty-four Bonny was a dozen years younger than Cait.

And divorced.

And childless.

For another—she was Jack Van Hooten's sister. Jack Van Hooten as in Best-Friend-Number-One.

Jack stood on the sidewalk outside the Blue Moon Gallery wondering how on earth he was going to get inside. With a cup of hot coffee in each hand, he couldn't press the old-fashioned latch on the gallery door. Apparently, automatic doors still hadn't made it to Pilchuck.

He couldn't even tap on the window to get his sister's attention. And she was standing right there behind the counter, her head bent over some unseen task, her long red hair falling like a curtain around her face. Her work had every ounce of her attention. Jack doubted Bonny would notice even if he got up the nerve and energy to dance a jig out here on the sidewalk.

He glanced up and down the street. No one coming. He leaned in closer to scan the store. Maybe a customer would happen to look up and notice his plight.

On the other side of the window a woman stood, her short blond hair shining in the morning sun that slanted through the window. She was gazing down at a display of shimmering glassware—perfume flasks, it looked like. She picked up a sapphire-colored bottle, rotated it in her hands, took out the stopper, put it back in again.

Hold it up to the light, Jack willed.

She tested the weight of the bottle, ran her fingers over its curves, held it out in front of her, head tilted…

Jack pressed his forehead against the window. Who bought glass without seeing how it caught the light? *Hold it up to the window!*

She turned toward him, lifting the blue flask high to catch the sun.

Cait!

Then everything seemed to happen at once.

Cait's brown eyes, wide and startled, met his through the window. She jumped, he jumped, hot coffee sloshed, blue light flashed. The plastic foam cups jumped out of Jack's hands, the bottle slipped through Cait's fingers—

Coffee splattered across the gallery window.

Glass shattered against the gallery floor.

"Cait-Cat!" Jack shouted, grinning from here to China.

Cait's face, too, was beaming. "Hoot-Owl!" he heard her muffled reply.

Only in the back of his mind did he hear his sister's howl of dismay.

Chapter Two

I was just thinking about you!"

"I was just thinking about *you!*"

Bonny came out from behind the counter with a broom and a dustpan. "I don't think *either* of you wants to know what I'm thinking about," she said darkly.

Cait wasn't sure if it was Bonny's words or the crunch of glass underfoot that brought her suddenly back to earth. She pulled away from Jack's bear hug and gazed at the mess on the floor. The blue flask she'd dropped when Jack's face appeared in the window like the Ghost of Christmas Past had been marked with a forty-five-dollar price tag. "Oh, Bonny. I *will* pay for it," she said, distressed.

"No, no—I'll pay for it," Jack broke in.

Cait grabbed the broom out of Bonny's hands and started sweeping. "Don't be silly, Hoot. It was my fault, Cait. Pretty scary seeing old Hoot-Owl's ugly mug appear out of nowhere like that, huh?"

She grinned. "You can say that again!"

"Pretty scary seeing old Hoot—"

"Spare me," Bonny interrupted, rolling her eyes. She handed Jack the dustpan and disappeared for a moment behind the counter. Jack knelt with the pan, tilting it up so Cait could sweep in the broken glass.

"You've got coffee all over your pants, Hoot," she said. They were nice slacks too, in a light-colored khaki that *might,* if he were lucky, have some kind of stain-resistant finish. "Do you have something to change into?"

"They'll dry," he said.

She shook her head. "If they do, you're in trouble. You need to get that stain rinsed out *before* they dry."

Bonny popped back up from behind the counter, a roll of paper towels and a bottle of glass cleaner in her hands. "Listen to her, Jack. Cait *knows* this stuff. You can rinse 'em out in the employee washroom. If you have a change of clothes, that is." She narrowed her eyes. "You wouldn't dare drive up without planning on staying the weekend, would you?"

"You mean you'd let me?" he teased. "After splashing coffee all over your clean window?" He put an arm around his sister's shoulders and pulled her close.

"Under advisement." Bonny wriggled out of his hug and thrust the ammonia and the paper towels toward him. "As long as you clean it up," she added.

"I'll get it," said Cait, intercepting the spray bottle and the roll of towels. "You get out of those pants, Hoot-Owl."

"Watch it," said Bonny jokingly. "That's my brother you're talking to."

Jack pushed the door open for Cait. "It seems a little silly—"

"Wasting a perfectly good pair of pants—now *that* would be silly," she said as he followed her outside. "You rinse 'em out, I'll take 'em home and throw 'em in the washer and dryer. Good as new in an hour."

He let the door swing closed behind him. "That's so much trouble—"

"I live two minutes away, Hoot. It's no trouble."

He crossed his arms and lifted his chin in a way she still

remembered from their childhood. "All right, then. If you'll let me pay for the perfume flask."

Cait sighed. Still as stubborn as all get-out. *Absurdly* stubborn. Just like his sister.

"Pigheaded," Cait called her Number-Three-Best-Friend on occasion.

"Tenacious," Bonny corrected her.

Cait didn't know what Jack called it, but whatever it was, the concept applied.

She ripped off several sheets of paper towel and sprayed some cleaner on the window where his coffee had muddied the view. "All right," she agreed. "Change your pants and pay the bill, and then I'm taking you home. Have you had lunch?"

"Oh, no you don't. You're not *feeding* me too. In fact—" He reopened the door to the gallery and called to his sister, "I really came by to see if I could take you to lunch, Bonny. Maybe Cait could join us?"

"You're on," Bonny said, looking up from the display shelf where she was rearranging the glassware. "Rosie comes in at noon, and Robin will be back from lunch around the same time. Meet you at the Kitsch 'n' Caboodle?"

He looked at Cait. She sighed again, then nodded.

As Jack settled up the bill with Bonny a few minutes later, his khakis traded for a pair of faded jeans, Cait leaned against the doorjamb, arms crossed, and considered the pair thoughtfully.

They didn't look a thing alike, Jack and Bonny—except for the freckles, maybe. Bonny was no midget, but Jack towered over her, as big and solid-looking as an old-growth cedar next to Bonny's willowy grace. In contrast to his sister's straight fall of red hair, Jack's hair was almost black, it was so dark. Great hair for a guy in his forties, she thought—thick and wavy, not even a touch of gray.

She couldn't see either of their eyes at the moment, but she knew both pairs well—Jack's, peering out at the world from under thick dark brows, as clear and blue as the shards of glass from the shattered perfume bottle; Bonny's the deepest brown, like bittersweet chocolate.

Thank goodness Bonny hadn't inherited the Van Hooten chin! Although it did look good on Jack, Cait mused. Strong, firm, resolute...

Ha! Try *stubborn.*

Best-Friend-Number-Three and Best-Friend-Number-One did share qualities other than their common pigheadedness—character traits Cait had come to know and love in Bonny over the last eight years the way she had in Jack so long ago. Passion, intelligence, resourcefulness—and underneath it all, the tenderest of hearts. Excellent qualities in a best friend.

"You look good, Jack," Bonny was saying. "Relaxed. Happy, even."

"I'm getting there," Jack said, signing his name to the charge slip. Then, as if that were enough about him, he turned the question back on his sister. "What about you? Still happy you quit teaching and went into business?"

"Best decision I ever made. The pay isn't as steady, but do I love being my own boss!"

"As if you weren't always. Yours and everyone else's, from age two on," Jack teased.

"As if you were ever around to let me," Bonny retorted.

Cait smiled to herself, enjoying the obvious ease and affection between them. She knew they didn't spend much time together—Bonny was pretty tied down with the store and Jack rarely came to Pilchuck—but they always seemed able to pick up where they'd left off without having to warm up to each other.

And it was the same with herself and Jack, Cait thought, shaking her head in bemusement. Hoot-Owl! Cait-Cat! Still the Owl and the Pussycat, even after all these years!

Cait's house was a little working-class Victorian just a few minutes from the heart of town, right across the street from Bonny's own working-class Victorian. Bonny's house, painted in muted shades of purple and lavender with ivory trim, was sedate compared to Cait's.

With its beige siding and multicolored trim—Jack counted no less than six colors—the Reilly home looked more like a ginger-bread house than an actual human dwelling. Two shades of pink, two shades of blue, a sort of lilac that tied the pinks and blues together—and a startling shade of green that shouldn't have worked with the other colors, but somehow did. It was that shade of green Helen had always called "new-leaf green." The color of hope. New life. New beginnings.

"My daughters chose the colors," Cait said when she pulled into the driveway, as if she thought she needed to explain. "We painted it together after Joe-Joe died. Great therapy."

"It's—"

"Don't say 'different' or I'll bop you."

"I wasn't going to. It's charming, Cait."

She smiled the sunny smile he'd always thought of as her trademark. "I'll take 'charming.' Come on in while I get your trousers in the wash. I'll fix us some coffee. If you think you can hang on to it," she teased.

"I'll try my best."

"You always do, Hoot-Owl."

He followed her up the brick sidewalk with its neat borders of ranunculus, marigolds, and sweet alyssum to the front porch, draped with wisteria. A Victorian porch swing painted the same cheery colors as the gingerbread trim hung from the rafters, facing the street, in front of a pair of tall casement windows where Jack caught a glimpse of white lace peeking through the glass.

Really, it was a fairy-tale cottage.

Cait must have seen him give the swing a gentle push as he walked by. "Joe-Joe made that for me," she said. "For our house-warming."

Jack had a sudden image of Cait and her husband sitting together on a warm summer evening, holding hands and talking about their day, calling out to friends and neighbors who passed by, watching the moon rise over the trees. He felt a surprising moment of longing.

When they'd first started out, Jack and Helen hadn't had a house to move into. For a long time they'd lived in a small apartment near the university, and later a duplex near the aeronautics plant where they'd both found work as engineers.

When it finally did come time to buy a house, they'd chosen Northwest contemporary, all wood and glass and stone. A beautiful home, made even more beautiful by the love within its walls.

But they'd never had a front porch, let alone a porch swing. Maybe that was why they'd never gotten to know their neighbors, never developed a sense of community where they lived.

"The world doesn't have enough porch swings," he said, holding the front door open for Cait and following her inside.

Somehow she knew exactly what he meant. "You're right, it doesn't." And then, smiling over her shoulder, "Now there's a calling, Hoot. Community-building by porch swing. I like it."

"Smart aleck."

"Who, me?" Wide-eyed and innocent. He remembered *that* expression. "Have a look around while I get the washer going. I'll be back in two shakes."

Two shakes didn't give him long enough to get past the hallway, lined on either side with a picture gallery he couldn't resist. One portrait in particular called to him: Cait and Joe-Joe with a pretty brown-eyed blonde who might have been Cait herself at sixteen or seventeen, and two younger girls, maybe nine or ten, identical in every detail—right down to their mischievous grins. Joe-Joe Reilly's grin.

Jack felt a sudden pang of envy. It must be comforting for Cait, he thought, to look into her children's faces and see Joe-Joe. What he wouldn't give for a child who mirrored Helen's smile and wit and grace!

The feeling passed. Yes, he and Helen had wanted children. But to tell the truth, he didn't know how he'd have managed these last three years as a single dad. To even one child, let alone the trio Cait had been left with.

Especially those twins! He stopped in front of a more recent photo and grinned. The teens were cute as a bug's ear, as Helen used to say—even with a pair of haircuts that would have done a boot-camp barber proud.

"Last year's stab at independence," Cait said from behind him, her voice wry. "You can probably guess I had a cow."

He turned his grin on her. "I know I would have! How are they anyhow? Your girls?"

"All grown up, I'm afraid. Cindy got married last Christmas, and since the twins turned eighteen I hardly ever see them."

"Still living at home?"

Cait nodded. "If you can call sleeping here at night living at home."

He wondered if she realized how wistful she sounded.

"You'll have to meet Cindy's husband sometime…" She was gesturing toward a picture of her eldest daughter with a nice-looking young man, but Jack's eyes slid past the portrait to another photo next to it. Cait and Joe-Joe's wedding portrait. Cait fell silent as she followed his gaze.

They'd made a handsome pair, Jack mused, the sweet Scandinavian farm girl and the rakish Irish rogue. Happiness radiated from Cait's face. And from Joe-Joe's, for that matter.

He remembered how anxious Cait had been that he approve of Joe-Joe when they'd first started dating. As anxious as she'd been for Joe-Joe to like Jack. He'd checked out Joe-Joe but good too, even though by that time he'd been at the university in Seattle, and checking out Joe-Joe meant long-distance phone calls and several trips back to Pilchuck. He'd always felt protective of Cait.

"You were a good match," he told her now.

"We were a great match," she said. She hesitated a moment before adding, "It took me a long time to get over losing him. I was *so* mad at God for taking him away!"

"And now?"

"Now, I'm just incredibly thankful for the years we did have together. For how much living and loving we did in those years."

Jack nodded, thinking suddenly of his spontaneous songfest on the way to Pilchuck this morning, realizing it had been an offering of praise, to God, to the universe, to Helen—*for* Helen. For a truly happy marriage, a marriage of body, mind, and soul.

"I've been around long enough to know most marriages aren't made in heaven," Cait was saying. "Mine and Joe-Joe's was. I believe that literally."

Again he understood. She didn't mean they had never had an argument, never hurt each other, never had to say "I'm sorry." She meant that heaven had had a hand in getting them together and in keeping them together. In getting them through the hard times and in growing their love. He knew about marriages made in heaven.

She touched him on the arm, startling him from his reverie. "Am I right in thinking you and Helen had what Joe-Joe and I did?" she asked quietly.

"You are. And you're right. It was rare."

"I'm sorry for your loss, Jack."

"And I'm sorry for yours."

She opened her arms—sweet Cait, who despite the minuscule amount of time they'd spent together over the last thirty years knew him better than any other living soul. They held each other for a silent moment, found comfort in their knowledge of each other and the kinship of their common loss.

Then Jack caught sight of a picture of Joe-Joe Reilly over Cait's shoulder, exactly at his own eye-level. Was it only his imagination—or was the brightly smiling Joe-Joe giving him the nod?

The nod! The thought brought him up short, and he released Cait hastily. *This is Cait!* he scolded himself. *Cait Anderson, who once upon a time was your very best friend. Your best friend, Jack! Whatever are you thinking?!*

Cait felt Jack's retreat even before he pulled away from her hug. One moment he was Hoot, her buddy, her sidekick, her oldest friend; the next he was a stranger.

By the time they sat down to coffee across the kitchen table from each other, he was even avoiding her eyes.

"Jack?" She reached across the table and laid a hand on his arm. "What's wrong?"

He jerked away from her touch like a two-year-old jerking away from a hot stove. His instinctive reaction might have stung, except that at first she was too surprised to feel hurt, and then, when it occurred to her what he was thinking, too embarrassed.

Her face flooded with heat. "You don't think I—"

"I'm sorry, Cait, I'm just not used—"

"I didn't mean—" She crossed her arms, tucking her hands out of sight.

"Of course you didn't! I just don't want you to think—"

"Oh, I don't, Jack! Really—the hug—I hug everyone!" Which was almost true. Kids, old people, her clients, her friends, her daughters. Even Pastor Bob at church. She didn't generally hug strangers, but then strangers were never strangers to Cait for long.

But there were hugs—and there were hugs. Jack had probably been on the receiving end of some not-so-innocent embraces since Helen's death. Why wouldn't he be? Not only was he easy on the eyes, and smart and funny and charming—he was a very nice man.

And gainfully employed, to boot. A combination Cait had run across only rarely since her traumatic reentry into singleness eight years ago.

Not that it worried her. She'd done just fine without romance since Joe-Joe died, thank you, and she would *do* just fine without romance until the Almighty decided it was her turn to go. With Joe-Joe, she'd had top sirloin. She wasn't about to settle for hot dogs just for the sake of saying she had a man in her life!

Besides—Jack Van Hooten? Old *Hoot-Owl?*

"Really, Jack!" she said again, her face still warm. "You and me? Can you *imagine?*"

"I'm sorry, Cait," he repeated, his voice rueful. "It isn't you. It's this entire…*situation.* Being single again after all those years with Helen."

Cait's embarrassment disappeared in a flood of empathy. "I know, Hoot," she said, her voice gentle. "I know. Of course no one could ever take her place. Just as no one could take Joe-Joe's place for me."

"Not when you've had what *we* had in our marriages," said Jack.

Cait nodded. "Exactly. Don't think of me as a woman, Hoot," she said, smiling across the table at him. "It's just me, Cait. Your good buddy, your old friend."

Jack stared at her thoughtfully for a moment, then returned her smile in kind. "Come here, you," he said after a moment, getting up from the table. He held out his arms.

"You're sure I don't have designs on you, Hoot?" she teased.

"Really, Cait!" he said, grinning broadly. "You and me? Can you *imagine?*"

Laughing, she rose from her chair and moved into his embrace. "Friends forever," she said against his chest.

"Friends forever," he agreed.

Chapter Three

L unch at the Kitsch 'n' Caboodle Café was an experience Jack would likely never forget. For one thing—as he was reminded the moment he walked through the doorway—the place itself was *designed* not to be forgotten. And more in the way of a howling northeaster than a beautiful sunset too.

The collection of kitsch in the diner screamed for attention. The velvet Elvis in its place of honor on the back wall, for instance. The deer antler chandelier hanging from the knotty-pine ceiling. The astounding assemblage of table lamps perched on practically every flat surface.

Neon lava lamps, Victorian bordello lamps, glowing white plastic night-light lamps in the form of famous statues: Michelangelo's *David,* the *Venus de Milo,* Rodin's *Thinker*—all with fig leaves circumspectly placed, so as not to offend any delicate sensibilities— and the arm of the Statue of Liberty, holding an ice-cream cone instead of a torch.

There was more: cutesy salt and pepper shakers on the tables, autographed photos of early film stars on the walls, Old Master jigsaw puzzles under the glass tabletops. Truly, it boggled the mind.

Matching the amazing collection of kitsch for whimsy and eccentricity was the collection of characters who frequented the diner. Oh, there were perfectly ordinary patrons scattered throughout, to be sure, as if to lend the place an air of respectability. But really, they only served to point out the oddities of everyone else.

Even the owners. *Especially* the owners, which wasn't really a surprise. The woman who showed them to their table was fiftyish, pleasantly plump, efficient, and affable, and wore a Donna Reed housewife dress, rhinestone-studded glasses shaped like cat's eyes, and a poufy hairdo it must have taken half a can of hair spray to hold in place. A man Cait murmured was the hostess's husband, wearing a white muscle tee, a white chef's hat, and a dark stubble, periodically poked his head through the window between the kitchen and the restaurant floor to bawl out a table number.

One of the customers caught Jack's eye immediately. The dignified elderly woman with the pink hair and the turquoise eyelids sitting across the table from a petite brunette was dressed impeccably in a mint-green suit, complete with a pillbox hat, white gloves, and a pair of the cleanest, whitest athletic shoes Jack had ever seen outside a shoebox. It was clear she polished them regularly.

Jack could have sworn it was Olga Pfefferkuchen, except that the Olga Pfefferkuchen he remembered always wore black and a sour expression, and *never* would have deigned to stop by their table to say hello. Cait Anderson and Jack Van Hooten, along with the "wild Wyatts" over on Hokanvander Street, had bedeviled the poor woman all their growing-up years.

"Olga, you're looking lovely," Cait said as the dowager approached. "You remember Jack Van Hooten?"

Jack raised his eyebrows in surprise. So it *was* Olga Pfefferkuchen!

"Indeed I do," she said, in a tone of voice that made him squirm in his seat. If she brought up the time he and "that Wyatt boy" had put her cat in the dryer for a spin, he didn't know what he'd do. He was pretty sure Bonny didn't know the story, and he was quite sure he didn't want her to.

Bonny had a particularly soft spot for animals, and even

though the cat-drying incident had been more an experiment than an act of meanness, he'd be hard put to explain it in a way that didn't sound like animal abuse. Which was something Jack would *never* stoop to.

But Mrs. Pfefferkuchen didn't bring up the incident. Nor, miraculously, any other reference to Jack's wilder days. Furthermore, to his surprise, the petite brunette in her company was a Wyatt! The youngest girl, Suzie, who'd been barely a babe in arms when Jack had palled around with her older brother.

"You've stayed away far too long, young man," Olga said instead of all the things she might have said. True, her tone was severe and she did waggle her finger at him. *Some* things hadn't changed.

But the glint of good humor in the elderly woman's dark eyes nearly left him speechless.

"I'll tell you later," Bonny whispered in response to his incredulous query after the old woman moved on.

"Hey, Mom! You didn't tell me you were coming in today. Hi, Bonny!"

Jack looked up at the sound of the cheerful voice to find himself staring at Cait Anderson Reilly twenty years earlier. And she was staring right back at him, too, with unabashed curiosity.

It wasn't Cait, of course. It was Cindy, Cait's daughter, with a trio of water glasses and a pot of coffee on a tray. He hadn't seen her in years, but dressed in a white camp shirt and pedal pushers, her blond hair pulled back in a ponytail, nodding and smiling in recognition as Cait introduced him, she looked so much like her mother had in younger days that Jack felt almost as if he'd been transported back in time.

Then he looked across the table at Cait and saw the warmth and humor and self-confidence reflected in her eyes and the depth of character etched in her expression, and he realized that Cindy might be pretty, and Cait had probably been pretty in her twenties too—but Cait at forty-six was utterly beautiful.

That was a revelation. In the old days Cait had been so close—and so much of a tomboy—he hadn't paid attention to how she looked.

Oh no? some inner voice niggled.

Well—not often anyhow. He did remember a couple of times he hadn't been able to help but notice. Her wedding day, for instance. And even earlier, the day she'd told him she was getting married.

She'd glowed with happiness that day, as if a light had been switched on inside her. He'd been pretty much bowled over, to tell the truth. Bowled over and a bit dismayed—as if perhaps he'd missed out on something...

Then he'd met Helen, and that, as far as his heart was concerned, had been that. As long as his parents had stayed in Pilchuck, he and Cait had stayed in touch, but after the elder Van Hootens had moved away, Jack and Cait's correspondence had eventually dwindled to once-a-year cards at Christmas, and over the last three years, not even that. Jack hadn't had the heart to send Christmas cards without Helen.

"What's Buster cooked up for the soup of the day, Cindy?" Cait asked her daughter, oblivious to Jack's eyes on her. "I don't want to eat too much, with a softball game at three."

"Shrimp and curry bisque," Cindy supplied as she upended their coffee mugs and filled them. Setting a cream pitcher shaped like a mooing cow in the center of the table, she added, "Mm-mm good!"

"Sold!" said Cait, closing her menu.

Bonny, too, snapped her menu shut. "The same."

"It comes with bread?" asked Jack.

"Extra-sour sourdough from Bilbo's," Cindy said.

"The bakery down the street," Bonny clarified.

"Fresh out of the oven this morning," said Cindy.

"Soup'll leave you room for dessert," Cait suggested. "You've *got* to try Biddy's apple betty, Hoot."

Jack's mouth watered. "Better make it three soups, Cindy."

"Done!" And Cindy whisked away, tray tucked under her arm, coffeepot and menus in hand.

Jack splashed cream into his coffee. "So you're still playing softball, Cait! Once a tomboy always a tomboy?"

"Huh! Women who play team sports aren't called tomboys, Hoot," she said. "Not anymore. Haven't you been paying attention to those Nike commercials?"

"Not close enough, I guess. You're playing for a church league?"

"City league. Coed. I play first base for the Fairley's Drug and Fountain team."

"First base on a coed team! You must be good."

Cindy materialized at the end of the booth with a basket of bread, a ramekin of butter, and a world of daughterly pride: "She's awesome!"

"Oh, pooh," Cait scoffed, true to form. "Softball gets me off my buns and out in the fresh air, that's all."

"Well, good for you," said Jack, reaching for a slice of bread. "I work out at the gym, but I can't remember the last time I played a team sport. Or got out in the fresh air, for that matter."

"You work too hard, Jack," Bonny said.

"Why don't you come cheer us on this afternoon?" Cait asked him. "If you don't have other plans?"

"No plans at all," he said, feeling pleased. "Except to have a good look around the gallery. I'd love to watch you play. And by the way, Bonny—"

His sister looked at him inquisitively.

"I may not be working hard much longer. At least not where I am now."

"You're not getting laid off!"

"Oh no! The company is downsizing again, though, and I'm coming up on twenty-five years—"

"You're retiring! At forty-six!"

"I can if I want to. And with a very attractive severance package too."

"What's this 'if you want to' business? Why wouldn't you want to?"

At which point Jack was sorry he'd brought up the subject.

He knew Bonny well enough to know that once she got hold of something, she was like a dog with a bone. And frankly, he wasn't sure he wanted to answer her question.

There were reasons, after all, he'd been working so hard the last few years. He hadn't had time to think about Helen, for one thing. He hadn't had time to be lonely.

"What in the world would I do with myself if I retired?" he said lightly, lifting his shoulders in a shrug.

"Might be time to start that porch-swing ministry," Cait popped in unexpectedly.

He looked at her blankly. "Porch-swing ministry…"

"Porch-swing ministry…" Bonny parroted, her expression as blank as Jack's.

"Oh!" He grinned as he suddenly remembered. "'Community-building by porch swing.' Now there's a thought."

"You know you were always Pasty Hasty's star pupil, Hoot. Maybe it's time to get a hammer back in hand."

"Pasty Hasty? Hammer?" Bonny sounded more exasperated than puzzled. "Would someone care to clue me in?"

"Sorry, Bonny," Cait said. "I forget you're so much younger than we are. Pasty Hasty must have been long gone by the time you got to Pilchuck High School."

"The shop teacher," Jack explained.

"It wasn't nice, calling him 'Pasty,'" Cait put in. "But you've never seen a man so pale!"

"Except when he was mad," added Jack. "When he was mad, he got red right out to the ends of his buzz cut."

"Right," Bonny said, rolling her eyes.

"No, really! He did!" Cait defended Jack.

Cindy appeared once more at the end of their table, this time with three steaming bowls of soup on her tray. Jack was glad for the interruption. Bonny seemed awfully testy all of a sudden.

"Save room for your apple betty," Cindy said as she set Jack's bowl in front of him.

"Oh, I will."

"So what's the deal about a porch-swing ministry?" Bonny prompted once again.

"A joke," said Cait, reaching for her spoon.

"I don't know about that," Jack said. "I think porch swings could go a long way toward building a sense of community. Bonny, you really ought to stock 'em in your store."

"If you don't have a sense of community in Pilchuck, I'm afraid a porch swing isn't going to help," Bonny said dryly.

Another member of the Wyatt clan came in with his family just as Jack and Cait and Bonny dipped into their shrimp bisque—which was, Jack noted, as delicious as Cindy had promised.

Simon Wyatt's family included a pretty wife whose short, curly hair was just a shade darker than Bonny's fall of red, a squalling baby, and a mop-haired imp of a kid who might as well have been *MAD Magazine*'s Alfred E. Neuman. He had that "What, me worry?" expression of practiced innocence down like syrup on a hot cake.

"That's Gordie," Cait whispered. "We're in for either trouble or entertainment, depending on your perspective."

Jack settled right away on "entertainment." Why go looking for trouble?

Simon recognized Jack and stopped at their table to say hello, taking a minute to fill him in on his older brother's whereabouts, and how his folks were doing, and to say how sorry he'd been to hear about Jack's wife.

"Is that still hard for you?" Cait asked quietly after Simon joined his family in the booth next to theirs.

He knew what she meant: having people bring up Helen. "Not so much," he said. "It gets easier." He was surprised to hear himself say it.

"Yes, it does."

"So, what is it about this Gordie character?" he asked, deliberately changing the subject. "Easier" wasn't the same as "easy." No sense in belaboring the point.

"Eavesdrop," Cait advised. "If you're lucky, you'll catch a Gordie-ism. The kid definitely has his own take on the world."

Jack didn't have long to wait for the promised entertainment.

Simon's wife had managed to get the baby quieted down. Jack, whose back was to the Wyatt family, didn't even think to wonder how. Not being used to crying babies, he was simply very glad the wailing had stopped.

He discovered Mrs. Wyatt's secret soon enough, however—along with everyone else in the restaurant. Cindy delivered their order a few minutes later, announcing the names of the dishes as she set them down.

"Excuse me—"

It was Gordie's voice, as polite as could be, interrupting Cindy in midsentence. Jack went on alert even before Cait held up a finger to signal a possible Gordie-ism.

"Excuse me, Cindy-relly," the little boy said in a loud voice, ever so serious. "But my mom can't eat right now. She's milking the baby."

Bonny snorted, Cait sputtered into her napkin, and Jack nearly lost a mouthful of hot coffee. Only the thought of Gordie's mortified mother kept him from howling, then and several other times throughout their meal. Gordie Wyatt was something else.

And my, did it feel fine to laugh!

Simon and Mrs. Pfefferkuchen weren't the only ghosts from Jack Van Hooten's past who stopped by their table at the Kitsch 'n' Caboodle over the lunch hour. In fact, it seemed that anyone in the restaurant who'd ever said so much as "boo" to Jack in his

Pilchuck days felt compelled to file by with a pleasant word and a handshake.

"We surely do miss your folks around here," the old town librarian told him. "How's your mother doing down there in Arizona, Jack?" The Van Hootens had retired to warmer climes a number of years before on account of Jack's mother's debilitating allergies.

"Very well, Miss Rafferty. Thank you for asking," he said. "I know they miss Pilchuck too. But there's just no getting away from mold and mildew in Pilchuck, is there?"

"More's the pity," Miss Rafferty said, sighing.

"You and Bonny'll have to come over for supper one evening," said Reese Fairley, the second generation Fairley of Fairley's Drug and Fountain, as he pumped Jack's hand.

Jack had worked for Reese as a soda jerk when he was a teenager, and Reese and his wife were Bonny's ex-in-laws. In fact, they were the reason Bonny hadn't changed her name back to Van Hooten the minute her husband left her—and left Pilchuck, presumably for good. In practical terms, she was more the Fairley's daughter than Timothy was their son.

"I'm only here for the weekend, Reese," Jack told his old employer now. "But it wouldn't surprise me if I started spending a little more time in Pilchuck. I'll let you know. I'd love to share supper with you and Donnabelle."

Bonny lifted her eyebrows in surprise as Mr. Fairley moved away. "Really?"

"Of course," he said, deliberately misunderstanding. "You know how much I like the Fairleys."

"You know that's not what I meant," she said impatiently. "I *mean*—you think you might be spending more time in Pilchuck?"

Cindy materialized yet again with her tray and set a dish of something golden and gooey topped with a scoop of ice cream in front of Jack. "I could name a few single women in town who'd be thrilled if you did," she said.

Once again Jack nearly choked on his coffee.

"Cindy!" her mother said, aghast.

"Well, it's true! A waitress in a busy restaurant hears things. Why, I've heard things just in the last half hour. Enjoy the apple betty, Jack."

And she tripped cheerfully away, as if she hadn't completely ruined his appetite.

Chapter Four

Cindy did have a special talent for upsetting the apple cart, Cait told herself as she wheeled her own cart into the produce section at the Apple Basket Market.

She could have gone back to the Blue Moon with Bonny and Jack—she hadn't done as much looking around as she'd wanted to before the unfortunate accident with the perfume bottle, and she did need a gift for Tuesday evening, when the Ladies' Missionary Sewing Circle at the Pilchuck Church of Saints and Sinners would have their annual secret-pal unveiling.

But truthfully, she'd have gone back to the gallery mostly to spend more time with Jack. And she simply couldn't let him disrupt her day entirely. There *were* tasks she'd set out for herself this weekend other than having fun.

She rummaged through the leaf lettuce bin, picked out a likely-looking bunch, and wedged it into a plastic bag before tossing it into the basket of her cart. Maybe she'd invite Jack and Bonny over for spaghetti, salad, and garlic bread tonight, she thought as she moved on to the tomato bin. That way Bonny wouldn't have to worry about fixing dinner after she got off work.

Be honest, Cait, she told herself as she selected several plump tomatoes. *That way you won't have to eat alone.*

She'd been eating alone an awful lot lately. She didn't like it either. Mealtimes were meant for company and conversation as well as good food. Like lunch this afternoon at the Kitsch 'n' Caboodle.

The thought reminded her once again of the startling comment Cindy had dished up to Jack along with Biddy's apple betty. Who in the world had she been talking about—the single women who'd be thrilled to have Jack back in town?

She tried to remember what single women had been in the restaurant that afternoon. Someone Cindy might have overheard. Someone who might even have purposely dropped Cindy a hint, hoping she'd pass it on: how attractive Jack was or how intriguing or how lonely he must be now that his wife was gone…

But to tell the truth, she'd been so engrossed in Jack herself she hadn't paid much attention to the other restaurant patrons. Jack and her own reactions to him. It was almost spooky how well she knew him, how in tune with him she felt even after all these years.

Like riding a bicycle, she thought. *Some things you never forget.*

Maybe Cindy had been referring to Ina Rafferty and Olga Pfefferkuchen. Single women who'd be happy to have Jack around as a surrogate son or grandson.

She rolled her cart along to the mushroom bin. Several younger women had traipsed by the table during lunchtime too, she reminded herself. Fluttering their eyelashes a tad more than was necessary, in Cait's opinion. She hardly thought any of them were Jack Van Hooten's type.

Jack Van Hooten's type. What would Jack's type be these days, she wondered? Someone like Helen, she supposed. Very smart, a little shy, on the serious side. Pretty—Cait couldn't imagine Jack with someone who wasn't pretty. Gracious to a fault. Possessed of a kind and generous heart.

Cait had a sudden and unexpected image of Lily Johansen sitting alone at the back of the Kitsch 'n' Caboodle Café during lunch that afternoon, lighting up the shadowed corner even with her head buried in a book. Lily hadn't dated at all in the two years she'd been back in Pilchuck. Had she decided it was time? Had the sudden appearance of Jack Van Hooten on the scene sparked her interest?

Gorgeous, flaxen-haired Lily Johansen—Lily Norland, she'd been then—had worn more Tillicum County beauty crowns as a teenager than any other Tillicum County resident before or since, including the coveted Tillicum County Merry Dairy Maid coronet. In fact, Lily had graced more floats in more parades around the state than roses graced Mrs. Pfefferkuchen's garden.

Cait didn't know Lily well, but she did know *of* her. Anyone who read the *Pilchuck Post* knew about Lily Norland Johansen. The beauty queen had been Big News in Pilchuck since she'd tap-danced her way to the Junior Division Talent Trophy at the Tillicum County Fair at the age of six. Of course, it didn't hurt that her mother was a reporter for the *Post*. Until two years ago, Lily's life had been an open book to anyone who cared to read it.

And not just any book either. With perfect grades in nursing school, a perfect job at a big-city hospital, a perfect wedding to a perfect prince of a husband, and two perfectly beautiful daughters, Lily's life had been a veritable fairy tale.

Unfortunately, Lily's perfect prince of a husband had been insanely jealous—if not simply insane—with regard to his lovely and gifted wife. According to Cindy, who'd heard it from her hairdresser, who'd heard it from Lily's second cousin once removed, Dr. Johansen had hit his wife on a fairly regular basis—and in front of the babies too.

None of which—no surprise—had made it to the local paper. Which wasn't to say no one knew.

Cait thought Lily was brave, coming back to Pilchuck when she had to know that everyone in the little town—in the way of little towns—would know the entire story of her failed marriage inside a week. Then again, maybe that was the reason she had come home. Everyone in the little town—again in the way of little towns—had welcomed and embraced her and her children. And without demanding that she explain herself to them.

Lily had found work as a nurse in a pediatrician's office in Bellingrath and made a little extra money teaching CPR and first-aid classes for the Red Cross, but Cait knew it must be a struggle trying to raise her girls alone.

She'd been there herself—and with a lot more help than Lily had. The word was Dr. Johansen wasn't even paying child support. And Mrs. Norland's continuing position at the *Pilchuck Post* might be prestigious in a town this size, but it paid in nickels and dimes— and, Cait suspected, not even as many nickels and dimes as Cindy collected in tips at the Kitsch 'n' Caboodle Café. Cait didn't know how she'd have made it without Cindy's contributions.

Under the circumstances, Lily was doing an outstanding job. If anyone deserved a second chance at happiness, she did.

But with Jack? Why did the idea send Cait's heart plummeting?

Furthermore—what in the world was she doing with enough produce in her grocery cart to feed the entire Fairley's Drug and Fountain softball team?

Bonny was in a snit. No question about it, Jack thought as he walked her back to the Blue Moon after lunch. He couldn't think of a thing he might have said or done to offend his sister, but she was definitely in a snit.

He knew she had a quick temper—but usually as quick to calm down as it was to ignite. It wasn't like her to keep her dander up.

He stopped her outside the gallery with a touch to her arm. "You mad at me, Squirt?"

Bonny slanted a look at him through her lashes, and for a moment Jack didn't know if she was going to answer. She did, finally: "Do you know that's the first time you've called me Squirt since you got into town?"

He wrinkled his brow in confusion. "That's why you're upset with me? Because I haven't been calling you Squirt?"

"No! Of course not. It's just—"

She stopped, shrugged, cast her eyes down. "It's nothing. I'm being petty."

"It *is* something," Jack insisted. "Besides, nothing's petty between two people who love each other."

He could see her features soften as he said the words. Maybe he hadn't told Bonny often enough that he loved her. Women needed that sort of thing, he knew from experience…

Face it, Jack, he told himself. *Men need that sort of thing. You need that sort of thing.*

I-love-yous had been in short supply, both on the receiving and the giving ends, since Helen had died. Maybe he really did need to spend more time in Pilchuck. More time with Bonny.

"That's very sweet, Jack," she was saying now, still looking at the sidewalk. "No wonder everyone made such a big deal over you at lunch."

He crossed his arms over his chest and stared at her, head tilted and eyes narrowed. She was withholding something, he was sure of it. But he knew he wasn't going to find out what by trying to force it out of her. Not *his* sister.

"So you're jealous of all the attention I got at the Kitsch 'n' Caboodle," he teased instead of pushing her.

She raised her head, and he was relieved to see a spark of humor in her eyes. His relief quickly dissipated at her words, however: "Don't you have an ego the size of Mount Balder!"

"Ego!" he sputtered.

She grinned as if she hadn't been out of sorts ten seconds earlier, tossed her head as if to say "You heard me, Buster!" and pulled open the door to go into the gallery. Jack grabbed it before the latch clicked shut and followed her inside.

"I do not have an ego the size of Mount Balder!" he protested. "And besides, you know very well all that glad-handing wasn't for Jack Van Hooten the person. *Really,* Bonny."

"Oh?"

"Absolutely not. It was for Jack Van Hooten the Prodigal-Son-Come-Home. You know Pilchuck. Even better than I do. Those old-timers at the Kitsch 'n' Caboodle would have acted the same with *any* native son. Or native daughter, for that matter."

Native son? Home? Was he actually referring to Pilchuck as *home?*

"Ah," said Bonny, somehow expressing a world of meaning with the simple syllable. He was about to protest further, but a cheerful stereophonic "Hey, Bonny!" stopped him.

The Reilly twins. One behind the counter printing price tags and the other in front, straightening handmade greeting cards in a wire rack. They wore identical flowered dresses. Their brown hair had grown out from last year's buzz cuts into sun-streaked Little Orphan Annie curls. They were still as cute as bug's ears.

"We sold one of those indoor fountains while you were gone," the twin behind the counter said proudly.

"The one with the shells and driftwood," the other twin expanded.

"You did! Well, good for you!" said Bonny. "A tourist or a local?"

"Garson Krueger," they said in unison.

"Garson Krueger," Jack said, joining the conversation as if he'd been invited. Bonny wasn't getting rid of him *that* easily. "How is Krueger anyhow?"

The twins' heads swiveled toward Jack, their dark eyes wide with curiosity.

"He's fine," the twin behind the counter said.

"Why shouldn't he be?" said the other. "With all that money?"

"Garson's a mogul, Jack," Bonny supplied. "An honest-to-goodness Tillicum County tycoon."

Jack supposed he shouldn't be surprised. Krueger had always known how to work the system.

"Pardon us for asking," the twin at the card rack said, "but—"

"Who are you?" the other finished for her.

"Allow me, girls," Bonny answered for Jack, flinging an arm toward him. "Robin, Rosie—meet Jack Van Hooten. My darling brother."

"Oh!" they said, once more in unison.

Jack still hadn't solved the mystery of Bonny's snit to his satisfaction, but as she seemed to have snapped out of it anyhow, and as she'd managed to throw him off entirely with that ego nonsense, he decided to drop it. At least for the moment.

Besides, he was as curious about Cait's younger daughters as they were about him.

"I graduated from high school with your mom," he told the twins, reaching out a hand to first one, then the other. "And Garson Krueger, too, for that matter."

"Oh!" they said again.

Then, from the twin in front of the counter, "I'm Robin."

"A pleasure to meet you, Robin."

"And I'm Rosie," said the other as she pumped his hand.

He inclined his head. "Rosie."

"We thought you looked familiar." That was Robin, speaking for both herself and her sister, although they clearly hadn't had the time to discuss the matter.

"We've seen pictures in Mom's old yearbooks," added Rosie.

"You've seen me in person," he told them. "Though I admit it's been a long time. When you were little girls you used to call me Uncle Jack."

"Uncle Jack!" they said together, even more wide-eyed.

They'd probably been only three or four, and Cindy ten or eleven, when he'd drifted out of their lives, Jack mused. After his parents had moved to Arizona the hundred miles between Seattle and Pilchuck might as well have been a thousand, even with a sister still in town. Maybe, he thought for the first time in his life, he and Helen had been a little selfish in their love. So involved in their own life together they'd neglected other important relationships.

"Uncle Jack," he confirmed, smiling.

The bell on the front door jangled as a customer came in, and Jack decided he'd better let his sister and her assistants get back to their jobs. He spent the next half-hour wandering around the gallery, impressed with the variety and quality of the handcrafted items on display—and with his sister's skill at merchandising. The store was as warm and inviting as the parlor in a country parson's home—but a lot more artfully decorated.

"So what do you think?" Bonny asked him as he approached the beautifully finished cherry dining table where she was arranging dried flowers in a trio of willow baskets.

"I think you're not so crazy as I thought you were when you gave up your teaching job," he said.

"Crazy! This from the man who once tried to spin a cat in a clothes dryer?"

Oops! So she *did* know that dark secret from his past. Had Olga Pfefferkuchen told on him? More likely Cait—the traitor!

Cait he would have to deal with later, but Bonny—

He grabbed her playfully from behind and pulled her against his chest. "You'd better watch it, Pipsqueak. I'm bigger than you are."

She wriggled out of his grasp. "Yeah, but if you want to sell your porch swings through the Blue Moon Gallery, you'd better be nice to me!"

"Oh, so *that's* the way it's going to be!"

"I'm the boss," she said.

"As always," he teased. He picked up one of the willow baskets and swung it by the handle, liking the way it felt in his hand. "So is this a challenge, Squirt?"

"Is what a challenge?"

"If I give up my job to make porch swings, you'll sell them for me?"

"I can't say that until I see a representative sample," Bonny said primly. "The Blue Moon does have standards, after all." She lifted her chin and looked down her nose at him—with difficulty, since she was a good six inches shorter than he was. "How long did Cait say it's been since you've swung a hammer?"

"It just so happens I'm still very handy with a hammer," Jack told her, rotating the willow basket, mentally deconstructing and then reconstructing it. The curse of being an engineer…

"Mm-hmm."

He tossed her an arch glance as he set the basket carefully back on the table. "I'll have you know, Cait doesn't know *everything* about me," he said.

"Mm-hmm," she said again.

Why did she sound so skeptical?

Chapter Five

Cait *didn't* know everything about Jack, of course. As Jack didn't know everything about Cait. How could they, with nothing but Christmas letters to go on over the last dozen years? Plus, more recently, snippets of information from Bonny, who only naturally talked to her best friend about her brother and to her brother about her best friend.

So much water under the bridge, Cait mused, since the years of their childhood! So much that had changed them both in significant and permanent ways. Their relationships, their responsibilities, their successes and failures. Their roles—especially Cait as mother and Jack as caretaker for his ailing wife.

And maybe most of all, their losses.

Yet the changes Cait saw in Jack didn't make him a stranger to her. In fact, even without knowing all the details of Jack's experience, by the end of the weekend Cait felt she knew him better than she ever had.

The wonder of it was, the ways he'd changed were the ways she'd changed as well. Maybe because, all those years ago, they'd absorbed the same small-town values, made them a permanent part of their lives. And adopted the same simple faith—faith in a God who didn't necessarily keep bad things from happening, but who would always be there when bad things did happen.

And good things, too, Cait reminded herself. For all their disappointments, failures, and losses, both she and Jack recognized the gifts God had bestowed on them. Not the least of which had been their exceptional marriages.

Was it possible, Cait wondered—sitting between Bonny and Jack for the Sunday-evening service at the Pilchuck Church of Saints and Sinners, listening to Cindy play a medley of spirituals on her flute for the offertory—was it possible she could be happy with another man? After Joe-Joe?

Jack shifted on the pew next to her, his arm brushing against Cait's as he did. It wasn't the first time this weekend they'd inadvertently touched. Or the first time since their spontaneous hug in the Blue Moon Gallery that they'd touched on purpose, for that matter.

Jack had sneaked up behind her when he showed up at the field for her softball game, covering her eyes with his hands and inquiring in a squeaky but readily identifiable falsetto, "Guess who?" Large, strong, capable hands they were. Warm, loving, gentle hands. Hands that sent a surprising but wonderful shiver up and down Cait's spine.

She'd talked him into playing shortstop and third-base coach for the Fairley's Drug and Fountain team when they'd turned up a player short. He hadn't needed much coaxing. In fact, he'd seemed eager to join the game.

After that—well, it seemed to Cait that every chance he got, Jack was there. Helping her to her feet after she'd slid into third base two seconds after the other team's third baseman had tagged her, for instance. "Wow, Cait," he'd said admiringly after determining she hadn't sustained any injuries worse than a skinned elbow. "Cindy was right. You're awesome!"

"If I'm so awesome, how come I'm out?" she'd grumbled, brushing herself off as she left the field. He'd slung an arm across her shoulders and pulled her close for a quick hug. "Could have gone either way, Cait-Cat. You took the chance, is the thing. And gave it your all."

After Jack's squeeze bunt in the ninth inning brought the winning run home, there he was again, whirling her around in an impromptu victory dance. A dance that had left her practically breathless. In more ways than one.

After the game there'd been Jack's hand at her elbow as he escorted her to her car. Jack's arm brushing against hers as they sat together on her Victorian porch swing later that afternoon, leafing through a stack of old how-to books to find the plans Joe-Joe had used to build the self-same swing all those years ago. Jack bumping into her every time he turned around in her one-cook kitchen when he insisted on helping her fix dinner. She was surprised at how well he knew his way around a kitchen until he reminded her he'd done most of the cooking during Helen's final, difficult year.

Even later, after dinner, when Bonny had excused herself to use the rest room, Cait had nearly jumped out of her chair when Jack reached over to lay a hand on hers. "Is it just me, Cait, or is Bonny upset about something?" he asked in a low voice.

Bonny *had* been a tad cranky during dinner, but not alarmingly so. Probably just her Monthly Moodies, Cait had already decided. A conclusion she wasn't about to tell Jack.

Truthfully, she was more surprised by Jack's perceptiveness than by Bonny's funk. In her experience—even with Joe-Joe—men usually didn't notice a woman's unhappiness until she was practically suicidal.

"I wouldn't worry about it," she'd said, trying to ignore the warmth of his hand on hers. "We're all allowed, once in a while. And if something's really bothering her, she'll let us know."

Bonny's mood hadn't improved much over a game of Scrabble though. Whose would have under the circumstances? Jack had trounced them both royally.

On Sunday morning—the church choir being on summer

hiatus—Jack and Cait had shared a hymnal, Jack singing the melodies in his rich baritone, Cait harmonizing, just the way they'd done in high school. After church, they'd gone back to Cait's house and once again bumped good-naturedly into each other in her tiny kitchen as they made sandwiches and packed a picnic lunch.

"Too bad Bonny couldn't take the afternoon off to come with us," Jack said, cutting through a thick ham and cheese on pumpernickel.

"That's the problem with running a retail store," said Cait, dropping a half-dozen homemade chocolate-chip cookies into a plastic baggie. "And she talks about *you* working too hard."

"I'm worried about her," he said.

Cait didn't say anything, but by now she was a little worried too. Bonny had been awfully snappish when she'd declined their invitation to lunch after church. She'd apologized immediately, but nevertheless, when they dropped off a sandwich and cookies at the gallery on their way out of town a half-hour later, she still seemed out of sorts.

Not Jack and Cait though. The sky was blue, the sun was warm, and the open road beckoned. Jack's Jeep Cherokee was a lot more comfortable than the old Chevy truck he'd driven in high school—but then, Jack hadn't been interested in lazy Sunday drives in high school either.

When an old pickup with several teenagers crammed into the front seat blasted by them on a narrow country road, horn honking and kids yelling, and they both clucked in irritation, Cait had to laugh. "We've turned into the old fogeys who used to get in our way on a Sunday afternoon," she said.

"We were never that rude!"

"Afraid we were. It's okay, Hoot, I probably wouldn't remember either, except that I've lived through three teenage drivers since then. Tends to remind you."

They'd spent an hour winding through the rolling pastureland and wooded foothills east of Pilchuck before pulling over to the side of the road, climbing a fence, and trekking across a field to spread out their picnic blanket. It was a lovely spot, under a willow tree and next to a bubbling brook. After lunch they'd stretched out on the blanket and talked about their lives: revisited the past, reflected on what they'd learned since then, mused aloud about what the future might still hold.

They'd walked along the stream, Jack taking Cait's hand to help her down the bank and over the boulders in the water and across a fallen log. Not that Cait couldn't have done all those things on her own—she just hadn't wanted to.

Cindy had been a huge help over the last eight years, Cait told herself now as her eldest daughter wrapped up her flute solo. And Bonny had been there for her too, in ways she knew she could never repay. But when you got right down to it, ever since Joe-Joe had died Cait had been doing her life on her own.

And she was tired of it. She hadn't known how tired until now.

As Cindy left the platform and sat down on the front pew, Jack touched Cait yet again. "She's so much like you," he murmured. "You must be proud."

She nodded without looking at him.

No—it wasn't the first time she and Jack had touched this weekend. Or the first time she'd responded with an involuntary shiver of pleasure. Did he know? Did he feel it too?

And—she asked herself as they rose for the benediction—was it really so ridiculous after all? She and Jack together? More than friends?

It felt right, Jack thought as he followed Cait and Bonny outside after the service. Being back in Pilchuck. Sharing a pew at the Pilchuck Church of Saints and Sinners with his sister and his good buddy Cait.

Astonishingly, absurdly right, considering how many times in his life he'd said he could never, ever live in a town like Pilchuck again. A town where everybody knew everybody else's business—where you could sneeze in the privacy of your own home, for heaven's sake, and hear a dozen "Gesundheit!"s up and down the street before you even reached for a Kleenex.

The subsequent parade of neighbors climbing the stairs to the front porch bearing cures—everything from foul-smelling herbal poultices the color and consistency of tar to steaming vats of jalapeño-seasoned chicken soup—would last from here till Tuesday.

And just what's so bad about that?

Jack started. Helen's voice again?

But Helen—being the private person she was—would have hated living in a little town like Pilchuck, some part of his mind protested. Not so long ago, *he* would have hated it.

Then again…

What if they'd had a Pilchuck in their lives when Helen had taken sick? Instead of their fenced-in house in a suburb where they didn't know their neighbors except to say "hello" and "how-are-you" and "fine, thanks" even when they weren't?

What if they'd been part of a busybody Saints and Sinners congregation instead of the politely distant church they'd chosen on purpose so as not to feel obliged to get involved?

What if a Pastor Bob had dropped by the house to pray with Helen every morning on his way to work? Or a Mrs. Pfefferkuchen had knocked on the door with a home-baked pie once a week? Or a Cait Reilly had offered to run whatever errands needed running—whenever they needed running?

Cait would have done that too. If he hadn't known it before this weekend, he knew it now. She was that kind of friend. She'd always been that kind of friend—or would have been, if their paths had crossed more often, day to day.

Maybe in Pilchuck he wouldn't have felt so overwhelmed with the burden of Helen's care. Or so all alone when she was gone.

"Hoot? Are you all right?"

Startled, he turned to see Cait staring at him, her brown eyes wide and her forehead creased in concern. Somehow they'd walked all the way from the church to the street where Cait and Bonny lived without his being aware. "Why do you ask?"

"You're so quiet. And you looked so far away."

"Far away?" He grinned. "No, I wasn't far away. In fact, I was right here in Pilchuck. A place I had better not stay much longer, by the way, as I have to get up for work tomorrow and I'm still more than an hour away from home."

"Then you don't have time for strawberry shortcake? You and Bonny?"

It wasn't the temptation of strawberry shortcake that made him waver. It was the fact that he hadn't had an entire weekend of such pure and unadulterated fun for years, and he didn't want it to end.

His songfest on the way to Pilchuck had started it, he guessed. Then running into his first best buddy, Cait. Lunch at the Kitsch 'n' Caboodle had been delightful. And then there was the adrenaline rush of winning the softball game. And the pleasure of cooking with Cait—learning her recipe for German spaghetti and sharing his own for honey-yogurt-dressed fruit-and-walnut salad.

And what a game of Scrabble he'd played with Cait and Bonny after supper! He couldn't remember ever playing a "z" on a triple word score *and* using all his tiles for fifty bonus points all in the same turn.

"There's no such word as 'mythicize'!" Cait had protested.

He couldn't say she was wrong, but he knew how to bluff. "Are you challenging?"

"Yes!" From Cait *and* Bonny.

Wonder of wonders, it was in the dictionary. To his relief and the ladies' chagrin.

Cait had forgiven him, he was pretty sure. She hadn't seemed upset during their afternoon jaunt to the countryside anyhow.

How long had it been since he'd been on a picnic? Or walked

on fallen logs, or jumped from rock to rock in a stream? At least as long as it had been since the whole idea of fun had occurred to him. Which, as he'd already determined, was far too long.

A good thing for him he'd run into Cait; fun seemed to follow her around. And how easily they'd picked up the threads of their friendship, after so many years!

She was just what he needed in his life. The perfect weekend comrade. Fun to be with, easy to talk to. Relaxing. Inspiring.

And *safe*. He didn't have to worry about Cait Reilly getting all misty-eyed and moony on him—like too many women had already gotten since Helen died. Well—only the one so far really. A work colleague who'd let him know in no uncertain terms that she was interested.

But one was more than enough. *Any* misty-eyed romantic was more than enough. He'd given everything he had to give in that department. He couldn't imagine ever again having what he'd had with Helen. Just like Cait couldn't imagine ever again having what she'd had with Joe-Joe.

Thank goodness they'd cleared *that* up early on!

"I'll stay for shortcake," he bargained with Cait now. "As long as we can have it with chocolate syrup drizzled over the berries."

"Sounds decadent. And whipped cream on top?"

"How else?"

Bonny made a noise Jack could have sworn was a snort of disgust. "Count me out."

"You don't *have* to put chocolate on yours, Bonny," Cait said cheerfully.

"I know that!"

Hmm, Jack mused. "Snappish" was hardly a strong enough term anymore.

"Come on, Squirt," he wheedled, slinging an arm around her shoulders.

She shrugged him off. Looking none too happy either. "I—said—*no*."

Jack frowned.

"Would you rather go out?" Cait asked, doing a better job at "polite" than Jack was feeling at the moment.

Bonny tossed her head impatiently. "Why do you just assume I want to be with you all the time?" No mistaking the exasperation in her voice now. Or the spark of anger in her eyes.

Cait's face crumpled. "I'm sorry, Bonny, I didn't—"

"Wait," Jack interrupted, his own anger rising. He could hardly stand the hurt on Cait's sweet face. "You don't have anything to apologize for, Cait. Bonny, that was totally uncalled for. It isn't like you to be cruel."

Now it was Bonny's face that crumpled.

Great, Jack thought. *How in the world did I get in the middle of this?*

"Oh, Cait, I'm sorry," Bonny said, sounding truly anguished. "I just—it's just—I'm just so *awful!*"

"Of course you're not awful," Cait quickly reassured her. She looked at Jack reproachfully. "Really, Jack! Talk about uncalled for!"

Jack's jaw dropped. Now *he* was the villain of the piece?

"Well, excuse me for breathing," he muttered under his breath.

"What is it, Bonny?" Cait asked her quietly, ignoring Jack. "Something's been bothering you all weekend."

"I'm so embarrassed…"

"Please."

Bonny took a deep breath and raised her eyes to Cait's. "All right then. I can't help but be a little jealous."

"Jealous!" Jack interrupted. So he'd been right after all! But why was she taking it out on Cait?

Bonny crossed her arms and stared at the sidewalk. "I told you it was petty, Jack."

"No, I didn't mean that." He paused. "Look, Squirt, I haven't been to town for a long, long time. The Kitsch 'n' Caboodle crowd was just catching up with me, that's all. You don't—"

"You don't get it, Jack," Bonny interrupted, shaking her head as if he really was the most clueless person she'd ever encountered.

"Okay! I don't get it! So tell me."

"I'm not jealous of *you*," she said, finally meeting his eyes. "I'm jealous of *you and Cait!*"

Chapter Six

Cait held her breath. If Jack hadn't yet guessed how she was start-ing to feel, he was sure as rain in Pilchuck going to find out in the next few minutes. And—whether she wanted to know or not—she was going to find out how Jack was feeling. If he was feeling anything at all.

On the one hand, she wasn't sure she wanted to know; some fantasies were better left alone.

On the other hand—wasn't it always best between friends to get things out in the open? Because whatever else she and Jack were or weren't, and whatever else they might or might not become, they were friends. *Good* friends.

Then again—something told her this wasn't the way the romance game was played, friends or not. Getting things out in the open, that is. At least it wasn't the way it happened in romance novels. And she'd dipped into a few of those, she wasn't ashamed to admit. Although her personal preference ran to suspense thrillers, the twins always had half a dozen Harlequins in the house. They were the only place Cait *went* for romance anymore.

In Harlequins, nobody ever told anybody what he or she was really feeling—not until the final, inevitable, happily-ever-after clinch on the very last page. The way it happened in *real* life, she couldn't exactly remember. It had been too long.

She guessed it didn't matter at this point anyhow. Bonny had set the train in motion, and nothing but a blizzard could derail it now. She should have known better, asking what was bothering Bonny in front of Jack—but somehow she hadn't seen it coming. Bonny's jealousy, that is. Even though it did make perfect sense.

Jack, meanwhile, seemed at a loss for words. "Jealous of me and Cait?" he finally asked, scratching his head. "I don't know what you mean."

Cait's heart sank. So he hadn't guessed. In fact, from the confusion on his face, the idea had never even crossed his mind.

Bonny sighed. "You're my brother, Jack. My one and only. Cait—" She glanced in Cait's direction, "—you're my best friend."

Cait nodded and tried to swallow the lump in her throat as Bonny kicked at a pebble on the sidewalk.

It skittered across the street toward the Reilly house, and Cait was tempted, just for a moment, to follow it home. She didn't have to hear the rest of the conversation to know how it would go.

"And?" Jack prompted.

"And—but—all of a sudden it's as if I don't exist. Or at least that I don't matter."

"Don't matter…" Jack repeated blankly.

"Oh, Bonny," Cait said sorrowfully.

Jack shook his head. "Am I missing something here?"

Cait and Bonny both turned to stare at him, Bonny's face expressing what Cait was feeling: *Men!*

"Apparently you are," said Bonny.

"Please enlighten me."

"She feels left out, Jack," Cait jumped in, trying to spare her friend.

"Left out?" Jack still looked as blank as ever.

Bonny sighed again. Cait braced herself.

"How could I not feel left out?" Bonny asked him. "You and

Cait have this…this…I don't know. *Connection.* Like the two of you together are *complete* somehow. And me—I'm just out there on the periphery. Hardly even a blip on the screen."

Cait winced. And Jack, finally, was getting a clue. His face was suddenly red as a tropical sunburn. "But—it's not—we don't—" he choked out.

"You *do,*" said Bonny. "I'm a big baby for minding, I know—but there you have it." And once again she sighed. "Sometimes I'm just a big baby."

"But—but—"

"I'm sorry, Bonny," Cait said when it was clear Jack hadn't yet gathered his wits about him. Poor Jack! "It isn't something we're doing on purpose. Leaving you out."

"I know it's not. Besides, if you're attracted to each other—"

"Attracted to each other!" Jack exploded, finding his voice at last.

Cait's heart sank even lower. Did he have to look so *horrified* at the idea?

"Whoa, Nellie! Cait and I—we're just friends, Squirt," he said emphatically. "You're reading us all wrong. We've never been attracted to each other! Tell her, Cait."

But Cait didn't say anything. *Couldn't* say anything. Would have choked on her words if she'd *tried* to say anything.

Quite frankly, she hadn't felt so embarrassed since Cindy's wedding reception last year, when she'd walked out of the rest room of Tillicum County's only four-star restaurant with the back of her skirt inadvertently tucked into her pantyhose.

From the expression on Jack's face, Cait knew he was finally getting the picture that Bonny had gotten without even trying. In Technicolor and big as life too.

He grabbed her arm and pulled her away from Bonny, whispering urgently, "Cait, what's going on? You told me yesterday—you said—I thought we agreed—"

But he couldn't seem to actually get the words out.

Now it was Cait's turn to cross her arms defensively. "That was yesterday, Jack," she whispered, her teeth clenched. She met his eyes briefly before hers nervously skipped away. "Things change."

She turned around and walked away from him with as much dignity as she could muster. Which wasn't much. Unbelievably, this was even worse than her skirt in her pantyhose.

If a person really could die from embarrassment—she only had moments to live.

Jack stared after Cait, dumbfounded.

Now wait a minute! he wanted to call after her. *Just what do you think you're doing here? This wasn't part of the bargain!*

But Cait was no longer paying any attention to him. "You're right, Bonny," he heard her say. "Jack came to Pilchuck to see you, and I've been hogging him all weekend. I'm sorry I wasn't more sensitive."

He shook his head, but the motion didn't seem to clear away the cobwebs in his brain. This didn't seem real somehow. He felt as if he were sitting in the back row of a theater at some play he didn't know he'd had tickets for—some play with a plot so confusing it could only be Theater of the Absurd. If ever he'd needed Cliffs Notes, now was the time!

"I'm sorry I've been such a pill," Bonny was saying.

"As if *I* never am. Spend some time with Jack before he leaves, girlfriend. I've got that latest Tom Clancy novel to keep me company tonight. And you and I can get together later this week, okay?"

The latest Tom Clancy novel. Probably the same one he'd stuffed in his overnight bag just in case boredom struck in Pilchuck.

Boredom? Hah! If only he'd been so lucky!

He'd have been a good deal better off with boredom. Why

hadn't he just holed up at Bonny's and read all weekend? Why hadn't he just holed up at *home* and read all weekend? This trip had turned into an utter disaster! His sister mad at him, and his oldest friend—his good *buddy* for crying out loud—getting all misty-eyed and moony on him! How *dare* Cait ruin their friendship by telling him she was—she had—she felt—

Well. She hadn't really said anything out and out. But she'd made it clear enough. And he was mad as a Hun about it! Mad as a *horde* of Huns. After all, he'd never told *her*—

He tried to stop the thought, but it was too late.

He'd never told her when he'd had a crush on *her*.

There was a reason, Jack, some part of his mind told another part. *You didn't know it yourself until she got engaged. And then you* couldn't *tell her.*

Cait turned around just then, and for a moment, with the lowering sun behind her, she glowed like an angel—the way she'd glowed that day almost three decades ago when she'd told him she was going to marry Joe-Joe Reilly. The day he realized he'd lost whatever chance he might have had to win her heart. The day he realized trying to win her heart was something he ought to have considered.

But it was too late then. And it was too late now. He wasn't going to fall in love again. He wasn't going to marry again. How could he, after Helen?

Still, just for a moment as he gazed at Cait against the golden sky and remembered, he wished he could.

Then the sun dropped behind the line of trees at the end of the street, and Cait blended into the shadows. Jack felt suddenly, ineffably sad.

Not to mention *exhausted.* All these uninvited feelings attacking him, one after the other!

She must have seen. Why were women so much better than men at that—reading expressions? Identifying emotions?

"Don't worry about it, Jack," she said gently. As if to comfort *him,* of all things! As if her *own* embarrassment meant nothing. "We had a great time this weekend. Let's leave it at that, okay?"

"I'm sorry, Cait—"

"Sorry?" she interrupted lightly. "Why not be flattered instead?"

"Flattered?"

"Sure." She fluffed her hair, struck a saucy pose, and fluttered her eyelashes outrageously. "I may not be a spring chicken anymore, but I'm told I'm quite the thing for an old hen."

Jack sputtered and then laughed outright. Leave it to Cait to turn the moment around. To make the whole thing funny.

And to make things right between them. Again. "*Quite* the thing," he said, grinning. "And can you make an old rooster crow!"

"Or an old owl hoot," she said, answering his grin. "I'll see you next time, Jack. Have a cup of coffee with your sis before you go."

"You're doing it again," Bonny said, her voice resigned, before Jack could answer.

"Doing what?"

"Talking like I'm not here."

"Oops!" Cait looked contrite. "Sorry, Bonny. I'm on my way. You do your own inviting. But could you give your brother a message for me?"

"Oh, I suppose."

"Great! Tell him I got over him once, and I'm quite sure I can do it again."

"I'll tell him," Bonny said, grinning at Jack, who was staring open-mouthed at Cait's backward retreat across the street. Gotten over him once! Could do it again!

"You want me to tell him about the first time?" Bonny called after her.

Cait waved. "I leave it to your discretion, girlfriend. Bye, Hoot!"

And she was gone.

Poor Hoot, Cait mused the next afternoon as she fitted the bodice for Camilla Thigpen's eighth-grade graduation dress.

Camilla and her mother, while Cait pulled and snipped and pinned, were arguing about whether or not fourteen was old enough for a girl to go out on an unchaperoned date—a squabble too painfully familiar to Cait, after raising three girls, to interest her ever again.

Jack, on the other hand—poor Jack…

She hadn't stopped thinking about Jack since last night when she'd seen him barrel down the street in his fancy Jeep Cherokee like the harpies were after him. He'd probably felt as if they were.

Jack had stayed for coffee and a visit with his sister, but not for long. And Bonny was on the phone to Cait even before the dust had settled on the street out front. "He didn't even finish one *cup* of coffee," she'd complained.

"Why not?"

"I don't think he liked what I had to say."

"About Mindy Vanderhoeven, you mean?" asked Cait. "But that was such a long time ago!"

"True. Though it did seem to shake him up a little. He had no idea."

Mindy Vanderhoeven wasn't the half of it; unfortunately, Bonny hadn't stopped at telling old tales. She'd also told Jack that he was in denial if he thought he wasn't attracted to Cait, that a happy first marriage was the best indicator of marital bliss the second time around, and that Jack's vow not to marry again had more to do with fear than it did with loyalty.

These theories Cait was quite familiar with as Bonny's friend. Bonny read self-help books like the twins read romance novels. And handed out opinions like a politician handed out kisses to babies.

Cait took her friend's axioms and advice with a grain of salt, and frankly found the whole thing highly entertaining. She was used to having her life scrutinized and analyzed—but Jack must have found it disconcerting, to say the least.

She hoped she and Bonny hadn't scared him away from Pilchuck for *another* three or four years, or however long it had been since the last time he'd come. That would really be too bad for Bonny, who could use a brother like Jack.

It would be too bad for Jack, too, because Jack could use a sister like Bonny, analysis and all. In fact, Jack could use a town like Pilchuck. And he could certainly use a whole lot more fun in his life than he'd had in a good long while. Hadn't he told Cait—before that last little scene between them—that his weekend in Pilchuck had felt like a week's vacation? That he hadn't felt so relaxed and alive since before Helen had taken sick?

Yes, it would really be too bad if they'd scared him away.

As for Jack's horrified shock at the very idea of Cait and romance—she was trying to be philosophical.

It wasn't as if she was looking to be with a man, after all. As she'd told herself often enough over the last eight years—and told Bonny, too, as Bonny pretty much got the inside scoop on everything Cait was thinking—she just couldn't see herself with anyone other than Joe-Joe. It was only Jack's nearness this weekend that had set her to wondering.

"The thing is," she'd told Bonny more than once, "I couldn't be fair. How could I not compare? How could any other relationship even come close? It's better not to think about it."

"Fear," Bonny opined. "Denial."

"Maybe." Cait never rejected Bonny's suggestions out of hand.

"Besides—don't you get lonely?" Bonny asked.

"I have the girls. And a whole houseful of memories."

Only she didn't have the girls in the same way anymore. They didn't need her the way they'd needed her when they were young.

And her memories didn't exactly keep her warm at night.

Of course she wasn't about to *settle* for someone just for the sake of keeping warm at night. No matter how hard those winter northeasters blew through Pilchuck, she could always find another log to throw on the fire, another blanket to throw on the bed. She did have plenty of blankets.

Not that being with Jack would be *settling*, she told herself. He was a very special person. In general, and in her life.

But really—they were just too *close* to be anything more than friends. It really *was* ridiculous. She'd figured that out the first time. Way back at their *own* eighth-grade graduation, when Mindy Vanderhoeven—

"Ouch!"

"Sorry," Cait murmured to her client around the pins in her mouth. *Concentrate, Cait,* she reprimanded herself.

She placed the last few pins and gave the bodice one last tug. "That's fine, Camilla. We've got a good fit. Come back tomorrow and I'll pin up the hem."

"Graduation's on Friday," Mrs. Thigpen said, sounding a bit worried.

"It won't take any time to hem," Cait soothed as Camilla, pouting, shrugged out of the bodice and into her crop top. A bit too cropped for Camilla's figure, in Cait's opinion. Camilla wasn't just blossoming; she was in full bloom.

In fact, Cait thought as Camilla primped in front of the sewing-room mirror, reapplying liberal amounts of lipstick, mascara, and eyeliner while her mother fidgeted near the door, in her opinion, Mrs. Thigpen had more to worry about than Camilla's dress being finished for graduation.

Eighth grade, Cait thought, shaking her head as she showed the Thigpen mother-daughter duo to the door and closed it behind them. How did anyone ever survive it? How did *mothers* survive it?

And did Mrs. Thigpen realize her daughter was a Mindy Vanderhoeven in the making?

Chapter Seven

Until last night, Cait hadn't thought of Mindy Vanderhoeven in years. Unconsciously blocked her from her memory probably; Mindy had ruined Cait's eighth-grade graduation. And almost ruined her friendship with Jack.

The graduates, as was the custom, had been lined up alphabetically for the ceremony—which put Cait Anderson at the front of the line and Jack Van Hooten at the back. Paired up with Mindy Vanderhoeven.

Mindy Vanderhoeven was *not* the kind of girl an innocent fourteen-year-old boy should have been paired up with for anything. And oh, had Jack been innocent! Nothing in his life had prepared him for the kiss Mindy gave him under the football bleachers the afternoon of graduation practice. Or for his enthusiastic reaction.

Cait hadn't heard about it from Jack either; she hadn't had to. Everybody in the entire Pilchuck Junior High School, including the teachers, knew about it by the time the actual ceremony took place that night.

Mindy liked to kiss and tell.

Jack liked the kissing so much he didn't care; he was gone on Mindy.

Eighth grade had already been a miserable year for Cait—as eighth grade often was, she'd been reminded twice since then, once with Cindy and once with the twins. But nothing was so miserable as finding out Jack had a crush on Mindy Vanderhoeven—and finding out in the same moment that she herself had a crush on Jack.

She'd gone home to her long-suffering mother, sobbing as if her heart would break. It wasn't fair! Jack was her best friend. If he was going to have a crush on someone, why couldn't he have a crush on *her*?

But that *was* why, her mother had gently tried to explain. Boys just didn't get crushes on their best buddies; they knew them too well. Romance required mystery…

"You'll see, sweetheart," Cait's mother had tried to console her. "There are boys out there who see you the same way Jack sees Mindy."

Which had proven to be true—and not so long afterward either. Her birthday was two weeks after graduation, and she'd received not one but *two* deliveries of fresh flowers, from Sam Hutchins and Garson Krueger—and both while Hoot was over too. She remembered it as a triumph.

At fourteen, of course, the whole boy-girl thing was so incredibly *confusing*. What on earth had the Creator been thinking, Cait wondered still, setting things up so that all those hormones exploded at once in a poor kid's body?

Thank goodness her mother had known what to say: That while crushes were truly intoxicating, and ought to be enjoyed for what they were, they rarely lasted—but true friendship always did. Better Jack's buddy for life than his fling for a week, she'd decided—a week being the length of Jack's interest in Mindy.

There'd been others, of course, for both of them—but none who'd interfered with their friendship. If Jack hadn't moved out of town, she doubted even Joe-Joe and Helen would have interfered with their friendship. Partners were partners. Pals were pals.

Not once since eighth grade had Cait ever again acknowledged—not until yesterday, that is—that she'd been interested in Jack Van Hooten "that way." Why the idea had even entered her mind now, she couldn't fathom.

Maybe it was the Mindy Vanderhoeven Effect all over again: Maybe imagining Jack attracted to Lily Johansen had triggered Cait's unacknowledged longings.

Or maybe it was hormones—she was getting to be that age when the silly things were scheduled to go wacky again. Another of the Creator's mysteries.

Or maybe it was simply the phase of the moon. Cait didn't discount the influence of the moon on human behavior. Wasn't the moon responsible for the ebb and flow of the ocean tides? And wasn't the human body ninety-eight percent water?

Whatever it was—it wasn't important. Not nearly as important as Jack's friendship was. She hadn't let those feelings ruin what she had with Jack in eighth grade, and she wasn't about to let them ruin what she had with him now.

She pulled a box of stationery out of the roll-top desk in her room and sat down with a pen.

Hey, Hoot-Owl! the note read when she was finished. *Hope we haven't scared you away from Pilchuck forever. Bonny told me she subjected you to one of her amateur headshrinking routines—guess I should have warned you. She can be pretty daunting in pop-shrink mode if you're not prepared.*

I so enjoyed reconnecting with you this weekend, Hoot. Hope you know I would never do anything to jeopardize our friendship. Like I said yesterday—I got over you once, and really—it was no big deal. Because like I said Saturday—you and me? Can you imagine?!

Come back to Pilchuck. Often. I made Bonny promise to lay off the analysis next time you come to town! She and I could both use a man's perspective once in a while—especially a man who can swing a hammer. Maybe we'll be good for you too. (Had you ever even thought of a porch-swing ministry before this weekend, for instance?)

Thanks for everything—
Friends forever—
Cait-Cat

Of course she was out of stamps. Oh well—it was a pleasant afternoon for a walk to the post office. After dealing with Camilla Thigpen and her mother, she needed a break.

Joe-Joe's old how-to book, *Porch Swings and Patio Furniture,* was sitting next to Cait's purse on the kitchen table. She picked it up, running her fingers along its worn edges and then leafing through its pages. Jack had seemed so excited when she'd dug out the manual and let him peruse it: "I can almost feel the hammer in my hand, Cait. This looks like so much fun!"

She tucked the manual in a side pocket of her large handbag. When she mailed her letter a few minutes later, it was inside a large Priority Mail envelope along with the book.

If it looked like fun to Jack, then he should have it.

Hoot clearly needed all the fun he could get.

By the time Jack found Cait's package in his mailbox, after work late Thursday afternoon, he didn't know which end was up. Which end of his life, that is. If only life came with a stamp in the upper right-hand corner! If only it came in such a neat package. Labeled so clearly *Priority.*

Priority label or not, Jack plowed through all the other mail first, reading everything from start to finish, even the notice from Publisher's Clearing House that he was definitely in the running for the ten million dollar super-prize. He actually read through the sheet of order stamps and wondered if he ought not subscribe to *WoodWorks* or *101 Home Projects* or *Hammer and Saw.* A subscription to *101 Home Projects* came with a genuine faux cowhide tool belt if he acted now.

But as much as he wished it could be, his mind wasn't really on genuine faux cowhide tool belts. It was on that package lying in front of him on his kitchen counter, as intriguing as Pandora's box. And as potentially filled with danger.

Hadn't Cait already turned his quiet, ordered, comfortable life completely upside down in the space of a couple of days? She and that bossy, meddlesome, know-it-all sister of his?

You mean your empty, sterile, humdrum life?

"No, I do not!" he said aloud, with feeling. He didn't know how, but Cait and Bonny had somehow fired up this pesky voice inside his head that had to put in its two cents worth about everything.

And it wasn't the only thing they'd fired up either. Take Jack's temper, for instance. He was *miffed.*

Maybe more than miffed, if the way he'd peeled out of Bonny's driveway Sunday night was any indication.

But really! When had Bonny turned into such a know-it-all anyhow? Telling him he was in denial! Attracted to Cait! *Afraid!* Psychoanalyzing him as if she knew the slightest thing about it! As if she knew the slightest thing about *him.*

So maybe Bonny had read every self-help book on the market since that nut case of a husband left her. So maybe she did know a thing or two about loss and grief herself. But Timothy Fairley and Helen Van Hooten had less in common than—than a toad and a princess!

How *dare* Bonny presume to understand his feelings? To *dissect* him, for pity's sake?

And Cait! The one person other than Helen he'd ever trusted with his secrets, and what had she done? As if it weren't enough that she'd spilled the beans to Bonny about the cat-in-the-dryer incident—

She'd actually told his little sister, his innocent little sister who'd always looked up to him, about his *first kiss!*

What other secrets had she given away?

And then there was that whole other thing. That piece of information Cait had shared with Bonny but had never shared with him. Cait—the one person other than Helen he thought had always told him everything.

She'd had a crush on him, for crying out loud! And never told him! Who knew how their lives might have been different if she had? Not that he'd have wanted to miss out on Helen. That wasn't the point. The point was that Cait had held out on him. Without a reason. He and Mindy hadn't been *engaged,* for pity's sake!

And now here Cait was *again* with a crush on him. *Telling* him this time. When it was the last thing on earth he wanted to hear!

That Cait. She can't do anything right, can she?

"What are you talking about? Of course she can!" he answered the pesky voice inside his head. "I can hardly think of a thing she *doesn't* do right."

But she was wrong for not *telling you thirty years ago, and she's wrong for* telling *you now.*

"Her timing's off, that's all."

She'd be a good match for you, Jack.

This time it wasn't his alter ego. It was Helen.

Jack dropped his head in his hands and sighed in frustration. It had been like this since the moment he'd peeled out of Bonny's driveway. Constant arguing inside his head! With himself, with Cait, with Bonny. Even with the Almighty.

And yes—with Helen, of all persons! He and Helen had never argued!

You have so much to give, Jack, he imagined her saying. *And so much still to savor! So much life. So much experience. So much love… Don't squander your love. It's far too precious.*

And as clear as if she'd been there in the flesh: *I want you to have the things we couldn't, Jack. The things I couldn't give you. Children. Grandchildren. A hand to hold during the rest of your journey. A hand to hold when you're old and gray.*

Remember—to everything there is a season, he could almost hear her gentle voice reminding. *A time to every purpose under heaven. A time to weep, and a time to laugh. A time to mourn, and a time to dance.*

A time to love…

Love again, Jack. Let yourself be loved.

He reached for the blue-and-white package and ripped it open across the top. What did he have to lose?

Porch Swings and Patio Furniture. Jack stared at the book in his hands, Joe-Joe Reilly's old how-to manual, the one Cait had dug out when he said he'd like to know where Joe-Joe had found his plans for her Victorian swing. The one that actually had made his fingers itch to hold a hammer. The one he'd said he'd like to find a copy of.

She'd be a good match, Jack, he heard Helen's voice murmur again.

"I'm not ready," he muttered.

He wasn't. There were no two ways about it. He wasn't ready to have another woman in his life. Not Cait. Not anyone.

Why?

That pesky alter-ego voice again. He didn't know which was worse, his alter ego or Helen.

"I'm just not, okay?" Not much of an argument, but at this point all he had.

Because when he thought about it—there wasn't a reason on earth he shouldn't enjoy the company of a good woman again. A woman like Cait. As more than a buddy, too. There wasn't a reason on earth he shouldn't remarry.

Except for Bonny's reason.

Why aren't you ready for a woman in your life? the voice insisted.

"Because I could never go through what I went through with Helen again, that's why! All right? Are you happy now?"

Jack sat up straight, mouth open. That hadn't been a voice in his head. That had been his own voice, saying out loud what he hadn't even let himself think until now.

Bonny was right. He was afraid. As much as he'd tried to deny it, he was afraid. As much as he'd tried to deny it, the thought of Cait as anything but his good buddy made him tremble with fear.

A verse came suddenly to mind: *Perfect love casts out fear.*

There was something worse than fearing death, Jack knew with sudden insight. Fearing life. Fearing life so much you missed out on the gifts God wanted desperately to give you.

Now you're getting it, Jack.

Helen's voice once more. Warm, loving, full of compassion.

His fingers trembled as he pulled the single sheet of Cait's letter from the smaller envelope that had come with Joe-Joe's book. He scanned it quickly, then went back to read it through again. Both times his eyes stopped at the same place. Both times the words jarred him: *I got over you once, and really—it was no big deal. Like I said on Saturday—you and me? Can you imagine?!*

"Got over me once," Jack muttered, scowling ferociously. And in a week, Bonny had informed him. A *week!*

That rankled. That really rankled! Did she think she could dismiss him so easily again, the way she'd done in junior high? Without giving him a chance? Without giving *herself* a chance? No big deal, she said! How did she think *that* made him feel?

And just what was it that was so ridiculous about them being together anyhow? Because, as a matter of fact, he *could* imagine it.

And did. Vividly. Between alternating bouts of indignation and terror, for the rest of the evening and most of the following day.

Nevertheless, when he jumped into his Jeep on Saturday morning and pointed it north, he told himself he had a particular reason for making this trip to Pilchuck, and it didn't have a thing to do with Cait Reilly. Though it did have to do with the book she'd sent him—specifically, the plans on pages 113-122 for a willow porch swing.

His trip to Pilchuck had nothing to do with Bonny either—though it did have to do with his sister's ex-in-laws and the pastureland they owned just outside the city limits. Specifically, the stand of willow trees that grew along their creek.

Most assuredly, his trip to Pilchuck had nothing whatsoever to do with the fact that once upon a time, Cait had had a crush on him and got over him in a week—and that nearly a week had passed since she'd made up her mind to get over him again.

No big deal, he thought, his grip tightening on the steering wheel. No big deal, she said!

Chapter Eight

"Cait? I thought I'd better warn you." Bonny's voice was a low, urgent murmur over the phone.

Cait's heartbeat quickened. "What? What's wrong?"

"Jack's in town."

"Jack's in town," Cait repeated blankly. "This is supposed to worry me?"

"Look, Cait, you can try to fool yourself, but you can't fool me." Bonny still spoke in an undertone, as if trying to keep someone from overhearing. Hoot, maybe?

As for her comment—Cait wasn't about to touch it. "Is he there?" she asked instead.

"He just left. Says he came to town to go cut willow boughs at my ex-in-laws'. Says he's going to make a willow swing."

"Really! I wonder if he's using the plans from Joe-Joe's book."

Bonny snorted. "Like you believe him!"

"I don't know why I shouldn't—"

"Oops, here comes Robin. You coming by later?"

Cait breathed a sigh of relief. At least Bonny was being discreet around the twins. All she needed was her eighteen-year-old daughters poking their noses into her love life.

Love life! She almost dropped the phone, she was so startled by the thought. Whatever was she thinking? Love life, indeed! She'd already had her turn at once-in-a-blue-moon love. That part of life was far behind her.

On top of which, Hoot had made it clear as a full-moon night last weekend what he thought about the whole idea of romance. Or at least the idea of romance with *her.*

"Cait?" Bonny prompted.

"Oh! Not today," she said. "I have a consultation this morning and a softball game after lunch."

"Well, keep your eye out for Jack," Bonny told her.

As if she had to instruct her! "I will," she said.

She did—all morning as she worked on a wardrobe plan with her client, a world-class pianist who'd been coming to Cait for her concert gowns for years. In fact, Cait glanced out the window of her sewing room so often as they discussed designs and fabrics and classical music that the pianist asked if Cait were expecting the Publisher's Clearing House Prize Patrol sometime today.

After that, she tried to be more circumspect.

But Jack didn't show.

Cait begged off her client's invitation to lunch at the Kitsch 'n' Caboodle and warmed up a bowl of leftover homemade garden-vegetable soup, then changed into her jeans and running shoes and her Fairley's Drug and Fountain team T-shirt.

By the time she left for her softball game, Jack still hadn't shown. Did it take that long to gather willow boughs? Or was he avoiding her?

It made her a little nervous that she wondered.

The problem was—though Cait hadn't breathed a word to any-one—Bonny was right. It hadn't been as easy as she'd thought it was going to be, letting go of Jack. Letting go of her attraction. He'd been popping up in her mind all week long.

And my, was he appealing! She was beginning to think it was

more than the Mindy Vanderhoeven Effect or hormones or the phase of the moon.

In fact, when she got home from her softball game Saturday afternoon and finally saw Jack's Jeep sitting in Bonny's driveway, and her heart skipped a beat and then began to flutter crazily—she suddenly realized she didn't *want* to let her feelings go. Not just yet anyhow.

The truth of the matter was, the idea of Jack—the idea of her and Jack together—made her feel about sixteen. On the very brink of life. So young! So hopeful! At forty-six, she wasn't about to give up *that* till she'd enjoyed it for a week or two. In fact, she'd thanked the good Lord more than once this week she still had it in her to *feel* the way she was feeling.

Hoot didn't have to know.

Hoot *wouldn't* know. She'd make sure of it. In whatever way she could. Because Hoot's friendship was more important even than feeling sixteen again.

She knew what Bonny would say to that—if she could talk to Bonny about it, which she couldn't.

Cait hated to hold out on her best friend. It didn't feel right not to confide in Bonny. But it didn't feel right talking to Bonny about Jack either. It complicated the situation, Hoot being Bonny's brother.

Anyhow, Cait knew that if she'd given Bonny half a chance, "You can try to fool yourself, but you can't fool me" would have been only the beginning. And she was fairly certain—knowing her friend the way she did—that Bonny's monologue would have been peppered with phrases like "empty-nest syndrome," "the need for primary connection," "fear of intimacy," and "ambivalent feelings."

Jack, because he'd made it clear he wasn't available for romance, felt *safe* to Cait, Bonny would undoubtedly say. Jack-as-Romantic-Interest was a nice, comfortable, nonthreatening fantasy.

"But you're going to have to face it sometime, Cait." She could almost hear the words. "You still have half your life to live, and you're all alone. Is that the way you want it?"

That particular question, at this particular moment in her life, Cait wasn't ready to answer. Two weeks ago, yes; but now, suddenly, she couldn't say. Which was another reason for avoiding the subject with Bonny.

Feeling sixteen again did have its downside, Cait discovered in short order. She should have known there'd be lows along with the highs. There always were, at sixteen. Excruciating self-doubt, for instance. A total lack of self-confidence and composure. In fact, when both the phone and the doorbell stayed silent the rest of the afternoon, Cait remembered vividly why it was a good thing sixteen came along only once in a person's lifetime. She was a nervous wreck.

Why didn't he call? Had she upset him? Made him mad? Scared him away forever?

Should *she* call *him?*

Had she offended him somehow? Said something wrong in her letter? Did he even *like* her anymore?

Why didn't he call?

Should she call him?

And on and on…

She didn't call him. After all, she'd made the last move, writing her letter, sending Joe-Joe's book. The ball, as they said, was in Jack's court. If he wasn't interested in being active in her life again—even as a friend—she wasn't going to force him. How could she?

Still, the questions kept rolling around in her head.

Without any answers.

Jack's hour and a half trip from Seattle to Pilchuck Saturday morning had been long enough that he'd talked himself into and out of Cait Reilly several times over. "Into" because he realized he did after all find her enormously attractive. And because both Helen and the Almighty seemed to him to have given him the go-ahead. And because when he stopped to think about it—he knew he didn't want to be alone the rest of his life.

"Out of" because the whole idea made his feet sweat. Jack didn't like it when his feet sweated.

So he hadn't stopped to say hello to Cait when he got into town, even though he wanted to. He stopped at the Blue Moon instead, to say hello to Bonny, and to tell her what he was up to. He didn't even mention Cait. After all the trouble last weekend, he wasn't sure he'd ever mention Cait to Bonny again.

But he thought about Cait the rest of the morning and into the afternoon. He thought about her with every lop of the pruning shears and every rip of the bow saw as he gathered the willow boughs he needed for his project.

He didn't know exactly why he'd chosen a willow swing for his first foray into furniture making, except that it was different than anything he'd ever done before. Most woodworking was so precise, the way his work as an engineer was precise. Making willow furniture looked more forgiving. More spontaneous and creative.

Jack could use a little spontaneity and creativity in his life. A little *fun*.

Then go for it with Cait, his alter ego intruded.

He didn't answer, but his socks were sopping.

He was still thinking about Cait when he drove back into town from the Fairleys', the Jeep loaded down with green willow branches, and pulled into Bonny's driveway. *I should thank her for the book,* he'd told himself.

You should, his alter ego agreed.

So he'd crossed the street, his feet practically sloshing around inside his shoes, and had rung her doorbell.

To his relief, Cait hadn't been home.

He raided Bonny's cupboards for a bite to eat, then walked into town to the Coast-to-Coast to buy nails—a pound and a half in varying types and sizes—and forty feet of manila rope, and a pair of two-inch welded rings.

The task took longer than it otherwise might have, as he kept running into people who recognized him. "I'd know that Van Hooten chin anywhere," one old woman had warbled. Everyone wanted an update on his life and wanted to update him. And not in twenty-five words or less either.

When he got back to Bonny's and saw that Cait's car was parked in her driveway, he *meant* to cross the street to see her, or at least to call her on the phone, after he showered and shaved and dressed for dinner with Bonny and the Fairleys.

But Bonny had a stack of old *Psychology for the New Century* magazines in the bathroom and he got so engrossed in an article called "The Tao of Kissing" that he barely had enough time to get to the Blue Moon before it closed. An extremely thought-provoking article, too, especially in the context of—

No—he didn't want to go there.

Or did he?

By the time the Jeep backed out of the driveway across the street just before six, still without word one from Jack, Cait was a complete and total basket case. And when the twins came home from work going on about "Uncle Jack," and how sweet he was to Bonny, and how he really was the *nicest* man, and so good-looking for a guy that old—

Well, it peeved her, is what it did. "Uncle Jack," her eyeball. What made him think he could traipse into town and "Uncle Jack" her daughters when he didn't even have the decency to pick up the phone to say hello to *her?*

It did help to hear from the twins that Jack and Bonny were having dinner at the Fairleys'. If Jack was back in town so soon, and using the book she'd sent him, and being civil to his sister, surely their own friendship was on solid ground. He'd probably been busy all afternoon and the time had gotten away from him, that's all. He wasn't avoiding her.

Was he?

She was glad he was spending time with Bonny too. Being brotherly. She *wanted* him to spend time with his sister.

Didn't she?

As long as it doesn't mean he won't spend time with me, she told herself, and then felt instantly guilty. *Love isn't jealous,* she reminded herself, quoting from one of her favorite Bible passages. *Love seeks not its own....*

She sighed, loud and long enough that the twins asked in unison, "What's wrong, Mom?"

"Oh, nothing," she said and sighed again. Then, before she could think better of it, she called Garson Krueger, who'd been divorced for three years and after Cait to go out with him for two, and asked him if he'd like to go to church with her in the morning.

Maybe if Jack saw her with an eligible bachelor, he'd realize that he didn't have a thing to worry about. That her attraction to him had been only momentary. An aberration. That their friendship didn't have to be affected. That he was *safe* with her.

Then again, maybe she'd better go the second mile and arrange for Jack to meet Lily Johansen.

Cait sighed once more as she hung up the phone with Lily a few minutes later. This feeling-like-a-teenager-again definitely wasn't all it was cracked up to be.

Jack couldn't believe it when he walked into the Pilchuck Church of Saints and Sinners the next morning, fully intending to share a pew and a hymnal with Cait, and found her standing in the foyer with "honest-to-goodness Tillicum County tycoon" Garson Krueger hovering at her elbow. Pompous, officious, self-absorbed Garson Krueger, Jack thought darkly. Balding, potbellied, rich-as-old-Croesus Garson Krueger.

That Cait would keep company with a man like that—well, it felt like a slap in the face, is what it felt like, Jack told himself. Sure, she'd told Jack not to worry about her, it was no big deal, she'd get over him soon enough. But moving on to a man like *Krueger?* In a *week?* How could she?

"Jack!" Cait waved across the crowd when she saw him. "Over here! There's someone I'd like you to meet."

He waved back, and would have left it at that and escaped up the stairs to the balcony, but Bonny grabbed his arm and maneuvered him through the crowd like a mother trying to get a curbside spot for her son at the big parade.

To his surprise, it wasn't Garson Krueger that Cait wanted him to meet, though the two men did exchange cursory greetings. It was a lovely young woman named Lily—extremely young, it seemed to Jack, and so shy she couldn't seem either to meet his eyes or to think of a word to say after their initial introduction.

"Garson and Lily are coming for dinner after church, Jack. Wouldn't you like to join us?" Cait offered.

"I certainly would," Jack answered without hesitation, not about to let Krueger loose with Cait, who automatically always thought the best of everyone. Krueger was just the kind of guy to take advantage of a sweet, affectionate, generous-natured woman like Cait.

"Good! Bonny, I'll save the leftovers if you want to come over after work." At Bonny's nod, she added, "Why don't we find a seat?"

Somehow—much to his consternation—Jack ended up on the opposite end of the pew from Cait, with Bonny on one side and Lily on the other. Krueger was already snaking his arm across the back of the pew behind Cait, and the service hadn't even started.

When it did, Jack tried very hard to remember where he was and why he was there. This was the house of God, he reminded himself, and he had come to fellowship and to worship.

But he was so agitated he could hardly manage the singing, and he fumbled around so long looking for the Scripture reading that he missed the first half, and after the sermon he couldn't have said for the world what Pastor Bob's main points had been.

All he could think about the entire hour was losing Cait. Again. Waiting too long. Letting her fall in love with someone else—Garson Krueger or anyone. He'd already lost one love—through no fault of his own, to a fate over which he had no control. But if he lost Cait...

If he lost Cait, he would have no one to blame but himself.

Chapter Nine

She'd put a pretty good face on things, Cait thought as Pastor Bob wrapped up the service with his benediction. A service she was afraid she hadn't gotten a whole lot out of, as putting a good face on things had required most of the energy she would otherwise have used for worship.

She'd managed to keep it light with Jack. Make enough of a pretense with Garson Krueger for Jack to get the idea.

But was that what she wanted to do? Put a good face on things? Make pretenses? Encourage the attentions of a man she could never be interested in while letting the man she could love with all her heart believe she could take him or leave him?

In other words—lie?

She stared down at her hands, gripping the back of the pew in front of her so hard her knuckles were white.

"Shall we go home and have roast preacher for dinner?" Garson Krueger murmured in her ear.

Cait jerked her head around, staring at him with what must have been an extremely disapproving frown, if his peeved reaction was any indication: "Hey, it's a joke. Lighten up."

She tried to smooth her expression. "I need a few minutes alone, Garson. Could I meet you and the others outside?" Without waiting for an answer she slipped out and made her way against the crowd toward the front of the church, where she dropped onto the first pew and sat silently for several minutes. She stared at the desert scene painted on the back wall of the baptistery as if the answers to all her questions were scripted on the gold-tinged clouds. Finally she bowed her head and prayed silently.

I didn't think it would ever happen again—but Lord, it has. I love him. Hoot, that is. As my oldest best friend. And as the one I want to go through the rest of my life with. I don't want to lie about it to anyone. Not to you or him or Bonny or Garson. Most of all, not to myself. So from here on out, it's in your hands, Lord. I leave it to you.

She didn't *hear* the Almighty say "OK," but she felt it. Along with an overwhelming flood of peace to her heart.

Now *that* was what prayer was made for.

Last week Bonny had gone straight to the store after church, but this morning, Jack noticed, she was hanging around. A table to one side of the walkway outdoors was set up with coffee and tea, and lots of people were hanging around. At the moment, Lily Johansen was pouring second cups of coffee for herself and Garson Krueger, who was hovering at her elbow the way he'd been hovering at Cait's before the service.

Jack frowned as he sipped at his own coffee. He didn't want Krueger within a hundred miles of Cait, but he didn't want Cait to see Krueger dallying with another woman either. Not if there was a chance it might hurt her.

Where *was* she? He glanced at the church doors for what seemed like the twentieth time, but still no sign of Cait.

"What's wrong with you, Jack? You're as wound up as a groom on his wedding day," Bonny's voice came from behind him.

He flushed at the metaphor. That Bonny! "Don't you have to open the gallery?" he asked tersely.

"Not for another half-hour. I want to see Cait before I go."

She wasn't the only one. Jack glanced once more toward the entrance of the little church, where Pastor Bob and his wife were still in conversation with a couple of parishioners. "You don't suppose anything's wrong?" He tried to sound casual.

"I think she's had a very difficult week," said Bonny, her voice fraught with meaning. *What* meaning, Jack wasn't sure, but from Bonny's expression he figured it must have something to do with him.

He brightened. So maybe Cait was having a harder time getting over him than she'd expected.

"You don't have to look so happy about it," Bonny said.

He started. His coffee sloshed in the plastic foam cup. "Happy about what?"

She looked at him strangely. "About Cait having a difficult week, of course. What's wrong with you, Jack?" she asked again.

His fingers tightened around the cup. "Nothing. Nothing at all. Not a thing."

"No?" She eyed him skeptically. "How've you been this week anyhow? You don't exactly look rested."

"After a night on your Hide-A-Bed?" he said lightly. But his feet were starting to sweat.

And Bonny wasn't about to be deterred. "You didn't come to Pilchuck for any old willow swing, Jack Van Hooten."

He pressed his lips together. She could fish all she wanted; she wasn't going to get a thing out of him.

Once again his eyes turned to the arched doorway of the chapel. Pastor Bob and his wife had finally given up their post by the door.

Where are you, Cait?

As if in answer to his silent question, Cait stepped out of the shadowed interior of the church and paused on the top step, blinking against the bright light. The morning sun slanted down over her, lighting her face and her halo of golden hair, and she glowed like an angel.

"If you let her go to Garson Krueger, I'll never forgive you," Bonny murmured.

His socks clung wetly to his toes. *If I let her go to Garson Krueger,* he thought, *I'll never forgive* myself.

Then Cait's eyes met his, and she smiled a smile that set his heart to thumping. A smile that might, just possibly, mean she *hadn't* gotten over him yet.

Or was it only a friendly smile? A smile as much for Bonny, standing next to him, as it was for him? A smile—horror of horrors—that might even include that blasted Krueger?

Suddenly, out of nowhere, the image of Cait sliding into third base at the softball game last weekend flashed across his mind, along with their brief exchange:

You're awesome, Cait!

If I'm so awesome, how come I'm out?

You took the chance, is the thing. And gave it your all.

She'd taken another chance last weekend too. And she had risked a whole lot more than a skinned elbow: her feelings, her heart, her dignity.

It's your turn now, Jack. Take the chance. Give it your all.

He didn't know if it was Helen, his alter ego, or God. He only knew it was time to take his own words to heart, sweaty feet and all.

"Looks to me like it's time for a Hallmark moment," Bonny murmured next to him. "Don't you think so, Jack?"

But Jack was no longer thinking. He was moving toward Cait, walking at first, then breaking into a run as she started down the stairs toward him, her face aglow.

"Cait-Cat!"

"Hoot-Owl!" So eager. So happy. So hopeful!

Whatever the risk—that look on her face was worth it.

Jack flung out his arms—forgetting he still held his cup half-filled with coffee.

"Cait-Cat!" he said again.

She moved into his embrace as if she'd just been waiting for the word. "Hoot-Owl!" she whispered, as oblivious to the brown stain spreading across his shirt and over her jacket as he was.

He held her tightly. "Don't get over me, Cait," he murmured. "Don't ever get over me. Promise."

"I promise, Jack. As long as you promise to love me."

He buried his face in her golden hair. "So long as we both shall live," he whispered in her ear.

"So long as we both shall live," she whispered back.

Postscript

And so it was, Gentle Reader, that for years afterward, Cait and Jack Van Hooten could be found of a warm summer evening on the front porch of the old Pilchuck house where they lived out the rest of their days, rocking slowly on a willow swing, holding hands, calling out to passing friends, watching the twilight descend...

And thanking the Almighty that true love had found them not just once, but "Twice in a Blue Moon."

Texas Two-Step

by Jane Orcutt

Chapter One

Crunk, Texas, population 532, prided itself on a great many things, among them its lofty claim to owning the most God-fearing cattle in Central Texas. It was an unprovable boast, of course, but everyone in Crunk knew no outsider was likely to question the morals of the local bovine.

So if the Good Book said the Lord hated divorce, it'd be easy to believe that Ernest Milton's Holsteins eyed Molly Merriweather Fuller with some skepticism as she rattled past in her red '69 Chevy pickup, its radio blaring the finale to Beethoven's Ninth Symphony.

Molly tooted the horn and waved out the open window. "Hey, ladies! I hope Ernest's been treating you right. Don't take any bull, you hear? Whee!" She jabbed her foot with its Cherry Fire–painted toenails against the accelerator and sped past the unblinking cows.

Leaning her head back, Molly laughed. She almost hated to admit it, but it felt good to be back in this neck of the woods again. She'd forgotten how green the rolling land looked after a spring rain, wide open and inviting, the sky touching down everywhere like a blue blanket plumped out over a bed. In Austin she could scarcely see the sky anymore for all the construction and highways being built, much less hear the squawk of grackles or the twitter of sparrows.

At one time in her life, she thought she'd never leave Crunk; in the past year, she thought she'd never return.

But no matter how pretty the scenery, she wasn't here to stay. She'd hear the reading of Great-Aunt Electra Merriweather's will, then Molly and Clay Fuller would lay to rest their five-year-old marriage as well. The Crunk locals would no doubt share a good laugh and more than one I-told-you-so, but Molly didn't intend to stick around to listen. She'd walk straight from the conclusion of the divorce proceedings, toss her shoes on the floor of the Chevy, and head back to Austin and her graduate studies at the University of Texas. She didn't care anymore what anybody had to say about that silly, longstanding Merriweather-Crunk feud. She and Clay had been foolish to think they could break it.

Molly straightened against the Chevy's cracked vinyl seat and ran a hand through her unruly curly hair. The city limits and newly erected tourist sign came into view.

Welcome to Crunk. Named after Odibe Crunk, fallen hero of the Republic.

Molly smiled. "Ila Crunk and her historical group have been busy, I see." She drew a deep breath. "Well, time to face the town. Tongues ought to wag in force over a returning prodigal."

The farm road widened into Main Street, familiar as ever with its row of brick buildings. First was the *Crunk Gazette* office, then Clovis's Comics and Curios, then the feed store. On the other side of the street was I. C. Easley's hardware store, the old Bijou theater, and the bank where Molly's daddy had been a vice president up until his stroke six months ago. He and Mama had moved to Amarillo to be near Molly's sister, Robin.

Set back from the road a bit was the Dew-Drop Inn. Molly noticed only two cars parked out front, even though it was nearly noon. When she was growing up, the Dew-Drop had been the social hub and agricultural exchange from dawn till dusk.

Molly headed down the street, casually studying the remaining buildings. Several bravely sported new coats of paint, but overall the town looked much older than it had a year ago, the last time she'd seen it.

Back then, she'd been happier to head home. She hadn't even bothered to collect her undergraduate diploma from the University of Texas. "Mail it to me," she'd muttered, then jumped into the truck and headed for Crunk.

And Clay.

On impulse, she cut over two streets and drove by her family's old home, then headed over five blocks and up three—a path she could walk in her sleep as well as she'd walked it in real life. Keeping her eyes fixed on the road, she deliberately avoided even a glance at the home Clay had once shared with his widowed daddy.

On Odibe Street, she passed a number of aging but well-tended homes. If Crunk could be said to have a wealthy section of town, this was it.

Positioned right in the middle of the block was Ila Crunk's sprawling home. Built in the Greek revival style popular during antebellum days, it was still a paragon of beauty. Monkey grass lined the flagstone walkway that perfectly bisected the manicured lawn from street to house. Azaleas, caladiums, and an assortment of lilies flanked the porch. The house rose, gracefully regal, to two stories and was painted a warm coral shade with smooth white columns and shutters. A shiny brass knocker adorned a sleek, black front door.

When she was growing up, Molly had always wanted to live in Ila Crunk's house.

Sighing, she pulled forward one more house and parked at the curb, next to a tumble-down picket fence and gate. Aunt Electra's home had never been in particularly stellar shape, but Molly was dismayed at its current appearance. Shingles were blown off the roof. White paint peeled from the second story to the bottom.

Window screens rotted within their frames and at the door. The old rattan porch swing hung by only one chain, and the porch itself had collapsed in two places.

Molly shook her head, tsking. She'd noticed last year that the place needed repairs, but Aunt Electra had confessed she was too tired to attempt them.

More than a hundred years ago, Cyrus Merriweather had built the home alongside that of William Crunk, oldest son of Alamo hero Odibe Crunk. They'd been business partners, and the homes had been handed down through the years to the oldest children of each line.

The feud began during the 1929 stock-market crash. Though family lore had been deliberately obscured over the years, the prevailing rumor was that Eustis Merriweather had secretly sold his stocks just before the crash and handily survived the Depression. His partner, Arnold Crunk, didn't fare so well, but once the business was severed, he had worked hard to regain the family fortune. Ever after, the Merriweathers and Crunks had shunned each other, a tradition that proved difficult to squelch.

So when Clay Fuller, second cousin twice removed to Ila Crunk, took a shine to Molly Merriweather—and vice versa—the young sweethearts had to see each other on the sly. It had been a difficult secret to keep in a small town, but if Molly headed for the Bijou with her friends and happened to encounter Clay and his friends, nobody thought anything of it. And if Molly happened to sit next to Clay, it still all seemed innocent enough. And if Clay happened to give Molly a quick kiss before the lights went up, no one had been the wiser.

Remembering, Molly stared at the dangling porch swing. The night of high school graduation, her maiden Great-Aunt Electra Merriweather—who had neither the time nor the inclination for family feuds—had thrown a party for the graduating class. Molly and Clay had sat on that very swing, careful to keep at least a foot's distance between them, lest Ila Crunk stare disapprovingly from her house next door.

"I hate this," Clay said in a low voice, kicking the swing into motion. "Why do we have to sneak around? What do we care about some stupid fight that happened years ago?"

"I sure don't," Molly said. "But it's only for a few more months anyway. You're going off to A&M this fall, and I'll be going to UT. When you get to College Station, you'll probably forget all about me."

"No, I won't." Clay braced his boot heels against the porch and stopped the swing's motion. He turned and looked at her. Even in the porch's dim light, she could see his blue eyes shining. He took her hands and inched closer, until their legs touched. "You're the only one for me, Molly-girl," he whispered, then kissed her. Slowly.

Molly drew in her breath so hard she thought her lungs would burst against the pink silk dress Mama'd ordered all the way from Houston. Or maybe it was her heart breaking. Why did love have to hurt? "It doesn't matter," she whispered. "We can't even tell anybody how we feel. Your pa doesn't like me. Daddy doesn't like you. They'd never approve of us being together."

Clay's eyes gleamed. "Then let's don't ask. Come on, Molly, let's do this thing right. Let's go get married."

"Take off, just like that? *Now?*" She frowned. Clay certainly had a peculiar way of trying to cheer her up.

"We're both eighteen—we don't need our parents' permission. Once we're married, they'll have to accept us."

Her heart caught in her throat. He really *was* serious. "But… but school…in the fall…"

"Don't worry about that now. Say yes, Molly. Marry me."

Molly stared into his eyes and felt her breathing quicken. Nobody else had ever made her feel the way she did when she was with Clay Fuller. It wasn't just what the preacher called lust, either, though plenty of Clay's kisses left her breathless. It was more the feeling of rightness. Security. Belonging.

"Okay," she whispered.

Clay whooped, nearly upsetting the swing. He grabbed her by the hand, and with a quick glance at the party going full blast inside Aunt Electra's, they raced down the front steps and toward his waiting Ford truck.

To avoid the chance of anyone alerting their parents, they drove to the first town in the next county and tracked down and roused from bed the justice of the peace. Once they had the legally signed license in hand, Clay proposed they spend their wedding night in Austin.

Halfway there, they realized they didn't have enough between them for gas money, food, and a room. They spent the night in a roadside Best Western and feasted on corn nuts and a bottle of Big Red soda pop.

The loving was heaven, but there was the devil to pay when they returned to Crunk. Molly's mother never stopped crying. Molly's father took one look at Clay and Molly's rumpled clothes and slugged Clay on the jaw. Even when Molly tearfully produced the marriage license from her purse, he didn't calm down. The newlyweds retreated from the yelling to Clay's father, but his reception wasn't any better. Daniel Fuller popped his son on the other side of the jaw.

Weeping, Molly poured Clay into the passenger side of the truck. She kicked off her shoes, started the engine, and headed for Aunt Electra's. There she tearfully related the story while Electra hastily thawed a New York strip for Clay's injured face. Then she offered them the entire upstairs of her home for their living quarters, which they gratefully accepted.

That summer was the best of Molly's life. She worked at the five-and-dime while Clay toted hay and tended crops for anyone who would hire him. Aunt Electra fed and pampered them, delighted that they'd taken up residence with her.

The nights were sweet and tender, and as she got to know her husband better, Molly was convinced they hadn't made a mistake. Clay was companionable and cheerful, conscientious and thrifty. They pooled their meager wages and paid ten percent off the top to their respective churches—five percent to her family's Methodist, and five percent to his family's Baptist. Clay insisted they pay Electra's household bills, as well as something for her trouble, even if they only had ten dollars to spare.

They attended both family churches, alternating weeks. They always sat on the back row, blissfully unaware of the mixed stares of curiosity, sympathy, and humor from the town, and the downright baleful glares from the family members in attendance. Sharing a hymnal, Molly and Clay relished the chance to join their voices in song—"Victory in Jesus" with the Baptists and "Are Ye Able, Said the Master" with the Methodists.

After a month, the families showed up, grim-faced, on Electra's doorstep. They'd accepted that they couldn't undo the marriage, but they didn't want to see Clay and Molly throw away their futures. If they would each go to their respective colleges in the fall, as planned, the parents would pay for their educations. After all, Crunk was halfway between Austin and College Station—they could still see each other on weekends, holidays, and summers. In four years, when they'd earned their degrees, they could resume their marriage in a normal fashion.

Molly argued in favor of abandoning her plans for an English degree, but Daniel Fuller flatly refused to pay one dime for Clay's education if Molly went to College Station with him. Conferring privately, Clay and Molly realized they didn't have a choice but to agree. He'd always wanted to own his own greenhouse business, and he needed to study horticulture.

For three years, their long-distance marriage amazingly survived. They studied hard while at college and spent every free day together in Crunk at Aunt Electra's. Then in their senior year, the work became more intense, the drive back home more of an effort. Molly learned to create jewelry to sell near campus and abandoned the country music she'd grown up listening to in favor of classical and jazz. She switched to an all-organic diet and wrote a health column for an Austin alternative newspaper. When she told Clay the first night home after graduation that she wanted to register for graduate studies in nutrition that fall, he exploded.

"We've been waiting for this time for four years, Molly. I've got my degree—I'm going to start my own business just like we planned. You can make your little jewelry and sell it here in Crunk."

Little jewelry. Stung by his words, she forced a laugh. "Who's going to buy handcrafted silver in Crunk? At least people in Austin have an appreciation for hard work."

"You don't think people work hard here? Don't you remember how hard it is to be an independent farmer? This is an agricultural community, Molly."

"Exactly. And an agricultural community doesn't have any need for the things I'm interested in now. Like jewelry. Or writing. Or nutrition."

Clay sighed and raked his hand through his hair. "Go on then. Go back and get your graduate degree. I don't want to hold you here against your will."

They continued to call each other regularly, but she never returned for a visit. The truth was that she missed him—even missed Crunk—but pride kept her from letting on. Besides, she had her jewelry and her studies to keep her busy. She'd grown up; she didn't need a social life.

Seven months later, after a spell of not even phoning, Clay abruptly called. He told her to come back. She wanted to say yes, was on the verge of saying yes, when she heard him sigh into the silence over the phone line.

She could see him leaning wearily against the glass phone booth just outside the Dew-Drop and hear Garth Brooks wailing from the jukebox inside. She could picture Clay, tired of chasing after a woman he wished he'd never married, tired of being saddled with a wife.

Trembling, she refused. There was another long moment of silence, then Clay suggested they call it quits. Molly hung up the phone, weeping, but when he called again five months later to tell her Electra had died, she had agreed it was time to make their separation final.

Molly took one long last look at Electra's home, then headed up the road to the law office.

Rudie Tyler was Crunk's only attorney, and the town stood in awe of her knowledge, grace, and blue-ribbon peach preserves. A tall, trim, fortyish black woman, educated at Harvard and SMU law school, Rudie had returned to Crunk presumably to care for her aging mother.

Dew-Drop speculation held that she was sweet on Junior Sites, the county extension agent.

Outside the one-story brick law office, Molly pulled up next to a late-model Ford Bronco. She slipped into her sandals and hopped out of her truck. Slamming the heavy door, she eyed the fully loaded Bronco and whistled. Judging from the vehicle's amenities, the lawyer business was good lately.

She didn't see Clay's old pickup truck anywhere. He must be running late.

"Why, Molly Fuller!" Jo Bell Grapple rose from behind a desk, her neon Spandex shimmying with her broad hips. She patted her lacquered bouffant hairdo, then put her hands on her hips. "Where you been keeping yourself, girl?"

Molly grimaced. Jo Bell had been the class flirt. "Here and there. How're you doing?"

"Right as rain, can't complain." Jo Bell giggled, then turned serious. "You best get yourself on in there. Ms. Tyler's just about had a fit three times, waiting on you." She shooed Molly down the hall, then opened a door marked *Rudolpha Tyler, Attorney-at-Law* and pushed Molly through. "Here she is!"

Molly caught herself from stumbling and turned to thank Jo Bell, who promptly shut the door in her face. When she turned back around, she saw a large cherry desk and Rudie Tyler standing straight as a flagpole behind it.

Resistol hat in hand, Clay Fuller stood to one side of the desk. "Hello, Molly," he said quietly.

She felt a rush of emotion. He looked tall and lean—handsome as ever with his short brown hair and angular face. "Hello, Clay."

They stood staring at each other until Rudie held out her hand. "It's good to see you again, Molly. I always intend to look you up when I'm in Austin, but time seems to get away from me."

"Time has a way of doing that," Molly said, glancing at Clay.

Rudie coughed. "Yes." She sat in her high-backed chair and put on her reading glasses, all business as she studied a document. Clay pulled out a chair for Molly beside his, and they sat, eyeing each other nervously.

Rudie glanced over the top of her glasses at Molly. "In all my years as an attorney, I've never been asked to draw up quite such a will. I drew up the original for Electra years ago, which leaves all her money to your father."

Molly frowned. "What's unusual about that?"

Rudie pushed her glasses to the bridge of her nose and studied the document. "Nothing. It's the codicil she added several weeks ago that makes things interesting."

Clay cleared his throat and rose. "Molly, I'll wait outside. When you're ready for—"

"Sit yourself back down, Clay Fuller," Rudie said, waving him to his seat. "This involves you too." She spread out the document.

"Your great-aunt left her money to your father, but she left you her house."

"Me?" Molly's voice came out in a squeak. "What will I do with it?"

Rudie smiled. "The question is what will you and *Clay* do with it. She left it to both of you." She paused. "But only on the condition that you live in it as husband and wife. For three months. 'The same amount of time,'" Rudie read from the paper, "'that you previously occupied my home when you were first married.'"

"Oh, for goodness' sake." Molly sighed. "Rudie, you know we also came to you to start a divorce. Aunt Electra must have known we'd talked about it too. You told her about it on one of your visits, didn't you, Clay?"

He nodded. "She knew."

"Then what was she thinking?"

"Apparently she wanted you two to stay together," Rudie said.

"Well, it's not going to work! She doesn't have any way of knowing whether we're staying there or not."

"No, but I do. The will further stipulates that if you don't reside in her home for at least three months, it must be razed."

Molly couldn't believe what she was hearing. "But it's been in the family for years! It needs repairs, but surely someone could fix it. It could at least be turned into a city museum or something."

"Electra seemed to think it still had potential too. She left you several thousand dollars to fix it up. If you refuse to live in the house, however, the money goes to charity."

"Fine. Then it will go to someone who needs it."

"What about the house itself?" Clay leaned forward. "It belongs to you Merriweathers, Molly. Your sister's family might want it one day, even if you don't."

Molly swallowed hard. She hadn't considered that. "But I can't live here for the summer. I have to go back to school in the fall."

Clay leaned back. "You've got plenty of time till then. This is

May. By the end of three months, you can get back to Austin in plenty of time to register for the fall semester."

Molly studied him closely. Didn't he realize what they'd have to do? *Live* in the same house!

"While you're thinking about it, let me execute the last item from Electra's will. This also involves both of you," Rudie said.

"There's more?" Molly was shocked. What else could Aunt Electra require of them?

Rudie reached beside her chair and brought up a covered, economy-sized Chock full o' Nuts can. Setting it on the desk, she pushed it between Molly and Clay.

Clay frowned. "She left us coffee?"

"Hardly. Those are Electra's ashes. She wanted to be part of the package." Rudie folded her hands across the document and smiled. "Take some time and talk this over."

To Molly's chagrin, Clay nodded his agreement. "Let's get some lunch, Molly. The Dew-Drop's special today is chicken-fried steak."

"But—" The last thing she needed was to pollute her body with a high-calorie, high-fat lunch. Or sit with Clay and make small talk.

He handed her the can, and before she knew it, he was steering her out the door, his hand planted gently at the small of her back. She shivered, wishing she'd worn something other than a short cotton dress. Like a broomstick skirt that fell all the way to her ankles. And a heavy sweater. Maybe even an overcoat.

Clay's touch was definitely unsettling.

He guided her outside, then dropped his hand. "I see you still drive that old Chevy."

She shrugged, relieved at the loss of physical contact. "It runs well enough. Where's your truck?"

"I traded it in about six months ago for this thing." Clay unlocked the Bronco's passenger door and held it open, waiting. "Well? Won't you even ride with me?"

"This is yours?"

"It will be when it's paid off. Come on, Molly." He extended his hand.

"Thanks, but I can manage by myself." Clutching the bulky can, she ignored his offer and climbed in. Clay shook his head and shut the door.

The drive to the Dew-Drop was mercifully short, and Clay took a path she hadn't seen on her way into town. Except for pointing out changed sites, he was silent.

At the restaurant, Molly set the can on the floorboard and scrambled out before he could help her down. He looked disappointed, but when they arrived at the door at the same time, he went through first.

The Dew-Drop had gained several patrons since she'd driven by earlier, and everyone—including Iris, the waitress, hefting a full serving tray—stared when Clay and Molly entered. "Well, it's about time you two got back together," Iris said loudly.

Clay ignored her. "Back booth?" he asked Molly.

She nodded, even though she figured she'd probably be more comfortable sitting on the black-and-white tile floor. The back booth had always been their favorite. Before they'd married, they'd sat there so they could keep an eye on the front door.

Clay slid across the black vinyl bench. Molly sat on the other side. She couldn't ever remember sitting across from him.

Clay set his hat, crown down, beside him. "I'm real sorry about Electra. I saw her at the nursing home two days before she passed on, and she looked fine." He paused. "She asked about you. Wondered when you were coming to visit."

"I wanted to," Molly said in a small voice. "If I'd known…"

Clay waved away her words. "No point in regretting things that can't be changed. She knew you loved her. She knew you had your reasons for staying away."

Do you *know my reasons?* Molly was surprised at how quickly the thought came to mind.

"Hello there, lovebirds!" Iris leaned over them, touching each of them on the shoulder. "Why, take me back five years and I see two starry-eyed high schoolers making calf eyes over their milkshakes. What finally brought her to her senses, Clay?"

"She isn't here for a reunion, Iris," he said tightly. "Just to hear Electra's will."

"Well, it'll be interesting to find out what the old girl left." Iris pulled a pencil from behind her ear and dug an order pad out of her skirt pocket. "What'll you have?"

"Two chicken-frieds, and don't skimp on the gravy."

Molly straightened. "No."

Iris held her pencil above the pad and raised her eyebrows. "No gravy?"

"No chicken-fried steak. I just want a salad—no dressing. Just squeeze a little lemon juice over it, please. And some whole-wheat crackers."

"Whole wheat?" Iris's eyebrows raised a fraction higher.

"Yes. Oh, and could I have a bottled water, please?"

Iris grinned, scribbling on the pad. "Sure, hon. What do you want to drink, Clay?"

"Coffee. Black." He sighed as Iris retreated. "So you're still into health food."

She nodded. "I've never felt better."

His gaze swept over her. "You do look good," he said gruffly.

"Thanks. You're looking well too."

He did indeed. His shoulders had never looked broader or his face quite so handsome. He'd aged in the year since she'd seen him, aged in a way that made him look more mature than she remembered. "How's your greenhouse business?" she asked, hoping to redirect the conversation.

Clay shrugged. "Right enough. I'm selling bedding plants to wholesalers as well as doing a little landscaping here and there. I do the upkeep on Ila's place."

"Hey there, Clay. Molly! I thought I recognized the sound of that old Chevy engine coming down Main Street. You in town just for a tuneup?"

A cheerful, heavyset woman in well-worn mechanic's coveralls stood at their table.

Molly leaned back and smiled. "Willie Bean, you're a sight for sore eyes. How're you doing? Have you and Bobby Giles set the date yet?"

Willie grinned and tucked back a strand of long blond hair, leaving a grease smear on her round cheek. "Shoot, Molly. He ain't never gonna ask me. You know Bobby. He's too busy worryin' about his cotton crop."

Her smile faded. "I'm right sorry about your Aunt Electra. There wasn't a finer lady in town. We was all kinda hopin' there'd be a good send-off for her, but Rudie Tyler said she wanted to be cremated. I guess it was in her will."

"That's why I'm in town. To find out what *was* in her will." She glanced at Clay. "She left us her house."

Willie cocked her head and squinted, shoving her hands in her coverall pockets. "Y'all ain't really gonna divorce, are you? A lot of folks haven't forgotten all the excitement you two caused when you ran off to get hitched. Why, I remember the stories about your daddies' tempers—"

"'Scuse me, Willie." Iris pointedly bumped her in the back with a full tray. "But I've got food for these folks."

"Oh, sorry." Willie stepped back. "Clay, you bring Molly over to see me and Mama. And Bobby'll want to see her too, don't you reckon?"

Clay nodded, his mouth a tight line.

Molly put her hand on Willie's arm. "Can I bring the truck by for your best once-over? I don't trust those Austin mechanics the way I trust you."

Willie beamed and headed toward her own table. "Bring 'er by anytime," she called over her shoulder. "I'm workin' on a tractor for I. C., but other'n that, things are pretty slow."

Iris stepped closer, lowering the tray. "All righty. One order of chicken-fried steak and a black coffee for Clay. And for Molly, one salad, hold the dressing, Melba toast, and one of God's lemonades—bottled."

Molly stared at a small bowl of iceberg lettuce adorned with a quartered tomato and a lemon slice. Annoyed, she picked up Iris's version of the requested drink—a tap water-filled Dr Pepper bottle. "This isn't what I—"

"Thanks, Iris." Clay's mouth twitched as he tried to smother a grin.

The waitress winked. "You're welcome, sweetie. Y'all let me know if you need anything."

Iris bustled away, and Molly leaned forward. "Why'd you send her off?" she whispered angrily. "This isn't what I wanted, and you know it."

Clay laughed. "And you should know the Dew-Drop thinks more of its customers than to sell them some highfalutin version of what comes natural from the sky. What happened to your sense of humor, Molly?"

She sat back, opening her mouth to speak, then thought better of it. She didn't want to fight. At least not in the Dew-Drop, where there would be witnesses. She was going to get out of this town with as much dignity as possible. Let everyone say that Clay Fuller had dumped her, but let them say it when she was a hundred miles away.

Concentrating on regaining her composure, Molly carefully squeezed the lemon over the salad and cut the quartered tomato into eighths. Her stomach rumbled, and she glanced hungrily at Clay's rapidly diminishing food. Nobody served up chicken-fried steak and mashed potatoes like the Dew-Drop.

She swallowed a large forkful of lettuce, feeling vaguely dissatisfied. "How's your pa?"

Clay looked up from his plate. "He died four months ago."

"You didn't tell me!"

"I didn't figure you'd be interested."

Fighting back hurt, Molly set down her fork. "Of course I would be. I'm so sorry. What happened?"

"Heart attack."

"Oh, Clay," she said mournfully.

"It's all right. I'd moved in with him when I came back to town after graduation. We had some good times together before he went, anyway. Now it's just me in the old place. I'd like to sell it and buy some land adjoining my greenhouses to build on." Clay glanced over her shoulder at the Dew-Drop clientele and sighed. "Some days this town seems to have too many people."

"Yes, I know." Molly could feel the stares being shot their way, and she heard Iris's laughter drift across the room. "Look, Clay, I can leave after three months, but this is your home. It'd be too hard on you, having to listen to the town gossip after our breakup."

"I can handle it," he interrupted, sawing vigorously at his steak. "They'll quit talking after a while. Our marriage has always been just a joke to them."

"It wasn't to Aunt Electra."

Clay speared a bite with his fork. "No, to her it wasn't."

"I drove by her house on my way in," Molly said. "How long has it looked so bad?"

"A few months. It seemed like everything just sort of went at the same time."

"Kind of like us," she said softly, without thinking.

Clay glanced at her with surprise, then his mouth tipped up ruefully. "Yeah. Kind of like us." He set down his knife and fork. "Why don't we go take a look at the old place together? You finished with that rabbit food?"

Molly nodded, no longer hungry. She drew some bills from

her wallet, but Clay pushed them back. "Keep it, Molly. You might need gas money to get to Austin."

He smiled, and she knew instinctively he was thinking of their wedding night. They'd never reached their planned destination, but it had been wonderful just the same.

Feeling unsettled, Molly quickly rose and nodded greetings at the other diners as she headed toward Clay's truck.

Chapter Two

Both hands holding tight, Molly braced the Chock full o' Nuts can atop her knees. The Bronco zoomed up Odibe Street, its occupants silent. Neither she nor Clay had spoken a word since they left the Dew-Drop.

The Bronco hit a bump, and the contents of the can sloshed up against the plastic lid. Molly pressed her lips together and shot Clay a look. He returned it with one of his own, his jaw clenched hard. Molly stared out the window, gripping the can tighter.

The Bronco screeched to a stop in front of Aunt Electra's. If possible, the place looked even more decrepit than before.

"We're not really going to do this, are we?" She slid out of the truck, hugging the can to her body.

Clay slammed his door shut. "We didn't make Rudie any promises. We're just going to take a look." He strode ahead and pushed at the wooden gate, which stuck fast. Clay muttered under his breath as he fiddled with the rusty latch. Unsuccessful, he stepped back and kicked it. The gate popped off its hinges and banged to the ground.

"Clay!"

"It's open, isn't it?" He took her by the elbow. "Let's go see what's left of the place. I haven't been inside since the last time you were here."

That surprised her, but she didn't say anything.

Clay guided her up the cement steps and around a gaping hole where the wooden porch had rotted away. "Careful," he said, gripping her elbow. Molly inched around the crater, praying that she wouldn't drop the coffee can.

Clay fumbled with a key in the lock. Molly noticed thankfully that the frosted glass oval inset was still intact, and she hoped Clay wouldn't kick the door in if it proved as stubborn as the gate.

To her relief, the door swung open, and Clay stood aside to allow her entry.

As she squinted in the dim light of the interior, her first impression was that it looked like an entirely different house from years past. Voluminous sheets covered the furniture, the rugs had frayed appreciably, and a heavy layer of dust covered the mantel and fireplace tools. The warm, cheerful home that Molly remembered from her childhood and newlywed days now seemed like a mausoleum.

She blew away a patch of dust from the mantel and set down the coffee can. She wrapped her arms around herself and walked aimlessly around the room, lifting a corner of a sheet here and there to peer underneath. When she came to the wing-backed chair Aunt Electra had favored, she stopped short.

She heard Clay move behind her. "It's hard to believe she's gone."

Molly nodded, unable to speak for a moment. She'd thought it would be easy to turn her back on this home. But memories came rushing back—under the sheet in the corner was the table where they'd taken their meals, Aunt Electra always first insisting on saying a blessing; under another sheet was the grand piano where they'd joyfully plunked out Christmas carols; there were the sofa and fireplace where Molly and Clay had curled up together on cold winter evenings and planned their future. Once, when Aunt

Electra had stayed overnight in Giddings to visit friends, Molly and Clay had—

"Maybe it's better that we just remember the good times and not try to resurrect them," Clay said quietly. "There's no point in going through any more grief."

Molly was on the verge of asking if he was talking about the house or their marriage, when a shadow fell across the floor. Ila Crunk stood in the doorway, her small frame obscured by her usual dress: a blue bandanna tied at her neck, a bright colored T-shirt, an elastic-waisted denim skirt that wasn't quite long enough to conceal her knee-high hose, and a pair of white Keds.

"I thought it was you two," she said. "Clayton Fuller, why didn't you tell me *she* was coming back to town?"

"Hello, Ila." Molly heard Clay sigh. "I just learned Molly was coming a few days ago myself. She's here about Electra's will."

"Hmmph. I've heard all about that crazy codicil."

"Good to see you too, Miss Crunk," Molly muttered. She'd forgotten how quickly news traveled in this town. Jo Bell must have been listening at Rudie's door.

Ila idled forward, swiping a slow finger across the dust on the sheets. "Electra never did take good care of this old place," she said mildly. "I'll swan that woman didn't have good sense. Course I wouldn't expect her to have all that much in the first place, being a Merriweather and all."

Molly closed her eyes and sighed. *Lord, give me strength.*

"Now, Ila…" Clay tightened his jaw.

"Oh, I'm sure Electra knew best. Why, she's probably smiling down from heaven right now, grateful that this rickety old home will soon be leveled."

Molly opened her eyes. "Who says that's going to happen?"

Ila looked surprised. "Why, surely you aren't considering carrying out her insane proposal!" She shook her head. "And I was beginning to have hope for you, Molly Merriweather. I thought you'd finally come to your senses and realized you weren't cut out to be part of the Crunk family. I'm sure Clayton will talk sense into you. At least he realizes you coerced him into marriage five years ago."

Molly turned toward Clay. Was that what he'd told Ila Crunk? The rest of the town?

"Molly…" he said gently.

Her face flushed, and she turned away, blinking. If she left right now, she could be back in Austin before sundown. It didn't matter that the house would be destroyed. She didn't want to be a Fuller or even a Merriweather any longer. She never wanted to set foot in Crunk again, and she certainly didn't want to see Clay Fuller, much less live with him for the summer.

Ila must have seen the expression on her face, for she smiled triumphantly. "Then it's settled."

"No." Clay stepped forward. "Molly and I are going to abide by Electra's will. We'll live here for three months, and I'm going to help her fix this place up. Electra was a great lady, and this house should stay with her kin. When our time's up, I'll give Molly my half, and she can do whatever she wants with it."

Ila's mouth dropped, then she quickly closed it. "I guess you aren't quite as bright as I'd hoped, Clayton. Still, you're descended from the Caldwell Fullers, and nobody in their family ever knew spit from Shinola."

"We can't all be direct descendants of the brave and glorious Odibe Crunk," Clay said. The corners of his mouth twitched, though Molly could see he was trying to keep a straight face.

Ila straightened. "No, indeed. Well then." She pulled a hand-kerchief from her T-shirt sleeve and held it against her nose as she glanced around the room. "If you two are determined to restore this place, then all I can do is wish you well. And warn you to expect no help from me, even if I am your neighbor."

She turned and marched out, her back ramrod straight as she let the screen door bang shut behind her. Molly and Clay watched her retreat, and when she was safely down the rickety porch and far down the path, they burst into laughter.

"Why is she so ornery?" Molly said, after she'd recovered.

"Pride. That's what kept the families fighting all these years. I think deep down she hates to see it end, but she knows she's the last of the Crunks. And with Electra gone, you're the last of the Merriweathers with any ties to this town. The last of the sworn enemy."

"You didn't have to let her get to you like that. I don't expect you want to stay cooped up here for three months." *With me,* she almost added.

Clay looked serious. "I meant what I said. I'd hate to see this home destroyed. If nothing else, we should do it for Electra. She put us in charge because she knew we were the only ones in town who cared, the only ones with any kind of stake in whether this house fell apart or made it."

"I think it's too far gone," she said quietly. "Electra herself always said you can't turn back the hands of time."

He studied her a moment, his blue eyes intense. "Where's your faith, Molly-girl?"

Molly caught her breath, and Clay smiled slowly. He peeled back a sheet from the sofa. "Look. The furniture's in good shape, and mostly this house just needs a thorough cleaning. I know we can get it back in living order."

"And when the summer's up, we'll file for the divorce, as planned."

Clay's smile fell, but he nodded. "We can do that."

"But until then, since we're still legally married..." Molly glanced significantly upstairs, to where they'd once lived. "Look, Clay, I don't know what you're thinking, but..."

He cleared his throat. "You can sleep up there, and I'll stay down here. We'll hardly have to see each other, if that's what you're afraid of."

She watched him stride toward the front door, and she wondered if she was more afraid that she wouldn't see him nearly enough.

Comic book and curio purveyor Clovis Hightower pushed open the door to I. C. Easley's hardware store. "Mornin'," he called up to the proprietor.

"Howdy, Clovis." I. C. didn't turn from his task, carefully setting the last can of paint atop a pyramid worthy of the ancient Egyptians. Letting out a whooshing breath of relief, he stepped down the ladder and found himself face to face with a grinning Clovis. "What's up? You look like a small dog with a big bone."

"Molly Merriweather's back in town, and she and Clay Fuller—"

"Save yourself some air; I already know."

Clovis's face fell. "You do?"

"Where you been? They've been out at Electra's for several days now. In fact, Clay came in here yesterday to buy supplies for the repairs they're planning to make. I let on like I didn't believe the talk about Electra's crazy will, and he 'lowed how it was true." I. C. dug an elbow into Clovis's ribs. "What d'ya think the odds are those two'll wind up sticking together after all?"

Clovis thought for a moment. "Living next door to Ila Crunk? I'd say their chances are slim and none, and slim's saddling up to leave town. Ila never cottoned to the notion of them kids being hitched in the first place. And Molly's changed, I. C. You should hear what Iris over to the Dew-Drop said that skin-and-bones girl ordered. She turned down chicken-fried steak and ordered salad— with no dressing! That's what big cities'll do to you."

I. C. shook his head, sighing. "What's happened to our little Molly?"

Clovis wagged his head in companionable dismay.

I. C. frowned. "The only divorce this town's ever seen has been next to Tammy Wynette's name on the Dew-Drop jukebox. Besides, Molly and Clay belong together. It'd be a shame to see them bust up after they ran off to get hitched, then faced down their families. That took more guts than you could hang on a fence."

Clovis looked doubtful. "I don't think they'll make a go of it. They're too different now."

I. C. squinted. "Care to make a friendly wager?"

"Why, Isaac Caleb Easley! You know I'm a Baptist and what we believe about gamblin'. I don't want to wind up as the main topic of the preacher's next meetin' day sermon."

"Aw, we won't bet money, Clovis. How about this: I say that before this summer's over, Molly and Clay Fuller will agree to stay married."

"And I say they won't."

"And if I'm right, you have to let me read all the new Sonic the Hedgehog comics that come to your store first."

Clovis's face fell. "Even before me?"

I. C. nodded.

"Well then," Clovis said. "You have to lend me your best huntin' rifle when deer season opens."

"Done. But don't let your trigger finger get itchy."

Frowning, Molly studied Aunt Electra's aging cookbook. The brittle pages had long since turned yellow, and flour and grease smudged nearly every recipe. Aunt Electra had enjoyed variety in her culinary efforts, and seeing each recipe brought back fond memories for Molly.

Unfortunately, scarcely a single recipe was low in fat, cholesterol, or sugar.

Molly closed the cookbook, sighing. She wished she'd paid more attention when she cooked, but she was the sort who had to have the recipe right in front of her. Ten minutes after she'd finished cooking, she couldn't remember exactly what she'd done. If only she could go back to Austin and pick up her *Healthy Eating for a Healthy Planet* cookbook.

Rudie had shaken her head when Molly originally made her request. "The will says you can't leave town unless there's a life-or-death emergency."

"But this *is* life or death!" Molly argued. "I only have a few clothes with me. And I have friends who will worry. And a jewelry business to run!"

"Buy some new clothes here. Phone your friends. And have somebody ship your jewelry here. Believe it or not, the Crunk post office handles overnight mail."

Even now, Molly bit her tongue to keep from complaining out loud. And not just about the cookbook.

She opened the old Frigidaire and studied her options critically. She wished she hadn't agreed to do the cooking, but she knew if she didn't, Clay would bring home a greasy packaged dinner from the Dew-Drop every night. Or some high-fat, low-nutrition TV dinner. Judging from her memory of the town's male population, she believed him when he said he'd never really learned how to cook.

They hadn't talked much since they'd become housemates again. Oh, they chatted over supper—what he'd done that day at the greenhouses, the progress she'd made on her jewelry, a new litter of pups at the McCrackens'—but never anything truly important. After supper, Clay would wash the dishes and clean up, and Molly would head straight upstairs to either continue her jewelry work or read a book from Aunt Electra's library.

Mostly, though, she'd catch herself staring at the wall, listening for sounds of Clay downstairs, wondering what he was up to. Once she almost went back down to check on him, but she stopped herself at the top of the stairs just in time. Sticking out these three months would be much harder if she started passing time with him. She had a life to get back to in Austin, after all.

The back screen door banged shut, and Clay clomped in. "Supper almost ready?"

"Yes, and…Hey, watch out! You're tracking mud on the floor."

Clay checked his boots, then slipped them off guiltily. "Sorry. I forgot Ernest and I were out in his field this afternoon."

Molly rattled a pan to show her annoyance. "Can you clean up the mess? I'm kind of busy here."

"Sure thing." Setting his boots outside the back door, he padded in his socks to fetch a wet towel. She watched him covertly as she worked and was pleased that he finished in record time. He washed up at the sink, then sat down at the table just as she laid out the last dinner plate. Immediately he said the blessing, then reached hungrily for the single serving bowl. Clay stared at the contents, then up at her.

"Go ahead." She motioned toward the bowl. "Baked mushrooms and tomatoes on a bed of brown rice. Healthy and full of vitamins."

He dished himself a heaping spoonful, silent for a long time. "You know, Molly," he finally said, "I've been lifting, toting, bending over the plants, watering…I appreciate your taking the time to cook and all—especially when I'm not very good at it—but you've probably forgotten how hungry a man gets when he's been working hard all day."

"Feel free to eat as much as you want," she said. "Just be sure to save a little room for dessert."

"Dessert?" His eyes lit up. "What are we having?"

She smiled. "I bought some low-fat, diet ice milk. I don't normally indulge like that, but I figured you were used to sweets."

Clay bent over his plate and didn't look up again. After he'd polished off two helpings, he set down his fork, mumbled something about doing the dishes later, and headed outside. Hurt that he hadn't wanted the dessert she'd gotten just for him, Molly went straight upstairs. She could hear Clay pounding with the hammer, as he had for several nights running. Since he had returned from Easley's hardware with an armload of lumber and nails, he'd spent every night working on the porch.

Once upstairs, she sat at her desk. Unfortunately, the air conditioner was out of kilter, and every noise from the front porch below drifted up to her open window on the early evening breeze.

Wham! Wham! Wham!

Molly put her hands over her ears against the pounding. She couldn't figure out how to tackle the scrollwork on her latest creation, a bracelet. Maybe a delicate flower pattern was what was needed. Or perhaps a bold Southwestern design.

The lilting opening notes of Ponchielli's "Dance of the Hours" wafted up from the old hi-fi. Molly lowered her hands from her ears. Wasn't that nice of Clay to play classical music for her? He was probably only familiar with the tune because it was part of the famous dancing hippos scene in *Fantasia,* but—

Bang! Blam! Boom!

Molly gritted her teeth. This wasn't one of Electra's classical records; it was a Spike Jones version, complete with gunshots, auto horns, and cowbells to puncutate the so-called music. If Molly remembered correctly—

"Good afternoon, ladies and gentlemen…"

She groaned, slamming her fists back over her ears to drown out the noise of Spike's sidekick, Doodles Weaver, and his loopy auto race play-by-play.

Zoom! Whiz! Screech!

Wham! Wham!

Clay's hammering competed with the trademark Spike Jones sound effects. Molly gave up trying to muffle the noise with her hands. Frowning, she made a few preliminary sketches on a sheet of graph paper.

Doodles Weaver pattered on, his voice rising with the fevered pitch of the crazy race.

Molly bit the end of her eraser, then rubbed it furiously against an offending line on the page.

Wham, wham, WHAM!

Molly leaned back in her chair and closed her eyes.

WHAM! Wham! WHAM! Wham!

Molly pushed back her chair and bolted downstairs. She covered her ears as the Spike Jones cacophony intensified, the cars squealing rubber for the finish line. *Errrrrrrrr!*

She jerked the hi-fi's arm, and the needle screeched full-volume across the record just before Doodles could announce the winner. "Ouch!" she heard Clay say. The hammer clunked onto the porch, and he stood in the doorway. "What gives, Molly?"

"What gives? I'll tell you what gives. It's this record!" She waved it accusingly. "It's your hammering! I can't concentrate!"

Clay looked like she'd slugged him in the gut. "I didn't realize I was bothering you. I had the record up loud because I couldn't hear it over my hammering. Listening to something keeps me from getting bored."

Immediately Molly felt foolish, and she let the hand holding the record drop to her side.

Clay ran a hand through his hair. "Look, I was thinking about heading for the Tastee-King for a hamburger. You want to come along?"

"For a *hamburger?*"

"I'll treat you to whatever you want."

She laughed. "I doubt that they have anything at the Tastee-King that I'd want."

Clay looked annoyed. "You used to like their food just fine. Remember when we'd sneak down there together? I'd buy you an ice-cream cone, and you'd eat every bite—even half of mine. Now you don't eat anything fun at all."

"Eating isn't about *fun*, Clay," she said hotly. "It's about nourishing your body."

"That's true, but I figure the good Lord wants us to enjoy what we eat. Otherwise, why'd he bother giving us taste buds? Or such a variety of things to eat? He invented Tastee-King ice cream right alongside mushrooms and tomatoes."

"Mushrooms and tomatoes are just as much *fun*, as you put it, as ice cream."

"Sure they are! When they're sitting next to a big, juicy steak. But by themselves, they're hardly more than a mouthful."

Molly crossed her arms. "You seemed to enjoy the mushrooms and tomatoes I made tonight. You ate like you were starving."

"I was!" Clay stepped forward, his eyes snapping. "Since we've been living here, I've had pita bread, couscous, and something called falafel. But I haven't eaten any meat or anything else substantial. I'm about to pass out from hunger! I've been so busy, I haven't had time to get anything on my own. I wanted to work on the porch tonight, but if you're just going to scream and break records, I'm heading out for the Tastee-King. Now do you want to come with me or not?"

Molly felt tears burn the back of her eyes. She'd thought she was helping him by cooking decent, healthy meals. And maybe she'd blown up at him, but she'd thought he was deliberately trying to annoy her with the hammering and the record's volume.

"Y'all doing all right over there?" Ila Crunk sang out from her yard. Molly glanced out a side window and saw the elderly woman tending her rose beds. Even from this distance, Molly could see the smirk on her face.

"Great. All we need now is Ila Crunk." Clay jammed his hand into his jeans pocket and came up with his truck keys. "I'll be back later, Molly." He smiled bitterly. "Don't bother waiting up."

Bereft, she lingered in the doorway and watched him zoom down Odibe Street. Cackling loudly, Ila shot her a glance then headed into her house.

Free from observation, Molly stepped out onto the porch. Clay had made progress on its repairs; one of the holes was partially covered. He was ripping up the old planks one at a time and laying down new ones.

Molly slumped against the door and studied his work, feeling guilty. She hadn't done much with the inside of the house other than to remove the sheets and air out the musty rooms. Since they'd moved in, she'd spent most of her time setting up a small work area in the upstairs room. Once that was completed to her satisfaction, she'd start in on the main rooms of the house. After she gave them a good dusting, the first thing she'd do would be to wash down the walls in preparation for painting.

Just thinking about it left her feeling exhausted. Working alone was slow going.

Jo Bell Grapple leaned back against the Tastee-King's hard plastic bench. "Well, if that don't blow up my dress. Willie, look who just walked in."

Willie Bean turned and stared openly at the glass door, then turned back, unimpressed. "Clay Fuller. So?"

"So…" Jo Bell leaned forward and whispered conspiratorially, "look at that big ol' frown on his face. I'd say that's the look of a man who ain't gettin' along with his wife."

Willie licked the hamburger grease from her fingers and rolled her eyes. "Jo Bell, you've been anglin' after him ever since high school. Ain't you ever gonna give up? He keeps tellin' you he's married, and you know Clay. He's so honest you could shoot dice with him over the phone. He won't even spend a minute with you as long as he's wearing Molly's ring."

"Well, it won't be much longer till he de-rings himself, and then he'll be footloose and fancy-free." Jo Bell yanked at the hem of her T-shirt so that the scoop neckline dipped lower. "And I don't aim to wait till the last minute to get myself planted in his mind."

Willie shot her friend a warning look. "Jo Bell, you leave Clay alone. Give him and Molly a chance to work things out. And quit trying to show yourself off! Ever since we graduated, you've been trolling for a breadwinner using a short skirt as bait."

"Oh, pooh." Jo Bell waved a hand and put on a grin. "I'm hungry for some dessert."

"Jo Bell…" Willie warned in a low voice, but the receptionist was already sashaying to the counter.

"Why, hi there, Clay!" Jo Bell said. She studied his tray as the server filled it. "You joinin' Molly for supper here?"

Clay's mouth tightened. "No, I'm here by myself."

Jo Bell laid a sympathetic hand on his arm. "You look like you could use some cheerin' up. Why don't you join me and Willie?"

"She's here too?" Clay glanced around the room.

"Right over there. Now go on and set yourself down." She gave him a small shove, smiling as she watched him go, then she turned to order.

When she returned with her ice-cream cone, Clay and Willie were deep in conversation about truck engines. Willie was blabbing a mile a minute about a Chevy she'd rebuilt, and Clay listened intently as he wolfed down his hamburger. Sighing, Jo Bell slid across the bench, next to Clay. "Enough of that old car talk. Let's talk about somethin' more fun."

"Like what?" Willie studied her suspiciously.

"Like our five-year class reunion this summer. Where should we have it?"

"Doesn't matter to me. I won't be going." Clay shoved a handful of French fries into his mouth.

Jo Bell licked around the edges of her slowly dripping cone. "Clay," she said in a sultry voice.

"Yeah?" He looked up, and she saw his gaze drop to her ice

cream. She continued to lick up the drips, then took a small bite off the top.

"Mmm." She closed her eyes. "I just love ice cream, don't you?"

Clay laughed, and her eyes flew open. Jo Bell's face flushed with embarrassment. "What's so funny?"

He shook his head. "Jo Bell, you're about as subtle as fire ants on a bare foot. Willie, keep her out of trouble, you hear? I have to get home." He wadded up his hamburger wrapper and tossed it on the tray, then placed his hat on his head. "See you ladies later."

Willie turned all the way around to watch him leave the Tastee-King. When the door banged shut behind him, she turned triumphantly to Jo Bell. "I told you so."

Jo Bell made a face. "You just wait, Willie Bean. He'll put up with Molly's crazy notions only so long, then he'll be lookin' for a real woman."

Willie smiled broadly. "When you find one, let me know."

Molly watched Clay pull into the driveway. It had been so hot, she hadn't wanted to go back inside. The silver bracelet design could wait; her creativity seemed shot for the day anyway.

Clay looked tired. He kept his eyes on the ground as he walked up the path and didn't notice her until he was on the steps. He seemed surprised. "You been out here all this time?"

It sounded more like an accusation than a question.

Molly swallowed hard. "How was the Tastee-King?"

Clay shrugged, not looking her in the eyes. "Same as ever." He put his hand on the screen door handle, but she quickly rose from her seat on the steps and stood beside him. He turned slowly, and their eyes met.

"I..." Oh Lord, he'd never believe her if she apologized. "I was thinking about driving out somewhere to see the sunset." She paused, fearing rejection, then plunged ahead. "I'd like it if you went with me."

His face relaxed, and he actually smiled. "The prettiest sunsets are on my acreage with the greenhouses...if you're interested in going there."

"I'd like that." She smiled back shyly. "Let me lock the door first."

"This is Crunk, remember?" Clay eased the door shut and guided her down the steps. He handed her his keys. "You drive."

"Your new Bronco?"

"Nope. Your Chevy. I haven't ridden in it in a long time. I've missed it."

Sure enough, there was her truck key on his ring. She'd forgotten she ever gave it to him.

When they got in the truck, he smiled admiringly as she kicked off her sandals. "You still drive barefoot."

"Uh-huh." She started the engine and headed down Odibe Street. "Which way?"

He told her, and they followed a farm road out of town. Molly kept one eye on the fading sun, hoping they'd beat its descent.

They crested the top of a hill, and at Clay's direction, Molly steered the truck into a field. They hopped out, and Molly lowered the tailgate. They perched on the edge of the bed and dangled their feet, staring in awe at the fading orange, purple, red, and yellow of a Central Texas sunset.

"It's beautiful," Molly said softly. "I haven't done this in a while."

"Me either. Every time I tried—" Clay trailed off into silence.

Molly turned. "Every time you tried, what happened?"

"I'd wind up thinking about you. Thinking about how we used to meet somewhere to watch the sun either set or rise." He paused, his gaze intense. "Do you remember?"

Her heart was pounding, but she forced a grin. "Of course I do, Clay. It hasn't been *that* long."

He turned to stare at the horizon again. "In a lot of ways, it seems like a lifetime."

They watched the sun disappear completely, then the sky began to darken. The first light of Venus twinkled, and still they watched. One by one, the stars came out, bright and big. Molly pulled her knees up under her chin and wrapped her arms around her legs. She yawned, but didn't want to leave. She felt more peaceful than she had in a long time.

"Why do you really want to stay in Austin?" Clay said at last, quietly. "Is there somebody else?"

"No." It seemed easier to talk in the darkness. "I haven't even dated anybody since I left Crunk five years ago. I'm married to you, Clay. We made a commitment."

She heard him sigh. "Yes, we did."

Molly hugged her legs tighter, afraid to ask, but she had to know. "How about you? Is there somebody you're interested in?"

He was silent for a long time. "There's never been anybody but you, Molly-girl."

Her heart pounded louder. "Clay..."

"Look, Molly, you don't have to say anything. I know you want a different life from what we had...what I still have...out here. It's not very exciting, that's for sure. And you're probably right about not being able to sell your jewelry in town. And unless you want to write for the *Gazette*, there probably isn't anybody interested in your writing either."

"There's overnight mail. There are faxes," she said. What was the matter with her? Did she *want* to stay in Crunk?

"We don't even like the same food anymore," he continued, ignoring her. "Or music. I've heard you listening to that classical stuff when you're upstairs. It drives me crazy." He leaned back on his elbows and looked up at the stars. "What's your life like in Austin?"

"Well..." She cleared her throat. "I go to school, then I come home and study for a while, then I work on my jewelry. I sell it on the weekends on the drag, near the campus. When I can, I work at a food co-op, and a couple of times a month, I write articles for a local newspaper."

"What do you like about living there instead of here?"

Hadn't he heard what she said? She couldn't do any of those things in Crunk. "It's a *city,* for starters. There are always new people to meet, unlike here, where I've known everybody since I was born. There's always something going on there, something exciting to do—plays, ballets, the symphony."

Clay rested his hands behind his head. "What about our marriage, Molly? Are you willing to chuck it just because it's not exciting enough?"

"What about you? You want to let go because I've changed. I know I'm not the same person anymore, Clay, and I can tell you don't feel the same way about me that you used to."

He touched her arm. "I don't?"

"You know what I mean." She shivered, wishing he'd move his hand.

"Lean back, Molly," he said softly. "Lean back and look at the stars with me like we used to do."

Sighing, she dropped back on her elbows. Clay eased them out from under her until she was lying beside him. He made a pillow of his arm and pulled her closer, till she was snug up against him, her cheek resting against his shoulder.

What in the world was she thinking? She didn't want to be here with Clay. She didn't want to go back to a time when stargazing with him was the best entertainment she knew. She didn't want to give up the opportunities waiting for her back in Austin.

But, oh Lord, she didn't want to break the promise she'd made to Clay Fuller five years before. She knew in her heart divorce wasn't the answer for them.

"Clay…"

"Hush, Molly-girl," he said softly. He raised up on one elbow, then leaned over her. Her heart beat so hard she was sure he could hear, and her throat constricted with emotion.

Yes, she wanted to say. *Yes, I still love you. Yes, I want to make this work.*

Clay leaned closer, and she shut her eyes for his kiss.

Which he placed gently on her forehead.

Chapter Three

Before Ila Crunk's pet rooster had crowed twice the next morning, Molly was up and about. She hoped to see Clay, but he had already headed out for his greenhouses. A note tacked by the front door said he wouldn't be back till suppertime.

Molly pinned back her hair with a bandanna, took a good long look at the dusty main room, and pushed up her tie-dyed sleeves. Aunt Electra used to say that the best way to eat an elephant was one bite at a time.

Straightening the Chock full o' Nuts can above the fireplace, Molly grinned. She wouldn't dream of moving the ashes to a more stately container. Or a different location. The mantel seemed like the spot of honor for Aunt Electra.

By late afternoon, Molly had dusted the room from top to bottom, washed the walls, and mopped with a special cleaner for wood floors that she purchased at I. C. Easley's.

"How're things at Electra's place, Molly?" I. C. had said as he bagged the cleaner. "How's Clay?"

"He's fine," she said, shoving back hurt at the thought of last night's brotherly kiss.

I. C. handed her the bag and winked. "I got a feeling about

you two, Molly. Just remember if you ever want to read the latest Sonic the Hedgehog comic to come see me."

"What? Sonic the…? *Comics?*" She obviously hadn't gotten enough sleep last night; she wasn't able to pay attention properly.

But I. C. never had explained himself.

Nor had Willie Bean. The mechanic had grinned foolishly when Molly dropped off the Chevy for a tuneup. Molly popped open the hood and tried to engage Willie in a discussion about spark plugs and pistons—the kind of talk Willie generally thrived on—but Willie just stood beside her grinning, not even leaning forward to study the truck's innards.

Molly straightened. "What on earth is wrong that you're smiling to beat the band?"

"Nothin'." Willie leaned over and fiddled with the battery with a monkey wrench. "I can't be near as happy as you." She turned her head and winked at Molly. "I heard you and Clay drove up to Spoon Hill together last night."

"Oh, good honk!" Molly said, using Aunt Electra's favorite expression. "Living in this town again is like living in a fish bowl."

Suppose someone had seen him kiss her on the forehead? Common sense said that was illogical, but what if instead everyone assumed she and Clay had…

She blushed. Word would no doubt get back to Clay, and he might think that she was the one spreading those rumors.

And that she wanted to get back together.

"Look, Willie," Molly said quickly. "Are you and Bobby doing anything tonight?"

Willie frowned. "Well, it ain't our bowling night, and the dance hall ain't open Wednesdays on account of the Baptists, so I guess we'll just be planted in front of the TV."

"Can I talk you and Bobby out of watching reruns? Come eat supper with Clay and me."

Willie's eyebrows drew together. "You know I'd go to the end of the trail with you, Molly Fuller, but Iris warned me about your newfangled eatin' habits. Salad fixin's is fine for some folks, but I'm not so certain Bobby would take to it. He works hard all day. He needs a solid meal."

"That's just what Clay said. Trust me, Willie. I'll have plenty of food."

"Well…" Willie closed one eye in concentration. "It'd be worth it just to see Jo Bell sore. When she hears about it, she'll be madder'n a wet hen that I got to pull up to your and Clay's trough instead of her."

"What does Jo Bell care?"

Willie's face looked stricken for a moment, then she relaxed. "What time do you want me'n Bobby to be at your place?"

No, just like I. C., Willie had never explained herself either.

Molly stood back and studied the front room. She'd frantically tried to get the house in order so she could start cooking before her guests even arrived. She and Clay had known Willie and Bobby ever since they'd all played in the sandbox together down at the park, but it still wouldn't be neighborly to make them wait on their supper.

She'd kill two birds with one stone by having Willie and Bobby over for supper. They would see there wasn't anything between Clay and Molly, which would hopefully stop the town tongues from wagging.

And more important, Molly would lay to rest any fears Clay might have that she was beginning to care. He obviously didn't care about her.

Satisfied that the downstairs was as tidy as it was going to be, Molly headed for the kitchen. Taking a deep breath, she opened Aunt Electra's cookbook and ran a finger down the index. Finding the right reference, she flipped past desserts, salads, vegetables, and went straight to meats.

And saw that the page with the recipe for fried chicken had been ripped clean out of the book.

"*Now* what am I going to do?" she wailed. She'd never fried chicken before in her life.

A voice dripping with false sincerity sailed through the open window. "Bye now! Thank you for coming. I'm *so* glad you found my genealogical studies fascinating!"

Molly grimaced. Ila Crunk was bidding farewell to her historical-society ladies. Oh fiddle. Why did she have to hold the county fair's blue ribbon recipe for fried chicken? Surely it was too much to hope that she'd help Molly out of this jam.

Molly couldn't believe she was even considering the request, but desperate battles called for desperate alliances.

She slammed out the front door and shot across the lawn after Ila Crunk, who was climbing the steps to her porch. "Miss Crunk! Wait!"

Ila shut the front door behind herself.

Molly charged up the steps and banged on the door. "Miss Crunk, please! I need your help! Believe me, I'd go to one of the other neighbors, but everybody knows you make the best chicken in town."

The door opened a foot's width, and Ila peered out suspiciously. "What does my chicken have to do with whatever situation you've gotten yourself into?"

"I'm having company for dinner, and I bought a chicken to fry. But Aunt Electra's cookbook doesn't have the recipe."

Ila snorted. "Since when does anybody need a recipe for fried chicken?"

"I've never made it before, Ila, and I'm running late. *Please* help me out. I promise I won't ask anything of you again. I don't want to take credit for your cooking; I just want to have food on the table when they show up."

Ila studied her, then grudgingly opened the door wider. "Let me get my good apron. Come inside, if you must."

Molly stepped inside, awed. In all her life, she'd never been invited inside Ila Crunk's home. The outside was so lovely, she'd always wondered what the inside looked like.

Rich mahogany furniture filled the front room, along with what had to be an antique harpsichord. A large oriental rug ran nearly wall to wall.

Above the ornate mantel hung an oil portrait of a somber-looking man clad in buckskins, clutching a rifle. A man in a coonskin cap had his arm thrown around him, and another man in dress uniform stood at attention on the other side.

"Who's the man in the middle, Miss Ila?" Molly said as the elderly woman bustled into the room.

"Why, a good Texas girl like you doesn't recognize Odibe Crunk? I suppose you don't know that's Davy Crockett with the coonskin cap and Captain William Barrett Travis either." Ila laid a hand over her heart. "They all died brave, glorious deaths at the Alamo, God rest their patriotic souls."

Molly smothered a grin. The Crunk Independent School District wasn't so far enamored of the town hero that they hadn't taught the truth. "Miss Ila, I'd hardly call dying from the measles a brave, glorious death. Odibe Crunk never saw so much as a sling-shot battle."

Ila snapped her apron strings tightly at her waist. "Hmmph. That's the sort of disrespect I've come to expect from all of you Merriweathers. You've always been jealous that we were related to Odibe and you weren't."

Molly laughed. Clay had certainly pegged Ila Crunk and her desire to keep up the family fight. It was pride, plain and simple, that kept her from people like Clay, people who just wanted to love her.

People like Clay.

"Well, come on, girl. Shake a leg, or we'll never get that chicken ready for your company. Can't anybody say that Ila Crunk let a neighbor go hungry."

Ila marched the distance next door and let herself in. "Place looks a mite run-down," was all she said as she headed straight for the kitchen. "Well, let's see what I've gotten myself into."

She pushed Electra's cookbook aside and barked out orders. Molly scurried to help by washing chicken, fetching bowls, and generally trying to stay out of the way. Ila soaked, dipped, and battered the chicken, then had it frying before Molly knew what had happened. All the while, Ila issued instructions and directions, and Molly wondered if anyone else in Crunk had ever had private lessons with Ila. When she asked, Ila looked embarrassed, then harrumphed. "Every Texas girl should know how to fry chicken for her man," she said gruffly.

"Clay and I won't be married anymore after the summer though. Why would you bother to teach me?"

Ila poked at the frying chicken. "In my day, divorce wasn't an option."

"Do you think it's an option now?" Molly leaned back against the counter. Strange that she should be having this conversation with Ila Crunk, of all people.

"I think there's things that women shouldn't have to put up with, that they used to have no say about." She turned slightly. "Is that your problem with Clay?"

"Do you mean does he beat me or is he unfaithful? No. Of course not. Clay's as good as they come."

"All the Crunk men have been good and decent."

Molly couldn't resist smiling. "Even those descended from the Caldwell Fullers?"

"The Crunk blood runs deep enough, I guess."

Molly laughed, pushing away from the counter. "Ila, you are truly a treasure to this town. I mean that. Why didn't you ever get married?"

"No one ever asked me," Ila said quietly, looking thoughtful as she rearranged the chicken. She straightened, as if she had revealed too much and wanted to collect herself. "I've always had my own interests. I never needed a husband or kids underfoot."

Molly thought about Ila rattling around that large house all alone. "Did you ever think about moving away from Crunk?"

Ila looked shocked. "Why on earth would I want to do that? This is my home. I know everybody here, and they're good, solid folks. I can sit outside of an evening and not have to worry about some lunatic drive-by shooting. I don't have to worry whether a car mechanic is going to take advantage of my age and overcharge me—Willie Bean is as honest as the day is long. And there's fresh air here, Molly Merriweather Fuller, something I'm sure you're not used to from living in Austin. And traffic? Why, the last traffic jam we had in these parts was when Ernest Milton's cows got loose and blocked the farm road for two hours."

"But what if you *had* a husband and had to choose between him and living in a place you didn't like, where it would be harder to pursue your interests? Wouldn't you choose to live where you wanted?"

Ila looked thoughtful. "When I was a girl, I took a Bible verse to heart. I thought it was the most romantic verse in the Good Book, and I promised the Lord I'd always adhere to it." She paused. "Trouble is, I never got a chance to keep that promise."

"What was the verse?"

"Whither thou goest, I will go; and where thou lodgest, I will lodge: thy people shall be my people, and thy God my God." Ila untied her apron and folded it over her arm. "Well, it looks like you're on your way to some first-class chicken. Just keep turning it and make sure it doesn't burn. Now don't bother walking me to the door. I can see myself out."

She turned, and Molly touched her arm, her own eyes damp. Ila looked up, surprise written in her eyes. "Thank you," Molly said softly, then impulsively kissed Ila's wrinkled cheek.

"Why…" Ila's hand stole up to touch the spot. She stared at Molly, then scurried out of the room. Molly heard the front door open, then Clay's voice.

"*Ila?*"

"Your wife's in the kitchen," Molly heard Ila say, then the front door closed.

Quickly she bustled around, trying to look busy. She knew when Clay had entered the room even before she saw him.

"What was Ila Crunk doing over here?"

For some reason, she felt shy about looking at him. Molly turned the frying chicken even though it didn't need it. "She was helping me cook supper. I invited Willie and Bobby over to eat with us."

"You did?" She heard Clay move forward, then he was right beside her. "You're frying...chicken? Listen, Molly, I hate to tell you this because you're liable to dump it all out, but the last time I heard, chicken was an animal. And when you fry it, it isn't exactly healthy eating."

Smiling, Molly turned. "Listen yourself, Clay Fuller, I..."

He was standing much nearer than she'd imagined, and she found herself nearly in his arms.

His eyes twinkled mischievously, and he moved even closer. "What?" he said, grinning, bracing his hands on either side of her against the counter.

Molly shivered. "I...I was just going to say..."

"Don't say a word," he whispered as he leaned down.

Molly crossed her arms in self-defense. Goodness, but she'd forgotten what this man could do to her. She felt tingles up and down her arms, tingles that...

"The chicken!" Molly pushed him away and rubbed her arm where the hot grease had popped onto her skin. Clay laughed, and she frantically lowered the heat under the skillet. "Clay Fuller, don't you dare think this is funny. I had to beg Ila Crunk to help me fix this chicken. She'll never let me hear the end of it if I burn it."

"If you don't eat meat anymore, why are you making chicken? And why the sudden urge to have Willie and Bobby over?"

"I saw Willie down at the garage today, and I thought it would be nice to talk about old times with her and Bobby." Molly casually flipped over a drumstick. "And I'm making chicken because I can't expect everybody else to eat the way I do."

Clay shifted uncomfortably. "If you're sore because I ran out last night…"

"No, you were right." She faced him squarely. "I'm sorry I haven't been feeding you enough. I said I'd do the cooking, and I should have considered what you needed…and wanted."

Clay's expression altered slightly, to something Molly could almost describe as pained. "I haven't always considered what you needed or wanted either, Molly," he said softly.

Molly watched him leave, and her heart twisted with confusion. She wasn't sure she knew anymore just exactly what her needs and wants really were.

"Willie, do we hafta go?" Bobby Giles whined as he helped her into his truck. "I wanted a chili dog for supper."

Willie slammed the door with finality and glared. "Bobby Wayne Giles, we've got a marriage to save, and if breaking bread with Clay and Molly is what it takes, it's the least we can do."

"Well, I wouldn't half mind, except I ain't so sure Molly's gonna have any bread for us *to* break. She'll probably have one of them Styrofoam-tastin' rice cakes served with sushi." Bobby's large frame shuddered at the thought. "I'll never understand how them city folks survive on those skimpy little portions of raw *fish,* of all things. My food's gotta be baked, boiled, or fried, Willie. I gotta eat!"

Willie sighed loudly. "I promised Molly we'd come. I figure if we can lay it on thick-like with the love talk, they'll start to remember what it's like themselves. Maybe we can even tell them we've set a weddin' date!"

Bobby wiped a hand across his suddenly sweaty brow. "Let's not stretch the facts, Willie. You know I'm waitin' till I have more than chicken feed to support us."

"Hmmph." She eyed him sideways. "Money don't matter when it comes to affairs of the heart. Clay Fuller didn't have two dimes to rub together when he asked Molly to marry him!"

Bobby sighed at the sound of the familiar strains Willie had been playing back to him for five years. Normally she didn't require a great deal of romantic maintenance—she didn't go in for flowers and such—but when it came to recounting Molly and Clay's elopement, Willie nearly swooned in her Dickies coveralls every time.

"All right, I'll go along," he said grudgingly. "But I won't eat no raw fish."

Willie patted him on the knee. "Don't fret, Bobby. If Molly's grub ain't fit for table grazin', you can take me to the Tastee-King afterward."

Molly couldn't remember when she'd passed a finer evening. The look of surprise on everyone's faces when she set out the fried chicken, mashed potatoes, cream gravy, and a steaming bowl of green beans was worth the time she'd spent cooking. She merely nibbled at the green beans and potatoes—without gravy.

Bobby wiped his mouth and leaned back with a contented sigh. "Molly, that had to be about the best meal I ate in a long spell. I didn't know you had it in ya to cook such a fine… Ow! Willie, stop kicking me under the table! What'd I say wrong?"

Molly laughed. "I didn't do it all by myself. I had help from Ila Crunk. This is her special chicken we're eating."

"Ila gave you her recipe?" Willie's jaw dropped.

"Not only that, she was over here herself helping Molly fry up this yard bird," Clay said. He smiled at Molly. "Seems like my wife has a way with people when she fixes her mind to it."

Wife. Molly rose to gather plates. "Clay, why don't you set up the card table and get out the dominoes. Anybody want to play some 42?"

"Only if we can play partners," Willie said, glancing significantly at Bobby. She batted her eyelashes dramatically and laid her hand over his. Bobby turned his head so she couldn't see and rolled his eyes.

Molly suppressed a smile. She'd never seen Willie in such a flirtatious mood.

Clay retrieved the table and set it down to wipe his brow. "Even with the ceiling fan, it's awful stuffy in here. How about if I set this up out on the porch? There's a good breeze blowing tonight."

Bobby shook off Willie's hand and leaped from his chair like a bull out of a chute. "Lemme help you with that, Clay."

They wrangled the table between them out the door, and Molly stacked the last of the plates. "What's with all the calf eyes you're making, Willie? You and Bobby have been going together too long for you to suddenly get all moony."

Willie smiled sweetly. "I heard on this afternoon talk show that a woman often takes her man for granted. The talk show woman said that if a gal'd just treat her man special-like, he'd appreciate her more too."

"I have a few women friends in Austin who would disagree." Molly chuckled.

"Are they hitched? Or even ringed?"

"No. They're single."

"Well, maybe that's why. Seems to me there's a whole lot of folks in the world who are too busy lookin' to see what they can get out of love instead of what they can give."

Molly plunked the silverware down on the stack of dishes and brushed her hands together. "Come on, Willie. Let's go see if they've got that contraption set up yet. I haven't played 42 in a long time. I hope I remember how."

Willie winked. "It's like fallin' in love, Molly. It's impossible to forget."

Molly intended to be partners with Willie—"women against the men," she'd said—but at the last minute, Bobby squeezed past her for the chair opposite Willie. Molly had no choice but to play partners with Clay.

He mixed the dominoes, grinning. "I bet we can set Bobby and Willie, Molly. Even if you're probably as rusty as a twenty-year-old windmill."

For some reason, his teasing pleased her. It reminded her of when they used to play dominoes with Aunt Electra, sometimes even out here on the porch. She'd make a big pitcher of lemonade or iced tea and set it on the table, the dominoes clinking comfortably against each other, laughter filling the air. Sometimes a neighbor stopped by to join in, and sometimes two or three would gather just to watch and offer unsolicited pointers.

Under the warm yellow glow of the porch light, Molly watched Clay's hands. She'd always been fascinated by the way they could nearly cover the entire set of dominoes, circling and counter-circling to mix them up. His hands were strong and tanned from outdoor work, his nails cut short and clean. The gold wedding ring gleamed, and she wondered if he'd ever removed it since she'd placed it on his finger five years ago.

Clay pulled back his hands, and Willie nudged her. "Come on, Molly. Take your dominoes. Surely you remember you have to do *that.*"

Molly smiled, embarrassed to be caught daydreaming. Clay winked at her, and she felt even more vulnerable.

As they played, talk turned to the latest doings in Crunk. Junior Sites and Rudie Tyler had been seen eating together at the Red Rooster Café in the next town, Mayor Spell's Toyota engine had to be completely rebuilt—you cain't always trust them foreign cars—and oh, Molly, did you hear that our class is having its five-year reunion this summer? Jo Bell's trying to find a place to hold it."

Molly frowned. "I hadn't heard."

"How about here?" Willie said. "It sure would be fittin', seein' as how Electra sponsored our graduation party." She nudged Bobby in the ribs. "And that's when Molly and Clay took off together and got so romantically hitched."

Bobby rolled his eyes. "I *know*, Willie. I was right here in the house, remember? And I agree. I think this'd be a great place to hold a reunion. There's only about ten of us—not countin' spouses, of course. But still, we could help you push back the furniture like Electra done so that we could dance."

Willie glanced hopefully at her friends. "Molly? Clay?"

"Well, the house really isn't in such great shape," Molly said. She didn't want to face the stares of her old classmates, and certainly not in her home.

"I can get the porch fixed up, and the inside looks just fine, Molly," Clay said. "Maybe we can even give it a lick of paint before the party."

"Well…"

She caught his gaze, and he smiled slowly, as slow as warm chocolate over ice cream.

"Yes," she breathed out, her heart fluttering.

"All right then." Clay grinned more broadly. "Willie, I think it's your turn to mix these dominoes. Molly and I are just a point away from setting you two."

Willie pretended to sulk. "It wouldn't be that much if Bobby hadn't bid so high three rounds back."

"Why, sugar!" Bobby laid a hand over hers. "What happened to my romantic gal?"

Willie crossed her arms and glared.

The others laughed, and she relaxed. "Aw, gimme those dominoes. I vowed I'd follow that talk show lady's advice, and she said the most important ingredient in a relationship was not to stay so mad you didn't talk to one another."

Molly glanced at Clay and caught his gaze. They both quickly looked away.

Soon everyone was yawning, and Bobby and Willie finally rose and admitted that as much as they hated to leave, it was time to head home. Willie's mama would worry if Willie was too late getting home.

"If we was married, we wouldn't have to worry about Mama," Willie said, digging an elbow into Bobby's ribs. "We could sit up all night together if we wanted, like Clay and Molly here."

The thought of staying up all night with Clay made Molly blush. He must have been nervous too, for he scuffed the toe of his boot so hard against the porch that it splintered the already fragile wood.

Bobby let out a whistle. "That ol' thing might just cave in altogether despite the work you've done, Clay. You need any help, you just give a holler."

"Thanks, Bobby. And thanks for coming over."

Willie squeezed Molly's arm. "Remember what that talk show lady said, you hear? Love is always worth the effort." She grinned. "And that's Willie Bean talkin'."

Molly smiled gamely. She didn't have an answer for the ever-optimistic Willie.

Amid a chorus of good-byes, Bobby and Willie took off in his battered truck. Molly stood on the top porch step and watched the taillights fade down the street.

"Sit with me for a while, Molly?" Clay said from behind her. "It's a lot cooler out here than inside."

She sat on the step, and he sat beside her, keeping a good distance between them. It felt strange to sit together, yet so far apart. When they'd lived here with Electra, they'd sat so close, Aunt Electra said you couldn't tell where one left off and the other began.

Molly rested her chin in her hands, elbows on her knees. Things weren't the same without Aunt Electra. Maybe she was the glue that had held their relationship together. Now all they had was this old house. She sighed. "I hate seeing it fall apart," she said without thinking.

"Seeing what fall apart?"

"Aunt Electra's house." She paused. "What'd you think I meant?"

"I didn't know." Clay stretched his legs out down the steps and leaned back on his elbows. She couldn't see his face, but she was certain he was studying her.

"I can help you with this porch, you know," she said. "All you had to do was ask."

"I didn't think you'd say yes. You usually seem pretty busy with other things."

She winced inwardly. It was true she'd shut herself upstairs so that she could work on her own interests first instead of helping him. "Well, let me know the next time you plan to work on it."

"I thought I'd put that old swing back up too," he said, then paused. "Would you have any objections?"

She turned to face him. "No. Why would I?"

He shrugged. "I don't know, Molly. I've been trying to figure that out for the past year."

She pulled her legs up a step and wrapped her arms around her knees. "What do you mean, Clay?"

"I mean that five years ago, you went away to college, but you never came home. You'd meet me here, and things were good and all, but when the time came to settle down, you didn't want that. This is your home, Molly. These are your folks. I saw what a good time you had tonight. You belong here."

"You can take the girl out of the country, but you can't take the country out of the girl, right?" she said.

"Something like that."

"Do you think our getting a divorce is all my fault?" she asked hotly.

Clay was silent for a moment. "I don't think any of it's your fault, Molly. I think we were doomed from the day I asked you to run off with me."

Molly shivered, as if a cold wind had suddenly blown across the porch. Hadn't he ever loved her? Hadn't it ever been true? "Then why did you ask?" she said in a small voice.

Clay ran a hand through his hair. "I guess part of it was that I just wanted to show up our folks for keeping us apart. And part of it was just plain being an eighteen-year-old kid who was lusting after you."

Her eyes filled with tears, and she stumbled to her feet. Then it was true. He'd never really loved her after all.

"Molly." He rose and gripped her arm, stopping her from fleeing into the house. "Molly-girl, aren't you listening? It's my fault."

She'd heard all right. She'd heard enough to know that Electra's house or not, she'd be in Austin by morning. "Let me go, Clay," she said, trying to hold back her tears. "Please just let me go."

"Not until I apologize to you. You were always a fine girl, and you're an even finer woman. But I never should have asked you to go against your family by running off. I should have courted you first, then we should have had a church wedding with all our friends and families present. Instead of starting off our marriage with a blessing, we started off—"

"With a curse?"

He shook his head. "Not that. We started off as two headstrong kids who didn't stop to think about what we were doing. And it's my fault for talking you into it." He dropped his hand from her arm. "I don't blame you for wanting to divorce me. I haven't been a good husband from the start."

"You've been fine," she said, touching his sleeve. "You haven't changed a bit since the day we got married."

"That's the problem," he said, stepping back, stepping away from her reach. "I haven't changed a bit. And certainly not enough to keep up with you." He ran his hand through his hair again, looking weary. "Guess I'd better tackle those dishes. That really was a fine meal you cooked."

She stepped toward him, wanting to say more, wanting to comfort. "Clay…"

He held her at arm's length. "Molly, it'd be awful easy right now for me to kiss you, but then I'd probably wind up asking you to sleep downstairs with me tonight. I think in the morning we'd both regret it."

"Even though we're married?" she said softly.

"Especially because we're married." He smiled ruefully and nodded at the house. "Go on upstairs. I want to do right by you for a change."

Blinking back a tear, Molly skirted the half-repaired porch hole and stumbled to her room.

Clay still hadn't said whether he had ever loved her.

The breeze all but died, and Molly tossed on her bed upstairs, unable to sleep. It wasn't just the warmth, it was the thought of Clay downstairs. How was he sleeping tonight?

Molly's stomach rumbled uncharacteristically. That was odd. She'd eaten a decent portion of potatoes and beans. Maybe it was because she'd saved room for just a bite of the peach cobbler she'd prepared, then had never eaten any. They'd all gotten so involved in the 42 match that she completely forgot about dessert.

I hope Clay remembered to put it in the refrigerator. It'd be a shame for it to spoil. Maybe I'd better go check.

"But what if he's still awake? Do I really want to see him?"

Come on, Molly, don't be in denial.

"What's the point of seeing him? He obviously said his piece. Nothing I can say would make a difference. He didn't want to hear it earlier."

Maybe you want to see him for other reasons?

Molly flung back the covers. The chance of running into Clay had to be better than arguing with herself.

Heart beating loudly, she tiptoed down the stairs to the main room. No light shone from the kitchen or from under his closed door. She paused with her hand on the knob. Holding her breath, she quietly gave it a turn.

Clay lay sprawled on his back, arms flung out, sound asleep. In the darkness she could barely see the gentle rise and fall of his chest. She leaned against the door and studied him, remembering what it had been like to sleep in those arms, to rest her head against that chest. His business demanded hard work from that body during the day, yet he looked so peaceful now.

The way she had no doubt looked when she was with him, when their souls were so close that even she couldn't tell where he left off and she began.

The way she had felt when she wasn't afraid to say she loved her husband.

The way she wanted to feel now, even though she was afraid.

Backing out quietly, Molly shut the door and crept upstairs to sleep alone in her double bed.

Chapter Four

When Ila Crunk opened her front door the next morning, Molly could have sworn she saw the elderly woman smile. Ila quickly recovered, however, and assumed her usual stern expression. "Molly Merriweather Fuller, what on earth brings you here? If you've come to complain about my chicken…"

"Not at all! Everybody loved it, Ila. I brought you this." Molly held out a covered aluminum pan. "We were all so full, I forgot about dessert. I made a peach cobbler, and there's no way Clay and I can eat all of it, so I want you to have half."

Ila took the pan, her face a mask of surprise. "Why, that's very kind of you."

"I hope you like it. I wanted to share with you, since you shared your chicken recipe with me." Molly stepped back. "Well, I'll see you around town, I guess."

"Wait, Molly." Ila touched her arm, then when Molly turned, she drew back, as if embarrassed. "Would you like to come in and have a bite with me? I just made some coffee." She paused. "If you're not busy, that is."

"To tell you the truth, I was just getting ready to clean the bathrooms." Molly winked. "I believe that chore can wait a spell."

Ila held the door open wider, and her face broke into a small but genuine smile this time.

Molly spent most of the morning next door, listening to Ila Crunk recount family history. Ila had a teacher's drone for a voice, but Molly was fascinated by the elderly woman's knowledge about how the Crunk and Merriweather families figured into the settling of Texas. It was even more fascinating when Molly considered that she and Clay were descendants of two such strong lines.

Before either woman realized it, the regulator clock on Ila's mantel was tolling noon. Ila invited Molly to stay for lunch, but fearing she was already way behind in her household chores, Molly graciously declined.

"I had a lovely time, Ila," she said at the door. "Would you join me and Clay for supper some night? As soon as I learn how to make your fried chicken on my own, that is."

"Truth is, I'm a bit tired of that old recipe, myself. I'd be content with a nice bowl of greens. Here. Take this cookbook of mine. I know all the recipes I'm ever going to make. You might find something in here you and Clay like."

"I can definitely put this to good use as far as he's concerned." Molly grinned, then impulsively gave Ila a quick hug. "Thank you again for inviting me. I'd love to hear more family history."

Ila winked. "There won't be any more family history to pass on if you and Clay don't add a limb to your branch of the family tree. I know your scatterbrained sister has kids, but she's not part of the Crunk line."

"I wish I could tell you we'd add that limb, Ila," Molly said. "But I don't hold out much hope."

"I hear hope isn't what's needed." Ila nudged her, then laughed at her shocked expression. "Scoot on home, girl. I'll be waiting for that supper invitation."

Molly waved good-bye, then buried her nose in the cookbook's index as she walked across the lawn. Most of the recipes were high-fat, high-calorie dishes, but with a little modification, she could make them tasty enough for Clay and healthy enough for herself.

"Miz Fuller?"

Startled, Molly stopped short at her porch steps. She hadn't noticed that a delivery truck waited at the curb. A teenage boy stood by her front door, holding out a long white box wrapped in a pink ribbon. She frowned. "Yes, I'm Mrs. Fuller."

"Flowers for you from Beamon's Florist."

Her heart skipped a beat. Crunk didn't have a florist; anyone who needed flowers had to go all the way to Sweetbriar. In all her years, no one had ever sent her flowers. Excited as a kid at Christmas, she slipped off the ribbon and opened the lid.

Six perfect yellow roses lay on a cloud of white tissue paper. Molly was speechless with joy.

"There should be a card."

"What? Oh...there is!" She handed the boy the box and tried to keep her fingers from shaking as she withdrew the card from its envelope.

Thinking about you. Clay

"Trim the ends of them roses and put 'em in a vase of water. They ought to last a long time," the boy said, then tipped his cap. "Have a nice day, Miz Fuller!"

"Thank you!" she called after him, then gathered the box, card, and cookbook and made her way into the house.

The phone was ringing off the wall. "Molly?" Clay said in a worried voice. "Where've you been? I've been calling all morning."

"I was over at Ila's. Oh, Clay, she has the most fascinating stories about our families."

"Really?" He sounded distracted. "Listen, Molly, I was calling to see if...did anything come to the house today?"

"The flowers just got here. They're beautiful. Thank you!"

He cleared his throat. "I wanted to see if you'd like to go to the Bijou with me tonight. The movie changes today, so it'll be something new."

Molly smiled. She'd probably seen the movie in Austin months ago. "I'd love to go, Clay."

"Great!" he sounded relieved, as though he'd thought she might turn him down. "The movie starts at five-thirty, so I thought maybe we could go over to the Dew-Drop afterward and have supper." He paused. "Shoot, Molly, I'm sorry. They won't have anything there to eat that you'd like. What am I thinking?"

"I'd love to do that too, Clay."

He was silent a moment. "You would?"

"Yep." She grinned into the phone.

"I'll be home to pick you up a little after five then." He sounded confident now, jubilant.

"See you then." Molly hung up the phone and smiled to herself. She studied the roses, then scrounged in the hall closet until she came up with a dusty glass vase. She rinsed it out, filled it with fresh water, clipped the roses' stem ends, and set them in the vase.

She set the vase on the mantel, at the end opposite the Chock full o' Nuts coffee can. "What do you think, Aunt Electra? I hope you don't mind the company, but I think the roses look pretty up here."

Molly stood back and examined the mantel, then decided Aunt Electra would no doubt agree.

Rudie Tyler took a stool at the Tastee-King counter and ordered the same thing she did every afternoon after visiting the Autumn Seasons Retirement Home. "A strawberry ice cream Dr Pepper float, Lexine."

"You got it. How's your mama, Rudie?" The counter girl expertly scooped the ice cream and flipped it into a soda glass.

Rudie shrugged. "She has her good days, she has her bad."

"Speaking of bad, that Junior Sites was through here a little while ago. He said that if a certain lady lawyer showed up, I was to tell her that he'd pick her up for dinner tonight over in Sweetbriar." Lexine handed over the float, then leaned her elbows against the counter. "Come on, Rudie. When are the two of you going to get married?"

"I'm getting too old for romance. And too busy for marriage. Junior and I like our friendship just the way it is. We'd probably get married and discover we really didn't like each other. We'd be headed for divorce court in no time flat."

"That's not what's happening to Clay and Molly Fuller, to hear Jo Bell talk."

Rudie dug her spoon into her drink. "Everybody knows Jo Bell talks too much." She ate a mouthful of ice cream, then looked at Lexine expectantly. "Why? What's she saying?"

Lexine laughed. "You mean she doesn't talk to you? And there she is, working for you and all. Girl, she heard it from I. C. who heard it from Iris. Molly and Clay went to the movies a few nights ago, then ate at the Dew-Drop." Lexine leaned closer and dropped her voice to a whisper. "Word has it that they were looking pretty friendly too. They were both smiling and laughing at each other, like we all remember them doing when they were just young pups trying to hide their love from their folks."

"The only person left they have to hide it from is Ila Crunk," Rudie said. "I suppose she could give them fits, if she set her mind to it."

Lexine stood up straight. "Well, now, I'm glad you mentioned her, Rudie, because I darn near forgot the funniest part of the story. While Molly and Clay were having supper at the Dew-Drop—by the way, she had a bowl of vegetable soup. That's all, can you imagine? And her with her skinny frame! Why, she could eat half a side of beef and not show an ounce of gain. Too skinny, I say. My Bert says he likes a woman with a little meat on her bones."

"What about Ila?"

"Oh. Ila. Well, she walked down to the Dew-Drop for her daily glass of buttermilk—said she didn't have any at home, and she didn't care for the Piggly-Wiggly brand. She usually goes all the way over to the SuperMart in the next county for her grocery shopping, you know."

"So Ila showed up at the Dew-Drop…" Rudie said patiently, hoping to get Lexine's gossip train back on track.

"And darned if Molly didn't wave her over and invite her to join her and Clay! Can you imagine?" Lexine put her hands on her ample hips.

"Well, they *are* neighbors, Lexine." Rudie poked around in the mush at the bottom of her soda glass. "Did Ila sit with them?"

"She sure did. And after they finished, she got in Clay's truck and rode home with them." Lexine shook her head and swiped at the Formica counter with a wet rag. "Mighty curious, I'd say. She's never had a good word to say about any of the Merriweathers. Or that marriage."

"Times change." Rudie shoved the empty glass toward Lexine and grinned. "Looks like old Electra knew what she was doing after all, leaving those kids her house. But I'll bet she never counted on Ila getting involved."

Lexine stopped wiping the counter. "I don't know, Rudie. Electra was always as smart as a thermos bottle. She knew how to keep hot things hot and cold things cold, without ever making a mistake. Maybe she knew Ila would eventually figure into the picture. Maybe this was her way of finally finishing that silly Crunk-Merriweather disagreement that'd been going on for years."

"She always did favor Clay and Molly being married, even when nobody else did."

"Hmm." Lexine tapped a finger against her forehead. "I wonder what Electra thought about you and Junior."

"Oh, give me another float, Lexine." Rudie sighed. "And stop playing matchmaker. One in the town is enough."

Lexine grinned. "Now that Electra's gone, I guess I might as well step in and fill the job."

Molly removed the nail from between her teeth and lined it up against the plank. *Wham! Wham!* She brought the hammer down in a clean first strike, then pounded again. *Wham! Wham!*

Clay had gone back to I. C. Easley's and purchased enough lumber to replace the entire front porch. He'd shown Molly the best way to lay the planks and drive the nails, then he'd ripped up the old, rotting wood. She worked on it during the day while he was at work, then they tackled it together, side by side, in the evening. They were now more than halfway finished.

Some evenings Clay would make Molly set down her hammer, and he'd take her out for dinner, a movie, or even just a walk into town. Several times he came home from work with a handful of new wildflowers.

The plank firmly in place, Molly rocked back on her heels and studied her work. Pleased, she wiped a wrist across her wet brow.

"Looks good, Molly." Clay stood in the front doorway and held out a pitcher of iced tea. "How about a break?"

"I'd love it. This is hard work."

Clay trod carefully along the finished portion of the porch to the steps. Molly sank down gratefully beside him and wiped her sweaty hands against her overalls. He poured her a glass, and she drank noisily.

Clay laughed. "Pounding nails is hard work, all right. But it'll sure feel good when it's done." He studied the still-unengraved silver bracelet on her wrist. "Haven't you decided on a design for that one yet?"

"I'm going to leave it plain. Sometimes that's best. And speaking of bracelets, I talked to Clovis today, and he said he'd place a few of mine with his curios. Maybe he'll sell one. Meanwhile, I can keep overnighting them to Austin. I've got a friend who's glad to sell them alongside her handmade scarves."

Clay leaned back against a column and studied her face. "Do you miss Austin, Molly?"

She took a long swallow of tea and wound up draining the glass while she considered. When she lowered the glass, he was still looking at her. "To be honest, it's nice not to have to fight traffic. Or to deal with people I don't know. I've forgotten how nice folks are here. People are always so friendly wherever we go."

Clay grinned. "I heard I. C. and Clovis have some sort of bet going on whether or not we're going to stick together."

"That's ridiculous." Molly tipped her glass to her mouth, ostensibly to catch the last remaining drops, but in reality to hide her expression.

"Yoo-hoo!"

Molly lowered the glass and inwardly groaned.

Jo Bell Grapple sashayed up the walk, her skirt so tight her hips rolled like two pigs trapped under a blanket. "How're y'all doing? Isn't it a *lovely* Saturday afternoon? Even if it is a mite warm." She fanned herself with her hand.

"Hi, Jo Bell," Clay said. "Would you like some tea?"

Molly closed her eyes briefly. *Clayton Fuller...*

"Why, I'd love a glass. I'll just plop myself on the step here while you go fetch me one."

"Sure thing." Clay headed inside, and Jo Bell took his spot.

"So how are *you*, Molly?" Jo Bell continued in her sugary voice. She gave her a once-over. "Truth to tell, you're looking like you've been rode hard and put up wet."

"Thank you, Jo Bell." Molly struggled to keep control of her voice. "And you're looking like—"

"Here we go." Clay stepped between them and sat two steps

below, handing Jo Bell a glass. "What have you girls been talking about?"

"Why, I was just fixing to tell Molly here that the reunion committee has decided that they want to have the get-together next Saturday. I told them you two would love to have it here."

"Well, I don't know…" Clay glanced around the porch. "We've still got a lot of—"

"We'd love to." Molly laid a hand on Clay's arm and looked straight at Jo Bell. "We'll be done by then."

Jo Bell's jaw dropped momentarily, then she quickly recovered. "All righty. I'll let the others know. We'll see you here next Saturday night at…seven?"

Molly nodded firmly. "That would be fine. Tell them not to worry about the food either. Willie volunteered to help."

Jo Bell rose, making a show of straightening her skirt. She smiled broadly at Clay. "I look forward to it. Bye now," she said, then swished back down the walk.

Clay's gaze followed her, and Molly poked him in the ribs. "We'd better get to work, Clay. This porch won't finish itself."

As they worked alongside each other—one holding a plank while the other pounded nails—Molly studied Clay. Shortly after they'd married, he told her that his parents had always pushed girls like Jo Bell Grapple on him. "Clay?"

"Mmm?" he said around a nail between his teeth.

Molly fussed with a loose plank, avoiding his gaze. "What do you think your life would be like now if you'd married Jo Bell like your parents wanted?"

Clay stopped hammering and removed the nail from his mouth. "What made you think of that?"

Molly shrugged. "I saw how she looked at you. I think she wishes you two had married. I think she…"

Clay picked up the hammer. "Quit thinking, Molly. I married you, didn't I?"

Molly started to reply, then thought better of it. Clay may have married her, but since she'd been back in town, he hadn't yet so much as kissed her. No point in bringing it up though. He might get the notion she wanted to stick around.

Clay gave the nail a final resounding smack, then set down the hammer. He tested the plank, and finding it sturdy, sat back. "Whew! That's enough for today. Let's get cleaned up, and I'll take you to that Mexican restaurant over in Sweetbriar. Casa Pedro, remember?"

She nodded. On homecoming night during their senior year, everyone from their class had gone there to eat. Because she couldn't go with Clay, Molly had accepted a date with Randy Reeves. Clay had taken Jo Bell.

All night long she and Clay had gazed longingly over two tables at each other. When they rode back to Crunk, Molly had found herself in the back of Bobby Giles's pickup with Clay, Jo Bell, and another couple. Randy had wrapped his arm around her and tried to steal kisses, and she'd miserably noticed Jo Bell attempting the same with Clay.

Now she wondered if she'd be forever condemned to live in the past of young love.

At the restaurant, Clay looked as nervous as he had that homecoming night five years ago, only speaking when spoken to, acting distracted.

Molly pretended to study the menu even though she wasn't the least bit hungry. Clay was probably so quiet because he was upset that she'd asked about Jo Bell.

After the waiter had taken their orders and left, Clay cleared his throat. "The porch is coming along."

"Yes," she said brightly, seizing on the first real topic of conversation they'd had all night. "You were right about it being hard work."

"I hope it'll be worth it." Clay cleared his throat again, then took her hand. "Molly, speaking of things being worth it...and hope, and all..."

"Ah, young lovers!" A strolling guitarist stopped beside their table. "For you, I will play a ballad of love."

Clay's face darkened. "Look, we're…"

The guitarist strummed a chord, then broke into a long Spanish ballad that, as near as Molly could make out, had something to do with a man and woman loving each other, falling out of love, falling back into love, falling out… The song went on and on, and by the time the guitarist finished, their food had arrived. Looking rather annoyed, Clay pressed some money into the beaming guitarist's hand.

Molly picked up her fork. "What were you going to say, Clay?"

"Molly…" Clay leaned forward, his expression serious.

"Señor, Señora. How is the food?" The waiter hovered over them, all smiles.

Clay leaned back, sighing, and picked up his fork. "Wonderful."

Molly stared at him curiously, waiting for him to speak again, but he started in on his food, so she did the same.

He was just as silent on the way home, and her thoughts turned anxious. What was on his mind tonight? He'd talked so little—maybe he was going to tell her that he couldn't last the summer living with her and why didn't they just give up the house and their marriage.

Once home, she mumbled something about being tired and headed up for bed without giving him a chance to speak. She'd rather have one more night before he gave her the bad news in the morning.

But he didn't. Not that Sunday or the next day or any day after. They worked together on the porch throughout the week, speaking when necessary, but not laughing and joking as they had in the past. Something ominous lay between them, but she couldn't bring herself to address it—or the truth she couldn't ignore any longer. She wanted to stay in Crunk. She wanted to stay married to Clay Fuller.

Her heart nearly ached with the realization, especially knowing that whatever good they'd had between them was now apparently gone. Maybe it left when he saw Jo Bell. Or maybe he'd just wanted Molly's help finishing the house before he told her he'd had enough of their marriage.

On the morning of the reunion, Molly awoke, irritated, feeling like she was ready to come apart at the seams. The past few days had been worse than the first ones they'd spent together. Clay had hardly spoken to her.

At least they'd finished the porch in time for the reunion party.

Getting dressed, Molly stomped around her bedroom, then headed downstairs. She wished she'd never agreed to having the party at their house. She wished she'd never come back to Crunk.

Almost.

"Mornin', Molly." Clay looked up from where he sat drinking coffee and reading the *Gazette* at the kitchen table. He leaned back and studied her. "You ready for tonight?"

He was probably ready himself. Ready to spend time with Jo Bell. "I guess." She brushed past him and opened the old Frigidaire for a glass of orange juice.

Nestled in a clear plastic box was a yellow-rose-and-baby's-breath corsage.

"Do you like it?"

Wordless, she opened the box and gently fingered the delicate arrangement. "It's beautiful," she finally said.

"I thought you should have something pretty for the party tonight." Clay glanced away as though embarrassed. "I didn't know what you'd like. I stood in the florist shop and realized that even though I've known you all my life and been to a million school dances, I'd never once gotten to take you."

She swallowed a lump in her throat. "It's beautiful," she said again, softly, then reluctantly closed the lid and put the box back in the Frigidaire.

"Well…" Clay folded the newspaper and stood. "I've got things to tend to. I'll be home in time for the party. And Willie will be here to help you set up the food, right?"

Molly nodded, her heart beating a little faster than normal. "And Ila volunteered to fry up some chicken wings. We'll have things under control here." She paused. "You're sure you'll be back?"

He smiled. "Of course, Molly. I wouldn't miss it for the world." He headed for the front door, then called back from the hallway. "Check the fence out front. I did some painting on it last night after you went upstairs."

"Okay," she called back, but the front door had already banged shut. Almost instantly, she heard a knock at the side door.

Ila Crunk. For the past few days, she'd started showing up at the door facing her house, claiming that neighbors didn't bother with the front door. That was for company.

"Here's your chicken wings." Ila handed over a large covered platter. "They'll keep till it's time to heat them. And didn't Clay do a wonderful job on that old fence? I saw him out there painting like mad last night, trying to catch the last of the light."

"I haven't seen it myself," Molly said, feeling guilty now that she'd hidden upstairs, sulking, while he'd been outside working alone.

"Well, come on, girl!" Ila pushed her out the door and into the side yard. "Take a look at it from the front, like you were just walking up."

Molly kept her gaze fixed on the ground until she was almost to the street, then looked up.

Days ago they'd painstakingly replaced the old fence and gate, but now each picket and slat was a bright, clean white. Molly tested the gate, and it swung open easily. She stepped inside the yard and critically studied the porch.

Each plank gleamed with raw newness. They hadn't had time to paint it, but somehow she found the incompletion comfortably reassuring. Along with repainting the house's exterior and reshingling the roof, painting the porch gave them something more to accomplish together.

Molly sucked in her breath. Clay had painted Electra's old rattan swing a soft green, fitted it with a plump floral seat cushion, and rehung it on two solid-looking chains.

Ila grinned and nudged her. "Turn around."

"What…" Confused, Molly complied.

"The fence." Ila pointed toward the gate. "Look what he painted."

On one side of the gate, Clay had vertically painted "Molly." On the other side, "Clay." Visible only to someone standing in the yard or inside the house, the words were like a secret from the rest of the world. Molly's pulse quickened. Did this mean that he wanted her to stay after all? Why hadn't he just come out and asked her?

"If you stand there with your mouth open much longer, you're bound to catch a fly," Ila said mildly. "I've got to go get ready for a historical meeting. Let me know if you need anything." She sauntered to the gate, paused to look at the names, then shook her head, laughing. "Electra, you sly old dog."

Molly watched until Ila was back inside her own home, then, checking to make sure no one was watching, she stepped onto the porch.

She sat in the swing, gingerly, as though she were afraid it would break. When had Clay had time to restore it? He must have taken it out to the greenhouses. He probably hadn't wanted her to see him working on it and think it held any sentimental value for him.

Giving the swing a gentle push with her feet, she closed her eyes and leaned her head back. It certainly held a lot of sentimental value for her.

"Hey, Molly."

Startled, she opened her eyes. Willie stood grinning down at her, her hands gripping a food-laden tray. "Well, ain't that a pretty swing! Where'd y'all get that?"

"This was Aunt Electra's." Molly rose quickly. "Here, let me help you with that. We'd better start setting things up. Time has a way of slipping by."

And not just when it comes to parties, Molly thought ruefully as she and Willie headed inside.

Everything was ready.

Willie had gone home to change clothes and to collect Bobby. The house was clean, the *Welcome Crunk High Alums* banner strung across the mantel beneath the Chock full o' Nuts can, and the furniture pushed back for dancing.

Molly stood in the kitchen, her fingers shaking as she tried to pin on the corsage. She couldn't decide whether she was nervous at seeing all her old classmates in one place or because she was anxious just to see Clay.

"Ouch!" she muttered, pricking her thumb. She held her hand out, careful not to smear any blood on her full cotton skirt.

"Here, let me pin that on."

Clay.

She turned, and he was right there, his strong hands nimbly pinning the corsage to the neckline of her off-the-shoulder white eyelet blouse. His fingers lingered on her bare skin a moment, then he stepped back and held her at arm's length. "You look beautiful, Molly. I seem to recollect you wore a fancy pink dress on graduation night."

She nodded, unable to speak because she suddenly remembered the feel of his hands at the zipper of that dress after they'd married. A slow smile spread across his face, as if he remembered too. "I think I like this outfit even better," he said.

"Thanks." Wearing a brand-new denim shirt, freshly pressed jeans, and shined-up boots, he looked pretty good himself. Like a hard-working small-town man, not one of the dime-store cowboys she frequently saw in Austin.

"Molly?"

Startled, she realized that he was watching her…watching her watch him. He took a step forward, a serious expression taking the place of his smile. "Molly, what did you think of the fence?"

"They're coming up the walk!" Willie burst into the kitchen, her beauty parlor–arranged bouffant slipping to one side. The buttons of her one-size-too-small dress strained at their holes with her heavy breathing.

"Relax, Willie." Bobby put an arm around her and winked at Clay. "This is just the old crowd—not visitin' royalty. Besides, we see purt near most of 'em on a regular basis."

Willie stiffened. "Not Jim. Or Ted. Or Allison. Why, she drove all the way up from Tomball!"

Clay laughed. "Come on, Molly. I guess we're hosts of this shindig. We'd better go greet our guests." He put his arm around her and led her into the front room, where just as Willie had reported, it seemed like the whole gang was surging into the house.

Molly thrilled to his touch, encouraged by the fact that his protective embrace seemed an affirmation of their relationship. They were a couple, the mysterious union of two into one.

Yet the good-natured backslapping and shoulder punching finally forced Clay to move his arm, and Molly found herself alone again. It seemed like he was pulled away by a powerful tide of male companions, and she by an equally forceful tide of females. The men were eager to relive their glory days and foretell great future personal feats. The women recounted childbirth tales, canning secrets, and gossip. Most people were either married off or seriously engaged, no longer prone to the high-school allure of the opposite sex in a social setting.

"Yoo-hoo!" Jo Bell paused dramatically in the doorway, then flatly ignored the women and sauntered over to the men's group. Her hips rolled in a tight leather skirt, and she leaned an arm on mousy little Randy Reeves's shoulder. She batted her mascara-laden eyelashes. "Why, if this isn't the finest bunch of Crunk High alumni I *ever* saw!"

Molly closed her eyes momentarily. *Good honk.*

Randy's eyes popped out at Jo Bell's attention, and his tongue went slack like one of Aunt Electra's old hound dogs during the middle of July. "Ain't you looking pretty, Jo Bell," he finally said. "Can I talk you into moving to Navasota to be near me?"

Jo Bell coyly smiled, glancing around the circle of men for dramatic effect. "You might. If I don't get a better offer."

The men laughed as though it were the funniest thing they'd ever heard. The women went completely silent, then put their heads together and cackled like a gaggle of geese at a new feeding ground.

"Did you ever see such a spectacle?"

"She always was a flirt."

"And a tad too big for her britches."

"In more ways than one."

That brought on a nervous round of laughter, but it was quickly drowned out by Jo Bell's own sounds of mirth. "Why, Bobby Giles, how you do go on!"

Willie's ears burned bright red. She thrust back her shoulders, and a button popped off her dress. "Why, that little—that's *my* Bobby!" The fingers of her sturdy mechanic's hands curled into fists, and she started to push through the ring of women.

Molly restrained her friend. "Why don't we eat, everyone?" she said in a loud voice. "There's plenty of time for catching up, but the food is getting cold."

She'd counted on the universal pacifier of food to calm the crowd, and she wasn't disappointed. Both groups broke up and merged into pockets of couples again as indignant wives and girl-friends claimed their male halves. Molly searched for Clay, but Jo Bell reached him first.

"I'm here all by myself, and it seems like everybody else is paired up," she said in a syrupy voice. "You don't mind being my supper partner, do you, Clay? After all, you *are* the host."

"Well…" Clay looked around for Molly, and spying her, arched his eyebrows in question.

Molly felt a moment's hesitation. There was truth in what Jo Bell said, and if Molly laid claim to Clay, Jo Bell would just latch on to some other unsuspecting man and leave *his* woman stranded. Besides, as the hostess, she had a multitude of chores to tend to. And Mama had always taught her that a good hostess made sure *all* her guests had a good time.

She gave Clay her approval with a slight nod, wishing miserably that her mama hadn't been in the habit of teaching her daughters good Southern etiquette. Jo Bell swept Clay toward the buffet table, and Molly was left staring up at the coffee can on the mantel.

"Is that really your great aunt?" an oily voice whispered.

Molly's stomach dropped, and she turned to face Randy Reeves. "It *was*. She's now no doubt in heaven enjoying the rewards of being a good and faithful servant."

"Oh, of course," Randy said hastily, as though he might have offended her. "She was a wonderful lady indeed." He held out his arm. "May I escort you to the buffet?"

Alarmed, Molly scanned the crowd to find a suitable partner for Randy, but everybody else was paired up. How had he slipped through the cracks? "Didn't you bring a date?" she said.

Randy shook his head. "I came by myself up from Navasota. I just had to see everybody again. We had such a good time our senior year." He edged closer and smiled. "Didn't we?"

Molly stepped back, deciding quickly that if he was eating, he wouldn't be able to talk. "And I seem to recall you're partial to Swedish meatballs. Willie Bean made a whole batch of them, and I'm sure she'll want your honest opinion. Let's go check them out."

Randy beamed at her ready agreement to dine with him, and they went through the buffet line, then squeezed together next to several others on Electra's old sofa. Molly miserably noticed that Jo Bell was off in a corner with Clay. She was laughing loudly, punctuating her one-sided conversation by touching Clay's sleeve periodically. Clay, to Molly's relief, scarcely looked up from his plate of food.

Molly sat through nearly an hour of inane conversation with Randy Reeves, who seemed bent on discussing his every decision as a certified public accountant for the City of Navasota. Every time someone approached them and tried to change the subject, Randy waved them away.

Molly wondered if Randy would notice if she stabbed herself in the eye with a fork, or if he would just go right on prattling about his meticulous financial statements and balance sheets.

At last it was time to gather plates, and Molly saw a chance to escape. But Randy trailed right behind her, still babbling as she collected dirty plates and silverware and headed to the kitchen.

Molly fumed as she set the dishes in the sink. Jo Bell hadn't even looked up as she thrust out her plate and kept right on chattering. Clay had cast her a "help me" glance, but hadn't moved an inch to get away from Jo Bell.

She ran hot water full force over the plates, wishing she had Jo Bell in the sink along with them. Clay too.

"Molly? Is anything wrong?"

Randy timidly touched her bare shoulder, and she whirled around. "Randy!"

He jumped back, blinking, and she lowered her voice to stay calm. "Why don't you go pick out some records to play on the hi-fi? Or turn on the radio? I'll finish up here while you do."

"S-sure, Molly." He all but scurried from the kitchen.

Molly sighed and plunged her hands into the scalding water. She'd apologize to him later for her curtness, but at least she had a few moments to herself.

Music wafted into the kitchen, softly, then gradually increased in volume. Molly dried her hands and headed into the front room, where she saw several couples dancing a lively two-step. She rested her folded arms against the back of Aunt Electra's old chair and watched them, smiling.

More couples joined in, and the tune quickly changed to a George Strait waltz. Someone dimmed the lights.

"Oh, Clay, I love this song," she heard Jo Bell purr from somewhere behind her—hidden in the dark, halfway up the stairs. "Let's dance."

Molly stiffened. She didn't know whether she wanted to run screaming through the front door or bound up those stairs and slug Clay Fuller.

"You'll have to find yourself another partner, Jo Bell." Molly heard the sound of Clay's boots coming down the stairs. Then she felt him standing right behind her. "I only dance with my wife."

Molly's anger vanished, and her pulse raced. She turned slowly, and Clay was holding out his hand. "Molly?" he said. "May I have this dance?"

Trembling, she nodded, then put her hand in his. She caught a glimpse of Jo Bell's angry expression, then Clay drew her into waltz position with an arm around her waist and clasped her free hand in his, and she forgot about everything except him.

When they'd first married, they occasionally danced in this very room, sometimes alone, sometimes for Aunt Electra, who had been a wonderful dancer in her younger days. She said she took great joy in watching Molly and Clay.

But the only time they'd danced together in public before tonight was when they were in high school, always as seemingly disinterested partners, never as dates. Molly had forgotten how she had wanted to melt against him then, but it all came back in a rush as they swayed to George Strait's singing.

Clay smiled and brought their clasped hands in toward their bodies, a tender, intimate move. Then the music changed rhythm, and with only a slight pause, he led her into another slow song, a two-step this time.

Though her right hand and his left remained clasped, they shifted subtly, moving even closer. Molly's left arm dropped to around Clay's waist, and his right elbow rested on her left to lead.

"Aunt Electra, I'm a good dancer, aren't I?" Molly had once asked anxiously.

Aunt Electra laughed softly. "Many a girl's imagined she was good because she could hold her own on the dance floor, but it turned out it was all because she had a good partner."

"But if that's true, why does it seem like there are so many better women than men dancers?"

Aunt Electra leaned forward, her expression sober. "Because it's harder for men, Molly. They have to lead. They have to know where the couple's going, watch the crowd so they don't run into anybody—all while they steer their partner with them and signal in advance where they're going." She had paused. "You're too young to realize it now, but Clay's a very good dancer."

Molly stopped suddenly, and her eyes filled with tears. She turned her head and swallowed hard.

"Molly?" Clay said softly, then lifted her chin. He took one look at her face, then wrapped an arm around her waist. "Let's get some air."

He led her to the porch, which thankfully was empty, then to the swing. She sank down and buried her face in her hands. Clay sat beside her, waiting patiently with his hands clasped between his knees. She tried to hold back the sobs, but one escaped. Suddenly he was holding her, and she was leaning against him, pressing her cheek against his shoulder as he smoothed her hair. "Molly...Molly-girl. What's wrong?"

She drew a deep, shaky breath, feeling the weight of guilt pressing on her soul. "Everything's wrong," she said miserably.

"Like what?"

He tried to hold her tighter, but she drew back. "*I've* been wrong, Clay. For the past year, I've ignored you and made my own decisions. That's not what marriage is supposed to be. I always thought when the preacher taught about the wife submitting to the husband that it meant she was supposed to be some sort of doormat."

"Some folks seem to think that."

"But it's not true. When we were dancing together, I felt safe with you. We were moving…together. Yet somebody has to lead. Just now I trusted you to do that." She drew another shaky breath. "But I haven't let you do that in our marriage."

"Molly…"

She raised her eyes to his. "Clay, I know it's too late now, I know these words can't make up for the wrong I've done, but I'm sorry. I'm so sorry. Please forgive me."

Clay cupped her face with his hand. "It's me that needs to be forgiven. I never courted you properly before we married. I never insisted a year ago that we get together and agree on our plans for the future. I'd always just assumed we'd live here. If you want to live in Austin, if you *need* to live in Austin…"

"No!" She covered his hand with her own. "I don't. I want to stay here in this town, in this house…with you, Clay. If you'll have me."

Laughing, he embraced her. She could feel him shaking with relief. "Of course I'll have you! I've been courting you the past few weeks just to show you how much I love you. I haven't even kissed you because I was afraid of where it would lead. I don't want just your body; I want your heart too."

Clay reached into his jeans pocket and withdrew a small box. "I've tried to ask several times, but I kept losing my nerve. I was afraid you'd say no."

Molly opened the box. A small but beautiful diamond ring nestled against the velvet.

Clay knelt beside the swing. "Molly, will you marry me? In church this time, with all our family and friends there to see our love and commitment to each other."

Molly slipped the ring on her finger and pressed it against her gold wedding band. "Yes," she said softly. "Oh yes."

Music spilled through the window, the Dixie Chicks singing about a young girl needing wide open spaces. Molly smiled, for she'd found freedom in her own heart, which she gladly gave to Clay Fuller for safekeeping.

Clay smiled too, taking her hand. "Dance with me, Molly," he said softly. "Be my partner for the rest of our lives."

And there on the porch they'd built together with hard work and determination, patience and laughter, Molly and Clay sealed their future with the tenderest of kisses.

Epilogue

Laughing, Molly leaned up against Clay and ran her fingers through his hair. "You've still got rice."

Clay gripped the steering wheel of Molly's Chevy and shook his head. Several grains flew out. "Jo Bell pelted me pretty hard. Did she get you too?"

"She would have, if Willie hadn't gotten her first."

Clay laughed and looped his right arm around Molly to pull her closer. Only the headlights of the truck cut through the darkness of the farm road. "It was quite a wedding."

"And I predict it'll be quite a night too." Molly put a hand on his knee and smiled.

Clay drew in his breath. "I can't believe we waited. Craziest thing I ever heard of a married couple doing."

Molly laughed softly. "Good thing we're almost there."

"It's a shame we can't go somewhere special. Like Austin." Clay grinned.

"I like where we're going just fine. There'll be time enough to travel when we've fulfilled Aunt Electra's will stipulations."

Clay guided the truck to the top of the hill, then cut off the engine. Together they clambered out of the cab, and by the half-moon's light, lowered the tailgate and climbed into the bed of the truck.

Molly bumped into something and felt it prick her arm. "Ouch!" She reached out and grasped a wicker basket. "What's this?"

Clay glanced up from where he was spreading out several quilts. "I don't know. Maybe it's a gift from somebody."

"It is!" Molly delved into the basket. "Fried chicken, with a note from Ila, a book of love poems from Willie, two bottles of Big Red from Bobby…"

"I hope Rudie Tyler didn't include a certain coffee can," Clay said, scooting up beside her.

Molly laughed. "No, I think that's it." She rummaged in the basket, then frowned. "Except for one more thing." She pulled out a comic book encased in protective plastic. "That's odd. The note says it's from I. C. Easley."

"What?" Clay moved even closer and squinted in the dark. "Sonic the Hedgehog? You'd think that would come from Clovis."

Molly shrugged. "You'd think. Why do you suppose I. C. sent this?"

Clay ran a hand up her arm. "Maybe it's for all the little Fullers."

"What little Fullers?"

"The ones we're going to have to fill up all of those bedrooms in Electra's house."

"Clay Fuller!" Molly laughed as he playfully wrestled her closer. Finally spent from tussling, they lay on their backs and stared up at the stars. Molly snuggled in close, and Clay held her tight.

"Aren't they beautiful, Molly-girl?" he said, pointing up at the brilliantly lit sky. "We could be looking at the same stars that our ancestors did—Odibe or William Crunk or Cyrus Merriweather." He grinned. "Maybe even the same stars that all the little Fullers after us will be looking at."

"What if they don't want to live here? What if they don't even want to live in Texas?"

"They will, darlin'," Clay said, raising up on his elbow to lean over her. He kissed her gently on the lips, then murmured, "We'll teach 'em to two-step as soon as they can walk."

The Boy Next Door

by Suzy Pizzuti

To the Lord, from whom all blessings flow, and
for my dear friend Betty Springer,
who faces life's valleys with uncommon
faith and grace. I love you, Betty Babe.

Chapter One

Lucy Burns pressed her nose against her living-room window. Trying to remain unobtrusive and retain a demeanor of serene maturity, she rubbed at the fog created by her excited puffs of breath. However, it was difficult not to revert nearly a dozen years to the age of twelve, especially with her childhood coming home to roost.

Trevor was back.

Amazing. After what seemed to Lucy like years.

A slight frown marred her brow. Come to think of it, it had been years. With a rapid motion, she whirled away from the window sill. Hair bouncing from a ponytail caught in a wild bunch at the crown of her head, Lucy hurried through her living room, over the front porch stairs, and down the cobblestone walk of the duplex where she had grown up. The very same duplex that her family had shared for two generations now with Trevor's family. As both she and Trevor had been born "only" children, he was the closest thing to a sibling that Lucy would ever have. She'd never been more eager to lay eyes on anyone in her life.

Trevor was just now pulling his moving truck up to the curb, and behind the reflections on the windshield, she could see his familiar grin. Lucy's heart crowded into her throat. It had been so long.

Coming to a halt on the grass between the sidewalk and curb, she reached out and knocked a welcoming tattoo on the hood of the truck and strained to get a better look at his familiar face.

"Hey, Sport-o!" His old nickname rolled as easily off her tongue as if she'd seen him only yesterday. "Park this bucket of bolts already. I want to get a good look at your ugly mug."

"Hang on to your hat, Squirt." His good-natured rejoinder reached her from the truck's cab, through the passenger window. "Boy, am I ever glad to see you. I can use some help carting my stuff inside."

Pretending to pout, Lucy moved to the passenger door and spoke to him through the window. "And here I thought you would be excited to see little old me because you missed me so much."

"Yeah," Trevor snorted as he yanked on the steering wheel and craned his neck to better see into the rearview mirrors. "Like I miss a bad case of poison oak."

"Oh, that's nice. Flattery like that will get you moved in real fast. I should probably remind you that I gave up being your slave the day you moved out to go to college. If you want help, you're going to have to ask real nice."

She tossed him a saucy grin. His mere presence filled her with a buoyancy that she hadn't felt in eons. Laughter bubbled into her throat as she watched him back up over the curb, then bounce back onto the street when he realized his error. Lucy had to admit, it couldn't be easy maneuvering that thing into place, especially since his car was hitched to the tail. Still, she couldn't resist ribbing him.

"Nice driving."

"Shut up." His face comically menacing, he shook his fist in her direction.

Lucy could hardly contain her joy. Trevor was home.

Even though the old mansion-turned-duplex was located on Main Street—at the edge of the quaint and busy area that comprised downtown McLaughlin—she had been lonely rattling around in the Victorian all by herself. Funny how hundreds of people could pass her stoop on their way to the delightful, historic shopping district only a few blocks away, and yet she could still feel so completely isolated.

Years ago, the house had been remodeled into two separate and very spacious apartments by her own—and Trevor's—parents. The Bacons and the Burnses had been best friends since long before Lucy or Trevor had been born and had maintained that friendship until death parted them. After Lucy's folks had passed away three years ago, she had inherited one-half of the duplex. The Bacons still owned the other half and lived there now.

However, Trevor's mom and dad were snowbirds, preferring to trade in the rather chilly winters of McLaughlin, Vermont, for the sunnier climes of Florida. So, with the exception of the brief summer months, Lucy lived alone in the old building. She missed Trevor's parents terribly when they were gone, for in the years since her parents had passed away, they'd taken her under their wing, serving as wise counselors and beloved family. She'd even taken to calling them Mom and Dad.

As Lucy stood watching, Trevor was at last satisfied that he'd parked to perfection, and cut the engine. She could see the top of his dark head as he climbed out of the cab and—with a slam of the door—strode around behind the truck bed's massive walls to inspect the hitch between the van and his car.

Her fists clenched and unclenched with impatience.

Because she and Trevor were less than twelve months apart in age, they had been best friends as children. Oh, they'd bickered and fought like average kids, but for the most part, they'd been inseparable. Trevor, being older, had been Lucy's staunch defender against the occasional bully, and she—kid sister fashion—had tagged along after him everywhere he went.

They shared secrets and adventures, built forts in the backyard, climbed trees, rode bikes, went swimming, kept each other company when they were sick, and hung out their bedroom windows late at night and whispered to each other.

That is, until Trevor went away to college in California. It was one of the saddest days in Lucy's life. She'd had no idea how much she'd depended on good old Trevor for company. But that was all a long time ago. She'd gone to college in Vermont and, while they'd managed to correspond, it simply wasn't the same as sharing the same roof.

After he'd graduated, Trevor had lived in an apartment in Montpelier, which wasn't really all that far away from McLaughlin. Nevertheless, Lucy rarely saw him anymore. Since he'd begun his career as an account executive for SystaServe Corporate Computer Systems, he was a man on the go. In fact, she couldn't remember the last time she'd laid eyes on him. Could it have been at a funeral service for one of her parents?

Through the grapevine, Lucy had been able to keep apprised of his comings and goings and sketchy love life, but now that his parents had taken to spending their winters in Florida, even that connection to Trevor was largely a thing of the past.

Until now.

Trevor rounded the back of his car, and his eyes lit with delight when he spied her. Arms open, he reached her in two giant steps and soon Lucy felt herself airborne, her body taking flight with her heart.

"Squirt!" He kissed her enthusiastically on the cheek.

Lucy wrapped her arms around his neck and hugged him hard.

"Sport-o!" Her gleeful squeals filled the air as she pounded him on the back. She buried her nose in his neck, then reared back and peered suspiciously at him, laughing all the while. "You don't stink as bad as you used to, buddy. What's the deal?"

Trevor's laugh was full-bodied as he let her down onto the sidewalk. "Neither do you, Squirt."

Heart pounding unnaturally, Lucy took a step back and looked up at him, registering surprise at the changes time had wrought. Gracious! He was really beginning to look like his dad.

Since she'd seen him last, his face had matured into that of a man. Now there were little smile crinkles gracing the corners of his dark brown eyes, and the dimple-like brackets at the sides of his mouth had deepened, giving his face more character and charm. The hands that held hers were large and warm, making her feel all the more frail and petite next to his impressive size.

Lucy dropped his hands and playfully slugged his arm to dispel this new and decidedly unnatural view of her old playmate. After all, this was good old Trevor. So he'd grown up a little. Big deal.

"Oww." Rubbing the spot on his arm where she'd nailed him, Trevor grinned. "You still trying to beat me up after all these years?"

"Yep." Her own grin mirrored his. "How long has it been anyway?"

"Too long, obviously. You've changed."

She narrowed her eyes. "What's that supposed to mean?"

Trevor laughed and raised an appreciative brow as he studied the changes he found in her. "Relax. I meant it in a nice way. C'mon, give me a hand unloading this thing, will you?" Without waiting for her reply, he moved to the back of the small moving van and rolled up the rear door.

She tagged along, her eyes widening at the mountain of boxes within. "Planning on staying awhile, are we?"

"Through the winter anyway." Trevor loaded her arms as he talked. "Mom and Dad are letting me stay rent free, if I play Mr. Fix-it around here. Since I'm saving up for a house, it's a win-win situation."

Lucy nodded. Sounded good to her. Her gaze strayed to the box of jumbled odds and ends he'd piled into her arms. "A lava lamp?" She rolled her eyes.

"Goes with my bean bag chair and my black light posters. It's a retro thing."

A wave of giddy laughter bubbled into her throat. "I see your taste is still as horrible as ever. You really haven't changed after all." She was relieved to find that at least he was the same on the inside.

"Nah. Still the same old boy next door."

His muscles bulged beneath his shirt as he lifted a heavier carton out of the van and into his arms. Lucy averted her gaze.

"C'mon. This stuff all goes into my old room."

With a mute nod, Lucy struggled after him, down the cobblestone walkway. Funny, she didn't remember his muscles being so big. Against her better judgment, she let her gaze wander over his rather impressive build as he carted his box into the house and up the stairs to his old room. What happened to the skinny kid who used to swing from the jungle gym in the backyard?

She shook her head. So he'd grown a little. So what? This was just goofy old Trevor, her best buddy from way back when.

"Here we go."

Trevor grappled with his old doorknob, then nudged open the door with the toe of his boot, and suddenly Lucy was transported back in time. From the model airplanes suspended in flight from the ceiling, to the sports trophies that lined his shelves, nothing had changed. The room even smelled the same. A little like his mother's laundry soap and air freshener, and a little like nails and snails and puppy dog tails. With the warm autumn sun streaming through the window, it was a dim memory come back to life.

"Just set that stuff down anywhere." Grunting, Trevor dropped his own box on the bed. He dusted off his hands and straightened to look around. "Mom refuses to clean out and pack up my room. I think she's in denial. Still can't believe that I'm twenty-four and not fourteen." His fond gaze wandered to hers. "It's good to be home. Really good."

Lucy swallowed. "It's good to have you home."

Her mouth went dry as an autumn leaf. The unusual way he was looking at her had her heart suddenly beating in fits and starts. Was there something stuck between her teeth? Slowly reaching up, she rubbed her front teeth with a fingertip, then smoothed her hair. No doubt she looked like the wreck of the Hesperus. But she'd never felt the need to tidy up for Trevor. At least not before now.

She was being ridiculous. He wasn't looking at her any differently than he ever had.

To redirect her thoughts, she dropped her box next to his on his bed. Then she held out her hand in the secret handshake position that the two of them had perfected in this very room a dozen years ago on Trevor's twelfth birthday.

A slow grin of recognition crossed his face, and Trevor's hand enveloped hers. They pumped twice, fluttered their fingers together, tapped elbows, performed a high-five, a low-five, and finally held each other by the forearm and slid their hands back together in a firm grip. For a moment, they stood, hands clasped, and regarded each other with smiling eyes.

And Lucy still couldn't get over the changes.

Blinking madly, she averted her gaze. Obviously, she'd been wandering alone in this big old monstrosity of a house for far too long. She needed to get out more often.

For pity's sake, if Trevor even suspected that she'd noticed his muscles or how handsome he'd become, he'd die laughing. Pulling her lower lip between her teeth, she nibbled it, deep in thought. She would have to keep uppermost in her mind that she and good old Trevor were just buddies. Practically family. She couldn't let these ludicrous thoughts keep flitting through her brain.

After all, what would his parents think, if she began to moon over their son? She couldn't jeopardize losing the love and affection of her last set of parents. Her only family. Not over something as juvenile as a crush.

For the rest of the afternoon, she and Trevor unloaded the moving van, their light, familiar teasing bringing the mood back to the normalcy of their youth. As they traipsed in and out of his parents' half of the house, Lucy would pause now and again, as poignant memories of her childhood with Trevor washed over her, bringing a lump to her throat and tears to the back of her eyes. They were happy tears though. It was just so wonderful to have family this near again.

Outside, the crisp, cloudless autumn day was typical for a Friday afternoon in September. The air was cool, so the sun that streamed down and beat upon their backs as they transported boxes was welcome in its warmth. Their plaid flannel jackets came off and lay in a heap on the lawn. In the woods on the hills behind the house, the leaves had changed, adorning the trees with a brilliant riot of color. Beneath their feet, more leaves crunched pleasantly, a melodic undertone to their banter. Now and again, a passerby would stop to chat and welcome Trevor back to the neighborhood.

Finally, after they'd unloaded the last of Trevor's worldly goods into his room, they flopped down on the porch steps to take a breather and share a pitcher of iced tea.

"Man, you have a lot of junk." Leaning back on her elbow, Lucy eyed him as he sat next to her.

"I beg your pardon." He feigned wounded feelings. "First of all, I'll have you know that I only invest in top quality material goods."

Lucy lolled her head to the side and shot him a skeptical look. "Oh, I'm sure that bean bag chair of yours is very valuable. Needs beans though. Looks like a giant pizza."

"If you think I have a lot of junk now, you should have seen all the stuff I got rid of last week in my yard sale." He buffed his nails on the cloth of his shirt as it stretched over the contours of his impressive chest. "I made some good money, selling that so-called junk."

"Well, I guess I can be thankful that I didn't have to cart any more of your quality goods. I'm pooped."

Trevor reached out and ruffled the curls that had escaped the clip at the crown of her head. "For a runt, you did pretty good. A regular Hercules."

"Gee, thanks. And, in case you haven't noticed, I'm not a runt anymore."

"I've noticed."

She ducked out from under his hand. The familiar touch threatened to bring back twinges of the ludicrous crush she was trying to forestall. "Anyway, you owe me." She peered up at him. "How about you run to the store and pick up a couple of steaks while I fire up the barbecue? We can eat here on the porch."

Trevor lifted an interested brow and rubbed his stomach. "Sounds good. I have to turn in the moving van anyway. Can you give me an hour?"

"Perfect." That would give her plenty of time to shower, blow-dry her hair, put on a little makeup, and maybe change into something a little more…comfortable.

Lucy stifled a groan at her recalcitrant mind. There she went again, going all mushy and stupid just because the kid next door grew some impressive muscles and was more charming than any other single man in the greater McLaughlin area.

Sighing, she rose to her feet and waved good-bye to Trevor as he strode to the van. She needed to have her head examined.

Chapter Two

"More iced tea?"

"Sure." Trevor slid his glass over to Lucy. Comfortable and satisfied, he leaned back in his wicker chair and regarded her across the matching wicker table.

They'd just polished off a barbecued steak dinner on the old front porch, in the cozy little cove created by the corner turret. As they finished their meal, the shadows of twilight were beginning to chase the last of the sun's rays over the horizon. The days of autumn were shortening, and before long, winter would be upon them. Trevor was glad Lucy had wanted to eat their dinner on the porch. He loved it out here, and hoped to spend all the time he could in this very spot before the weather changed.

As Lucy squeezed lemons and spooned sugar into the pitcher of iced tea, Trevor had the opportunity to really study the changes in her that had so mysteriously taken place in his absence.

She was a woman now.

A pretty woman, to boot. Very pretty. To say that he'd been taken aback when he'd first laid eyes on her that afternoon was an understatement. The smattering of freckles across the bridge of her nose had faded, and her shoulder-length mass of curls had darkened from the flaming red of her youth into a chestnutty auburn that Trevor found eye-catching. He doubted that many of the other bachelors in the area had missed that terrific head of hair either. Or the amazingly translucent green of her eyes, for that matter. Such a piercing gaze. It was as if she could see right through him, into his very soul. Which was very disconcerting, considering the nature of his thoughts on and off all day long.

For some oddball reason, he was seeing Lucy in an entirely new light. A mature, and very…desirable light. This caught him off guard because, though there were glimmers of his childhood buddy, teasing and playful, this new womanly persona she projected kept interfering with his reception.

Not that he objected really. It's just that it was kind of messing with his mind.

Lucy as a woman.

Strange.

Lucy as an attractive, poised, well-educated woman, stranger still. Although why he should be surprised was a mystery. It was ridiculous to think that she wouldn't eventually grow up. He rubbed the muscles at the back of his neck and shrugged.

At any rate, it was great to spend time with her again. He'd forgotten how much he'd enjoyed her company. She was still just as spirited and ready to laugh as he'd remembered. It would be fun living next door to her all winter.

That is, if he could keep his brotherly view of her intact. He watched a little uncomfortably as she pulled her full lower lip between her teeth in concentration and, filling his glass, set it back down in front of him. Her smile was so compelling. It filled his belly with a warm glow.

Man, what was with him anyway? He'd have to keep reminding himself that Lucy still thought of herself as his kid sister.

That much had been obvious from the moment she had flown into his arms today. She'd probably haul off and slug him in the gut if he ever expressed any interest other than platonic. No. He couldn't go and get any ideas about asking her out on a date, or something nutty like that. Couldn't chance ruining a great friendship. Dating always messed up a good deal.

Inhaling deeply, Trevor held his breath for a moment, then heaved a regretful sigh. Too bad. She was a cutie. Ah, well. She made a great sister too.

"Full?" Lucy crumpled her napkin and, setting it on her plate, looked over the candles that lit the table and surrounding area.

Trevor patted his belly. "Umm. Yep. Thanks. It was really good. You're not a bad cook. That rice dish was great."

"Yeah, well, a box of this, a can of that, and a bag of the other and presto! Dinner."

"Well, you open a mean box of rice. And that Caesar salad was just right. What'd you put in there anyway?"

Lucy's gaze flitted to her hands. "Just added all the stuff that came in the bag."

"Oh. Those little crab appetizers?"

"Frozen section down at the MiniMart. I just followed the directions on heating them up." Her eyes lit with sheepish fun. "If it's not premade, or something I can toss on the grill, I'm pretty much sunk."

Trevor grinned. Same old carefree, undomesticated Lucy. "Well, everything was delicious. Thanks." Before he could stop to analyze his next question, it had escaped his mouth and hung in the air between them. "So, is there someone special that you…er, cook for out here on the porch on a regular basis?"

Lucy paused, her glass halfway to her lips, suspended between her fingertips. A tiny, philosophical smile tipped the corner of her mouth. "Not anymore. At least not since Freddy and I broke up."

"Freddy? Freddy Goldman? The kid in the third grade who used to constantly pick his nose?" Trevor hooted, then managed to look contrite.

Lucy narrowed her eyes and set her glass down with a thud. "He outgrew that."

"Good thing." Biting back a grin, Trevor picked up his own

glass and took a sip. "How is good old Freddy these days? I wouldn't recognize him without a finger up his nose, I'm afraid."

Lucy scowled the same petulant way she used to when she was peeved as a kid. "I wouldn't know. He moved away."

"Oh. Too bad. Any other prospects?"

"No. All the worthwhile single men from around here seemed to move on to bigger cities with bigger opportunities."

"Like Freddy?"

"Like Freddy, yes. Among others."

"So Freddy was a worthwhile guy, huh?" Trevor didn't know why he was pressing the issue. But for some odd reason, he wanted to know what this Freddy guy meant to her and if she might be nursing a broken heart. Not that he even knew why that mattered.

Must be that she still brought out that brotherly, protective streak.

Lucy shook her head in exasperation. "Freddy was a very worthwhile guy. He just wasn't my type."

"Why not?"

"We…" Lucy lifted and dropped a shoulder. "I don't know. We were dull together, I guess. It was time for both of us to move on." Her gaze shot to his. "As long as we're being nosy, what about you? Dating anyone special?"

Trevor shook his head. "Not anymore."

"Why not?"

"I don't know. I guess I travel too much to really form much of a history with anyone."

A devilish grin transformed her delicate features. "How is the life of a traveling salesman anyway?"

"Very funny." He returned her grin, in spite of himself. It felt good just to be spending time with Lucy. "And, to answer your question, good. I don't really have to travel all that much anymore, since they reassigned my territory last summer. Just a few days a month really. SystaServe is a good company, and the pay's not bad. I'm saving up for a house. That's why I moved back here for the winter."

"You mentioned that. Good for you. Need a loan?"

"Why? You offering?"

Lucy giggled. "Not in a million years. I have enough trouble just keeping my side of the house from falling apart. But interest rates at the bank are beginning to come down. I could get you some information."

"Thanks. That would be great. How goes the banking battle? Still like being a teller?"

Bristling slightly, Lucy straightened in her seat and, with a haughty tilt of her chin, regarded him. "I haven't been a teller for years now."

"Do tell."

"I'll have you know that I'm branch manager now. You're not the only one to have graduated from college, you know."

He bit back a smile. Still as feisty as ever too. "Congratulations on your promotion. How do you like being branch manager?"

"I love it." She relaxed and exhaled in contentment. "I think I enjoy it so much because the people who live around here are awfully nice. I get to keep up with everyone in McLaughlin. You know, who died, who had a baby, who got married, all the local comings and goings."

"You'll have to fill me in."

"Don't worry. Before the end of winter, you'll be back in the know." Gathering the stray auburn locks that were obstructing her view, Lucy tossed her curls over her shoulder and, leaning on her elbows, regarded him in the candlelight. "So where is this house you are going to be buying?"

"I don't know exactly. I'm not in any particular hurry. My folks have been trying to talk me into buying the old Miller house, up on the hill."

Her face lit, and Trevor, unable to help himself, stared, transfixed. "Oh, I love that place. I didn't know you were considering moving back to McLaughlin permanently."

He cleared his throat. He hadn't known either. Until just now.

"Uh, yeah. The old Miller place is an option, I guess. It's…unique. Kind of like this place." He forced himself to tear his gaze from her and look around the porch. "Although," he mused aloud, "the porch on the Miller place is nothing compared to this."

Lucy nodded. "But less work, I bet." Her glance swept the ornate bric-a-brac of a bygone era and she pointed at a space where a spindle was missing. "A lot of this is starting to fall apart."

"I know. It's on my to-do list."

"Good. I hope that list includes cleaning the gutters, painting some of the trim, and wrapping the pipes. Last year the pipes broke, and I got to see what it would look like if we had a pool in the basement."

"I bet it was cool."

"Oh yeah. Real cool. Real, real cool. And real, real expensive. Anyway, this year, I don't want it to happen again. Maybe you could move that to the top of your list."

"Who appointed you head slave driver?" Propping his chin in his hands, he cocked his head and grinned.

"Oh, now, Sport-o old buddy, don't go and get all bent out of shape. I'll help, I promise. Actually, I've become pretty adept at house maintenance in the last few years."

"Was the pool one of your projects?" He just couldn't resist teasing her. She was so cute when she was riled up.

"Funny boy. That was a fluke. We had a freak storm in the middle of the night. By the time I woke up, it was too late to build the ark. Anyway, I'm learning, slowly but surely. The truth of the matter is, I've had to handle a lot of the confusing maintenance stuff around here, since your folks have been heading south each year and my mom and dad passed away."

The melancholy look that passed over her gamine face tugged at his heartstrings. Lucy's parents were nearly as close to Trevor as his own, and their deaths had affected him more than he cared to admit. He was never any good about expressing his condolences. Come to think of it, he probably hadn't done much of a job of expressing his sympathy back at the funerals several years ago. But the massive lump in his throat had prevented him from approaching Lucy. Both times.

Luckily, on each occasion, Lucy had been surrounded by her multitude of friends and his own parents. His verbal contribution hadn't been all that necessary at the time. Still, he felt duty bound to say something to her now. Something that proved how much he cared. But what? He was rotten at this stuff.

"I…uh…" He touched his tongue to his lips and swallowed. "I was really sorry about your folks. Especially how it happened so close together and everything. They were like family to me. Like my own mom and dad." Absently, he scratched at his five o'clock shadow with his fingertips. He wished he could sound more empathetic or poetic or something. Instead, he just sounded nervous and tongue-tied and dreading to dredge up painful memories. "How are you doing?"

Lucy smiled, her face soft in the waning evening light. "Better now, thank you. Thanks in large part to your parents. They were really wonderful."

A stab of guilt shot through his gut. Tongue-tied or not, he should have been there for her, for more than just the afternoon of the funeral. Especially when her mother died. But he was just getting started with SystaServe, and he'd been on the road. Even so, that was no excuse.

"I miss them every day," she confessed.

"I can imagine."

"You know, after my dad died of cancer, I don't think it was the pneumonia that killed my mom that winter."

"No?"

"No. I think the real reason she died was a broken heart." Lucy's smile was poignant. "Mom and Dad had the kind of friendship that I think every married couple should have. Your folks do."

That made Trevor smile. "True. They are good friends to each other. All four of them were special in that regard."

Lucy hummed in agreement. "It's not everyone who can live side by side in harmony with another family—under the same roof yet—without even so much as a cross word." Nudging her plate to the side, she rested her elbows on the tabletop and smiled at him. "I love the story of how they decided to share the house. I can't remember who saw the house first, my folks or yours."

"I thought it was your parents, but we could always ask my mom. She'd remember."

"Didn't they both make an offer on the house at the same time? And then, when each couple discovered that their best friends wanted the house, they kept trying to bow out of the deal and let the other couple have it?"

"Something like that. Then, I think the realtor got so fed up with their gushy, 'you-take-it-no-you-take-it' arguing, he finally told them to cut the doggone thing in half and share it."

"And so they did."

"I'm glad." Trevor never meant those words more than he did at that moment.

"Me too."

For a long while, they sat smiling at their past and at each other. Somewhere off in the distance a cat yowled. A light breeze caused the flames on the candle tips to dance and flicker. The aroma of their still-smoking barbecue grill floated on the air, and about half a block down Main Street, the voice of a neighbor out for an early evening stroll grew close.

"No, Popeye! Bad dog. Not on the sidewalk!" A tired sigh floated through the shadows.

The commotion pulled Trevor and Lucy from their reminiscing. Feeling the need to put some distance between himself and the increasingly intriguing Lucy, Trevor stood and leaned over the porch rail. That voice was familiar. He peered beyond the candlelight and into the darkness.

"Conrad? Conrad Troutman, is that you?"

"Uh, yeah…" came the uncertain reply. "I was just going to pick it up, honest."

"Conrad, it's me! Trevor Bacon." Trevor felt a smile tug at his mouth. He and Conrad had taken swimming lessons together down at the public pool when they were kids.

"Trevor? Why, you old son of a gun!" Suddenly Conrad was unceremoniously dragged through the soft pool of light from the front porch and halfway up the steps by his giant mastiff, Popeye, and Popeye's giant wife, Olive Oyl. Seemed Conrad's dogs appreciated the smell of a still-smoldering barbecue. Unfazed by this uncoordinated maneuvering, Conrad plunged up the rest of the steps and came to rest in front of Trevor. He nodded at Lucy.

"Hey, Lucy."

"Hey, Conrad."

"So, Trevor Bacon! What in thunder are you doing here in McLaughlin? I thought your folks had headed south for the winter already."

Popeye, jowls drooling, greeted Trevor by propping his giant head on his lap and proceeding to drip body fluid on his knee. Not to be outdone, Olive Oyl followed suit, snorting and sniffing and licking Trevor's fingers in a most obnoxious manner. Droplets of saliva hung from his hands.

"They…uh…" Trevor stared at the slobber, and after some awkward deliberation, opted not to shake Conrad's extended hand. "…they have."

Conrad seemed to understand and handed Trevor his linen handkerchief. It didn't, however, occur to him to control his dogs' disgusting advances. Soon Trevor was being bathed in kisses while Popeye's owner looked on, wearing a benign smile.

Lucy tried to disguise her blossoming grin behind her hands until Popeye noticed her and, abandoning Trevor, proceeded to soak her with his greeting.

"Trevor, how long are you in town for?" Conrad settled into a spare chair, obviously having nowhere pressing to be at the moment.

"The winter. Mom and Dad are letting me stay here for free in exchange for some odd handyman-type jobs."

"Well now, isn't that great! You know, my place, the old Thompson place up the street a piece? Did you know I bought that? Well, anyway, my place is a lot like this one. A ton of work, I tell you. You know about fixin' up old houses, huh?"

"A little."

"You know, I've been thinkin' I need to build me a shed. Maybe you could answer a few questions for me…"

Lucy stood and waved behind her at the kitchen. "I'll just get us some coffee."

Conrad nodded in a distracted manner, not pausing for a moment in his monologue about his shed. With a shrug, she disappeared inside.

As Lucy prepared a tray for the freshly perked coffee, she listened to the constant drone of Conrad's voice and felt guilty for wishing he'd leave. Conrad had a reputation in town for his endless visits and nonstop talking. A tiny smile nudged the frown from Lucy's lips. Apparently Trevor had forgotten that about Conrad. Ah well, soon enough he'd be back in the swing of things. It was a small town, and folks didn't stay strangers for long.

A loud crash thundered from the porch, rattling the dishes in her kitchen. Outside, Conrad was hollering at Popeye for something or other, and Trevor was trying to control Olive Oyl.

Grabbing the coffee tray, Lucy went running to see what had happened. When she reached the porch, her jaw fell open, her shoulders sagged, and her eyes bugged.

The barbecue was lying on its side, and the still-glowing coals from dinner were burning numerous little black holes into the porch floor. The dogs circled the mess, sniffing and snorting through the wreckage, looking for any leftover tidbits of barbecue that were not too hot to gobble. Trevor and Conrad were scrambling to herd the burning coals back into the metal basin of the grill, but considering the teaspoons they were using as tools, the going was slow.

Lucy set the tray on the sideboard and, fetching some paper plates, joined the men in scooping and cleaning. Unfortunately, they'd no sooner rounded up all the coals than Popeye and Olive Oyl discovered the potted mums. As the dogs romped playfully among the plants, their leashes pulled the pots over and rolled them about, further scarring the old porch floor and leaving piles of dirt as they went.

The dogs were as delighted as Lucy was exasperated.

Trevor swept the excess dirt into a pile and then shoveled it and the mangled mums back into the pots that had survived.

"Don't worry about this," Trevor muttered to Lucy, motioning toward the damage to the floor. "I can fix it."

Lucy shot him a droll look. "I hope so. Your mother will have a cow."

After considerable effort and lots of shouting at the dogs, a modicum of order was achieved. Finally, Conrad—flush-faced and apologetic—had regained some control of his overgrown beasts.

"I'm…so sorry. It's just that they are so excited to be here." His breathing was labored as the dogs jerked him about. "We don't get invited to visit that much."

Lucy could see why.

Once the dogs were reclining and Conrad had taken his seat, she began to pour steaming mugs of coffee and pass them out. Unfortunately, the sweet moments of reacquaintance conversation between her and Trevor were over for the evening. The new shed Conrad wanted to build was uppermost in his mind, and picking Trevor's brain about construction materials and tools was all that seemed to interest him.

For the rest of the evening.

Maybe for the rest of her natural life.

Bored out of her gourd, Lucy sat slumped, concentrating on her coffee. After a few minutes of that, and afraid she was beginning to nod off, Lucy set her mug on the table and decided to call it an evening. Trevor could fend for himself. After all, it had been his idea to invite the oblivious Conrad and his mischievous mutts into the middle of a perfectly nice evening.

"I'm not sure if I want to pour a concrete foundation or just go with cement blocks. I suppose I could save myself a bunch of time if I just contracted it out, but I figure it would be a whole lot cheaper to do it myself. Concrete pad would probably be the way to go. Could put a nifty little dog run out there too." Conrad pursed his lips into a thoughtful line. "I could probably knock out the forms in about a week…Think I'd need a permit? Probably. Need a permit to blow your nose, these days—"

Trevor watched with envy as Lucy set about clearing off the coffee tray and slipped into her side of the house. He sighed a heavy sigh. The evening had lost a lot of luster when she left. Smiling weakly, Trevor turned his attention back to the talkative Conrad.

However, try as he might to concentrate on his old friend's conversation, Trevor's thoughts kept drifting back to the softly humming redhead who, after tidying up the kitchen, clicked off the lights and disappeared for the night.

From the open window overhead, Trevor could swear he heard her muffled giggling.

He owed her one, he decided, doing his best to tune back into Conrad's musings over a metal versus a shingled roof for his shed. It was going to be a long night.

Nevertheless, Trevor sighed with contentment.

It was good to be home.

Chapter Three

The sounds of hammering and construction work filtered into Lucy's groggy consciousness from somewhere beneath her bedroom window. The autumn sun's first morning rays streamed through her gauzy curtains, bathing her in warmth and gently prodding her awake. Lazily, she stretched beneath her patchwork comforter and, blinking the sleep from her eyes, tried to remember why today felt different.

A high-pitched whine—sounding suspiciously like a power saw—interfered with her thoughts. She glanced at the clock on her nightstand and groaned. What kind of a nut would be up at this hour on a Saturday morning? Again, the whine, followed by some thuds and then some muffled muttering had her suddenly sitting straight up in bed and smiling.

Trevor was home.

And, if she didn't get downstairs soon, she had to wonder how long their home would be standing. Throwing back the covers, Lucy bounded out of bed with an eagerness to face Saturday chores that she hadn't felt in ages.

After a quick shower, she slid into a pair of jeans, pulled her unruly mop into a ponytail, and brushed her teeth. As she stared at her reflection, she decided to apply just a hint of makeup. Not for Trevor's sake, of course. Viewing her as the pesky kid sister the way he did, he probably wouldn't notice one way or another. However, she would be out on the front porch giving him a hand. People were always passing her place on their way to the multitude of charming shops just a few blocks down the street. It wouldn't do to look like a slob.

Once she'd rationalized this uncustomary Saturday morning makeup routine, she finished getting ready and headed to the kitchen for a cup of coffee.

Carrying two freshly brewed cups of steaming java, Lucy emerged onto the sunlit porch to find Trevor hard at work. He was wearing jeans and a faded T-shirt that clung to his torso like morning glory to an arbor. He wore a tool belt slung low around his hips, and from where she stood, he looked like a million bucks. Who'd have thought that the skinny Sport-o next door would have grown up to be such a capable man?

There was a brand-new gaping hole in the porch floor, and Lucy could only pray that he knew how to put it back together again. She leaned against the jamb of her front door and took a sip of coffee before she spoke.

"You always up and working hard this early on a weekend morning?"

Trevor glanced up from the board he was measuring and grinned. "Yep." He gestured to the extra cup of coffee she held. "That for me?"

"Mm-hmm." Maneuvering around the hole, she handed off the cup. "What happened here?"

"Dry rot. Tons of it. I'm surprised no one has fallen through yet." He took a sip of the coffee and grinned. "Although, to look on the bright side, you can't see where Conrad's dogs messed up the paint anymore."

"Wow." Her gaze swept the entire porch. "Think we have to tear the whole floor up out here?"

"I don't know. So far it seems to be concentrated over here on this side. Must have a leak up there." He squinted at the porch ceiling directly above and pointed out a water stain.

"We do. I haven't worried about it, because it was outside."

"Yeah, well, I'll get to it pretty soon. We don't want the same thing happening to the new floor."

Lucy nodded. "What can I do to help?"

"Know how to read a tape measure?"

Rolling her eyes, Lucy stepped forward and grabbed the tape from his hand. "I think I can handle it."

"How about using a saw?"

"I told you I was doing the maintenance around here before you arrived."

"Hammer?"

She pursed her lips. "Keep it up and I'll show you on that hard head of yours."

Trevor stroked his chin with a fingertip for a moment, as if deliberating over his vast array of prospective helpers, then nodded. "You're hired." There was a twinkle in his brown eyes.

"Gee, thanks."

"You're welcome. You can start your duties by pulling some of those new boards Dad bought for this project out of the garage and bringing them up here. Then"—he handed her a scrap of paper with a list of measurements—"I need you to measure 'em, cut 'em and bring 'em to me."

Planting her free hand on her hip, Lucy smiled sardonically. "And just what are you going to be doing?"

"Watching."

A lazy grin deepened the creases in his cheeks, and Lucy found herself flushing. He wasn't flirting with her. She knew that. But she couldn't help wishing he was. Just a little bit.

For the next five hours, they worked side by side, pulling up rotten floorboards and cutting new ones to take their places. The conversation was a hodgepodge of topics, everything from what needed to be done around the house over the next six months to what they'd been doing over the last six years.

More than once, Lucy had to set down her tools and lean against the porch posts, doubled over with laughter. Nobody could make her laugh like Trevor. It had been that way when they were kids, and nothing had changed. He had hilarious tales of college life, and some of his stories about his various clients were priceless. The more they talked, the more Lucy knew, deep in her soul, that she was treading on thin ice.

Everything about Trevor suited her to a T. Their shared history, their work ethic, their sense of humor, their common interests, their love of old buildings, their love of God and family, and, most frightening of all, their basic love of each other.

With a sigh, Lucy realized that she was going to have to do some serious praying about this situation. Loving thy neighbor was one thing. Being in love with him was quite another altogether. When they weren't chatting, Lucy prayed silently for wisdom and strength. But mostly, she pleaded for sanity.

Lord, she murmured under her breath, as she sawed a pile of boards to length, *please don't let me make a fool of myself over this man. Please help me to remember that you have given him to me as a brother. A member of my dwindling family. Please, Lord, help me not to blow it. Amen.*

Feeling a little more confident, Lucy dragged the boards over to Trevor and, just to prove that she was feeling very sisterlike, playfully whapped him in the arm, marveling at the steel-belted radials that passed for his biceps. Then she felt like an idiot for being so childish. For pity's sake, what twenty-three-year-old woman punched men in the arm? This new version of Trevor was really beginning to play havoc with her maturity level.

Determined, Lucy squared her shoulders and went back to work, vowing to remain sophisticated and poised if it killed her.

Finally, much to her relief, the noon whistle sounded down at the fire station.

"I'm pooped." She set down her hammer and rubbed her wrist. "How about we take a break and I make us some sandwiches for lunch?"

Absently, Trevor glanced up at her from where he lay hanging over the edge of the hole they'd created in the porch floor, perusing the underbelly for more rot. "Already?" His eyes focused on his watch. "Wow. Noon. Yeah, a sandwich sounds great. I can eat while I work."

Lucy gave her head a vehement shake. "Oh no. We're going to sit down like civilized people and have lunch. We can eat out here, but I'm not eating with one hand and hammering with the other."

That rakish grin she was beginning to fear came out of hiding once more. She fought the urge to leap up and slug him in the arm, just to prove how his charm only made her feel that much more sisterly. Clasping her hands behind her back, she gritted her teeth and chanted silently to herself. *Poise. Sophistication. Poise. Sophistication.*

Trevor stood, unfolding his lanky body to its full height, and cocked a playful brow. "My, aren't we the bossy one?" He hooked his thumbs through his belt loops, rocked back on his heels, and regarded her with amusement.

A slow flush crawled from her neck and came to rest in her cheeks. "I'll be back in a few minutes."

Thick roast-beef sandwiches and piles of potato chips rested on the paper plates that Lucy ferried from her kitchen to the wicker table on the porch. A pitcher of lemonade, a bowl of fruit, and a basket of cookies were already waiting there.

All morning long, a parade of local folk strolling or driving toward town had passed by out front—former teachers, folks from church, neighbors, and friends from school. Many of these people had called greetings to the pair, wondering what they were up to. Now and then, an old schoolmate would stop to chitchat with Trevor and welcome him home.

While Lucy poured the lemonade into glasses, the distinctive voice of her old school chum DeeDee Waterman grew steadily louder as she drove down Main Street and called a greeting to one of Lucy's neighbors. The noises of Trevor's construction must have caught her attention, because DeeDee applied the brakes and, pausing in a patch of sunlight, peered up into the shadows of the porch.

"Trevor? Iss that you?" DeeDee had a noticeable gap between her front teeth that caused her to whistle when she spoke. Her braying giggle reached the porch long before she did.

Head snapping to attention, Trevor looked around until he spotted DeeDee whipping her car into a spot at the curb.

"DeeDee? DeeDee Waterman?"

"Yess!" DeeDee squealed, then dissolved into a fit of giggles.

"Well, what do you know! Come here and give me a hug."

Self-conscious nervousness evident in her giggle, DeeDee got out of her car. She came up the stairs and over to the edge of the hole in the porch, where she made an awkward attempt at returning Trevor's bear hug.

"Why, DeeDee Waterman, you've sure gone and grown up." Holding her at arm's length, he looked her up and down and whistled in appreciation. "It is still Waterman, isn't it?"

"Yess." DeeDee's teeth were bared, and her unrestrained laughter brought to Lucy's mind the image of a horse suffering a fatal asthma attack.

Trevor didn't seem to notice. "How can that be? I'd have

thought you'd be married to some lucky guy and have several cute little kids trailing behind you by now."

"Oh, Trevor. You're still such a silly goose!"

"Yep. That's me, all right." With a rakish grin, Trevor draped a casual arm around DeeDee's shoulders and steered her around the hole and toward a safer area on the porch.

The gesture, though hardly intimate, had Lucy suddenly suffering an unwanted, and quite searing, pang of jealousy. Disgusted with herself, she watched the two old schoolmates make light conversation and tried to figure out why she was having such an idiotic reaction to their mild flirtation. It wasn't as if it had anything to do with her.

In her head, Lucy knew that she had nothing to fear. Trevor cared for her and always would, brother to sister. If he wanted to flirt with DeeDee and give her big old obnoxious bear hugs and say all kinds of sloppy, gushy things about how super it was to see DeeDee, then by all means, he should be able to do just that.

Lucy squinted at them, her jaw clenched as tight as the clamp Trevor used to glue boards together. So if all of this was so fine with her, then why was she fighting the insane urge to push the heehawing DeeDee into the hole in the floor?

Suddenly contrite, she gazed at the cloudless blue sky and felt the conviction about her uncharitable thoughts deep in her soul.

I'm sorry, Lord, she repented silently in her heart. *Please forgive me.*

Knowing she must take the high road, Lucy poured DeeDee a glass of lemonade and moved to stand beside Trevor.

DeeDee was clinging to Trevor's bulging bicep. "I just can't believe that you're back! What brings you to McLaughlin? Are you here to stay?"

"For the winter, yes—"

Lucy interrupted by handing DeeDee the lemonade and was satisfied to see that she had to release Trevor's arm in order to accept the glass. "DeeDee, why don't you join us for lunch? We were just

sitting down to eat, and I know you and Trevor have a lot of"—
she swallowed—"catching up to do."

"Seriously?"

DeeDee was delighted.

"Seriously."

Trevor frowned at his watch.

"Oh, Trevor, relax," Lucy admonished, proud of how poised
and sophisticated she sounded. "You've worked hard all morning.
A little socializing won't kill you."

He lifted and dropped a shoulder in mute resignation.

Lucy beamed at DeeDee and gestured to the table, offering her
seat to their guest. Then she moved into the kitchen to make herself another sandwich. From the porch, she could hear DeeDee's
enthusiastic whistles and Trevor's rumbling replies. They were
having a grand old time. Which was as it should be. DeeDee was
single. Young. Attractive. A good catch—if you liked her type.

As obviously Trevor did. His amused laughter had rung out
more than once since they'd sat down at the table.

"Trevor and DeeDee. DeeDee and Trevor." As she peeked at
them from behind the kitchen curtains, Lucy tested the whispered
phrase on her tongue much the way a wine connoisseur sampled
wine. Though it was not to her liking, she resisted the urge to spit.

Feeling despondent, Lucy slapped her roast-beef sandwich on
a paper plate and slogged toward the door. That did it. She was
going to have to get over this little infatuation she had with Trevor.
But how? With a heartfelt sigh, she pondered this quandary as she
moved to join Trevor and DeeDee at the table.

"Oh, Trevor!" DeeDee's honking laughter shot up the scales.
"You are still such a tease!"

Trevor's grin had DeeDee shivering with delight, and it was
then that Lucy knew. For her to successfully refocus her less-than-
sisterly thoughts toward Trevor, he would need to find a girlfriend.
Stunned at her brilliance, Lucy plopped into the chair next to

DeeDee and considered the light bulb that had just flashed on. Yes! That was it!

If he was no longer eligible, she would easily be able to stop thinking of him in any light other than brother. Sibling. Family member. Best buddy.

Mm-hmm. Yessiree. Trevor needed a girlfriend.

The wheels began to turn in Lucy's fertile mind. He would need to begin dating. Right away. The sooner the better. Her gaze strayed to the woman seated right here on her front porch— whistling and snorting with laughter—and Lucy decided that DeeDee Waterman was most likely the answer to her prayer. DeeDee was a lovely—if one could overlook the whistle and the unbridled laughter—single Christian girl. She would be a perfect place to start.

Perhaps now that he was back in town, he and DeeDee would find the time to get reacquainted. To date.

Lucy stared as a red-faced DeeDee wheezed and whistled into her napkin.

Okay. Trevor and DeeDee. The very thought was like chewing tinfoil, but they seemed to be getting on like gangbusters.

Lucy was determined. Soon, she would figure out a way to get them together.

And to get on with her own life.

Chapter Four

Trevor rubbed at his throbbing temples with his thumbs and struggled to continue smiling. DeeDee's piercing whistle had gone from a charming affectation to a lethal weapon during the course of their noon meal. With every sibilant sound that escaped the gap in her teeth, the pain grew sharper.

Wincing, he glanced at Lucy. She didn't seem to notice the irritating sound in the least. In fact, she encouraged DeeDee to continue regaling them endlessly with tidbits about her life as a single in McLaughlin. He glanced at his watch, then squeezed his eyes shut and sent up a quick prayer for deliverance.

Luckily, the answer to his prayer arrived without delay, for not a minute had passed before his salvation arrived in the form of one husky Don Sandler, former high-school-football teammate.

Trevor gave his head a slight shake. It was amazing how many of his and Lucy's old classmates still lived in the area. Didn't anyone ever move away from McLaughlin? From the enthusiastic reaction he was getting from everyone who passed the porch, it seemed he was the only prodigal son in these parts.

"Trevor?" Don's questioning baritone rose above DeeDee's dental-drill laughter.

Before Trevor could respond, Don was bounding up the stairs

to investigate. Don was a good guy. Not the sharpest knife in the drawer, but just about as nice as they come. Back in high school, he was affectionately known as Don "the Dunderhead" Sandler, but he never seemed to take offense. Probably because he could have torn the head off any kid in school, had he put his mind to it. Don was as burly as he was dim, but boy howdy, the guy could play football.

"Trevor! It *is* you!"

"Sure is, buddy!" Trevor grinned at the former defensive tackle. Don always had a knack for stating the obvious.

"You're back!"

"Sure am!"

Beaming, Don glanced around. "Hi, DeeDee."

"Hi, Don."

His gaze strayed to Lucy and lingered, a touch of longing tipping the corners of his smile. "Hi, Lucy."

"Hello, Don."

Noting the sparkle in Lucy's eye, Trevor glanced back and forth between the two, and for a split second wondered if there was something budding between them there. Nah. He gave his head a tiny shake. He was simply imagining things. A guy like Don would never appeal to a sharp cookie like Lucy.

"Why don't you join us, buddy?" Trevor motioned to the unoccupied wicker chair and shot him a hopeful glance. He figured Don would have to do some of the talking, which would give his ears a much-needed rest from DeeDee's shrill harangue.

"Oh, I can't stay. I gotta get into town and pick up my truck from the auto body shop. I was in a little accident last week. I was just passing by and thought I'd stop and say hi." Again, Don favored Lucy with a bashful smile.

"Oh, c'mon. Stay awhile." *Please.* After shaking Don's hand, Trevor nudged him into the empty seat. "Take a load off, buddy."

"Well, okay, for a minute, I guess." The old wicker chair

creaked and groaned and sagged alarmingly beneath Don's fearsome bulk.

As Trevor made small talk with their guests, Lucy slipped into the kitchen and grabbed an empty glass for Don.

Upon arriving back at the porch, Lucy handed the glass to Don and then held up the pitcher. "Lemonade?"

Entranced, Don nodded mutely and, unable to tear his eyes from Lucy's face, smashed his glass into the rim of the waiting pitcher. Shards of glass rained down on his hand and arm and the tabletop.

For once, DeeDee looked on in silence.

"Oh, man!" Startled, Don stared at his hand. Pinpricks of blood dotted his skin and began to run. "I'm such an idiot! I'm so sorry!" Mortified, he abruptly stood, tipping the table and causing an avalanche of glassware and silver to topple and begin rolling to the edge.

"Hey, buddy! Better have a seat," Trevor shouted, making a grab for the table before it turned over. Not comprehending, Don flailed about, struggling to extricate his legs and feet from beneath his chair. His attempts to stand only further upset the table.

"Don! Buddy! Better sit down! We're losin' her." With a valiant effort, Trevor and DeeDee juggled rolling dishes and silver, saving all but a few unlucky pieces of glassware.

As docilely as a puppy, Don dropped into his seat, his face flushed crimson with his humiliation. Unfortunately, the sudden stress was more than the old wicker could take. With a snap, the chair gave way, and the former McLaughlin High School football star found himself seated on the floor amid a pile of toothpicks that had once been a chair.

"Aw, man." Don's plaintive groan came from where he rolled, somewhere under the table.

Concern etched on her delicate brow, Lucy flew to Don's side and knelt to inspect the damage. "Trevor! Quick! Run into my laundry room and find the first-aid kit. It's in the cupboard over the washer."

"Okay."

On his way into Lucy's place, Trevor looked over his shoulder to see Lucy helping poor old Don to his feet. A scrap of wicker clung to his hair, and blood was now dripping from his hand. His shell-shocked apologies were soothed by Lucy's sweet and understanding murmurings.

"Don't worry, Don. That chair was really old. No harm done. Really, I'm much more worried about you than some rotten old chair. Let me see your hand."

She tsked and sighed and—cradling his meaty fist in her graceful hands—peered into the cuts. As Trevor bounded into the laundry room in search of the first aid kit, he could hear the sound of their voices. There was something vaguely irritating about the intimate quality he heard in Lucy's tone. She was being so sweet his fillings began to throb.

For crying out loud, if *he'd* been the proverbial bull in the china shop, she'd have slugged him in the arm and handed him the broom. Trevor opened and closed several cupboard doors before he spotted the first-aid kit. He seriously doubted that she'd have used that gooey tone of voice and inspected his wounds with such tender care. Feeling grumpy for some odd reason, he grabbed the kit and strode back to the porch.

Reaching the turret area, he froze and stared.

Don was now sitting in one of the three remaining chairs, gazing all dopey-eyed at Lucy while she dabbed at his cuts with a napkin.

"Gee, I feel like such an idiot."

"Don, hon, it was an accident. Could have happened to anyone."

Don, hon. Yeesh. Trevor closed his eyes so no one could see him roll them at the water-stained ceiling.

"Here you go." Three strides brought him near, and he held out the medical kit to Lucy.

"Thanks." Without giving him a second glance, she grabbed the kit and began to sort through it. "We'll have you all fixed up in no time."

The solicitous note in her voice and the positively smitten look on Don's face sent the pain that had been in Trevor's head to his stomach. Disgruntled, he moved over to the porch's decorative railing and, crossing his arms over his chest, perched on the balustrade directly behind DeeDee.

DeeDee giggled and smiled up at him. Trevor knew his answering smile was strained, but he couldn't seem to help himself. For some reason, with every sympathetic cluck that came from Lucy's lips, the pain in his gut churned and began to turn to nausea.

Man. Trevor rubbed savagely at the tightly strung muscles in the back of his neck. Why did he care who Lucy fawned over? He wasn't jealous, for Pete's sake. Trevor didn't have a jealous bone in his body. Never had.

Until now.

Was he...*jealous?*

Trevor couldn't believe it.

He *was!* The emotion was so foreign to him. And to be jealous over a kid who was for all intents and purposes his sister? Well, that was just downright weird.

Ah, for pity's sake. Who was he kidding? Lucy wasn't his sister. She was a grown woman, and he was beginning to develop some kind of feelings where she was concerned. Well, that would have to stop. Immediately.

"So," Lucy's soothing murmur continued as she cleansed and wrapped Don's multiple wounds, "tell me about this accident you had. Weren't you on your way to pick up your truck from the auto body shop?"

Don nodded. "Right. It was just a stupid little accident really. I was in my driveway and thought I was in reverse, when I was actually in drive." An embarrassed grimace seized his pliant face, twisting it into a wad of remorse. "The garage door will never be the same..."

"Oh, Don. I'm so sorry."

As Don stared in a complete daze at Lucy, Trevor began to see the light. Yes, right then and there, he realized that he needed to get a handle on these possessive feelings he was developing toward Lucy and her love life. He could never let on that he felt even the tiniest twinge of jealousy. She would hate him for sure.

All morning, she'd treated him like her long-lost buddy, punching him in the arm and teasing him unmercifully. It was clear that she could never look at him as anything other than the boy next door. Yeah. He needed to avoid all unnecessary time alone with Lucy. But that would be impossible, what with them living right next door to each other and all.

Trevor lifted his throbbing head and stared blearily at Don and Lucy.

Maybe…maybe if Lucy was spoken for, he wouldn't have to fight this budding attraction. That was a decent idea. Lucy needed a boyfriend. As much as that idea depressed Trevor, he knew it was necessary. And as Providence would have it, one boyfriend in the works, complete with budding crush, was currently putty in Lucy's capable hands.

"Well, I should be on my way." Don, now fully doctored and ready for action, stood and pushed his chair back. "I'm really sorry about all the mess."

Lucy tsked. "Don't give it another thought, Don."

Yep. Don-hon and Lucy. They would make a decent couple, he guessed.

"You have to leave so soon?" Trevor leaped to his feet and chased Don to the stairs before he lost his nerve.

"Yeah, I gotta get to the auto body shop and pick up my truck. They close at two on Saturdays."

Trevor glanced at his watch. "Listen, buddy, I didn't get much of a chance to catch up with you just now. Say—why don't you come back tonight? Have dinner with me and Lucy?"

Don was clearly amazed by the offer. "But I…" He gestured helplessly at the pile of broken wicker and glass that still lay on the porch floor.

"Oh, never mind that." Trevor gave the mess a dismissive wave. "We have more chairs. Sturdy chairs. Right, Lucy?"

"Right." Lucy sprang to her feet. "Do join us, Don."

Trevor allowed his eyes to slide closed at her encouraging tone. Man, this was going to be tougher than he'd thought.

"And DeeDee," she enthused, "you're invited too."

Trevor winced. Much tougher.

"We'll make it a foursome. We can put a chicken on the grill and I'll make some salads and rolls and baked beans and corn on the cob. Seven o'clock. What do you say?" Lucy glanced expectantly from face to face.

DeeDee's abrasive laughter skittered in electric jolts up and down Trevor's spine. "I ssay great! I'll bring desssert."

Don's eyes lit at the mention of food. "I'm free. Besides, I'd like to bring you a new chair, to replace the one I broke."

Lucy looked at Trevor and clasped her hands in victory. "Then it's a date!"

"It's a date." Trevor's echo was weak. Smiling, he clutched his aching gut and tried to project an attitude of anticipation he was nowhere near feeling.

Chapter Five

Lucy let out a heartfelt sigh of relief and, as she relaxed in one of the comfortable wicker chairs on the front porch, pulled an afghan more closely about her shoulders. It was nearly midnight now, and the warm, sunny fall air of the afternoon had taken on a decided chill. Blessedly, the evening with DeeDee and Don had just concluded, and both guests were on their way home.

The little white twinkle lights she'd strung around the porch and over the bushes cast a pleasant glow into the inky night. A large, golden harvest moon now high in the sky added to this soft, romantic light, and Lucy loved the way it gave the porch a magical quality. Then again, it might not be the light, but the man seated in the chair next to her that was creating the feeling of magic.

Trevor, his feet resting on the porch's balustrade, seemed as exhausted as she was by the long day. He rolled his head lazily to the side, and Lucy could feel his gaze come to rest on her.

"Well," he began tentatively, probing his temples with his fingertips, "that was…nice."

"Mmm. Nice." About as nice as having her teeth cleaned with a pickax.

"I don't suppose you have an aspirin handy?" He squinted hopefully at her.

"Head hurt?"

"Killing me."

"Mine too." She tossed a listless wave at the buffet table, set up against the wall behind him. "Can you reach the first-aid kit? It's just over your shoulder there." She'd opted to keep it on hand just for Don, and she'd been glad she had. The man was a walking disaster.

"Uh, yeah. I can reach it." Trevor grunted, reached over his shoulder, and snagged the kit. He rummaged for a bottle of pain reliever and shook several into his palm. He swallowed them without water, then held the bottle out to her. "Want one?"

"Two. No, three."

"That bad?"

"Worse."

"I'm sorry."

She drew in a deep breath and, slowly letting it out, smiled at him. "You know, you really shouldn't take pills without something to drink. It'll turn your liver into Swiss cheese or your kidneys into Brillo pads or something."

"Yeah, I know." Tucking his chin into his chest, Trevor again reached over his shoulder and grabbed the water pitcher. Handing it to her, he chuckled. "I'd offer you a glass, but I think Don broke them all tonight."

"He did. Hence, my headache," Lucy moaned. She should have known better than to use crystal for a front-porch barbecue. Especially one that Don "the Dunderhead" Sandler was attending. She tossed her pills into her mouth, took a healthy slug of water from the pitcher, then passed it to Trevor. "Here. Do your kidneys a favor."

As he took several swallows of water, Lucy, fascinated, watched his Adam's apple bob up and down. When he was finished, he set the pitcher on the table behind him and flopped back in his chair with a groan.

"So," she wondered aloud, "what caused your headache?"

"You have to ask?"

"DeeDee?"

"I can't believe that all that whistling and chain-saw laughter doesn't get on your nerves."

Lucy laughed in spite of the throbbing in her head. Though she was disappointed that her attempt at matchmaking had failed, there was a recalcitrant corner of her heart that was rejoicing. Not because she had any claim on him, of course. It was just that she had to agree. DeeDee was all wrong for Trevor. She could see that now.

"You know, I'd never really considered DeeDee's whistle anything other than cute."

"You have got to be kidding." Slack-jawed, he stared at her.

"Well, not until tonight anyway. But then, I've never really spent that much time with her before now. I guess it's when she started to tell us about her 'college dayss,' when she 'sstudied ssociology,' that I began to get a little edgy."

"You mean to tell me that chalkboard-scraping laugh didn't have you out of your mind long before she got to her college days?"

"I guess I was too busy keeping Don from tearing down the rest of the porch to really notice." With a weak grin, Lucy tucked her foot up under her leg and wriggled in her chair to face Trevor. "I take it you won't want to be seeing DeeDee socially in the future."

A look of consternation crossed his brow. "Why would I want to do that? I saw plenty of her today. I now know enough about DeeDee to last a lifetime, thank you very much."

"Oh." Lucy pretended to study her nails. "Is it the voice?"

"Is what the voice?"

"Is it DeeDee's whistle and her laugh that keep you from wanting to date her?"

"Who said anything about *dating?* I just got back in town, for heaven's sake. Give me a break."

"Well, I just thought that you might want some, you know, companionship. Some friends. Now that you're back."

"Why would I want that, when I have you to slug me in the arm and call me names?"

Lucy rolled her eyes. It seemed she was back to the drawing board on getting Trevor fixed up with a woman. She pushed her hair out of her face and over her shoulder. That was okay. There were plenty of available women here in McLaughlin. Surely one of them would fit the bill. It was simply a matter of time.

A low chuckle rumbled from deep within Trevor's chest.

"What?" Lucy shot him a curious glance, his contagious laughter tugging at her lips.

"You know, I think we should keep that hole in the porch floor. It makes cleanup a snap, doesn't it?"

"Oh, I think your mother would just love that idea."

"We could tell her it's a built-in compost pile." He tossed a corncob into the hole to demonstrate his point. "We could tell her that we did it on purpose. It would sure make cleaning up after someone like Don a whole lot easier."

"Think she'd buy it?"

"She'd get used to the smell. Eventually." Trevor's laughter rumbled from deep in his chest. "I could build a decorative railing around the edge. For safety."

"You're nuts." Falling helplessly back against her chair, Lucy let the mirth flow. Oh, there was nothing better than laughing with Trevor. Never, in all her years of dating, had she ever met another man who could have her giggling the way he could. She wiped at her eyes with the edge of her afghan.

"I'm sorry," she groaned. "I know my laughing must be adding to your headache."

"Nah. I like your laugh. Always have."

Lucy sniffed. "You'd better. You're the one who is always making me laugh."

"You mean to tell me that you don't laugh when I'm not around?"

"Not half as much. I'll tell you that right now."

"Well, in that case, I'm glad I'm back."

"Me too."

In the dim light, they drank each other in with their eyes, allowing their gazes to rove over the other's face, unabashed. It was a bittersweet moment for Lucy. She wished with all her heart that this lovely moment was something she could count on for years to come, until one day, she and Trevor would trade in the wicker chairs for rockers and bounce their grandchildren on their knees. But that was not to be. Someday, Trevor would live up the hill in the old Miller house. Maybe not with DeeDee. But with somebody.

Somebody who wasn't herself.

Knowing her eyes must reflect the melancholy she was suddenly feeling, she diverted her gaze to the golden yellow glow of the harvest moon. It wouldn't do to let Trevor see her feeling all sorry for herself. He'd ask questions, and he was not one she could distract with diversionary tactics.

Luckily, he didn't seem to notice the change in her mood.

"Speaking of my mom, did I mention that my folks called?"

Lucy brightened. "They did? When?"

"When you were getting ready for dinner tonight."

"What did they have to say?" Lucy was always thirsty for news from Trevor's mom and dad. Talking with them was like talking with her own parents.

"Oh, they wondered if I'd settled in yet and how we were getting along."

"What did you tell them?"

"I said aside from the fact that you still liked to beat up on me, we were getting along just fine. I told them you not only made a good little Hercules, but that you were shaping up to be a pretty decent carpenter and that you swung a mean hammer. Sometimes at me."

"You did not." Lucy blushed.

"Did too." Trevor's grin faded. "I also mentioned the hole in the porch floor."

"What did they say?"

"Well, when Mom was done giving me an endless list of instructions, she handed the phone to Dad."

"Yikes. What did he say?"

"That he trusted us to put it back together correctly. I told him no sweat. And when we were done, we were going to go for a swim. In the basement."

"You did not."

A mischievous twinkle danced in his eye. "No, I didn't." Reaching out, he took her hand in his, and Lucy felt her pulse quicken. "They did say to give you a hug and a kiss for them. I told them that you might slug me if I did."

No. No, she wouldn't slug him if he did that. She couldn't be sure exactly what she would do, but she knew for sure that hitting him would be the last thing on her mind.

With deliberate slowness, Trevor brought her fingertips up to his lips and pressed them to the warm softness there. Her heart leaped into her throat and her mouth went dry as a tumbleweed.

"That's from Mom and Dad."

"Oh. Thanks." Funny, she had never felt that way when his mom and dad kissed her before. Must be the deliveryman.

He held her hand much longer than was strictly necessary, his gaze probing hers, a strange look on his face. Lucy wondered if his heart was pounding as hard as hers was right then. Probably not. Brothers usually didn't go all atwitter from giving their sisters a simple peck on the hand. But this was far from simple. At least to Lucy.

She cleared her throat and looked at their hands as they lay clasped together. Any minute now, she was going to make a complete fool of herself by admitting to him how she was feeling. Time to get out of there.

"It's late." She hated the abruptness of her words, but couldn't for the life of her think of a graceful way to get out of this situation.

"Yeah." He nodded in agreement.

"It's been a long day."

Trevor yawned. "We should probably clean up this mess." He shot a pointed look at the pile of glass under Don's chair. "Wouldn't take but a minute to sweep it into the hole…"

"No." She stared at their hands, their fingers still intertwined. "No, I vote we wait until tomorrow. The food is all put away. The only thing we have to do is turn out the lights."

An enigmatic look flitted through Trevor's eyes, passing as quickly as it had come. With a brotherly squeeze of her fingers, he extracted his hand from hers and stood.

"I'll turn out the lights. You go."

Lucy looked up at him from where she sat snuggled in her afghan. "In a minute. I just want to sit here for a moment longer. I'll catch the lights."

"You sure?"

"Mm-hmm."

"Okay then. Good night."

"'Night."

For many minutes after Trevor had turned in, Lucy sat alone on the old porch and contemplated their complex relationship. It was beyond her ability to reckon with, and she knew that earnest prayer would be her only solution.

"Dear Lord." She murmured these words into her clenched fists. *"Please, oh please, help me get this nutty, romantic idea of Trevor out of my mind. A crush is counterproductive, Lord. He is the only brother-type person I can count on in my life. Please help me not to mess up a good thing. Thank you for listening, Lord. Amen."*

With a heavy sigh, Lucy opened her eyes. She'd hoped for an immediate sense of peace and well-being to flood her soul, but she was still just as confused as she'd been before bowing her head. She knew the Lord would answer her prayer in his own way, in his own time. But that was frustrating. She was impatient to get this over with. A feeling of hopelessness washed over her. Was it always to be this way between her and Trevor? She didn't think she could stand that.

Dispirited, Lucy gathered her afghan into her arms and moved around the porch, switching off the twinkle lights and blowing out the candles on the table. With the exception of the last hour spent alone with Trevor, the evening had been a flop. She was no closer to getting Trevor hitched up with some nice girl than she had been before this fiasco of a dinner party.

Oh well. As she moved into the dark interior of her half of the old Victorian, she lifted a resigned shoulder. Tomorrow was another day. One of these times, she would find Trevor his dream woman. Until then, she could only hope that her prayers for her renegade heart would be answered. Sooner rather than later.

Chapter Six

The lazy days of fall passed in a crisp, sunny, and blissful blur. Trevor and Lucy continued to work on the front porch in their spare time, finishing up the brand-new floor and then tackling the railing and overhead decoration to replace rotted spindles and spokes and other ornate bric-a-brac. Lucy would paint while Trevor sanded and puttied.

Before the first week of Trevor's return was up, they were both in the habit of eating together—on the old porch if it was warm enough, in Lucy's kitchen if it wasn't. Though the evening light was waning sooner as the end of daylight-saving time approached, they were able to accomplish a lot in the time they had: small tasks for the evenings after work, larger tasks on Saturday. Sundays were always reserved for church and, in the afternoon, some type of relaxation. Shopping, sightseeing, seasonal festivals, and simple games of cards on the porch were some of the activities they enjoyed together.

Lucy knew that she'd been remiss, lately, in her search to find Trevor a date. The more time she spent in his wonderful company, the more this problem weighed on her mind. After more than two weeks had passed, Lucy was spending the greater part of each day struggling to maintain status quo. Struggling to convince herself, and everyone else, that she thought of her handsome duplex partner as nothing more than a buddy. In a depressed fog, she knew she had to make a move to find Trevor's dream woman.

Because it was becoming increasingly clear, in the privacy of her own heart, that she was falling in love.

"Oh, hey there, Bess! Hi! How are you doing?" Lucy hung over the porch railing the following Saturday morning and waved at her friend Bess Clemmons. "Here I am! Up here on the porch, hon. Come on over here for a second. I have someone I want you to meet."

From the ladder on which he stood reattaching a loose section of gutter, Trevor sagged and slung his hammer into its loop in his tool belt. Too late to escape. Lucy had caught him off guard—again. Good grief. For the last several days, Lucy had done nothing but call the attention of the female population of McLaughlin to the fact that he was single and looking for a soul mate.

It was embarrassing, to say the least.

He was stymied by Lucy's suddenly energetic crusade to find companionship for him. He simply couldn't understand her fervor. Hadn't the fiasco with DeeDee taught her anything? It wasn't, after all, as if he came home from work every night and moped around and complained about being lonely. Quite the opposite actually. Between his work at SystaServe, the fix-it jobs on the house, and Lucy's rousing company, he hadn't had five free seconds to feel the least bit alone or sorry for himself. The constant parade of neighbors who stopped to chat could keep him from feeling lonely for the rest of his natural life.

From his perch atop the ladder, Trevor watched this next young woman approach.

Ducking her head as if she wished the ground would swallow her whole, Bess lifted her fingers in a tiny wave and trudged stoop-shouldered toward the wildly waving Lucy.

"Bess! I'm so glad you happened by! I've been wanting to introduce you to my neighbor, Trevor, for weeks now! Trevor?" Hands looped around the porch pillar, Lucy leaned back over the railing and craned her neck toward the ladder. "Trevor? You up there?"

Busted.

"Yeah. I'm here."

"Well, come on down here for a second, will ya? I have someone I want you to meet."

Trevor emitted a deep sigh. "Just a sec." Maybe if he fiddled around up here on the roof long enough, Bess would grow impatient and move on. From where he stood, he could hear the murmur of conversation. He cocked his head to listen better. No, that was no conversation. That was a monologue. Bess would occasionally interject a syllable, but for the most part she was silent. A blessed relief compared to DeeDee, Trevor had to admit.

"Trevor!"

Lucy was growing impatient.

"Coming."

Might as well climb down and get it over with. The sooner Bess was on her way, the sooner he could get the gutter fixed. He glanced at the sky. Weather report predicted the rains to begin by the first of the week. And by the look of the clouds beginning to gather, Trevor believed it.

"Here he is." Lucy practically dragged Trevor off the ladder in her enthusiasm.

"Don't knock me over, woman." As he came even with the railing, Trevor stepped onto the balustrade and leaped onto the porch floor. Removing his leather gloves, he tucked them into his back pocket and extended a hand to Bess. "Hi. I'm Lucy's neighbor, Trevor."

"Hi."

Bess extended a cool, clammy hand and gave his fingers a limp shake. Trevor had to fight the urge to wipe his hand on his pants. He'd never liked a mushy handshake. In his opinion, one could tell a lot about a person's character by the way he or she shook hands. Darting a quick glance at Lucy, he recalled shaking hands with her in their secret, age-old ritual and knew that he much preferred a strong, firm handshake in a woman. The way Lucy shook hands.

"Bess and I work together, down at the bank," Lucy explained, nudging Trevor to stand just a little closer to her friend. "Don't we, Bess?"

"Yes." Bess nodded, her face flushing from the neck up, much like the mercury rising on a thermometer.

"Oh, we have lots of fun down at the bank, don't we, Bess?"

"Yes."

Trevor shrugged affably. "I can imagine."

"How long have we worked together now, Bess?" Lucy was probing, desperate to encourage Bess to speak. "Two years now? Or three?"

"Three."

"That long?" Trevor rocked back on his heels and studied Bess's flaming face. The poor thing looked about ready to faint.

"Yes."

"That's right." Lucy nodded. "You started at the same time Becky started."

"Right."

"Well, well, well, how about that," Lucy murmured.

As she cast her gaze about, Trevor could tell that Lucy was searching for a way to breathe life into this lead balloon of a conversation. When her eyes focused on the barbecue, Trevor had to stifle an inward groan. *No. No, not another barbecue party.*

Lucy reached out and grasped Bess by the arm. "Bess, I was just wondering if you were free for dinner tonight."

After a long pause, Bess answered, "Yes."

"You are? Great! Isn't that great, Trevor?"

"Great," Trevor repeated dully. Why was it great? It wasn't great at all. It was irritating as all get-out. He didn't want to have dinner with the painfully shy Bess. He liked having dinner alone with

Lucy, just fine. The excruciatingly bashful Bess was not his cup of tea and never would be. He didn't have a clue how to act around timid people. Something about people who wouldn't talk made him blather on about things he would never dream of talking about otherwise. Rotating his tires, the five-year weather forecast, would Christmas fall on a weekend this year?

For the love of Mike, why was she doing this to him? Had he done something unforgivable to her when they were children? Because, for the life of him, he couldn't figure it out. He was a simple man. By now, she should know that. All Trevor wanted out of life these days was to spend his weekends working on the house and to have a quiet little dinner with Lucy. Beyond that, he simply wanted to be left alone.

The idea of having to pull a conversation out of Bess was exhausting. Nevertheless, Trevor smiled as Lucy unfolded her impromptu plans.

"Trevor and I were going to have the last barbecue of the season out here on the porch tonight, and we were looking for some company, weren't we, Trevor?"

"Oh yeah, sure we were."

"We are delighted that you can join us. Is six-thirty okay?"

"Yes."

"Great! We'll see you then."

"Bye." Bess, her face still burning like a house on fire, turned and stumbled down the stairs as if the hounds of hell were nipping at her heels.

The minute she opened her mouth to invite Bess over for dinner, Lucy knew it was a mistake. A terrible, horrible mistake that she couldn't take back. At seven that evening, from her vantage point in the kitchen, she peered through the window to the porch and watched Trevor struggle to yank a little conversation out of the terminally shy Bess. Right now, he'd pretty much exhausted the subject of tire rotation and was moving on to the projected five-year weather forecast he'd found in the *Farmer's Almanac*.

Leaning against the counter, Lucy sagged and bowed her head. *Oh, Lord, I know I bumbled into this without asking for your wise counsel or for your blessing.* With one eye, Lucy darted a quick peek to the porch. Trevor was already winding down on the weather issue and was moving toward wondering if Christmas would fall on a weekend this year. *I'm so very sorry, Lord. I don't know what to do. I thought Bess might make a nice match for Trevor. Am I wrong? Lord, if I'm wrong, please make that perfectly clear. And if they are meant to be, please help me to point that out to them both. Thank you, Lord, for listening and caring. Amen.*

Lucy's eyes fluttered open and she felt just a little better. She could only do so much to smooth the way for these two. The rest was up to God. Jaw set with determination, she wiped her hands on her apron. For now, anyway, she would simply make the best of a bad situation.

Grabbing two heaping platters of picnic-style fare, Lucy forced herself to hum a carefree little ditty as she swept out to the porch. At her arrival, Trevor's face flooded with relief. Lucy grimaced. That was not a good sign. He shouldn't be so dependent on her presence. Not that it didn't make her feel really good, but it was counterproductive.

Perhaps she simply needed to get the conversational ball rolling.

"Bess! Did you know that Trevor is an account executive for SystaServe Computers? Isn't that a coincidence?"

"Yes."

"It sure is. Why, Trevor, did you know that Bess is our computer expert down at the bank?"

"No, can't say that I did."

"Well, she is!" Bustling about, Lucy readied the table, checked on the chops that sizzled on the grill, and poured everyone a refill. "Isn't that interesting, you both knowing so much about computers and all! Well, I just bet you have a ton of stuff to talk about."

Bess shrugged.

Trevor grunted.

Okay, so that was a dead end. Lucy racked her brain for another topic as she dealt paper plates and napkins like so many playing cards. The sooner this evening was over, the sooner she could go throw herself out her bedroom window.

"Trevor! Did you know that Bess lives up on the hill next to the old Miller house now? You know, the old place your parents have been encouraging you to buy?"

Trevor glanced at Bess. "No. Can't say that I knew that."

"Well, it's true. Right, Bess?"

"Right."

"Yes, right next door. I bet Bess could really tell you all about the history of that old place!"

Eyes twinkling now, Trevor bit down on his lower lip. "I'll bet."

Lucy bristled. He was enjoying the torture she was putting herself through. No doubt he thought she deserved every miserable minute. Well, doggone it anyway. She was doing this for his own good.

"Bess! You should take Trevor up to your place sometime so he can see the old Miller place from your yard."

Bess went from pink to white. "Okay."

"That way, you could show him your computer too!" Lucy beamed at her flash of inspiration.

"Okay."

Lucy held up a forefinger and backed toward the kitchen. "Just need to get the salad out of the fridge, and we're ready to eat. You two visit. I'll be right back."

From the kitchen Lucy strained to hear above the roar of

silence. Nothing. They weren't talking. Not a word. Oh, this was not good. Tiptoeing to the curtains, she spied on them and her fists clenched in agony. Crumb. They weren't even looking at each other. This was worse than not good. This was horrible.

Doggedly, Lucy grabbed the salad, marched back out to the porch, and, chattering ninety miles an hour, proceeded to pile their plates with food. As dinner progressed, Lucy consistently tossed the conversational ball to Bess. Unfortunately, the blushing Bess sat like a lump, too fearful to lob it back over the net.

Lucy simply couldn't understand it. Though not the boldest of creatures, at the bank Bess could string together entire sentences. Paragraphs even. It was a mystery as to why a simple barbecue had her so conversationally challenged.

About halfway through the meal, Lucy was mentally and physically exhausted. That did it. She couldn't leap down the poor kid's throat and yank a conversation out. If Bess was more comfortable sitting in silence, then that was all right. She understood. Some people preferred to enjoy the conversation of others.

Lucy turned her attention to Trevor.

"Get the gutters done?"

"Yeah. All but those ones at the very top. I gotta rig some kind of a safety rope before I climb all the way up there."

"Good idea. You could clip it to the ironwork at the peak."

"I thought of that, but I'm not sure how secure that is. Might loop a rope around that chimney on the south side of the house."

"Oh, now you're thinking. Probably better get to it tomorrow afternoon. The weather is supposed to be changing."

Trevor nodded. "I know." He pointed to the honey-glazed chops with his knife. "This is really good."

"Thanks. It's one of those new bottled glazes. Just pour it on and *voilà!* Hey, Trevor, you know, if you can get those gutters cleaned out tomorrow after we get back from church, I bet we could make it to the Apple Festival and Heritage Fair out at the Kilmer Farms. Might be fun."

"Sounds great."

The conversation swirled and whirled about in this fashion until Bess simply seemed to fade away. In fact, at one point, after she excused herself to go to the powder room, they didn't really notice that she was still gone until over a quarter of an hour had passed and they were just getting ready to serve up the brownies and ice cream with a cup of coffee.

"That's funny," Lucy muttered as she came out of her place and met Trevor on the porch. "She's not in my bathroom."

Trevor scratched his head. "Mine either."

"Do you think she left?"

"Must have."

Lucy moaned. "Oh, I feel just terrible! We ignored her, Trevor! How rude of us."

"If you ask me, she preferred it that way. Listen, Lucy, don't fret. I don't think Bess wanted to be here from the get-go. If she wanted to slip away, that's okay too. No harm done."

Lucy flopped into her seat and heaved a dispirited sigh. "It's just that I really wanted her to have a nice time. To get to know you."

"You did the best you could. She's a hard one to get to know."

Plunging her hands through her hair, Lucy leaned back and smiled a wobbly smile. "You're right. I'll call her in a few minutes and apologize."

"That might be nice."

From somewhere down the street, strains of Conrad Troutman's voice reached them, as he herded Popeye and Olive Oyl through their evening routine.

"No, Popeye! Not there! That's a bad neighbor. Someone could step in that, Pop, old boy!"

Lucy didn't like the sudden mischievous light that entered Trevor's eyes. "Trevor—" she began, but was cut off by his enthusiastic shout.

"Conrad? Conrad Troutman? Is that you?"

"Trevor?"

"Hey, buddy! Lucy and I were just sitting down to a plate of brownies and ice cream. Why don't you join us? Bring the dogs!"

"Well, now, don't mind if I do!" Conrad's grateful acceptance reached them through the evening shadows.

Eyes narrowed, Lucy planted her hands on her hips, her expression glacial. "I guess you felt you had to do that."

Deep creases bracketed Trevor's mouth, causing her heart to flip most unmercifully. "Yep. Paybacks can be rough, no? And this time, no escaping to the kitchen."

"Well, batten down the hatches. Those dogs are nearly as bad as Don."

Throwing back his head, Trevor laughed with delight for the first time that evening.

Chapter Seven

The brownies were piping hot as Lucy pulled them from the oven. She added them to the waiting tray, already loaded with a carton of ice cream and a pot of coffee. With a long, tired exhalation, she battled a now-familiar wave of the blues. From where she stood, she could hear Conrad and Trevor greeting each other and settling into their seats.

Shuffling to the refrigerator, Lucy found the chocolate sauce and whipped topping. Then she listlessly searched the cabinets for some chopped nuts and the jar of maraschino cherries that she'd bought several weeks ago.

Outside, the dogs were running amuck yet again. Lucy heaved another weary sigh. It seemed that Trevor was just as anxious to get her socializing with the single men of McLaughlin as she was to get him involved in a relationship.

Too bad their reasons were so different.

Her motives were to save him from her stupid crush. His were…well, she wasn't exactly sure what his were. But she suspected they were something as simple as getting rid of his pesky, love-struck kid sister.

Ah well. She'd sulked in the kitchen long enough. Time to

socialize. Lucy took the dessert tray to the porch table and, trying to maintain a chipper facade, began to section the brownies into generous chunks, scoop them into bowls, and load them with toppings. The dogs sniffed at the perimeter of the tray but, sensing that Lucy meant business with her knife, eventually settled under the table and over her feet for a snooze.

Luckily, pulling a conversation out of the talkative Conrad was no problem at all. His progress on the new shed he was beginning to build was still uppermost in his mind and all he seemed interested in discussing. Many times, Trevor would try to steer the conversation back to Lucy and encourage a dialogue between the two. But Conrad would simply force a tolerant smile, then turn the conversation back to the shed.

That was fine with Lucy as she was still mentally fried from her efforts with Bess. She paused for a moment, her fork halfway to her mouth as inspiration struck. *Conrad and Bess!* They'd be perfect for each other! Tucking that little touch of brilliance into the back of her mind for future reference, Lucy concentrated on her brownie.

Well over an hour later, long after she normally headed for bed, some kind of nocturnal animal—to which Lucy would be eternally grateful—decided to take its life in its paws and scurry across their lawn and down the sidewalk. Popeye's head reared up, tipping the table, as he snuffed the air. Olive Oyl followed suit, sending the dessert tray into Lucy's lap. Before Conrad could say "see-ya-later-bye-bye," the dogs were off like a shot, with their owner hot on their heels.

As the three disappeared down the street in a cacophony of frenzied shouts and barks, Lucy turned to Trevor with a sardonic look. Bits of brownie and chocolate sauce clung to her blouse.

"I vote that you clean up tonight. I'm going upstairs to shower. I'll have my coffee after I muck the whipped cream and nuts out of my hair."

Trevor was laughing too hard to argue.

A little later, Lucy and Trevor burrowed down in their chairs with a couple of blankets and two steaming cups of decaf coffee. The air had a decided feel of fall to it. Every so often a breeze would kick up and dry leaves would swirl to the ground and crackle across the sidewalk. Far too soon the weather would no longer permit these lazy evenings spent relaxing on the porch. It was only a matter of days, Trevor knew.

Something about spending these last few days on the old porch with Lucy made him sad. Before they knew it, winter would drive them indoors and they would no doubt see much less of each other, without this common ground on which to come together every evening. Then, when the snow had melted and the green shoots of spring began to poke through the soil, his parents would return, and it would be time for Trevor to move on.

The thought was more depressing than he ever could have anticipated. It had been rough leaving Lucy when he moved out to California to attend college. But that was nothing compared to the way he felt about leaving her now.

As casually as he could, he looked sideways at her sweet face, scrubbed fresh and clean and so adorable in the moonlight. He couldn't imagine a face he'd rather look at for the rest of his days.

Her eyes were downcast, her lashes resting just above her cheeks as she puckered her lips and blew across the rim of her cup.

Something painful seared Trevor's heart in that moment of stark realization. This was as good as it would get. Aside from his relationship with God, for him, there would be no greater love. Anyone that he ended up married to in the future would pale in comparison to Lucy. That hardly seemed fair to his future bride.

But there it was, the truth: Trevor was in love with Lucy. Always had been since they were kids, and there wasn't a thing he could do about it. Too bad. He drew in a deep lungful of air and slowly let it hiss though his lips. They'd have had real cute kids. Feisty little red-headed things. Like their mom.

"What?" She cast a lazy glance in his direction.

"What, what?"

"You sighed that big old sigh. Just wondered what you were thinking."

His smile was rueful. She didn't want to know what he'd been thinking. Not really. He couldn't tell her that. But he could divulge a few of the fleeting thoughts that had crossed his mind over the last moments.

"Oh, nothing really. I was just thinking about when we were kids."

Lucy smiled. "Anything in particular?"

"Not really. Just remembering how we always used to pal around together. How you used to tag along after me everywhere." He lifted a teasing brow.

"I was kinda pesky, huh?"

"No. I loved it. I was never lonely when you were around."

"Same here." Her lips twitched with mirth. "Some of my little girlfriends used to think that when we grew up, we'd get married."

Trevor froze. When he could speak again, he asked, "And what did you tell them?"

"That there was no way, of course."

Trevor's heart stopped beating and plummeted into his stomach where it landed with a thud. "Why not?"

"Because if I married you, I'd be Lucy Burns-Bacon." Her giggle rang out into the quiet autumn night.

A slow grin tugged at his lips. "So, what's wrong with that? I think it has a very nice ring."

Lucy stilled, her hands wrapped tightly around her coffee mug. "You do?"

"Very nice."

They were sitting close together, the old wicker chairs separated only by the width of the armrests. Their heads were cradled against the simply caned backs and they faced each other, their noses mere inches apart. It would be so easy, Trevor mused, to lean forward just a bit and touch his lips to hers.

Her eyes were flashing as they searched his face for the meaning hidden behind his words. Fortunately for him, the shadows prevented her from seeing the stark truth that was no doubt written all over his face. At least he hoped she couldn't see. Never before had he felt so vulnerable.

"Me too," she whispered.

"You too what?" he whispered back.

"I think it has a nice ring."

Trevor leaned forward. He was going to kiss her. And if he wasn't mistaken, she didn't seem inclined to prevent him from doing so. His heart began to pound. Lucy leaned imperceptibly closer. He angled his head so that his mouth would oh-so-perfectly fit hers. She melted toward him.

And just as he was about to plant a tender kiss on her lips, Popeye and Olive Oyl—with Conrad in hot pursuit—shot down the street.

The mood was ruined.

As if she suddenly realized that she was about to make the mistake of a lifetime, Lucy reared back and blinked rapidly. A nervous twitter escaped her throat, and she cast her gaze about, letting it land everywhere but on his face.

Trevor's heart fell. All he could think about was how much he wanted to let Lucy know that he loved her and how much she was trying to escape. Never had he been in such a miserable position in all his life.

It was time to get Lucy involved with Mr. Right.

Before he lost his ever-lovin' mind.

"I should probably turn in." Lucy looked at him, a question that he knew he couldn't answer burning in her eyes.

"Sounds like a plan."

She sighed a sad sigh and, gathering up her blanket and mug, stood and moved toward her front door. "We still on for the Apple Festival and Heritage Fair tomorrow afternoon?"

His heart clinging to the back of his throat, Trevor nodded, knowing even as he did that it was a terrible mistake to spend any more social time with Lucy. "Yeah. Sounds like fun." Far, far too much fun.

"Okay then. 'Night," she called softly over her shoulder.

"'Night."

Trevor sat there, still in a daze, for many minutes after Lucy had trundled off to bed. What on earth had just happened back there? Well, whatever it was, it shouldn't happen again. Somehow, tomorrow at the festival, he'd show Lucy just what a wonderful platonic buddy he could be. Even if it killed him.

Bending forward, Trevor buried his face in his hands. Only God could bail him out of this jam.

"Oh, Lord," he prayed, his voice muffled by his palms, *"I've really made a mess of my life lately. It seems I've gone and fallen in love with a woman who does not love me back. So, since there is nothing I can do about that, I was wondering if you could please help me get over her. I think maybe if she found someone to love, someone to take good care of her, well, maybe I'd have to accept that and get on with my life. So, Lord, I pray that soon, as soon as you can, you help Lucy to find the man that she should be spending the rest of her life with. Amen."*

Trevor sat for another hour, pondering life and trying to imagine Lucy with any name other than Burns-Bacon.

And no matter how hard he tried, he couldn't.

It just had much too nice a ring.

Chapter Eight

After church the next morning, Trevor cleaned the gutters while Lucy put some finishing touches on the porch paint. When they were finished, they washed up, changed from their work clothes into clean, casual clothes, then hopped into Trevor's car for the scenic drive out to the Kilmer Farm.

Every October the famous historic homestead would host the marvelous Apple Festival and Heritage Fair with events as colorful as the hills among which it lay. A farmers' and flea market in the giant red barn, a sea of craft tables flowing over the farmhouse lawn, hayrides, boiled lobsters, fresh apples, chicken-pie suppers, fiddle concerts, hot-air balloons, and a horse show. There was something for everyone.

Trevor guided the car toward the farm along the back roads that ran through the small hamlets and villages that distinguished Vermont from every other state. Lucy decided to put aside her qualms about the direction of their relationship and simply enjoy the day. And a brilliantly beautiful day it was. The sugar maples had turned the hillsides into a breathtaking rainbow of reds, oranges, and yellows. Steep mountain peaks stood out majestically in front of the bright azure sky. Golden fields of corn and winding rivers sporting covered bridges never ceased to enthrall Lucy, even though she'd grown up in this beautiful state.

Trevor seemed to be in a relaxed mood as well, and when they reached the farm, the tension of the night before had virtually disappeared. Hands linked casually, they strolled past the various booths and attractions, sampling this and that, pausing to watch demonstrations on everything from spinning wool to the age-old art of making maple sugar candy.

"Want another caramel apple?" Trevor shot a longing look at a table loaded with delicacies as they wandered past.

With her free hand, Lucy clutched her stomach and moaned. "Are you kidding?"

"How about some fudge?"

"No!"

"A hunk of that apple pie?"

"No, no, no! Are you trying to kill me?"

"You can't be full."

"Why not? We just ate our way across ten of the twenty acres that make up this place."

"What are you talking about? We haven't even had dinner yet."

"You want *dinner?*"

"Don't you?"

"Trevor, since we've been here, I've eaten apple cobbler, apple pie, apple dumplings, caramel apples, candy apples, apple strudel, apple candy, and sour apple taffy. And that's just the apple products. That doesn't even count the boiled lobster, the chunks of honey-glazed ham, the maple sugar candy, the corn on the cob—"

"Yeah, okay, but none of that counts as dinner."

Lucy stopped in her tracks, her laughter incredulous. "Where do you put it all?"

He lifted a shoulder and grinned that adorable, vulnerable grin that could melt her insides. "I'm a growing boy."

Of their own volition, her eyes flicked over his impressive physique. *So I'd noticed.*

His hand tightened on hers, when it would have been prudent for her to take a step back. Leading her over to the table, he bought yet another caramel apple.

"C'mon." Tone cajoling, he looked deeply into her eyes, his brows lifted rakishly. "Live a little. You can have a bite of mine. I'll be happy to share with you." He held the candy to her lips.

Suddenly mush-brained, Lucy could only stare at him and nod mutely. Something about sharing this apple with him had the warning bells of reason sounding in her head. But taking a bite of his apple, she pushed these niggling worries to the back of her mind. She would worry about steering clear and finding Trevor a dream woman tomorrow. Today, she would simply enjoy the magic of his company.

Three days later, by Wednesday evening after work, the weather had changed enough that they needed to end their fix-it projects outside. Trevor's mom had wanted her living room to have a fresh coat of paint before they returned, and now seemed to Trevor as good a time as any to get started. Besides, if he kept busy, he wouldn't have time to think about Lucy and how much he missed her company as they worked on the old porch. Since the Apple Festival and Heritage Fair, he hadn't seen much of her at all, except to wave hello and good-bye as they ran back and forth to work.

Trevor was restless. And for the first time in his life, lonely.

Outside, the wind blew and a high-pitched whistle droned from under the front door. He made a distracted mental note to fix the worn-out threshold. A fire crackled merrily in the fireplace, and sparks swirled up the chimney with an occasional pop. The cozy picture was missing something though.

Trevor rubbed the five o'clock shadow at his chin and forced his attention away from thoughts of Lucy to the task at hand. The furniture was covered with tarps, and the paint was mixed to the shade his mother had specified. All woodwork and flooring had been taped off, and a pile of rags and rollers and various other tools was sitting on the dining-room table ready to use. Trevor pulled his rattiest sweatshirt on over his head and surveyed the job. Wouldn't take all that long, but it sure wouldn't be any fun without Lucy.

He wondered what she was doing.

He didn't have to wonder long. The doorbell rang before he could pick up his brush.

It was Lucy.

"Hi." Trevor felt his mood soar and hated himself for his weakness.

"Hi." She looked suddenly shy. "I just dropped by to talk to you, if you have a second."

Did he have a second? That was a dumb question. For her, he had a lifetime.

"Sure, sure. Come on in." After shutting the door he took her coat and motioned her to a seat on one of the dining room chairs. "Can I get you anything to drink? Juice? Soft drink? Coffee? Tea?"

Me? he wanted to add, but didn't think she'd see the humor in that considering how he'd been about to plant a big kiss on her last Saturday night. A kiss that unfortunately, he mused, raking a hand over his jaw, would not have been welcome coming from nothing but a pseudo older brother.

"No, no thanks. I'm fine." Her gaze drifted around the living room. "Looks like you're all set to paint."

"Yep. I got a brush with your name on it." He was teasing, but he hoped she'd bite.

"Sure. I'll help. Got an old shirt I can wear?"

"For you, I've got a *new* shirt." The second the words were out of his mouth, he regretted them. He rushed on, hoping she didn't notice how love-struck and dopey he sounded. "So, you said you had something to talk to me about. Shoot."

"Oh. That." She cleared her throat. "Well, there is a brand-new teller down at the bank. Amber Olafson. She just started about two weeks ago."

A suspicious shade of pink suddenly stained her cheeks, and Trevor leaned back to scrutinize her face. Just what on earth was she up to now? Luckily, it was too late in the year for another barbecue party out on the porch.

"Anyway, she's new in town. Doesn't know anybody. I feel kind of sorry for her. She's really, really gorgeous. Stunning is I guess how you'd best describe her. A beauty queen kind of gal. Blond, blue-eyed. Real tall, but not too tall. Statuesque. And she is one of those women who is perfectly dressed at all times." Lucy's smile was rueful. "Not a hair out of place."

Trevor had to school his face into a mask of indifference because her description of this Amber woman made him want to jump up and down and pound on the wall with his fists. Why on earth would Lucy think that he was looking for a beauty queen? Didn't she know that a pixie face surrounded by a riot of auburn hair was his idea of perfect beauty? He wanted to shake some sense into her, but instead nodded placidly and pretended interest.

"She's single. Did I mention that?"

"No, but I gathered as much."

"Well, anyway, I was thinking that maybe you could take her out, sometime soon. She's really nice. I told her all about you and she's interested. I don't think she'd be too surprised if you called her or anything."

Trevor ran a hand over his face, across his jaw, and to the back of his neck. There, he found a painful knot of muscles that he began to knead. Valiantly, he tried not to show how much her words stung. With all his heart, he wished that she could someday view him as something other than good old Trevor, the brother next door. It was so frustrating.

However, something told him deep in his gut that it was time to finally let go once and for all. To let God take over. Maybe this Amber person was part of the answer to his prayer. Personally, he doubted it, but he felt obligated to try.

"Okay." Reluctantly, he agreed. "I'll give her a call."

Lucy was taken aback. "You will?"

"Sure. I'll call her and ask her out for this Friday night, on one condition."

Her eyes narrowed. "What's that?"

"That you consider going out on a date with one of the guys from my office down at SystaServe. Phil Gunderson. He's single too, and he's just your cup of tea."

Lucy swallowed and looked up at him, her eyes wide. "Just my cup of tea?"

"Yep. He's outgoing and adventurous and a regular laugh a minute. And he lives right here in McLaughlin. Moved here last spring." Actually, Trevor thought that Phil—although basically a good guy—was a bit of a braggart. Full of hot air. Then again, maybe all he needed was a good woman like Lucy to bring out the best in him. Besides, all the gals in the office seemed to think that Phil was a pretty hot property. "To die for," they all said. Even the grandmotherly types agreed that Phil was a "charming boy." Trevor didn't have a clue what made a man attractive, so he decided that taking his coworkers' word for it would be his best bet.

Too bad the thought of Lucy and Phil going out on a date together tore him up inside. So much so that he began to feel physically ill as he stood there, looking at her sweet face.

However, he was beginning to realize that the longer he tried to stay in control of the situation, the longer he would simply be in God's way. Trevor realized that if he were meant to spend the rest of his life with Lucy by his side, God would have to work that out. If it were not meant to be, well, then the good Lord must have his reasons. With a quick silent prayer for strength and fortitude, Trevor moved to the phone and picked up the receiver.

"What's Amber's number?"

"You're going to call...*now?*"

If he wasn't mistaken, there was a note of uncertainty in her voice. He glanced over his shoulder at her and nodded. "Sure, I figure now is as good a time as any. Why? Is there some reason I should wait?"

Lucy cleared her throat and gave her head a vigorous shake. "No. No, no. That's...that's fine! I was just...surprised, is all, I guess." She fished a scrap of paper out of her pocket and pressed it into his hand. "Go ahead. I'm sure she's home by now."

As he tapped Amber's number into his keypad, he winked at Lucy. "As soon as I'm done here, I'll give Phil a call and see when he's got a free evening."

"Oh?"

"Sure. I figure, why wait?"

"Right."

"Anyway, Phil is a good guy. Kind of out there, you know, but—"

Lucy frowned, and before he could elaborate, Amber picked up on her end.

Trevor could feel Lucy's eyes practically boring a hole in the back of his neck as he began his conversation with Amber. After a brief introduction, Trevor told Amber that Lucy had suggested that he call. Amber was enthusiastic and easy to talk to, and soon he had a date all sewn up with her for the coming Friday night. They would meet at a local restaurant and, from there, catch a movie at the ancient movie house on Main Street in downtown McLaughlin.

Slowly, Trevor placed the handset back in the cradle and turned to face Lucy. The whole idea of meeting and taking this Amber person out was exhausting. He hated blind dates. Especially ones that Lucy instigated. But it was too late now. The deed was done. This Friday night he had a date with the dishy Amber Olafson, whether he liked it or not.

Lucy clapped her hands, and the sharp report echoed around the room. "So you're on for Friday night!"

Trevor nodded. "She said she remembered me from last week when I stopped in at the bank to pick up that stuff on home loans." He wiggled his brows and tossed her a playful grin. "She likes my dimples."

"Great!" Lucy's voice was louder than normal, and her eyes were suspiciously bright. "Well. Now that that is over with, how about you dig me out an old shirt, or better yet, some coveralls, and we'll get this painting show on the road."

"Oh no. Not so fast. I still have to call Phil."

Lucy sighed.

"C'mon. Phil will love you." He looked up the number, picked up the phone, and began to dial. "Just think. This may be your lucky day." The very thought made him want to punch a hole in the wall. He took a deep, cleansing breath and slowly let it out while he waited for Phil to pick up on his end.

Let go, he reminded himself for the umpteenth time. *Let go and let God.*

For Lucy, Friday night passed in an excruciating lineup of mundane tasks designed to keep her mind off Trevor and Amber and their date. So far that evening she'd polished her mother's antique silver tea service, cleaned and alphabetically organized the spice cabinet, paid all of her bills, given herself a facial, painted her toenails a shocking shade of pink, picked out an outfit to wear on her date with Phil tomorrow night, clipped some coupons for eggs and paper towels, and prayed the entire time for release from this emotional nightmare that had begun the day Trevor pulled up in his moving van.

Now, cuddled on her couch with a cup of hot lemon tea and a blanket, she tried to concentrate on a novel she'd begun at least half a dozen times in the last hour, but it was futile. Was the clock on her mantel broken? No. Couldn't be. The dining-room clock and her watch both said the same thing. Five minutes had passed since she last checked. She could have sworn an hour had ticked by.

Images of Amber and Trevor together, laughing and sharing a bag of popcorn, began to plague her anew. What if their hands collided as they were reaching for popcorn? What if there were sparks? What if those sparks led to a look? Or worse, a kiss? What if they decided to get married? What if they…*what if, what if, what if?* Lucy couldn't stand it anymore. She needed to do something constructive.

With a heavy sigh, she reached into the end-table drawer behind her and withdrew a pad and pencil.

"Let's see…" Lucy murmured as she scratched a rough story problem out on a sheet of paper. "If a couple…no, no, it's not like they're a couple." A nervous chuckle tickled her throat. "Okay. If two strangers meet for dinner at half past six, that would give them an hour and a half to eat before the movie at the McLaughlin Cinema begins."

The movie always started at eight and had ever since Lucy could remember.

"So, if the movie started at eight and was three hours long, that would make it…uh…eleven o' clock when they got out."

Surely, the movie wouldn't be more than three hours long, she figured. It would take less than five minutes for Trevor to drive Amber home, as she lived only two blocks down from the movie house. Then, it would take a few minutes—maybe ten at the most—to say their good-byes, and then, with his five-minute commute home, that would put him back here at…after some quick scribbling, Lucy threw in an extra ten minutes for good measure and came up with the grand total of 11:30 P.M.

And that was an hour ago.

Where on earth were they? Should she begin calling the police or hospital? Or should she mind her own business like the self-actualized woman she usually was and sit here in agony until Trevor came home?

Why, oh why had she suggested that Trevor ask Amber out on a date? It had seemed like such a grand idea at the time. Until Trevor had picked up the phone and called her. Lucy hadn't been able to draw a full breath of air into her lungs since that moment.

Knowing it was nosy and futile, Lucy drew herself up onto her knees and peeked out her window and into the silent calm of the street in front of her house. Still no Trevor. She was being ridiculous.

With a resigned huff, she tossed her notepad and pencil on the coffee table and grabbed her blanket. It was time to head for bed. Trevor would tell her all about his date in the morning. Sitting here wondering and worrying was a waste of time and energy.

No sooner had Lucy folded her blanket and put her empty teacup on the kitchen drainboard than she heard the familiar rumble of Trevor's car engine. Rushing back into the living room, she switched off the lamp. She didn't want him to think she'd been waiting up, so she grabbed her blanket and tiptoed toward the staircase that led to her bedroom.

A soft knock at the door halted her progress just as she mounted the stairs. Lucy vacillated. She was dying of curiosity, but at the same time, she didn't want Trevor to know that she'd been ticking off the minutes until he returned.

"Lucy? Are you still downstairs?" Trevor's low voice filtered through the leaded glass in her front door. She could see his shadow hovering just outside. "I saw you turn your light off and just thought maybe..." His hopeful voice trailed away on a heavy sigh. "That's okay. I'll just catch you tomorrow."

Curiosity won out, and before he could leave, Lucy hurried across her little foyer and yanked open her door. Then, realizing that she seemed a little overanxious, she tried to act as if she'd just awakened.

"Trevor!" She rubbed at her eyes and blinked. "What are you doing here? I thought you'd still be out having a wonderful time with Amber."

Trevor turned and stepped back to her door. His smile was sheepish. "I'm really sorry. I didn't mean to wake you up. It's just that I saw your light on and I thought…well, never mind. You go back to bed. I'll talk to you in the morning."

"No!" Lucy laughed in what she hoped sounded like a sleepy and relaxed—yet carefree and happy—manner. "I mean, no, it's fine. Come on in."

She flipped on the lights as she moved toward the living room. Once she and Trevor were settled in on the couch, she turned and favored him with her brightest smile. "What's up?"

Trevor pulled his ankle up over his knee and sighed the sigh of a man who has just been through the experience of a lifetime. Lucy felt her heart skid to a halt and claw its way into her throat. He was in love. *She knew it!* How could any man in his right mind resist Amber Olafson's many charms?

She wanted to throw up.

She wanted to faint.

She wanted to die.

She was too filled with shock and sorrow to do anything. "You two really hit it off, huh?" Her voice squeaked around the broken and battered lump in her throat.

"Hardly."

"I knew that you would really like her, once you had a chance to meet her."

"*Like* her?"

Lucy's life flashed before her eyes. Is this how the Lord planned on taking her to glory? Because it sure felt as if she were having a heart attack. She could hear the beeps on the heart monitor stop in her runaway imagination, the high-pitched flat-line tone screaming a death knell throughout her brain.

"Is it…" She touched her tongue to her lips and whispered haltingly, "is it…love already?"

A chuckle rumbled from deep within Trevor's chest and he slapped his thighs with glee. *"Love?"*

"So…soon?"

"Oh, Lucy." Trevor threw back his head and let the laughter flow. "Lucy, I have to hand it to you. When it comes to fixing me up with a woman, you don't have a clue."

Unable to do anything but stare, Lucy could hear the faint echo of the heart machine in her brain begin to tentatively beep again. "You mean, you don't love her?"

"Honey, I'd have to say that even liking her would be a stretch."

"Really? But, but she's so beautiful!"

"Ah. Yes. Did she tell you that? She sure told me. Spent the entire evening regaling me with tales of the old beauty-pageant days." Running his hands through his thick brown hair, Trevor leaned back against the couch and grinned. "Man, I'm glad that's over."

Lucy could swear that the heavens opened at that moment and the angels began a rousing rendition of the "Hallelujah" chorus. For several minutes, Trevor regaled Lucy with the dull details of his date, causing her heart to soar with unbridled joy. All her worries had been so much wasted time. She was humming under her breath when Trevor leaned forward and prepared to stand.

"Listen, Lucy. Next time you get the urge to fix me up on a date…don't. Okay?"

"Okay." She fought back the wide grin she felt tugging at her mouth and nodded in contrition. "I promise."

"Good." Then with a quick peck on her temple that left her breathless, Trevor left.

Later that night, knowing she needed to repent and work on getting her heart right with God, Lucy sat on the edge of her bed and, clenching her fists beneath her jaw, began to pray.

"Dear Lord, I'm so sorry that I was happy that Trevor and Amber didn't hit it off. Amber is a really sweet gal, and the pure joy I felt over the fact that Trevor didn't find her appealing was wrong. I should have been disappointed that things did not work out, not gleeful. Especially since it was my prayer that Trevor find someone to love. Oh, Lord," she whispered earnestly, *"please help Trevor find someone wonderful to love. And whoever it is that you choose for him, please help me to be eternally grateful. Amen."*

Chapter Nine

The next night, Trevor paced like a caged animal in his freshly painted living room. He snapped yet another quick look at his watch. It was officially after midnight. Saturday had slipped into Sunday now, and Lucy was still not home. Filled with dread and irritation, Trevor looked out the glass panels of his front door again.

All evening his imagination had tortured him with images of Lucy on her date with Phil. No doubt Phil would know a little gem when he saw one. Phil might be a bit of a blowhard, but he was no dummy. He'd snap her up like a holiday bonus. Trevor groaned as visions of himself someday visiting Phil and Lucy's cozy country cottage flitted through his head. In his mind's eye, he could see himself tossing one of their multitude of charming tykes into the air. Phil would be flourishing under Lucy's tutelage, a regular saint of a husband and father.

Giving his head a vicious shake to dispel the depressing scene, he began to pace once more.

He couldn't begin to fathom what was taking so long. The movie let out at 10:30. He knew this for a fact, as he'd been there just last night. Of course, Amber had insisted that he come in over at her place, have a cup of coffee, and see some fashion layout or another that she'd done when she was a kid. It had been all he could do to stay awake for her endless beauty show-and-tell session, even with the caffeine.

Trevor's jaw clenched. Phil had better not be showing Lucy any "etchings" over at his place. He stopped pacing. Maybe he should go over there and just make sure that everything was okay. But what could he possibly use as an excuse that wouldn't make him look like a first-class lunatic?

As he searched his brain for an answer, a high-powered engine roared to a halt, just outside the front door. Pressing his face to the leaded-glass panels in the door, Trevor could see Phil helping Lucy out of the car.

Standing as he was, with the lights on full force and the front door completely transparent, Trevor was in a jam. Trying to remain unobtrusive, he pressed his body back against the row of coats that hung on decorative hooks in the entryway and prayed that he blended in well enough to avoid detection.

The sound of footsteps mounting the stairs reached him where he hid. Soon, he could hear Phil's flirtatious laughter and Lucy's low murmur.

For a long time, the murmuring continued. Trevor frowned. What on earth could be taking so long? What were they talking about? Battling back the coats that surrounded him, he strained to hear. Phil was being ultracharming, that much was clear, but he still couldn't hear what he was saying.

Frustration made him bold and he moved closer to the door.

What was that?

It sounded like Lucy was annoyed, as strains of the conversation filtered though the glass. Trevor inched closer to the door.

"No, Phil," Lucy protested, a definite note of irritation in her voice. "I know that to *you* the night may be young, but I really don't want to make coffee now. I have to get up early for church. It's already past my bedtime. Thank you for a lovely evening, but really, I need to get my beauty rest."

"Someone as beautiful as you needing beauty rest?" Phil guffawed. "No way. Any more beauty rest and you'd be lethal."

A muscle jumped in Trevor's jaw.

"Be that as it may, Phil, I have to go. Good night now."

Not getting the message, Phil continued his unrelenting pursuit. "But you haven't even kissed me good night yet." His pouting tone was meant to be endearing.

Lucy sighed. "Give me your cheek."

Trevor tensed, his entire body ready for battle. Taking a chance on being discovered, he moved out of the safety zone of the coats and pressed his face against the glass.

A cocky grin on his face, Phil angled his head.

As Lucy tried to bestow a chaste peck on his cheek, Phil turned, pulled her into his embrace, and crushed his lips to hers in a kiss that had Trevor ready to burst through the glass.

From the way she pushed against his chest, it was obvious that Lucy was not amused.

"No, Phil, stop. I said…" Lucy grunted and huffed, trying to extricate herself from his clutches. "I…said…*no!*"

The tearful panic in her voice was all the urging Trevor needed to yank open his door, barrel out onto the porch, and grab Phil by the back of his collar.

"Didn't you hear the lady?"

The menacing tone of his voice suddenly had Phil frozen and searching for an explanation. Tucking his chin into his shoulder, Phil strained to look back into his captor's face. "Oh, hey, Trevor." His nervous laugh was a sharp contrast to his forceful demeanor of only moments ago. "You can relax, buddy. It's just me. I was just tellin' Lucy here good night."

"Seems to me that she doesn't want to hear it from you. Why don't you just be on your way?" With a none too gentle shove, Trevor released Phil toward the stairs.

Pausing at the top of the stairs to straighten his shirt, Phil sent a scathing look at the two of them. "I get it. You want her for yourself. I don't know why I didn't see that when I got here. The phony father act when I picked her up, telling me when to have her home." He snorted with disgust. "Why didn't you just tell me that you were in love with her in the first place?" A sneer twisted his handsome face. "Could have saved me a boatload of time and money."

Hands clenched at his sides, Trevor took a menacing step toward him, and Phil bounded down the stairs two at a time, muttering pithy expletives all the way. The angry squeal of his tires could be heard from one end of Main Street to the other as he shot off into the night.

Trevor turned to Lucy, who stood shivering before her front door. "Are you all right?"

"Yes." She blinked back her tears and laughed, her voice shaky with emotion. "Now that you're here."

With a groan, Trevor closed the gap between them, pulled her into his arms, and gently rocked her back and forth. "I'm so sorry I suggested that you go out with him. I had no idea he would act that way. I don't know what I'd have done if he'd so much as touched a single hair on your beautiful head."

"Oh, Trevor." Snuggling against his shirt placket, she spoke quietly, her voice muffled by the heavy fabric. "It's not your fault. Really, he was very nice and charming all evening. I…just didn't want to—I couldn't give him a chance. I had a bad attitude about this date from the beginning, and I think he sensed that. His ego was a little bruised. I'm so sorry. I hope I haven't ruined your working relationship with him."

"Lucy, Lucy, Lucy," he murmured into the soft curls atop her head. "I don't care about that guy's ego. It's plenty big enough. Don't you know how much more important you are to me than some stupid working relationship?"

She leaned back in his arms and looked up into his face, her eyes brimming with tears. "Really?"

"Really."

The love and adoration Trevor found there suddenly took his breath away. Could she be feeling the same things he was? Maybe. Maybe not. At any rate, it was beyond time to say something. Deciding the hour was finally here to take the risk of a lifetime, he cupped Lucy's face in his hands and felt his heart begin to pound as their gazes met. "Phil was right about the way I feel about you. Don't you know how very, very important you are to me?"

Between his palms, Lucy gave her head a tiny shake. "No." The word was barely more audible than the beat of a butterfly's wings.

He'd been holding his breath. Well, he guessed now was as good a time as any to demonstrate his feelings. Slowly, Trevor lowered his head and tilted her mouth to meet his lips. He was amazed to discover that she wasn't pulling away. Not only was she not pulling away, she was pressing against him and looping her arms around his neck. He took a step forward and deepened the kiss, and she followed suit by threading her fingers in the hair at his nape. Suddenly Trevor was transported to a level of ecstasy he'd never enjoyed before with any other woman.

As his breathing picked up speed, so did hers, until Trevor thought surely he must have fallen asleep while waiting for her to come home and was having the dream of a lifetime. Luckily for him, it was no dream. It was really happening. Right here on the old front porch, for all the world to see. Nothing had ever felt more right in his entire life.

After a moment, Trevor needed oxygen. A lopsided grin tugging at his mouth, he leaned away from Lucy and looked deep into her hazy, happy gaze.

"I haven't wanted to say anything to you about my true feelings, because it would kill me if I thought that kissing you this way, and telling you how much I love you, would jeopardize our friendship."

Lucy nodded dumbly, her eyes still filled with an adoration that gave Trevor courage to continue.

"But," he lifted and dropped a shoulder, "now that the cat is out of the bag, I guess I might as well tell you everything." He took a deep breath and plunged ahead. "I don't want you dating anyone else. Ever again. Unless…" he peered into her face for her reaction, "it's me. There. I've said it. I love you and I want you all to myself. Hate me?"

Lucy didn't answer. Instead, she pulled at his neck, urging him to lower his mouth to hers once more for yet another wonderful kiss. "How could I hate someone I've loved my entire life?" she whispered against his lips. "I thought the reason you were trying to get me to date other men is because you knew I was in love with you and you were gently trying to get rid of me."

Trevor's head dropped back on his shoulders, and he laughed out loud. "That's what I thought *you* were trying to do!"

Lucy grinned. "Never."

"Does this mean you don't hate me?"

"I love you with all my heart."

With a sigh of contentment, Trevor pulled Lucy's head against his shoulder. "You know, I've always been partial to the name Lucy Burns-Bacon."

"It kind of grows on you, doesn't it?" Lucy giggled. "Besides, it's a pretty accurate description."

"Then you'll marry me?"

Brows knit, Lucy reared back and looked up into his face, a mischievous glint in her eye. "You know I'll be depriving the single women in McLaughlin of its most eligible bachelor."

Trevor bent to kiss Lucy again. "That's the best news I've heard all day."

"Umm. Then yes," she whispered just before his mouth covered hers, "I'd love to be your wife."

Epilogue

The following summer, on a lovely warm June evening, Lucy burst out of the Bacons' front door onto the old front porch. Swathed in a cloud of taffeta, satin, and lace and clutching her bridal bouquet at her waist, she smiled at the crowd of well-wishers now standing on the front lawn. Only moments ago, this crowd had attended her and Trevor's wedding in the Bacons' spacious living room.

Lucy was married.

She could scarcely believe how happy she was. Giddy with excitement, she sent a silent prayer skyward, thanking the Lord for knowing far better than she ever could what a perfect match she and Trevor would make.

Resplendent in his tux, Trevor joined his wife on the front porch, followed by his beaming parents. The happy quartet stood together for a moment, waving at the cheering, birdseed-throwing, bubble-blowing crowd, a real family at last.

If only her own parents could have been here for this moment, Lucy reflected, too happy to feel melancholy. They would have been thrilled.

After they'd hugged and kissed their son and new daughter-in-law, Trevor's mother and father stepped off the porch to mingle with the crowd.

"Time to throw the bouquet." There was a slight note of impatience in her husband's voice that thrilled Lucy to her toes. She was more than a little anxious herself to move from the wedding to the honeymoon.

"Okay." With Trevor's assistance, she gathered her voluminous skirt and turned her back on the excited and giggling faction of single ladies that waited at the bottom of the stairs. "Are they all ready?"

"If the blood in their eyes is any indication, they're ready. Fire at will."

Giggling, Lucy gave the bouquet of white roses a wild toss. A flurry of squeals and laughter followed as the floral missile seemed to float in slow motion through the air until it landed in Bess's arms. Her broad smile of pleasure belied the twin spots of mortification that burned in her cheeks.

"Bess!" Lucy squeezed Trevor's hand. "Bess will be getting married next!"

"Whatever." Trevor was unimpressed. "Let's get this show on the road." Kneeling on the floor, he reached beneath the hem of Lucy's dress.

"Trevor, what are you *doing?*" She gasped in surprise as he lifted her skirt above her knees.

"Time to toss the garter. Then we are outta here." Locating the object of his search, Trevor pulled the scrap of lace over Lucy's satin pump. Without ceremony he slingshotted the garter to where the men stood, only to hit Conrad in his open mouth.

Lucy stared, slack-jawed. "Conrad! I knew it!"

Trevor shrugged. "What?"

"Bess and Conrad!"

"Getting married next?" His gaze traveled from Conrad to Bess, and then Trevor let his laughter ring out. "I guess I shouldn't doubt you. After all, you were right about Amber and Phil getting engaged. Not to mention DeeDee and Don dating all spring. I have to admit, when it comes to true love, you have a knack."

"They all seem pretty happy, all right. But none could ever be as happy as I am with you." Eyes shining, Lucy gazed at the man she'd loved her whole life.

"That's because, Lucy Burns-Bacon," Trevor murmured, taking her hand and pressing it to his lips, "out of all the people in the world, we were each lucky enough to marry our best friend."

If you enjoyed "Tarnished Silver" by Lisa Tawn Bergren,
ask for her Northern Lights trilogy in your local bookstore!

*From the gentle hills of Norway to the rocky coast of Maine...across the
crashing, danger-filled waves of the open sea...readers will experience an epic
saga of perseverance and passion, faith and fidelity. Three powerful stories of life,
love, and new beginnings in a promising, but challenging, new land.*

#1 *The Captain's Bride* (Available now; ISBN 1-57856-013-6)
#2 *Deep Harbor* (Available now; ISBN 1-57856-045-4)
#3 *Midnight Sun* (Available March 2000)

Praise for *The Captain's Bride*

"Lisa Tawn Bergren has a straightforward, evocative style of writing that makes her
characters breathe. They walk right across the page and straight into your heart."

—FRANCINE RIVERS

"Bergren at her very best! What an incredible tale of adventure, from Norway's
sparkling fjords to the high seas of the Cape Horn, to the rocky shores and plains
of America in the 1880s. I loved it!" —LIZ CURTIS HIGGS

"A rare pleasure...a terrific tale, told with extraordinary honesty and insight.
God's compassion and grace illuminate each page." —DIANE NOBLE

"*The Captain's Bride* rides the swells of history into the reader's imagination. A tri-
umphant saga!" —THE LITERARY TIMES

"4 ½ stars. Inspirational pick of the month. Bergren is a rare talent in historical fiction, writing with exquisite style as she immerses lucky readers in the powerful emotions of her full-bodied characters." —ROMANTIC TIMES

If you enjoyed Barbara Jean Hicks's "Twice in a Blue Moon," ask for her Once Upon a Dream series at your local bookstore!

Loosely based on fairy tales, and set in Pilchuck, Washington, these romantic comedies will grab your heart and your imagination.

#1 *An Unlikely Prince:* Suzie Wyatt's dream of running her own daycare center comes true. But her neighbors—handsome Harrison Hunt and crotchety Mrs. Pfefferkuchen—are horrified by the prospect of having seven noisy children around. Suzie and her charges endear themselves to Harrison, who captures Suzie's heart. Then she discovers he's joined forces with Mrs. Pfefferkuchen to close her doors. Can she forgive her *Unlikely Prince?* (Available now; ISBN 1-57856-122-1)

#2 *All That Glitters:* After years of waiting tables in Pilchuck, aspiring apparel designer Cindy Reilly is starting to despair that she'll ever see a line of evening dresses with her name on them. And when her longtime boyfriend falls for a classy big-city girl, her future appears even bleaker. Enter Franklin Cameron Fitz III, of Seattle's Strawbridge & Fitz department store fame. He wants nothing more than to help her sell her designs. Nothing except to win her heart, that is! But will she choose her ex-boyfriend, who has rediscovered the spark they once shared? (Available now; ISBN 1-57856-123-X)

#3 *Perfect Stranger:* Beautiful Bonny wants nothing to do with her handsome beast of an ex-husband, Timothy Fairley. But what she doesn't know is that Timothy has learned a lot about himself—and what led him to make the worst mistake of his life in leaving her. He's armed with a new commitment to Christ and a determination to win Bonny back, but will Bonny give him a chance? (Available February 2000)

Praise for *An Unlikely Prince*

"Need a vacation? Enter into a story so pleasing, so refreshing, it will be to your mind a summer breeze, a seaside respite. Pick up Barbara Jean Hicks's *An Unlikely Prince.*"
—PATSY CLAIRMONT

If you enjoyed Jane Orcutt's "Texas Two-Step," ask for her moving and critically acclaimed novels, *The Fugitive Heart* and *The Hidden Heart,* at your local bookstore.

The Fugitive Heart: When Samantha Martin's childhood sweetheart returns from the Civil War, he is no longer the gentle boy she's always adored. He's a physically and emotionally scarred man on the run, dodging charges of theft—and murder. Can Samantha lead him from darkness to light and to the only one who can provide true refuge for *The Fugitive Heart?* (Available now; ISBN 1-57856-022-5)

The Hidden Heart: Elizabeth Cameron joins a religious group in Belton, Texas, where she and her five-year-old Indian charge, Joseph, hope to hide from a cruel world. Former gunfighter and robber Caleb Martin—who'll do anything for a governor's pardon—escorts Elizabeth to Belton. Caleb and Elizabeth soon find their lives, and hearts, entwined. But can their love break through their shields of self-protection and secrecy? (Available now; ISBN 1-57856-053-5)

Praise for *The Fugitive Heart*

"This historical romance is a tale of God's relentless love and searching for His own. Sin and repentance are strong themes woven throughout in a way that touches the reader's heart and causes one to examine his or her own spiritual condition—a wonderful story that blesses and entertains."

—CHURCH LIBRARIES

"4 ½ stars. Top pick. Jane Orcutt's name may be relatively new to readers, but her work is every bit as fantastic as veteran authors, and like cream, she's certain to rise to the top."

—ROMANTIC TIMES

"Recommended. The [main] character makes this book stand out among the many prairie romances."

—LIBRARY JOURNAL

If you enjoyed Suzy Pizzuti's "The Boy Next Door," be sure to ask for her romantic comedies also set in McLaughlin, Vermont. They're guaranteed to tickle your funny bone and steal your heart!

#1 *Say Uncle…and Aunt:* Hattie Hopkins's tenants have to be careful what they ask her to pray for. This hard-of-hearing woman's prayers are always answered—but rarely in the expected way. That's what two high-powered single boarders discover when they end up caring for a baby. When it's all over will they return to life as normal? Or will their hearts *Say Uncle…and Aunt?* (Available now; ISBN 1-57856-044-6)

#2 *Raising Cain…and His Sisters:* Olivia Harmon is still recovering from a tragic loss, and although she loves her job at Vermont's department of tourism, she longs for something more in life. When she asks Hattie to pray for her, things don't work out exactly as planned, and soon Olivia finds herself bursting out of her cocoon to take care of three rambunctious street children. Can a woman so accustomed to solitude adjust to a new life, a new love, and a new challenge of *Raising Cain…and His Sisters?* (Available now; ISBN 1-57856-141-8)

Praise for *Say Uncle…and Aunt*

"This fresh, light and funny read is certainly a welcome change of pace."
—LIBRARY JOURNAL

"*Say Uncle* is a lighthearted comedy romance novel. It is meant for a refreshing break and a well-needed laugh. Yet the story reflects God's faithfulness in the lives of those who seek Him."
—CHRISTIAN RETAILING

"Suzy Pizzuti tickles my funny bone, big time. In *Say Uncle…and Aunt,* she guides her zany cast of characters through one hilarious situation after another on their roller coaster ride toward 'happily ever after.' What a hoot!"
—LIZ CURTIS HIGGS